SEAGRASS MAGGIE

Book I of the
Seagrass Maggie Trilogy

Charles Allen

Arcanus Press ®
dba of *Emmergen, LLC*
Post Falls, Idaho

This is a work of fiction. Names, characters, business, events and incidents are the products of the author's imagination. Any resemblance to actual persons, living or dead, or actual events is purely coincidental.

Copyright © 2020 by Charles Allen

All rights are reserved, including the right to reproduce this book or portions thereof in any form whatsoever.

Arcanus Press and design are registered trademarks of Emmergen, LLC.

Any questions, comments or reviews: arcanuspress@gmail.com

Author's website: www.charlesdallen.com

Interior Layout by Evan Kerver

Internal Chapter-Facing Illustrations by Matt Seff Barnes

Cover design by Matt Seff Barnes

Library of Congress Cataloging-in-production Data has been applied for.

1st Edition

ISBN (hardcover) 978-1-7354705-3-5
ISBN (softcover) 978-1-7354705-4-2
ISBN (ebook) 978-1-0880-9573-7

*To Paul Allen,
who I owed this book
for pushing me toward my dreams.*

SEAGRASS MAGGIE

CONTENTS

Preface - *ix*

Prelude - 1

I. The Pale Seal - 7

II. Deirdre - 61

III. Doran's Play - 105

IV. The Key & The Hollow - 133

V. The Great Kárpáti! - 181

VI. The Devil's Breath - 239

VII. Into the Caverns - 287

Epilogue - 335

Glossary - 343

Preface

The setting of this book is very much Ireland and its mythology. To keep things authentic (as much as one can when writing fiction) I have chosen to use Irish *Gaeilge* in some parts of the book. But fear not, for below is a pronunciation guide for the few important terms that you will find in this book. While there are some lines of Gaelic that also appear outside this guide (to borrow from what Clive Barker once wrote), feel free to let you tongue slip over the words how you wish. The pronunciation isn't as important as the atmosphere of the language itself.

Aisling (Ash-LEEN)
Arrachtaigh (AR-rock-tog)
Cailleach (Kal-LEE-eck)
Cuán (Coo-ehn)
Demidian (dem ee dee ehn)
Geas (gehS)
Maidí Uaimh (Mi-dun oo-ev)
Ó Fionnáin (oh-FAN-nuhn)
piocadh (pee-OH-kah)
Ri Elieris (REE El-AH-ris)
Shillelagh (shuh-LAY-luh)
siofra (shiff-RAH)
sióg (shIG)
Sionnach Silíní (SHEN-ah she-LEEN)
Tuatha Dé Danann (TUE-eh de DAN-en)

Prelude

A.D. 1823
Kilkee, Ireland

Colum drove his carriage down the country roads, a cigar stuck in his mouth, half-lit, when he saw the girl. Trying to keep himself as warm as possible from the nightly chill that he saw in his breath, he tucked his arms into his sides as he held the reins. He was daydreaming about his wife and newborn child, and a good day at the market in town, when down the road he saw a dark figure jumping up and down, waving her arms about. A dark, curly-haired girl was trying to get his attention. He slowed the horses down, realizing that the woman was young and in old rags. Beside her was a weave basket with a lid and carrying strap.

"Oh, God bless you, Mister," the girl said, giving him a large smile. "I fought with my brother, and he left me here like a sack of potatoes. Mind if I catch a ride to town?"

Colum shrugged, pulled the cigar from his mouth, saying: "Not heading to town, Miss. Heading home. This cold, it isn't pleasant either."

"Oh," she said, her face turned down in disappointment, and then up at the sky, "I see. It's so dark."

Colum nodded, puffed on his cigar some more, and withdrew it again. "If you don't mind stayin' the night with me and the Misses, then I can give you a ride in the morning. I only live up 'ere around the bend."

The girl stood on her toes for a moment and landed on her heels again as her face once again lit up. Did she not have shoes? Poor girl. "Sir, I will take you up on that. Better a warm roof than a cold ground."

Colum chuckled. "Hop on up. Don't be keeping me, colleen."

The girl leaned down and grabbed her basket, putting it over her shoulder. Colum briefly wondered what she had in it but didn't feel like prying. She didn't want to scare the young thing.

"Name's Colum."

The girl sat beside him on the carriage. To his surprise, she smelled rather pleasant. Like flowers. One looking dirty as she, nobody would suspect the sweetness. "Aisling, Sir. Glad to meet you."

Colum got the horses going again. The ride was a little bumpy, and it was fun watching the girl trying to stay balanced. She was holding on to the seat with white knuckles.

"It can be a bumpy ride," he said, snorting.

"Aye," Aisling said.

They rounded the hill, and the old farmhouse came into view. The windows were glowing. The lanterns were lit as his wife was finishing supper. He was going to say something to Aisling about his wife, but when he glanced at her, he saw that her face was stiff, her eyes staring off as if she'd turned into a statue. Her stillness seemed wholly unnatural. When he attempted another glance, she was looking at him, smiling again. Her eyes seemed so black in the darkness.

He stopped the carriage and decided to introduce Aisling to the wife, who had heard the carriage pull up. His wife opened the door, coming out as she wrapped her neck in her red scarf. They hopped down, and Aisling held her hand out to shake the Miss's hand, the girl still holding on to the basket over her shoulder.

"This is Aisling, dear. Do we have enough to get something in her belly? It looks like she needs to stay the night, and I'll take her to town in the morning," Colum said.

"Well, hello, my girl," his wife, Mona, beamed. "Where did you find her?"

"Just around the bend," Colum said.

"My brother and I were on the road, and he got upset with me," Aisling said. "He told me to walk the rest of the way and shoved me out."

"Oh dear," Mona said. "That is almost an hour by carriage. Yes, yes, come in dear, and we'll get you fed and a place to rest."

Colum nodded at his wife, saying, "I'll hitch the horses and bring in the supplies."

When Colum was done putting the horses up, feeding them, and carrying the supplies into the house, he found the girl sleeping near the fireplace.

He enjoyed the warmth of the crackling fire in the hearth for the first time today, the fresh scent of cut onions in the kitchen, and his wife came in, smiling at him.

"She ate a little bread and passed right out. Poor thing. If they are not from around here, they've probably been on the road for quite a while. And did you notice that she has no shoes?" his wife said.

Colum grunted in agreement, not knowing what else to say, looking at the basket in Aisling's arms. She was holding it much like a child. After a moment, he heard his daughter cooing. Colum grinned, ready to see his little girl. He kissed his wife on the way past her, and he entered the small room where the crib was kept. His daughter had wide, silver eyes, and curly red hair. He picked her tiny body up and held her close to his chest. She was warm, and he almost felt bad for taking her heat. She didn't seem to mind as she gave him a small, short smile before grabbing for his shirt. She cooed again. Colum was always amazed seeing her, feeling her little body in his arms, knowing how much she changed their lives for the better.

Colum kissed her on the forehead.

"She won't sleep if you keep picking her up," Mona chided in half jest.

Colum kissed his daughter's cheek. Hopefully, the farm would continue to do well, and hopefully, he could keep putting food in their mouths. It was all he could think about as he toiled throughout the day, even in the best of times.

These two people were everything—all that mattered—and he wasn't going to fail them.

Aisling opened her eyes. She could hear the couple's soft breathing and slumberous murmurs nearby, and she sensed the baby in the air, the mother's milk, and the slight lingering scent of her mother's womb. They were all sleeping.

Being as quiet as possible, she stood up and carried the basket to the infant's room. Again, she waited, listening. The couple continued to sleep deeply.

Aisling opened her basket and removed the larval-like soul, the plasmic creature given to her by her once-lover. To her people, it was called a siofra. It squirmed and wriggled in her hands, feeling slimy and cold.

"For Doran!" she whispered joyfully and placed the siofra into the crib. The baby started opening its eyes. Needing her to remain quiet, Aisling incanted: "*Leanbh codlata.*" And the baby rolled her eyes back, and her lids closed.

In the meantime, the larval creature became semi-transparent. Inside itself, it constructed a skeleton, veins, organs, sinews, and flesh. Aisling put Colum's sleeping daughter into her basket, put it back on her shoulder, and softly removed herself from the home.

Despite the chill of the night, Aisling removed her clothes and removed her glamour to walk as herself amongst her Spring Squill. She could feel her long, twisted horns sticking up from her head and the length of her pointed ears again. Her flesh was back to its natural, light purple tone. But instead of returning to the Spring Squill right away, she made her way to the cliffs and down the path to the water's edge. It was high tide, so she didn't have to go down the path too far.

While the baby slept, Aisling tossed the basket into the ocean waters as she cried: "*Seo é an síofra. Do Rí Elieris é seo!*" The waters splashed up before the basket came bobbing back to the surface, drifting along on the roiling black tide.

She could see the vaguely anthropomorphous spirits writhing beneath the surface as the basket bounced on top of the waters. They were dark or pale and ever shifting in their details as they smoothed along with the currents of the sea. Sometimes they had eyes, or they didn't. Sometimes they had mouths or hair, and sometimes they didn't. The dark ones would froth white when they crashed against the crags and drifted back to darkness.

For a short moment, she enjoyed the ocean winds, and the sharp, briny wafts of the waters that poured as rain onto her bed for many centuries, but soon enough, black hands came up and pulled the basket under. There... and then *gone*.

"*Go mbeannaítear thú*," she hissed and turned to make the climb back to her flowers. There she would rest for as long as she could as the world turned on, all but forgetting the ancient and primordial *sióg*.

In Colum Ó Fionnáin's house, the larval flesh of the siofra sucked into the new form of the infant and adapted a pigment that resembled Colum's daughter perfectly. It sprouted red, curly hair and opened her eyes for the first time. So accurate in form, it would be impossible for anyone to know that this was not Deirdre Ó Fionnáin, daughter of Colum and Morna Ó Fionnáin.

...but something other.

I. The Pale Seal

I.

A.D. 1841
Kilkee, Ireland

All her life Deirdre grew up near the western sea, looking out at its expanse, and feared it with her very soul. In her nightmares, Deirdre would dream of swimming far out into the ocean as if the ocean would embrace her with its puissance, but she would feel *hands* grabbing her feet, pulling her under into its cloudy darkness. There was something in the water, wanting to hurt her. Wanting her to die.

The strange creature was some dark reflection of herself—rainbow refracted blue eyes, light teal-tone skin with her dark, Irish red hair—and she held onto Deirdre's feet, eyes lit as if on fire, pulling her ever downward into the black abyss.

Deirdre would struggle in panic before waking, gasping for breath. Her dreams felt so real. Waking itself was like breaching the surface after almost drowning. Huffing arduously as she sat up in her bed, feeling the sweat trickle down her forehead.

Sometimes she would dream that the creature was even more monstrous: dark, glistening sea-green flesh, bioluminescent patterns glowing all over her body, and several sharp teeth like some deep-sea predator. Truly frightening, and the image of this creature-self would stay with her throughout the day before finally fading for a month or two.

But the nightmares would always return. Over and over again. As she grew up, as hard as she tried, she did not get used to them. The only explanation she had for them was that she was afraid of the waters.

A young boy who grew up nearby—Cuán—confided with her that he didn't want to grow up to be a fisherman like his father. Going to *Gilroy's* shop in the village for lemon drops with him as kids, he revealed that he loved books and wanted to learn more about the world at the university in Dublin. Cuán knew his parents would not be happy about this. Deirdre, though, she understood it. Kilkee was a small fisherman's village. If you didn't fish or support fishermen, there was nothing to do here.

It got her thinking. While she didn't care for books or university, she knew that Kilkee would stunt her growth. Perhaps her dreams were trying to tell her that she'd kill herself if she stayed here? Yes, she thought. Her gut knew that she was not supposed to be here.

The more she thought about it, the more imperative it was for her to get away. She craved excitement. Maybe a little danger. She pined for what she knew she couldn't get here.

Deirdre never felt like she belonged either. Her parents stopped making her go to church when she was six because she would have panic attacks and would sometimes throw up in the pews. Some whispered it was a sign that there was something wrong with her.

Deirdre had to agree with them.

The dreams.

The discomfort of being around the church.

She was alien to everyone around her, and she never understood why. Not really.

You're no alien. Not like me.

It was a faint voice in the back of her head. It always spoke up at the strangest times, and she didn't understand whether it was her own subconscious or someone else speaking to her through her mind. She had tried talking to the voice many times, but it never answered her back.

No, I am alien and... I'm different. This place isn't right for me, she thought.

It was why Deirdre went to her parents, Colum and Mona, just before her eighteenth birthday, and asked them to sit down after stoking up a warm fire. Colum smiled, lit himself a cigar, and asked her what was on her mind. Her mother went to her knitting with her bony fingers, merely waiting for her to go on.

Deirdre sighed, conjuring up what courage she had, and said, "Have you heard of photography?"

Her mother shook her head. Her da scratched his hairy chin.

"Can't say that I have," her da said.

"Well, it's really difficult to explain, but it's a chemical process of capturing an image and putting it on a plate. It's, um... an image of life that gets frozen in time like an illustration so that you can look at it forever."

Mona nodded. "Oh, yes, I have heard Oona speak of it. She mentioned it once when she came back from Dublin. A very new technique, yes? A chemical painting."

Deirdre lit up. Her mam did understand! "Yes! Well, I heard that people who work in advertising in certain print companies and for the newspapers, they use models to make their illustrations as real as possible. I wrote to them, and one got back to me by the name of Toal Mullins. He said that he wanted to attempt using photography and selling it as a sort of new way to illustrate the papers, including pamphlets and such."

"Extraordinary, Deirdre. I didn't know you were fascinated by such things," Colum said.

Deirdre smiled at her father. "I am, but, uh, I—" Sometimes she didn't know how to say these things, but she took a deep breath and forced herself to say it anyway: "Mammy. Daddy. I want to go to Dublin and work as a model. Mister Mullins said that he would photograph me and pay me for every sitting. He said the exposures took a while, and it wouldn't always be the most comfortable work, but he could pay good money for my attendants. Also, he said, there were other illustrators and painters who would pay me to sit in for their artistic endeavors as well, so I'd have plenty of work to do."

It would be exciting, she thought. And dare she even think of the idea of men gazing at her? Drawing her? Taking her pictures?

Colum and Mona were both staring at her now with expressionless faces. Colum looked at Mona and cleared his throat. Deirdre was holding her breath, worried they wouldn't understand.

This was it.

"You want to leave for Dublin for this job?" Mona said, almost sounding offended.

(*Oh, boy, 'ere we go...*)

"Mams, I am almost eighteen. I should get out there and work in this world and be a productive person in society, yes? I won't find much around here that will keep me satisfied. My spirit needs to move beyond Kilkee."

To the excitement.

"I just had no idea you felt this way," Mona said. Deirdre could see fear in her eyes.

Neither seemed to realize—or neither seemed to approach the subject—how Mr. Mullins would be able to pick her as a model without laying eyes on her. Deirdre didn't want to tell them how she met a photographer in Galway and paid an excessive amount of money that she saved up from skinning and deboning fish, to have the picture taken and sent in the post. And seeing her mother's eyes, she knew it wouldn't be convenient to tell them now.

The photographer had known Mr. Mullins and sent her photograph for him to decide on whether to hire her or not. It had only been a few days before the school got a telegraph that Deirdre had been selected for the job opportunity, should she arrive in Dublin within a few months.

"I love ye, Mammy, but I have to do this. I have nothing here. No man I'm interested in. No future. And if I make as much money as Mister Mullins says I will, I should have no trouble coming home to see you every year. Perhaps more."

Deirdre did notice that her daddy no longer looked at her.

"Da?"

His eyes remained down, and it weighed on her.

What she wouldn't give for him to say something.

A few days later, on the night of her birthday, her da took Deirdre to the pub and bought her a drink once the feast was over. Over the boisterous chatter and obnoxious laughter, Colum put an arm around her and said, "I'm sorry it hit me so hard, but you are right, Deirdre. You have a strong spirit, and it's too big for Kilkee. I just wanted to say that I love you, and I support yeh. You have to promise me that you have to be safe, and you have to be smart, eh? And... And if you need to come back for any reason, me and your Mams will always be here for you. Always."

Deirdre gave her daddy a kiss on the cheek. "Thanks, Da. I knew you'd come around."

Swimming out into the cold waters, Deirdre felt the familiar hands grabbing her ankles, yanking her under. She gasped for breath, unable to shout for help. The dark yet glowing creature pulled her under into the near blackness, holding her under so that she couldn't breathe, telling her: "You are a terrible thing—a terrible, *damned* thing, and you deserve to drown 'ere with me!"

"We're the same person!" Deirdre demanded.

The creature who looked like her—her hair, her eyes, her face—laughed. "No. We are not the same, and we will *never* be the same."

She woke up. Her body and bed were drenched in her sweat—its odor reminded her of sea water. Cursing herself, she crawled out of bed, opened her window and crawled onto the floor next to it. The breeze poured over her sweaty body.

The next morning, she started packing for Galway, where she'd board a train for Dublin. She couldn't wait to get away from here.

II.

The dogger, *The Orna*, rested far off the coast, surrounded in mist, bobbing gently on the sea. Cuán Foley couldn't see the coast beyond the fog, but he knew it was there. Not too far off, he could see the comfort of the lighthouse flare, cutting through the gray haze every few seconds.

In his mind, Cuán was too young to be stuck on a boat with his father out at sea. He should be on the shore, hanging with his mates or having his adventures. After all, he was only twelve. On the other hand, his father wanted him to grow up learning how to run the family business, even though Cuán hadn't once met his father's eagerness with any real interest.

No, Cuán had his heart set on the university. Biology. Science. That sort of thing. However, he wasn't sure he knew what to do with it yet. So here, stuck on *The Orna*, he was silently biding his time, working alongside his da.

He helped his father pull up the large trawl. They were heavy, burdened with squirming fish, and his da beamed when he saw the results. They pulled the trawl taught again and prepared the lines for bearing homeward.

"Good catch. I hope The Maggie is doing just as good," his da said, his breath misting in the icy air.

His da owned two fishing boats and was one of the most prominent fishers in Kilkee. He was proud of his da and what he had accomplished, though, at times, it was hard to have the same fascination for it that he had. Fishing wasn't in his blood as much as his da hoped. If Cuán were to be honest with himself, it left him feeling lonely, despite his da being right there with him.

Ponc, Cuán's furry Irish wolfhound, barked when his da hit the bell so that *The Maggie* would know that they were heading in. Ponc knew it was time to go ashore, and it made the hound dance and spin.

Ponc helped with the loneliness from time to time, he thought. He loved his dog and knew it would be much harder without the wolfhound by his side.

Cuán laughed and gave the dog a few strokes through his feathery gray fur. "Aye, boyo, we're heading home."

His da clanged the bell a good while, and Cuán achingly helped him lift the sails. Once they completed this, Cuán hugged himself against the weather as they looked for the lighthouse. They made their way closer to the cliffs to follow the land as much as they could, but it wasn't without its problems. They had to be careful of the sharp crags dotting the shoreline though they had made this journey thousands of times before. Cuán felt as if he knew these shores better than he did his own home.

Ponc licked Cuán in the face, so Cuán patted him again. He kept his eyes on the rocks and the cliffs. The tide was rising, and Cuán could see the seals leaving the rocks for higher grounds. Watching all the dark figures flip-flopping or diving into the waters, he couldn't believe his eyes when he thought he saw a tall, bleached seal rise on a crag. The longer he looked, the more he realized the form was humanoid. It wobbled on a rock as the waters crashed froth-white at its feet.

It? No... *Her.* The longer he looked through the mists at the creature, the more he realized he was looking at a fair, bare-skinned girl with long red hair clinging to her shoulders. She was trying to balance, crouching to catch the rocks at her feet. Her slim legs were bent and teetering. Her arms were out so that she could stand, but unable to do it, she crouched and grabbed the rock at her feet with her hands.

"Da," he said, but he knew he was already too late. Just as he pointed, saying, "Look!" he watched as the girl dove back into the water. His da turned, and of course, saw nothing.

"What was it, boy? Séala?"

Cuán shook his head. "I swear I saw a girl on those rocks, and she went right into the water! I think she was naked, Da!"

His da looked at him. This time he was the one giving him the side-eye. "You havin' me on for fun?"

"No, I swear, Da!"

His da laughed. "Well, I suppose you have your first fish story for your friends then, aye? Mermaids, and all. It was most probably a pale seal."

Cuán sighed, wishing his da had seen what he had seen. He decided to drop it and pulled Ponc close for warmth for the remaining journey.

A few days later—on the holy Sunday—Cuán walked the coast after church, Ponc running about him, a muddy blur, searching for animals that had washed ashore to play with or eat. His da joined his friends at the pub, and his mam was heading home for tea with her bible group. This gave him plenty of opportunity to enjoy the shoreline with his wolfhound.

The day was reasonably sunny, and he relished the warmth of it. There were white cottony clouds in the sky, and the sandy, sometimes rocky shoreline looked vibrant, which was rather inviting with the fresh sea air.

Ponc barked and brought him a wet stick that he must have snatched from the waters, so Cuán gave it a toss and watched the wolfhound sprint after it. Cuán loved the ocean, loved watching the waters and the cliffs and birds... and at the same time, he couldn't see his whole life trapped here.

Trying not to think about it, he turned his mind on the Pale Seal that had looked very much like a human girl with red hair. Had she looked back at him? Did her eyes fall on him as well? And what was she doing out there all alone, or at all?

The cliffs and waters of Kilkee could be very dangerous. Cuán wouldn't have wanted to be out in those waters, especially in a fog and definitely not naked. It didn't make any sense.

Had she been naked, though? Cuán wondered. Maybe she had on a gown, and the water was making the gown cling in such a way that it made it appear that she had been naked? It was hard to say, as foggy as it was.

Cuán wished he had another glance at the Pale Seal. Could it have been a *seal*? Was his mind imagining all of it? Perhaps it was the stress of fishing or the anxiety of knowing how upset his da would be when he learned of his plans to leave for Dublin when he was eighteen. Perhaps the Pale Seal hadn't been there at all.

Cuán could clearly see her when he shut his eyes. Maybe his mind made up all the details he saw now: the red, curly hair clinging to her scalp, her shoulders. Her back. The white skin with the light blue hue. The big black eyes.

It was as if his imagination was all made up about it.

Of course, he considered the old tales—as far-fetched as it would be. Cuán thought of the Scottish selkie, or the *maighdean mhara*, the mermaid. Female creatures that changed form so that they could be on land or sea. In most tales, men would steal their skin to keep them for lovers, and when the creatures were able to relocate it, they returned to the waters, for no man or thing could keep these creatures from the sea.

These were legends, of course. *Superstitious nonsense*, as his da would call them.

Could the girl he'd seen been from the shore?

Cuán knew of only one family in the area with the red hair: the Ó Fionnáns. Was the Pale Seal their daughter, Deirdre? They couldn't possibly be the same girl, could they? When Cuán thought of Deirdre, there was a deep longing at the pit of his stomach. It had been there since he had first met her. Deirdre never showed up for church, though, and he wondered why sometimes. Instead, he mostly saw her when her parents came to town for shop supplies and tools.

No, no, Cuán told himself. Nobody's dumb enough to swim off the cliffs during a fog or a storm. It's unquestionably dangerous. She would have drowned or would have been dashed into a bloody mess on the rocks. There was no way someone would risk that.

Taking him out of his head, he heard Ponc barking more excitedly than usual. Cuán went to his dog and realized that Ponc was looking down through some pointed crags at something. Cuán had to get down prone to look between the rocks, but he saw what his dog was barking at. It looked like a...

...*a Pale Seal*...

...wrapped in long, narrow seaweed. It was like dark green hair, tangled around her body and her thin limbs.

The seal wasn't moving. He couldn't see it very well from where he was, so he got up and went around the rocks, his wolfhound following him. Going around the rocks revealed where they could climb down.

Once upon it, he inhaled the sulfur and other sharp odors of the body, and he could see what he had first suspected: this was *no* seal. It was a skinny young lady with long red hair. Nose full of freckles. Naked and colorless otherwise. She was wrapped in the green algae, and it looked as though she had crashed against the rocks and knocked herself unconscious. He could see her chest rising and falling as she breathed, but barely.

And shockingly, he noticed that she had to be eight or nine years old. Maybe ten, but no older than that.

Cuán knelt to her and looked her over for wounds, not seeing any at first as he pried some of the slimy seaweed away. Ponc licked her face, but she wasn't waking. She was cold to the touch. Being fully aware of how dangerous hypothermia was, Cuán pulled off his jacket and wrapped it around the girl.

"We have to find someone to help us," Cuán told Ponc, who looked up at him as if he were actually paying attention. Ponc barked back at him.

He couldn't leave her. She looked small enough to carry, so he scooped her up in his arms and started carrying her up through the rocks.

"*Ní hea, stad, stad...*" —No, stop, stop.

It was Gaelic.

The delicate voice startled him, and one of her small hands touched his cheek. Her big blue eyes opened, and she added: "*Ní hea, stad. Ní gá d'éinne mise a fheiceáil.*"

He looked at the cracked lips around her small mouth, and back at her gorgeous blue eyes.

"I— I found you. Are you hurt?" he said.

"*Táim lag. Impím ort. Ní gá d'éinne mise a fheiceail,*" she said, strenuously grasping for each syllable.

Cuán's mam was fluent in Gaelic, and Cuán himself was raised with it his whole life, though he didn't use it much except with private talks with her. The girl in his arms spoke rather delicately and almost too softly to hear, but he pieced together that she felt weak and still didn't want to be seen by anyone.

"I need to get you somewhere where you are safe. You will die if you stay out here."

The girl rested her eyelids, taking deep breaths, and she opened her eyes again and looked into his. "*Tá a fhios agam an áit. Thall ansin. Thall ansin. Gabh thall.*" She pointed down the rocks with one long bony arm, towards what looked like a raised cave, where the tides might not be able to reach so easily. "*Le do thoil,*" she added, her voice almost gone.

She licked her lips with a lavender tongue.

Cuán watched as she passed out again in his arms. A part of him thought he should take her up to his folks because this was way over his head. His parents should know what to do. Surely, she would be safer that way. Besides, what would he do if she died?

Something deeper in him understood her fears of being found out. If she were in danger and he outed her, whatever happened next would be his fault. As long as she could think and communicate, she had every right to be listened to. *I should listen to her*, he thought. Carefully, he took her to the cave and tightened the jacket around her body after laying her down on the cold ground. Deep enough into the cave, the ground was dry and a bit softer.

Ponc barked again, watching him look at her. It was as if the dog knew that he was lost in his own thinking. He knew he couldn't leave her in this cold cave alone, but what other choice did he have? He needed to get some blankets, and perhaps a way to start a fire to get her warm. Maybe some food.

Something gnawed at him. Before he knew what he was doing, he pushed her lips apart with his fingers and pried on the teeth until she opened her mouth.

Her tongue was pink.

Had he imagined the lavender tongue? Cuán had so many questions, and he knew he wasn't going to get them right away.

Was she the same Pale Seal he saw just a few days before?

Obviously...

She was a little girl that somehow got washed away and miraculously washed back ashore for him to find. That was all.

At least, that was what he was trying to tell himself.

It was more important to save the girl, Cuán.

Right.

Cuán whistled at Ponc. "Come on, boy. Let's get her some food."

Cuán's mammy and her bible group were chattering away when he got home, barely acknowledging him as he made his way through the house, and through his mam's kitchen. He grabbed a lamp, pan, matches, and a blanket, and a turbot that they had in an ice cooler, putting it into a basket. He grabbed a knife and some old clothes that didn't fit him anymore. After gathering all of this, he made his way back to the cave before his ma had the chance to ask him about anything. Ponc once again prancing around behind him, following him wherever he went.

The girl was still asleep, so he unwound the hairy algae from her body, trying not to look at her nakedness out of respect. He dressed her in his old clothes. They were too small for him, but large on her. It didn't matter. They'd keep her warmer.

He wondered where she came from. She wasn't Deirdre. Too young. Could a ship have been going by, heading north, and could she have fallen overboard?

The only way he was going to find out was if he could get her to wake up.

Once she was dressed, he gathered rocks and some wood from outside so that he could make a fire at the mouth of the cave. After a few tries with the matches, he had a good, contained fire going. He took the turbot to the water's edge and cleaned it, taking out the bones and guts with the knife. A few minutes later, he had a flat pan in the middle of the fire, and the fish fillets crackling on top of it.

While the fish cooked, Cuán picked the girl up and brought her closer to the fire. It seemed to work as moments later, her eyes opened again, and she lifted herself into a sitting position. Her eyes darted around the cave.

She was frightened, the poor thing.

"Do you speak English?" Cuán said. "I mean, you have Gaelic down, haven't yeh?"

The girl looked at the clothes she was now wearing and hugged herself as she looked at him. Slowly she said, "This language? Aye. When I dreamed through the Hollow, I 'eard it many times."

"Good." Cuán smiled at her, not completely understanding what she meant, while Ponc walked around her, sniffing her. She watched the dog and gave a small giggle.

"Do yeh remember anything else? Do yeh have a name?"

The girl reached out and touched Ponc's snout. His tongue came out and licked her hand. She said: "I have a memberin', but it's so strange. I think I 'member lights and songs. I 'member drinkin' from a... um... a nipple? My ma... My da... They called me..."

"You remember that far back? That's, um, some memory," Cuán said. "My earliest memory is playin' ball with the other boys at the church. I think I had to be four or so."

"Four or so?" The girl licked her lips.

Cuán noticed her pink tongue, confusing him.

"More is comin' back to me," the girl said. "But it is comin' back slowly."

"Well, I will call yeh Maggie, until you are certain of yer name. Seagrass Maggie," Cuán said. He always liked that name. "Maggie, my name is Cuán Foley, and I brought a fish for us to eat. Will that do?"

The girl sat forward, sniffing deeply, smiling again. She looked almost as excited as the dog sitting beside her. *Such a weird girl*, he thought. He had never seen anyone act like this, and it was bewildering to him.

"Oh aye, please," she said. "I love a good turbot."

That took Cuán back. He looked at the meat crackling on the pan, unable to see how she could know what specific sort of fish this was. "How did you know it's a turbot?"

"Oh, I know the scent of every fish around the Éire," Maggie said, the firelight flickering in her big blue eyes.

They ate together. Cuán watched her in wonder. Part of her almost seemed as if she had to be raised in the wild, but she seemed to know some basic human things. It all seemed a little off, however.

"Yeh cannot tell anyone that I am 'ere. I have somethin' to tell yeh, and if yeh cannot believe me, then you must leave the cave and never turn back. Do yeh follow what I'm sayin'?"

Cuán nodded, certain he wanted to hear this story, as he fed the fire more wood.

The girl, her lips still a little greasy from the fish, hugged herself as Ponc laid across her lap, panting away.

"I don't know about how I got lost. I think I was taken by these demons—the fomori. I want to say they took me to a cave under the ocean, but I don't know if this was in this world or another, or somehow both? It's all fuzzy. It's blurry, like a hallucination that ye understand was once a memory," the girl said.

The fomori, or Fomorians. Hadn't Cuán heard of them before? He remembered a little about some of the myths he learned from his third-class teacher, Mrs. Donoghue. She described them as sea monsters or demons that reigned over Ireland before the Children of Danu came. They always had a terrible king that drove them into battle, plaguing the Irish people until finally they were driven into the sea.

"Anyway, I been there fer a long time. The fomori were always around me. Some of them acted with cruelty and... *harmed* me. Others ignored me as though I were not there. I don't have the memberin' the way I thought I did.

"But I know that it felt like a long time before I found this old woman's hand with an arm as slender as a snake, but so long I could not see who it belonged to, and the hand raised me up from the waters, and I was on the rocks," she said. Maggie started tearing up. "I know I once had a mam and da. I once had a bed and a teddy. They took me, and they took my life, and somehow some old woman helped me find the surface. I think I almost forgot there was a surface until I came 'ere. That's my memberin' anyway."

Cuán didn't know what to think. He watched her sob. Cuán wanted to go over to her and hug her close, let her know that she was no longer alone anymore. But he was partially frightened of her at the same time. Here she was, looking eight or nine years of age, and yet she spoke much older, though with a thick accent and a way that was rather strange. It was charming and a little adorable, too, and that's why his heart reached out to her.

Instead of hugging her, he leaned toward her. "I won't let anything bad happen to you. You're safe here with me, a'right?"

Maggie shivered. Her hands trembled. "If yeh tell others, they may find me. They may come back fer me. I am frightened that they will come back fer me, Cuán. I'm more afraid of that than death."

Cuán nodded, knowing already that he would do anything to help her. He could see that she didn't deserve whatever fate brought her to this point, and he couldn't resist himself. "I understand. I'll tell no one. I promise. But yeh can't just stay here. What will you do? What is it that yeh want me to do?"

Maggie seemed to think about this a moment. She was stroking Ponc's coat.

"I want to find my real parents. The 'membering is hard, but I know that these are the same cliffs of my mam and da. Will yeh help me find them?"

Cuán sighed. "It's a small village. It should be easy enough. Why don't yeh stay low, 'ere in the caves, and I will ask around? Once I know, I will bring yeh what I know."

Maggie got up. "Yeh will not be gone long?"

"I'll check on you every day. It will be harder when I am out with my da on The Orna. My da and I are fishermen. But when I'm on land, I'll come check on yeh. I mean it, Maggie. You'll be safe with me," Cuán said as softly as he could.

This time he forced himself to get up and go around the fire to her. He hugged her, and he let her go just as quickly as not to frighten her. Looking for a way to make this easier for her, he thought of a way she could be certain to know when he would be back. As she looked at him with those big blue eyes, he reached into his pocket and took out his pocket watch. His da had purchased it for him in Galway for his twelfth birthday, marking his first chance to go out with his da on the boats. It was made of coin silver and depicted ocean waves, and a sailing ship on the surface.

Cuán sighed, popped it open, wound it, and handed it to her. Her small fingers took it quickly and gave him a huge grin as she looked it over.

"What is this? I love how it shines!"

Cuán chuckled. "My da gave it to me. It tells the time. Yeh know, tells you when it is. The small hand points to the hour."

He gave her a moment to scrutinize it and pointed at the shorter hand.

"When this little tick points at the six, I should be here soon. I want yeh to keep this with you so you know when I will be here."

The fascinated girl twirled the watch and thumbed the short chain on it.

"It's very smooth, too," she said.

Cuán patted his leg so that Ponc would come, and he grabbed his lamp. As he left her, he added, "I'll try to find clothes that fit you. Get as much rest as yeh can and feed the wood to the fire when it gets weak, okay? Remember, the six."

Maggie nodded. "The six."

III.

"Maggie," she thought. *Seagrass Maggie.* She did sort of like that. She didn't know what to make of the boy. He had these beautiful seal-brown eyes, dark, feathery hair, and he was so... *friendly*. It was something that she had never experienced before. But could this all be a trick? Could the boy mean her harm?

She didn't know, but it had to be on the back of her mind. It was safer that way. What she learned in the Deep Dens—that *otherworld place* between the deep ocean and the fae-worlds, constructed and ruled by the fomori—was that cruelty could absolutely be found in everything and anyone. And Fomorian cruelty would extend from the Deep Dens, and they would look to return her to that place, compelled by their malevolence alone.

Maggie felt her hands shaking. She closed and stuffed the watch into the pants. There was so much behind her that it was dangerous. Things from the sea, hiding in its dark tunnels and chasms, that wanted to find her and kill her. If she wanted to survive, she needed to repeat what had kept her alive so far. Seeing the firelight playing on the walls of the stony cave, Maggie knew that though the fire was keeping her warm, it was dangerous. She could be seen. Maggie was so used to hiding in the dark, and it was a risk, exposing her.

Maggie started grabbing cool mud and started throwing it onto the fire. You could never be too careful. It was better in the dark. Even the deep-dwelling monsters found it harder to see in it.

She went deeper into the dark cave.

Maggie was already cold and shivering, and yet the coldness in her bones grew when she heard the long, dark whisper of an old, croaky woman: *"Seagrassssssss Maggie, is it now?"*

"Wh-Who are ye?"

A giant crone's skeletal face appeared out of the darkness of the deeper recesses of the cave. She filled the cave with her twisted body, half-lit by the lamp it carried between two branch-like fingers. The crone drew along a scent of deep, muddy earth and decay. Maggie recognized her as the old woman who held out her hand, plucking her from the Deep Dens. Around the old giantess were other whispers of other creatures, all chanting: *"Cailleach! Cailleach! Cailleach!"*

Maggie got down on her knees and bowed before the Cailleach, terror setting into her bones.

The crone was the Queen of Winter, a powerful goddess, and her savior. The crone's kindness so far had only been to rescue her, not to protect her from the Fomorians. Maggie had no idea why and it concerned her, but part of her feared that it was because she was condemned for reasons beyond her understanding. That was Cailleach's way. Benefice or malefactor. Neither good nor bad. She was the coming of winter on the land, and what ushered in the rain waters for the earth. She was ancient and probably an avatar of the mother goddess Danu, though nobody knew for sure. The only thing that was for sure: one worshipped the Cailleach with the same respect that one gives to the edge of a cliff.

Cailleach! Cailleach! Cailleach!

"Is this my time to die?" Maggie said.

"You may live, aye? Find your ma and your da. Find them. In ten years' time, return 'ere. Then you will repay me... repay me for this new chance at life, aye?"

Maggie looked up where there was now only darkness. The smell of earth and death vaguely left behind.

Cailleach! Cailleach! Cailleach...

"Fillfidh mé ar ais," Maggie said. "Fillfidh." I will return. I will. She was overwhelmed with relief and gratitude. Nothing in life had ever been fair to her, and with the Cailleach's benevolence, she knew that she would be able to live and would be able to seek out her parents.

This would be her chance to live, and her eyes welled up with tears, and she had to force herself to control the sobs.

"In the meantime... listen all around you. For the keen of Muirgen and her ilk. They will be plotting for you, my dear."

With that, Maggie could no longer feel the presence of the Cailleach, but she could hear keening and crying far off somewhere. Wiping her tears with the back of her hand, she told herself to be brave, and she left the cave, listening for the crying. The wind carried it for a spell before it wandered off, and she lost it.

Muirgen? Why did that name sound so familiar?

Maybe the caves were not as safe as she thought they would be. She needed to get to higher ground, more inland, so that the Fomorians would find it more challenging to find her.

When she mustered her braver side, she left the shoreline and looked around from the tops of the cliffs. First, she looked out to sea and looked for the Fomorians. Unable to see them, she turned and looked around the land. A short distance away, she could see the warm glow of a home, its hearth lit, and she could feel the life within it.

She decided to make her way there. It would be safer than being near the water's edge.

Her pants kept falling down, so she bunched and knotted them and pulled up the pant legs so that they would not drag across the wet grass. In several minutes she had crossed the grassy land and was at the walls of the home.

She placed her body up against the rugged gray wall, hoping she could feel its heat, though Maggie didn't feel any. There was an open window, but she couldn't hear anyone inside. There was a lattice nearby, so she made the climb to the nearest window.

When she got inside, she felt happily warm again. She could tell she was in some sort of bathroom, though the lights were off. She remembered bathtubs vaguely. Maggie remembered her mammy washing her down as she played in the tub. For a moment, she could almost see her face again.

Feeling her chest heave as sadness came upon her, she went to the glass... (*mirror?*). Mirror! Yes, that is what it was. It was showing her a reflection of herself—a *filthy* redhead child wearing rags with watery eyes and a heaving chest.

Much less a child. She felt older than this body. Maggie didn't know how she knew, but something didn't seem right to her. This body was definitely hers, but it wasn't old enough. She should be much older. Taller.

Weaker, she thought. As it were, she felt as though she were as strong as the earth, and she didn't know how to exactly tell herself that ever since she left the surface for the Deep Dens, her body felt unnatural. It wasn't something that she could sense logically. It was instinctive. Inside her. Like everything else.

Her body was changed by the Deep Dens. There was no doubt. The Otherworld was about Primordial Creation, the essence of which formed both the physical and spiritual worlds, bonding them together. And when someone got closer to the Primordial—a power that transformed everything—they were always changed by it. Since the Deep Dens were a part of the Otherworld realms, her time spent there naturally changed her and adapted her to its environs.

There were footsteps outside the door. Maggie wiped away her tears and listened for the steps to get closer.

Whoever owned this home was coming to check on the noises. Heart leaping into her throat, she darted for the window again. Once outside, huffing to catch her breath, she heard the door rattle and open. After a moment, it closed.

That's when Maggie saw a vent. She quietly reached for it, tugged on it, and it came loose. She slowly climbed through it, trying to keep as silent as possible, and found herself in a small, unfinished attic. It was much warmer here.

Hopefully, she could sleep peacefully now.

Maggie returned the vent covering and crawled prone a few feet deeper into the warmth of the home, and curled up to sleep. Her hand reached into her pocket, and she pulled out the silvery watch, popping it open as the boy had when he first showed it to her. She liked believing him and liked his help. It was comforting, though it was hard to see him holding his tongue.

Maggie was sure that if the creatures of the Deep Dens ever caught her, she'd suffer until the end of her days.

Her body felt very tired, though. It didn't take long for sleep to come, and all of this anxiousness to be forgotten for a spell.

IV.

Everything began in darkness. That's what they say, and in Maggie's case, it was true.

Maggie was taken under the sea when she was a babe, given Nathaira's blood, and quickly drowned as she gulped for air that wasn't there. Somehow, in some mysterious and magical way, the water fed her the oxygen that she needed, and she did not die. It was dark for a long time, and as the pressures surmounted over her tiny body, her body adapted remarkably to its crushing weight and coldness.

Her skin darkened, turning green. It thickened.

Maggie's toothless gums grew sharp, white teeth that filled her young mouth. Claws sprouted from her toes and her fingers. Her hands became webbed, and she grew spiked dorsal fins that ran over the middle of her scalp, down her back, and along the powerful tail that grew there. When it was all over, she had become a hybrid: a human baby that resembled a slender yet hearty eel-shark-thing.

An Altered One—an *athraithe*.

A grotesque thing, she thought, which was an inescapable and horrid thought that she would have to learn to live with.

The Fomorians gathered around. They were hybrids as well in their own, unique ways: some crustaceous, some octopoid, and others very fishlike. Some were mixtures of everything. The only thing they had in common was their deep, ugly faces, the terrible long teeth, and claws. Maggie was afraid of them, but they grabbed her, and they started carving into her flesh with their claws. Some of it was *ogham*—the ancient Gaelic writing—and others were arcane symbols that belonged only to the fae kin.

It was excruciating. Her flesh bled into the waters like a smoke around them. Her skin opened and scarred over as they scratched and bit. She would later learn that the scars adapted into a vague, blue bioluminescence that she would have to learn how to dim so that she wouldn't be seen by predators.

Once the fomori were done clawing at her, drawing their symbols, another came up. It had a large, red head that made it look like a burn victim; its teeth the same blood-red color, and the other fomori called it Fangtooth.

"By Ri Elieris, I take a piece of your soul, and I will it to the Deep Dens!" Fangtooth said, grinning at her. It reached into her body and pulled out a piece of her soul. It shined in Fangtooth's claws and broke into two. Fangtooth tried grabbing both pieces, but a part of it floated up and away into the caverns.

Fangtooth hissed at the other Fomorians to retrieve it, and fashioned the shine in its claws into a crystal shard. He held it in front of her, saying, "You are now bound to Elieris and the Deep Dens, child. By the Great Contracts, you are married to our tribe!"

The fomori took her through the caverns of the Deep Dens—a place of the spirit and of the physical, deep beneath the oceans—and took her to a chamber with eggs. They told her that she was to watch the eggs from other deep-sea predators.

Over the years, Maggie would watch horrible creatures being born from these eggs.

One egg was very old. It was the Egg of Muirgen, one of the Fomorian King's ancient lovers. Muirgen would never come in person to see the egg, but sometimes she would breach the Hollow in an almost transparent astral form to come and see it.

Maggie thought Muirgen was beautiful. The snow-pale skin, the mature female body with all its curves, and the abyssal black hair. Maggie knew that her own form was horrid and eelish. And she would be that way for as long as she lived amongst the fomori.

Muirgen would always go to the egg and put her ear to it, listening to what was happening inside. One day Maggie swam up to her, shy but curious. "What do you 'ear?"

"The life I will never have," Muirgen said.

"Out of all the Fomorian eggs, this one in particular hasn't hatched," Maggie said.

"Because it's not yet time. One day the Fomorian King, Ri Elieris, will say that I have earned my boon, and our egg will be hatched."

"You will come for it then?"

Muirgen smiled at her. Maggie could see that she had long, pointed canine teeth. She was no normal human either.

"Yes."

A few years later, Muirgen returned. Maggie felt more confident, going to her.

"How do yeh travel in such a way? 'Ere and not 'ere?"

Muirgen put her ear to the egg.

"I go through the Hollow—it is a place of psychic energy—mind, word, and deed; past, present, and future. It's like the water or wind that moves between the rocks of the earth. Only it's made up of its own energy. All minds are connected to it and can influence it. If you connect with it, you can move through it, and you can travel through it with your psychic resonance. It's called astral projection."

"I wish I could go beyond the Deep Dens. I would like to see the world," Maggie said.

Muirgen again smiled at her, letting her hands run across the surface of her egg. "I tell you what. If you protect this egg—make it yer priority—I will teach you how to use the Hollow."

Maggie grinned, probably the first time she'd ever been slightly happy since her imprisonment within the Deep Dens.

"Yer egg is me chief concern!" Maggie said. "I swear it."

Over the next couple of years, Muirgen taught Maggie how to use the Hollow. And Maggie started to see how people within the Hollow were 'doorways' into their own dreams. She didn't know why, but she was most drawn to one that looked like a trickling waterfall of caustic lights. A doorway that Maggie started calling The Fall. When she went through it, she didn't remember much, except that she would go in angry and come out feeling better. It would wash away her fear and her hatred for a few short days.

The other athraithe—the other altered human hybrids—that worked with the eggs were taught how to fight off predators from the Fomorian General, Ceithlinn. Fangtooth had told them that she was the only fomor who ever wounded the Dagda. Ceithlinn hated Lugh, her grandson, for killing her husband, Balor. (Though there were rumors that Lugh only wounded him and another of the sióg made the final blow later.) In Ceithlinn's hatred, she became one of the cruelest warriors amongst the Fomorian ranks. She would often take them and teach them how to wound the enemy and remove their heads.

"You take the head as a trophy," she said, grinning with her giant, crooked teeth. "But only the head of the mightiest. It is your reward for the kill. It is your glory. And if the head is truly worthy, it will often give you a boon."

While Maggie pondered this cruel idea, some of the other Altered Ones—Egg Keepers—started practicing this wickedness with the eggs. They would open one by tapping it, and when the fomor came out biting, they would kill it and remove its head.

Maggie was horrified when she saw it for the first time. "If the fomori catch you, they will kill yeh."

"So?" one of the other hybrids said. "Look at us. They have perverted us! They have taken our lives. Why should we stand for it? No, I'd rather die than live this way forever. If I'm to be trapped here, I take my fun as I please."

Maggie understood it. They only knew cruelty. But how could she tell them that this was wrong? That this wasn't the way? Deep inside her, she knew she didn't want to see this continue. There was no escape from the Deep Dens. Guarding the eggs was the only way they were all going to survive. The Fomorians were everywhere, and beyond the Deep Dens, they'd be lost in the ocean's immensity, possibly killed by creatures that Maggie hadn't seen before that lurked in the great deep.

"This disgusts me!" Maggie cried. "You attack the weak! It's pitiful! It's a crime of a coward."

But it didn't do any good. Over the next year, they continued tapping eggs and taking their heads. None of them were ever caught, and the fomori never realized it because they bred quickly, rarely rearing their young past a few days.

Maggie remembered when another athraithe child was brought to the Dens, looking much more like a crab. The fomori called her Crab Eye because, in her transformation, only one of her eyes extended out on a stalk. They found it cruelly entertaining and left her that way. Maggie took Crab Eye under her wing and tried showing her the ways, but the child was frightened of everything.

Early one morning, the other Egg Keepers were tapping Muirgen's egg to get it to hatch before Maggie found them. After a long moment, the egg started cracking open, spewing blood into the waters in ribbons that sprouted out like smoke. The female creature slithered out of the egg, and Maggie rushed to get to her before the others killed her. Though she was a child, the pale thing had fangs and attacked and killed a couple of the Altered Ones, and grabbed Crab Eye herself.

Maggie, afraid for Crab Eye, grabbed a hold of the newborn creature and bit deep into her neck, tearing half her neck away as Maggie yanked her teeth back. Maggie twisted the head off by the hair and tossed it to the ocean floor as the others watched in horror.

Crab Eye screamed in terror, and the other Altered Ones gathered around her.

Maggie, too, gawked, starting to feel sick in the pit of her stomach. This was Muirgen's daughter—the life Muirgen came to see, who Maggie had promised to protect.

What the hell did she do?

"We will help you bury the egg and the body," one of the Altered Ones said. "We owe you this."

Maggie didn't know what she was going to do.

She remembered her last words with Muirgen, sitting near the egg as she once again embraced it in her astral form.

"Why do you come through the Hollow by astral projection?" Maggie asked.

"Because I am in a sleep until Elieris needs me," Muirgen said. "And when I wake, I will conquer for Ri Elieris! I will earn my daughter's birth."

"How long do you have to wait?"

Muirgen looked doleful for a moment. "Perhaps a long time still. Who knows, my dear."

Until her final days in the Deep Dens, Maggie hid from Muirgen, leaving the egg chambers when she saw Muirgen's astral form project itself near where her egg was once kept. She heard Muirgen's awful cries when she discovered what had happened. Maggie found herself weeping. Not just in her terror, but because she was so ashamed of what had happened.

When the Cailleach reached for her and pulled her out of the depths, Maggie felt her body shifting again—transforming—returning to her more natural human form. She started forgetting most of what she'd experienced in the depths as her mind tried to wrap itself around what was happening to her. Drunk-like, feeling vertigo as the oceans crashed around her, she climbed onto a rock above the surface. She tried to stand, wobbled for a moment, and fell back into the waters, which pushed and pulled her around, flinging her against the rocks and pushed her with its waves onto the Kilkee shores under its cliffs.

The whole time she heard the Cailleach's cackling laughter all around as if they bounced off the ocean waves. It was as if the sea stirred everything up in her head and buried the horrors of the Deep Dens deep into her own mind where it could hide.

Only in dreams, laying there safe in a bed, Maggie could begin to remember where she had been or what she was.

And everything she remembered was cruel and awful, and she knew she could never go back there.

V.

A few days later, a storm came brewing in. So busy with work, Cuán was only able to sneak out at night to find Maggie waiting for him at the caves. He wished he could go see her more, make sure she remained comfortable, but it was the best he could do. She looked like she was getting healthy. She looked good.

He would always bring her leftovers from his dinner, which seemed to work just fine for her. Before he left, each time, he would point on the watch where the hand would be when he returned.

When the storm came through, he was able to sneak off to the Ó Fionnáin's farmhouse. Having time to think about it, Cuán knew the Ó Fionnáin's were the only ones with red hair. And in fact, as he was thinking about it more, he realized that Seagrass Maggie looked a lot like Deirdre if she were shy of ten. Cuán had only been four or five when Deirdre was that age, but he could see it for sure.

Could Seagrass Maggie be a lost sister? The idea intrigued him, though he didn't ever recall the Ó Fionnáin's mentioning having lost a child.

Of course, you couldn't say that to a person, could you? You had to have tact.

Cuán figured that he would maybe come up with some excuse to hang with Deirdre and maybe get her to spill something about it. (If she even knew about it. He'd have to be careful there.)

Cuán climbed their steps and knocked on the door, expecting Deirdre to answer. His heart sank when Colum opened the door instead, wearing his paddy cap, a cigar stuck in his mouth. Colum didn't fancy many of the boys hanging around his daughter, especially when she had started growing her ladylike endowments.

What Cuán had been noticing over the last few weeks was Colum's somber demeanor. Something changed in him, and Cuán wasn't sure what. To Cuán, Colum was always a quiet, low-key man who loved his farm and spending time with his family. Deirdre was a daddy's girl, and Cuán understood why. The man was attentive and showed nothing but kindness.

"Hi, Mister Ó Fionnáin. I was wondering if I could speak with Deirdre for a few minutes? I wanted to discuss a teacher she had once. You mind?"

Colum surprised him and waved him into the house, moving out of his way.

"Come on in, out of the rain, Cuán," he said. "Would you like some tea?"

Cuán nodded, offering a warm smile. "Yes, Sir. Tea would warm me up quite nicely."

Colum gestured toward the old, worn couch, and Cuán peeled out of his coat, hung it up on a hook by the door, and took a seat. It was warmer than the rainy day in the house, but not by much. Colum returned with some tea with steam twirling up like dancing snakes above the brim and sat down on the chair beside him.

"Sorry," Colum said. "Deirdre isn't here. I thought most people knew. She's in Dublin."

"Dublin?" Cuán was surprised again. Now, what was he going to do?

"Yes, she had some photographs done by a Galway picture maker a while back. The picture maker told her that he knew of a company in Dublin that modeled women for their illustrations and prints in advertising. They offered a salary, and she thought to use that salary in one of the Dublin colleges," Colum said. He was proud of his daughter and was happy to be telling him this, Cuán could tell. "Imagine that! Deirdre helping sell perfumes and clothing in the newspapers and pamphlets."

Cuán smiled. Yet inside, he didn't know what else to do, but Cuán was starting to understand why Colum's mood had been 'off' lately. The man was missing his precious daughter. Cuán didn't know how he'd fare in the same situation. If he could be a great father like his own da, or Mister Ó Fionnáin, Cuán would be proud of himself.

"Imagine that," Cuán said. "Deirdre finding her way in this world."

"Aye. She's crafty."

"Aye."

"And thrifty—Methinks."

"It's not like it used to be. Progress has changed a great many things. Kings no longer control things. Businesses do," Colum said.

Cuán thought of Queen Victoria and didn't know if he totally agreed with that yet.

"Sir, I had to ask you, and this may seem very odd, but was Deirdre an only child?"

Colum gave him a strange look then. It was somewhere between concern and curiosity. "Why would you say that, Cuán?"

Cuán chuckled and shook his head. "I don't know. I guess I've been thinking about it a lot since growing up. Maybe it was a dream. I don't know. I thought maybe Deirdre had a younger sister. Maybe eight or nine years ago? I don't know. I was so young."

Colum laughed and shook his head. "No, that's preposterous, Cuán. Deirdre is the only child we ever had. You know that."

Cuán felt like an idiot. His neck felt hot, his shoulders were tight, and he didn't like it at all. When Cuán spent so much time trying to earn respect, here he was, blowing it.

"Sorry. I don't know why—" He didn't know where he was going with that either. I'm a complete ape! He got up and added: "Sorry. I have to be going now. I wish you and your Misses a good day."

Colum shook his head, showing Cuán the door.

"No worries, son," Colum said, holding the door after Cuán stepped out. "Twelve is always an awkward age."

Colum shut the door, and Cuán turned around, rolling his eyes on himself. There wasn't any information here, and he took a nosedive for it. *Yeah, I'm a foolish eejit.*

VI.

Séala Bán Bay, Ireland—North of Kilkee

Creatures crawled and swam, half in shadows within the Deep Dens—their horrible, mutant bodies with hooks, barnacles, and frightening oceanic mugs. These creatures—the fomori—always seemed to be seeking flesh to rend and devour, only answering to the call at the back of the Den's caverns.

At the deepest place within the Dens, a large, horrible creature appeared to be half stone, partially crustaceous, and made of dark, rubbery meat. The cavern was its shell. It had crab-like claws, several octopoid arms, and tentacles roaming and shifting about. But if one looked at the center of the seemingly infinite logarithmic spirals, they could see his face and crown, his more humanlike form.

Elieris was once the most beautiful of the fomori, and now he was this horrible, gargantuan monster that had become part of the Deep Dens itself—a deep abyss of caverns under the ocean, located in deeper realms of the Otherworld, where the Fomorians called their home.

Elieris, humiliated and furious, reached out with his mind through the Hollow into the sleeping darkness of the bay. Deep in a cave to the south, there was a cave that legends often called the Feast Pit. Many centuries ago, the Milesian Druids would bring out one boy and one girl, both thirteen of age. Torches would be lit around the Feast Pit, and they would be lowered down to the creatures there, never to be seen again. Sacrifices to the monsters so that they would not come to the village and gorge themselves or attack their fishing vessels. In this Feast Pit, under the dark waters of these caverns, there was the lair of the *maighdean uaimh*. The humanoid yet undead sisters slept on the water cavern's floor, covered in centuries of mud and oceanic debris. They awoke at once when they heard Elieris calling, and they awoke hungry. They twisted and turned out from underneath the mud, naked and crying out. They roiled and thrashed in the waters, rising to the surface.

Their queen, Muirgen, crawled slick and naked from the waters onto the cave's rocky embankment around the edges of the main cavern, and raised her hands in supplication to the fomori, as her sisters swam around the ancient underwater cages behind her that were hanging down in the water by great rusted chains that were fixed to the cave ceiling.

She turned to her sisters and spoke to them in their ancient tongue: *"Ri Elieris commands us. We will call the mists of the Commination, and we will feed."*

The sisters all keened their hunger, but Muirgen stayed fast and started raising the mists. In her mind, the Ri of the Fomorians planted an image of a redheaded girl that escaped them. Oh yes, she remembered that face. They were to find her and return her to the Dens. Muirgen was only too happy to comply, feeling joy fill her with the waking that she so desperately needed.

VII.

For nearly a week, Oona was sure she heard something in her house. First, it was her bathroom. She thought somebody was inside it, but when she opened the door... nothing was there. She heard footsteps in the night, usually after she had just crawled into bed. Oona checked her attic whenever she heard something and didn't happen upon the culprit once.

After a few days of this, she was sure her home was haunted. Oona went to her closest friend, Orna, in Kilkee. Not wanting Orna's husband to hear and laugh at her, she waited for him to leave on the boat that he named after his wife, taking his son, Cuán, with him. Oona knocked on her door. Orna was happy to see her, letting her in and making her tea.

"Do you believe in ghosts, Orna?"

Orna smiled at her. "Of course. The Holy Ghost is the most famous of them."

Oona sighed. "I think my house is haunted. I hear footsteps at night in different rooms, but when I go to check on it, there's nothing there. Do you think I'm losing my mind, or do you think it might be a specter wandering through?"

Orna said, "Tell me everything."

Oona did. She told her about how clothes have been stolen, and food—the noises.

"No, I don't think you have a specter," Orna said. "They don't bloody eat."

Oona was perplexed. "Then what do I have?"

"Sounds like a faerie to me," Orna said matter-of-factly.

Oona took a sharp breath, her hands covering her mouth. She stared at Orna with wide eyes. "That's it! I have a faerie living in my home! That explains so much!"

Orna nodded. "You don't want to piss off the aos sí. I'd try to feed it and see if it goes away."

Oona was very aware of the *sí*, but her family didn't speak much of them. Not only did the Church sort of frown on it, but it was often considered impolite to mention the good folk if you could help it.

"Do you know how to feed them?"

Orna sipped at her tea and said, "Of course. I'll help you out with this. I wouldn't want you to try it alone and mess things up. When the sidhe curses you, it's a fair amount of work to turn your fortune. Don't want to mess that up. Not in Kilkee."

VIII.

"It's simple science," Cuán said. "You have red hair, so there would be other redheads in your family. And the only redheads I know are the Ó Fionnáin's. Though Colum was insisting that they only had one daughter. That's Deirdre."

Seagrass Maggie sat listening to him, eating the crab that Cuán saved for her while he stoked the fire in the cave for warmth. At the name 'Deirdre', she stopped and looked up at him.

"What is it?" he said. He loved looking into the girl's surreal blue eyes when she looked at him.

Ever since he'd been coming back to see her, she started to soften up, becoming at ease with him. Cuán was glad. He didn't know why, but something deep in his heart wanted her to like him. It was absurd, but there it was.

"Dee-uh-druh."

"Aye. Close enough, I suppose."

Maggie ran a finger down her lower lip when her eyes turned up. "I'm rememberin' this name. It's faint, though. The farther in me mind, the harder it's getting in rememberin'."

Cuán wiped his face in exhaustion, seeing her crystalline eyes following his hand with some thirst, and handed her a canteen with water. She drank it.

Cuán thought it out some more.

His third-class teacher used to be full of fairy stories and old legends. Cuán stood up and started pacing. Wasn't there a creature that stole babies, swapping them with their own? Something like that? He knocked on his head and said, "Fettlings... Seachangers... something like that."

"What words are these?" Maggie said. Her eyebrows were scrunched over her freckled nose.

Cuán shook his head, getting excited now. He was onto something. He knew it.

Cuán had never seen Deirdre in church. Why was that? She seemed so human, so normal, even if pretty. But could she be some sort of fae creature?

It all sounded so absurd. All of this. Except here he was, in a cave with a girl that was obviously touched by some *other world*. No matter how hard he tried, the unnatural was making more and more sense. He couldn't find any other logical explanation for any of it. There were no missing girl reports in Kilkee, nor any of the surrounding areas. The girl swam in dangerous waters and survived them. She didn't suffer from hyperthermia, and when he looked into her face, he did see Deirdre. She was right there. Surely.

"There's somebody I must talk to," he told Maggie. "She might be able to make some sense of this."

Maggie got up, holding her pants up as she shuffled quickly to him.

"Yeh won't tell her about me." Worry thick in her voice.

"No, I promise." *Trust me*, he thought.

Seagrass Maggie touched his face and let her fingers trace his jaw. He patiently let her soft fingers run over his face, though he caught a whiff of her foul smell.

Once she stopped, she pulled out her watch from her pocket.

Cuán took it and popped it open for her. After winding it, he pointed out an hour from then. "Very soon," he added.

Maggie nodded, taking the watch back, staring at it.

"Yer the only one I can count on," Maggie said. "I have no one else."

Cuán nodded, something inside him swelling. "I swear. You're safe with me. I promise."

Cuán made his way back to town. He stopped in a shop for a small bag of lemon drops and walked to his third-class teacher's—Mrs. Donoghue's—home. She answered shortly and pulled Cuán in for a hug. They retreated inside for some tea, and Cuán came right out with it: "One thing I really enjoyed were some of your fairy stories."

Mrs. Donoghue was one of Cuán's favorite teachers. She had an aura of wisdom as well as a sharp intellect, something that many of the other teachers lacked. The others seemed so caught up in the small world of Kilkee and its surroundings, while Mrs. Donoghue was always so worldly. She was a very good storyteller and would go into great detail about whatever experience she was relaying. Some of them were about her observations on people in general and the superstitions of the world—like faeries.

"Most kind, Cuán." She handed him his warm tea, and he took a sip before putting it down.

He enjoyed the warmth running through him for a moment. "I was trying to remember one of them specifically. They were the fairies that stole children and replaced them with their own?"

Mrs. Donoghue sat down beside him, nodding. "Aye. You mean the siofra. In other countries, they're often called changelings. Fairies would steal away the child and leave a changeling behind to grow up in their place. I believe a lot of medieval parents used to use this excuse to get rid of deformed or other unwanted children."

"That's horrible," Cuán said. He contemplated that horrible idea for a moment and decided to continue on in spite of it. "But let's say fairies were real. They're not just excuses fer bad parents. Why would a fairy steal a child?"

Mrs. Donoghue humored him, took a sip of tea, and said: "Well, I would suppose it could be the unseelie fairies. They love tricking people and do all kinds of nasty things. Maybe they do it to purposefully cause harm or are malicious enough that they enjoy such terrible tricks. Or perhaps it's because they want the child for some reason. There's something special about them, and they're willing to exchange their own child for it.

"The one thing about fairies that you must understand, Cuán, is that they are not like us. They're not human. They are something else entirely. A different kind of creature with their own habits and motivations. The thing is, if fairies were real, how would we begin to understand why they do what they do?"

Cuán nodded, understanding. It may be the reason why Seagrass Maggie seemed so human but had alien mannerisms that he didn't quite understand yet. She had spent eighteen years with—

Cuán stopped and thought about that for a moment. Assuming Deirdre was a changeling and Maggie was the real Deirdre Ó Fionnáin, it has been about eighteen years since she was taken. But Seagrass Maggie looked shy of ten, or maybe a little older. If she was indeed the child, how did she not grow up like Deirdre? There was another story. It involved a white horse, and man growing very old upon returning from *Tír na nÓg*, if he remembered correctly.

"One more question, Mrs. Donoghue, if you don't mind."

"Sure, Cuán. Ask away, boy."

"In this other place—this Otherworld—how does time manage?"

Mrs. Donoghue chuckled. She took another sip of her tea, beaming at him. "Well, there are stories of Tír na nÓg—the Land of Youth. It is said that when you die, this is where your soul goes for the rest of eternity. It is, ultimately, where the gods and other fairies retreated from the world when man came to power. The Milesians, specifically.

"In one particular legend, there was a fae girl named Niamh. She loved to leave Tír na nÓg for the mortal world from time to time, and she found love there in a man named Oisín. Not wanting to return to Tír na nÓg without him, Niamh took Oisín back with her on a pallid horse that could walk across the waters between worlds.

"It's said that they lived several months in happiness, love, and pleasure, but after a while, Oisín began to get homesick for Ireland. Niamh couldn't bear seeing him so depressed, so she sent for her horse and placed him upon it, saying, 'This horse can travel the waters between the worlds. While you are on her, Tír na nÓg will be with you. Be careful not to touch the ground.'

"So, the horse took Oisín back to Ireland, where he discovered that everyone he knew had passed away and the world had moved on three hundred years. Upset and frightened, Oisín did not know what to do, but in his shock, he fell from the horse and landed on the ground.

"In a span of several minutes, Oisín aged three hundred years and passed away. When the horse returned without him to Tír na nÓg, Niamh's heart broke, and it's said that he was the last lover she ever had."

"So, time is much different on the other side?" Cuán said.

"Sometimes, time there is faster, and sometimes it is much slower. Again, these are fairies, and fairy worlds. Our logic does not apply to them, their culture, or their worlds," Mrs. Donoghue said.

Cuán sipped at his tea and changed the subject to have a pleasant chat. Inward, Cuán thought about how this could make sense. Seagrass Maggie could very well be eighteen years old, but her body had only grown to eight or nine. Deirdre, on the other hand, having been here the whole eighteen years, would have aged as normal. This explained why Maggie spoke and thought much older than she was. Her mind was ten years older than her body.

Maggie *was* the same age as Deirdre. Her body just hadn't caught up with the world yet.

Once he was finished with his tea, he tossed a lemon drop in his mouth and bade farewell to Mrs. Donoghue. His father would be expecting him soon, but he wanted to share what he discovered with Maggie. He quickly made his way down to the cave, surprised not to see her there. Cuán looked around for her, but there was no sign of her. Unable to wait any longer, Cuán headed for home.

IX.

After Cuán left her, Maggie started getting scared of being alone. Unable to wait for him, she returned to the house where she had been sleeping. She crawled into the attic and found a strange ring of different things by the attic door: a small assemblage of twigs, lichen, small rocks, and pinecones laid out around a bowl with a small cake in it.

She sniffed the cake, and her belly grumbled. Thinking that it seemed pleasant enough, Maggie put it into her mouth and found the cake sweet and delightful.

She curled up again and fell asleep, hoping to empty her mind of all the nightmarish recollections and confusions that she had about her new life in this new world. She thought it would be a short nap, and when the pocket watch was close to the time, she'd go back to the cave to catch Cuán.

A little later, she woke up, hearing the far-off keening again. It wasn't a normal noise by any means, as it was one that seemed to be conjured up inside her head. She knew it was a cry made north of here, but it still only rang in her mind.

Maggie tried to block it out, but the tone crept into her bones like cockroaches. There was something dark and hungry about this keening. She had tried a few times to join her mind with the Hollow to travel north and see what it was, but she had somehow lost connection with it. Maggie didn't know why.

At the attic vent, she peered through to the garden down below and saw the middle-aged woman tending it. Over the last few days, she learned that the woman's name was Oona. She had lost her husband only the year before and made meager means by trading in town from her garden and the two goats that she kept in the small shed.

Maggie watched her work. Sometimes other women from town came by and gave her donations of food or clothes. Most didn't fit her, but she took them all with a graceful smile. They would chat awhile, and she would offer them some tea. Through their conversations Maggie began to know some of the people of Kilkee.

Maggie loved her. She was a sweet, older woman who cared for her animals and enjoyed everyone's company that Maggie saw her converse with. It was nice to see. It was different from the Fomorians, and their foul screeching and snapping. Maggie didn't have to watch the abuse they inflicted on everything around them, or fear the terrible eyes searching for her, locking onto her with their hate.

One of Oona's friends happened to be Cuán's mammy, Orna. Orna and Oona would get together, and Maggie could tell right away that Orna made Oona the happiest. They'd gossip and joke all through their visit, and they would hug deeply before they went their separate ways.

Maggie yearned for all of it, and yet was afraid to be seen. If they all knew that she was there, their minds would think of her and dream of her, and all thoughts and dreams flowed through the Hollow. She wouldn't be able to explain it to them in any real words, but the Hollow was a psychic atmosphere between the physical world and the astral plane that surrounded the Otherworld. To mortals, it was invisible, or 'hollow,' as if it didn't exist. To the fae and the fomori, the Hollow was an atmospheric projection of the mind: thought, word, and idea from the past, present and future, manifesting in an invisible dimension superimposed over the physical world. Maggie thought of it as a psychic cornea between two worlds. And if people thought about her or dreamed of her, the fomori could see this in the Hollow and know where to find her. It was already dangerous enough that Cuán knew who she was.

Maggie sometimes assumed a part of her own subconscious self knew how to project her being into the Hollow when she slept. A part of her searched for *The Fall*, wanting to torment them in their dream, but it was all so foggy afterward. She remembered little of it when she woke. Over time, however, Maggie started to suspect that in the Hollow, people became doorways to the innermost dreams, and her subconscious made connections that Maggie couldn't yet understand.

Maggie sighed, turned to look over her shoulder, and jumped up, crying out. Before she could move, she saw the blur of a woman coming at her, open arms grabbing for her. Maggie screamed, but the arms ensnared her, pulling her into the woman's warm body. It was Cuán's mother, Orna.

Oona was coming into the house under the attic door, saying, "It's a girl?"

"Let me go! Let me go! *Lig dom imeacht!*" Maggie cried.

"Calm down, calm down, little one. We're not going to hurt you. Are we, Oona?"

Orna held her tight, as Oona climbed the steep stairs, so that Oona could grab her wrist. Maggie made another attempt to escape, tugging as hard as she could, but Oona and Orna held tight.

Oona bent over to be more her height to not seem too scary. "I'm Oona. Who are you?"

Maggie didn't say anything. She teared up, unable to stop herself from doing so. She was too tired to fight anymore, and who knows how they now vibrated within the Hollow?

"Who are you, girl?" Oona demanded again.

Maggie looked at her, tears running down her cheeks: "Do not tell anyone. Please. They can't find me. Not ever."

Oona looked up at Orna and back at Maggie. Slowly, holding her hand tight, they worked together to bring Maggie down from the attic by the stairs. They directed her into the sitting room.

"There is no need to cry or be alarmed. Are you hungry? I think we should all sit down and eat, and have us a chat, okay? Nobody is telling anyone anything. We're just going to talk," Oona said.

Maggie looked at the door. It was closed. The windows were as well. There was nowhere to run, so she nodded her head.

Maggie didn't know what she would say to them. What could she say without giving herself away? She liked both women and didn't want to hurt them. But what would she do for her own preservation? Maggie couldn't answer that.

"What's your name, girl?" Oona asked again.

"Cuán calls me Seagrass Maggie. I don't have a 'membering on me real name."

Though 'Deirdre' still rang through her mind.

"What's this with Cuán?" Orna said. "What does he have to do with this?"

Maggie turned to look back at Orna, saying, "He showed me the cave and brought me these clothes. And food. He's been feeding me ever since—"

"Since when?" Orna said.

Orna looked off in wonderment, and Oona grabbed Maggie's shoulders to draw her eyes once again. Once they were looking into each other's, Oona said, "Well, let's get you some more food. And let's see if we can find clothes that fit you a bit better."

Oona and Orna sat down with her and decided that whether Maggie was telling the whole truth, she definitely wasn't from one of the families here in Kilkee. (Though she did look vaguely familiar to them.) They had no idea how she ended up here. Had no guesses at all, really. So they were not going to worry about this for now. They promised her that they wouldn't tell everyone in town about her either. Maggie was relieved, but she couldn't escape the idea that through them, she would be seen in the Hollow.

Twenty minutes later, they had all eaten their plates. The two women seemed to be engaged as if she weren't there. Maggie listened, waiting for them to change their minds or come up with a terrible plan that put them all in danger.

"Someone is bound to ask who this child is," Orna said.

Oona nodded. "For now, until we can figure things out, she can stay with me. I'll tell everyone she's a niece from Dublin. That should stop further questions for now."

The only thing Maggie kept to herself was the remembering of the Deep Dens, and the creatures that hurt her for countless years. She didn't mention the women keening that she heard ringing around in her mind. Maggie was sure they wouldn't believe her, and she didn't want Orna to take Cuán away from her either.

She was scared, to be certain.

The women seemed nice enough, and they knew Cuán. Over the last few days, she had begun to trust him, and though it was hard for her, she decided that if he could trust Cuán, she could trust them. The only thing she worried about was how their minds would vibrate in the Hollow. The Fomorians would be clever, waiting for the right signs that manifested in that invisible place. There was no denying it. Maggie would have to watch the shores carefully.

She hoped with all her heart that she could trust them.

"Tomorrow, I'll go by the church and see if there's any donations for girls about her size. We'll get her some clothes," Orna said.

"What will you say to Cuán?"

"Well, I don't understand why he didn't come to me with this right away, but under the circumstances, I'm not going to tan his hide for it. He obviously was frightened for her and wanted to help."

Oona nodded. "He'll be a good man one day."

Orna nodded and looked at Maggie.

Maggie wanted to agree, but she thought Cuán was already a good person. What did 'being a man' have anything to do with being good?

After Orna left, Oona showed Maggie to a spare room. It had a bed, fully made out for her, and a short dresser with three drawers. Otherwise, the room was empty.

"You can sleep in the bed. It's far better than sleeping on a dirty hardwood floor, for sure. It was going to be a nursery until I lost my husband," Oona said. "Now it sits empty. You'll be more comfortable down here."

Maggie turned to her and took her hand. "I'm sorry for your late husband."

This brought a sudden tear to Oona's eyes. "How did you know about him? Oh, oh, no. It's okay, Maggie," she said.

"It still hurts," Maggie said.

Oona nodded, wiping the tears away with her fingers. "Yes, but that's enough. You understand me?"

Maggie went to the bed and sat down, feeling its soft mattress and the duvets. She was grateful, but unable to express herself.

Oona returned with a nightgown and a robe.

"I heated water for a bath. Climb into it and wash your body. You should be clean before you go to bed."

"Bath?"

Oona tilted her head. "Have you never had a bath?"

Maggie didn't know what the word meant.

Oona took her hand and took her down the hall to the bathroom. The clearest water she ever saw filled a cast iron tub. It was steamy. Oona placed a hand in the water for a moment. She took a white bar, dipped it into the water, and lathered up her hands. She spread it out with the water and rinsed her hand in the tub.

"You do this with your body and not just your hands," she explained. "You remove all your clothes, and you use this soap bar to get the dirt off you. The water rinses it away, and you come out clean."

Maggie nodded. She remembered her mother washing her down in a tub again. "I think I understand."

Oona smiled at her and put the bar of soap in her hand.

"Take as long as you like. Baths can feel quite soothing if you're in no hurry. Once you're done, we'll try to brush some of that hair out."

Oona left, closing the door behind her. Maggie went to the water, expecting it to be cold, and found that the water was pleasantly warm. She smelled the soap and enjoyed the flowery fragrance. This is very nice, and she felt tears running down her cheeks. It was a kindness she had never felt before.

X.

Cuán, sucking on a lemon drop, helped his da clean out the two doggers to get them ready for the next morning's trip. The work was hard, and by the time he was done, his hands were sore, his clothes were filthy, and he stank of the sea, fish, and his own dankness.

They returned home and found that his mam was still out. His da mumbled about her visiting Oona, and he went in to take a bath. They only had one tub, so he was sitting on the porch, looking out at the night when he found his mam walking up the path. She seemed to be carrying a few things, so he went down to help her, grabbing a basket from her. In her arms, she was carrying several women's clothes.

"Cuán, my boy, I'm going to ask you once, and I don't want lies," his ma said.

Cuán knew this tone. She was being serious. He swallowed the small left-over shard of his lemon drop. What could she possibly know?

"I don't know if I follow," Cuán said.

"Why didn't you tell me there was a girl you found, and you was helpin'?"

Cuán felt his blood run cold. She found out.

"How did—?"

"...I know? Well, the girl in question has been sneaking in and sleeping in Oona's attic. She thought the girl was a fairy and we left her a cake, but when we checked the attic, we found her sleeping. We decided to catch her to find out what she was doin' there."

A fairy, Cuán thought. She was. If not really, she was in spirit.

"She must have been scared."

"She was, but she came clean. Even told us about how you warmed her up, got her some old clothes, and fed her over the last couple of weeks."

"Sorry, Ma. She was so scared, and she thinks that if people find out about her, she'll be caught and taken back."

"Take back to whom?"

They were at the door. Cuán thought to open the door for her, but da was inside. He wasn't sure if he was ready for his da to get in on this conversation, so he held still and looked at his mam.

"She says that she escaped from these bad people. Maggie's afraid that if word gets out, the people will find her and take her back. They were horrible to her," Cuán said. "You won't tell Da, will you?"

His ma looked him in the eyes, and after a brief moment of doubt, she shook her head, sighing. "I've no mind to tell anyone. The girl—Maggie—she's afraid of something. We decided she'll stay with Oona for now. I got these clothes from the church. They should fit the girl better. I'll take them to her tomorrow when you and your da are out on the dogger."

Relieved, Cuán kissed his mam's cheek. "Thanks, Ma."

"You stink, Cuán. Go take a bath. Tired of smellin' ye chisler's body odor."

Cuán opened the door for his mam. "Sure thing, Ma."

XI.

Séala Bán Bay, Ireland

Where did the fog come from? It was thick and Síle could barely recognize her home, where now the greens of her land were dashed by the hazy grayness of the mists. Síle shuddered, holding herself in a desperate attempt to be warm. The light dress she wore was short-sleeved, and the winds played with the ends of her skirt, annoying her.

Síle's father was a fisherman and so was her lover, Aengus. The two of them spent most of their time at the pubs or taking long walks through the fields when they didn't want to be home. It got late, and it was stupid, really. The fog had been around for several days now, and they knew there'd be some trouble getting home in the dark.

They had been walking down the path that ran along the shores when they decided to turn back for the village. Aengus had stopped to kiss her, holding her tight. They laughed, enjoyed the warmth of each other's bodies, and she felt him get aroused.

"You think anybody would see us with the fog so soupy?" Aengus said. "We're all alone. We should take advantage of the situation."

"You mean take advantage of me," she'd said, giggling. She pried herself free from his arms and spun around from him. "We can't have that."

In truth, she was nervous. It felt like someone watched them, and it made her shiver to think that it had malicious intent. Knowing his male ego would probably be hurt, she spun back around to tell him, "If you wanna fuck, you've got to take me home." Only he was no longer there. Only the fog.

"Aengus? *Aengus!*"

He was either refusing to talk to her, or...

"Aengus! Where the bloody fuck are you?"

Something watched her. In the air, something—not a stench, or sound—but something heavy in the misty air put thoughts into her head she didn't want to think about. Hunger. Hatred. *Blood.*

Síle frowned, cheeks burning, almost ready to sob as her chest got tight.

Something moved. She caught it in the corner of her eye. It was a blur, but something was there.

Laughter... Not Aengus. It sounded like a woman.

Something hissed behind her, and she spun around to see. Nothing. More leaden fog.

She knew it wasn't Aengus, but she cried out, "Aengus! I'll bloody break your nose if you don't stop this."

A long, breathy *hiss* oozed around her.

Close by, she heard a woman crying, adding its din to the hissing noises around her. Not just one person, or thing. No, there were many of them, and they were all around her. Clenching her teeth, heart beating fast and hard, she damned herself for not running when she had the chance.

Was there still time to run? Maybe if she ran, they wouldn't be able to catch her.

Who were *they*?

She didn't know, didn't care. *Run*, she told herself. *They're going to hurt you. RUN!*

Síle picked up her dress and she ran, watching the path at her feet, hoping that whatever was out there was only playing games.

She knew they weren't.

There was hunger and hatred in them.

"Stay away!" she cried. *"Stay away!"*

Pale faces were in the fog. They had large black eyes and pallid blue lips. Black hair. One opened their mouth, showing off rows and rows of long, barbed teeth. As soon as she saw a couple of them, they were gone in the whiteness of the fog behind her.

"Please!" she begged them. "Don't hurt me! I've done nothing!"

Hot tears were pouring down her cheeks now. They followed her. She could still feel them. They were reaching with their hands...

They wanted to bite her. They desired to tear Síle's flesh from her bones. Eat her internal organs. And though she thought they might be imaginings, she truly believed that she knew their very desire.

It was in the blackness of their eyes.

With the Hunger. The hatred.

"No! *No!*"

Through the fog, she could see the first home. It was whitewashed in the haze. Síle tried to think whose home it could be, but it didn't matter. She would be safer if she could get inside, she thought.

"Help! Help! Someone HELP!"

Cold hands grabbed her ankles, and she fell forward. Her arms hit first, then her pelvis, and her face bounced off the ground. The blow to her face shocked her, took her breath from her. She tried to cry out, except the breath she lost was the life in the words she needed to desperately use.

More hands were grabbing her, holding her down. The hands tore at her clothes, and she felt one of them bite into her calf. The burning agony of those teeth rending her tissues and muscles induced a terror that made her heart almost explode in her chest.

White skeletal faces.

Long, black, corpse-hair.

More teeth clamped onto her; more pieces of her flesh torn from her body.

They licked and sucked up her juices with white, viscous tongues that splayed out like webbing around their teeth, hands prying and clawing as they went.

She never felt her whole body in this much pain before. There were no words to describe what she was feeling. It didn't matter anyway. Her last thoughts were of Aengus. Bloody, *fuck-all* Aengus, and she wondered where he was before her mind found oblivion.

When the fog came off the sea in the Séala Bán village, the commissioners, Eamon and Patrick, began getting reports of people being found dead on the roads, torn apart, and drained of blood. Those who were terrified of what was happening around them attempted to leave, but many seemed to fall under a similar demise. Dead. Bloodless. After two months, the people of Séala Bán started to realize that the fog was never going to go away. This was no ordinary fog. This was the Devil's Work.

Patrick wanted to get the town's people out and started coming up with a plan to get the people on the boats and escape via the bay. Eamon fought with his fellow commissioner about how this would destroy Séala Bán, and how it would destroy their positions, but Patrick wanted nothing more than to get his family out of this fog.

It seemed most of the people sided with Patrick, and Eamon spent one evening drinking brandy, trying not to let his anger get the better of him.

His parlor windows opened, and the fog rolled in. Eamon was sure that he had closed his balcony and locked it. Through the fog came a very pale woman with long black hair. She was naked and wet, dripping on the floor, seaweed caught in her dark locks. This woman moved like a graceful animal rather than a human. She was ethereal as she made her way to his chair.

Eamon cried out, thinking, *Could this be the banshee?* His heart pumped hard in his chest as she drew near, and he knew that this could be the murderer that left bodies on the village roads. His eyes found the knife that she had buried into her left breast, sheathed there, dripping a black ichor down her torso.

What sort of creature would use its own flesh to sheathe a blade?

"*I am Muirgen*," the woman whispered. She leaned in close to his face, and her white tongue licked the air between them. "*I bring the Commination to your village.*"

"Wh-Wh-What do you want from m-m-m-me?" Even his voice betrayed him.

"*I know Patrick. He has spoken with the people,*" she said.

"Yes. They plan to leave the village."

Muirgen grinned, and he saw her sharp, inhuman teeth. He was sure that there were fishbones trapped between them. Her breath stank of something rotting in the sea.

"*You will stop him this night,*" Muirgen said. She grabbed the hilt of the dagger resting in her breast, and she pulled it free without so much as a wince. Her black eyes, he realized, never blinked.

Muirgen put the hilt of the dagger in his hand.

"I'm no murderer," Eamon said, trying to gulp the large lump in his throat down.

Muirgen grinned and nodded toward his balcony. At first, he thought he saw a wall of skulls in the darkness outside his home. His eyes widened when he saw all the pale faces. Black eyes and dark yawning mouths. Black hair sweeping about in the unseen wind. Otherwise, they were all still.

"Oh my Lord God," he said. The undead.

He looked back at Muirgen as she licked the air between them again, this time her tongue spider-webbing out like some gelatinous, white mucusy web before pulling back in between her bluish lips.

"*You are a murderer tonight, Eamon,*" Muirgen said. "*Or my sisters will run through your home and savor your wife, your elderly father, and all your children. Nothing will be left of them but bones.*"

"But why me," he sobbed, letting himself tremble, "when your sisters could—?"

Muirgen chuckled. "*Because I want to feel your agony and humiliation.*"

Eamon's hands tightened hard around the dagger's hilt so that his knuckles hurt. By the time he wiped his tears away, the demons were gone.

That night Eamon went into Patrick's home and struck him with a dagger. When Patrick fell dead, Eamon had his bodyguards take Patrick's family to the church, where he started ringing the bells. Once most of the townsfolk gathered, Eamon told them that demons roamed the fog. He said that if they were all to venture an escape, the demons planned to kill them all.

"Our only choice is to trust in God and remain here," he said. "Or we will all die, and we will find only an eternity in Hell."

Some of the folk argued, but Eamon put a stop to it.

"You will not put this village or anyone in it in jeopardy! Should you not listen to me, you will be hung for treason. This is for all our safety. Mark my words. This is the only way we will survive this."

After that, after a few days, the villagers began to realize that no other murders were being committed around the village. Some suspected Eamon made a dark bargain with the vampyric creatures, but nobody was willing to face him or the creatures.

By the end of that week, however, Muirgen returned to Eamon's lonely parlor.

"You have done well," Muirgen said. "But me and my sisters must feed. When you hear the keening, you will make a sacrifice at the old Feast Pit. If we do not have a sacrifice, we will take three for the one and have a feast. Do you understand?"

Eamon nodded.

"We need this fog to remain for a while. I need you to become our font—it's very source," she said. "Your lifeforce will feed the fog like a gush of blood for Ri Elieris!"

Muirgen drew closer and grabbed his manhood. Her fingers massaged him exquisitely before pulling his pants apart and down. She pushed him back in his chair and climbed on him. Her cold body took him in, and she worked him until he exploded inside her. Muirgen bit into his neck, her teeth sinking deep, and she began sucking blood from him. He could feel the blood rushing through his flesh into her mouth and it hurt, and he hated it.

Her tongue sprayed out in its web-like form, splattering across his chest. It felt like millions of long needles pierced his flesh and pumped fire into his muscles.

When she retracted her tongue, she climbed off, and he found himself falling to the floor, unable to move. He thought he was dying as the chemical fire within him swept through him wholly, stopping his heart, making everything go black.

Eamon later woke up in darkness. The air was short. He felt around. His heart leapt.

I've been buried alive, he thought. Panic swept through him, his muscles tightened, and he started pushing and pounding on the coffin.

"What is happening?" It was a voice from outside the coffin.

He stopped. Listened. He heard rustling around him. Someone fidgeted with latches.

"Help me!" he shouted. "Get me out of this thing!"

The coffin opened, and he scurried from it as quickly as he could. When he stood, he saw everyone looking at him with awe and horror. It was his wake! How long had he been out?

"You almost fucking buried me alive!" Eamon shouted.

His wife's mouth gaped. "The doctor couldn't find your heart. Nobody saw you breathing."

His eldest daughter fainted, and one of her brothers went to her to help her.

Eamon, terrified, shoved the coffin over until it crashed to the floor. Nobody in the room knew what to do or say.

So, he broke the silence: "I need a bath. Can one of you fine gobshite kindly pour one for me?"

Eamon thought of Muirgen and her cold, lifeless body enveloping his sex, thought of her teeth and her slimy sluglike tongue flickering around. His gut reacted, pumped heavily, and he threw up as he fell to his knees. That hag creature! What has she done to him?

Your lifeforce will feed the fog like a gush of blood for Ri Elieris!

Was he even alive anymore? What had she done to him?

What had she *done*?

Luckily, Eamon didn't have to see Muirgen again for several long years.

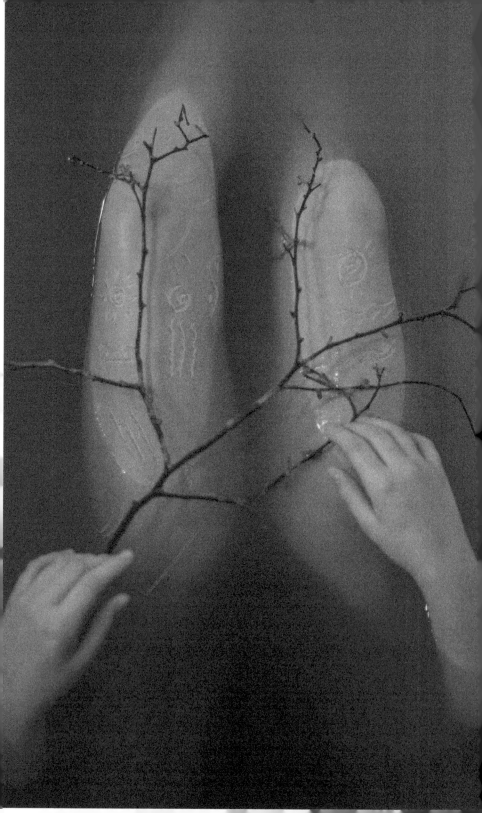

II. Deirdre

I.

Over the next ten years, Maggie and Cuán became closer while Oona raised her.

Closer. Maggie would always giggle at this.

Cuán tried to be the older brother as long as he could, but he couldn't deny how much of a crush he had for her for long. Maggie grew into herself, and she noticed how Cuán started looking at her, and how he lovingly tended her. She began to feel more comfortable with him every passing year. More than comfortable. When she began to sense his arousal when he was close to her—his look, his breath, his lips slightly parting—she couldn't deny that it excited her, giving her tingles throughout her body. Cuán wasn't just the cute older boy anymore, and their first kiss was electric. It danced across her chest, down to her legs and to her feet, like lightning trying to meet the ground.

Oona reared Maggie as if she were her own daughter, declaring to everyone in town that she was her niece. Nobody questioned it, since Oona was from Wexford, south of Dublin. Having married her fisherman husband, she moved to Kilkee when he wanted to return to his family roots. Nobody knew much about her family outside of what Oona shared with them.

Shortly after Oona's birthday, they realized Maggie didn't have one, so they chose a birthday for her to give her a special day. Cuán suggested the day he'd found her, and Oona would always bake Maggie the same faerie cake she gave Maggie when she didn't know any better. The joke remained between them, Orna and Cuán, of course.

When she wasn't thinking about Cuán or the other aspects of her life, Maggie spent each day and night longing to be with her blood parents. While Oona became more of a mother to her, Maggie was still haunted by the lingering division between her, Mona, and Colum. She followed them around, learned from them when she could, and helped them out whenever possible. They got to know her, and she got to know them, but Maggie found it impossible to tell them the truth of what happened. Of *who* she was.

How do you tell someone that you were their *real* daughter, and the one they have loved the whole time happened to be a fake?

You didn't, Maggie thought. The Ó Fionnáin's were happy with their memories of their daughter, Deirdre. The *siofra*. Maggie couldn't bring herself to destroy their dreams. But her rage with the siofra grew every day, and Maggie wanted to confront her, scream at her... *kill* her. Could she fix the mess without hurting anyone that she loved? She didn't know, but there was a rage in her that was unlike anything else. Whenever she thought of Deirdre taking away her life, or whenever she heard Deirdre's name, Maggie would sometimes seek the crashing ocean waves and scream as she dove into them.

Only the battle with the waves seemed to tire her anger.

Other times Maggie found herself returning to the Hollow, peering through the rippling *Fall*. As it was with her in the Deep Dens, these dreams were crazy, and she didn't quite understand them. Focusing her anger through *The Fall* always made it feel better though. For a while.

However, it was only a matter of time before Maggie realized what The Fall was inside the Hollow: it was a doorway into Deirdre's subconscious mind. And inside this door, Maggie could give Deirdre nightmares, tell Deirdre she was coming for her. *One day.*

"I will bring yeh back to the waters, and I will drown yeh for what you have done! Yer lungs will take in the cold waters, shoot agony through yer body, and you will die wracked in the worst pain imaginable, equal only to the pain yeh have given me!"

But taking out her anger in a dream or in the waves was one thing. Actually fixing the mess she'd made? It all seemed impossible. And eventually, Deirdre began to learn to hide her doorway or lock her out, making the ability to enter her dreams more and more uncommon.

And behind all of this was the fomori. Crooked, twisted, nightmare creatures that Maggie knew were still looking for her, wanting to take her back to the sea.

As the years progressed and life happened to be good for Maggie, the thought never left the dark corners of her mind that the Fomorians wanted to capture her. Though Maggie feared how her new family 'vibrated' in the psychic Hollow, the Fomorians either did not key into it, or hadn't made their move.

The mystery of it only disturbed her more. It wasn't until Maggie went looking for the Cailleach at fourteen, that Maggie learned why.

Oona sent Maggie to the small village shop for some supplies. Mona, carrying a basket filled with fruits, saw her and had stopped her, beaming with joy.

"The older you get, the more and more I think you look so much like Deirdre," Mona said. She sobbed, apologizing. "I have not seen her for so long. It's probably why I see so much of her in you."

For Maggie, this was profound. She had never wanted to be a reminder of anyone's sorrow, let alone her own biological mother. Leaving the shop, Maggie teared up. It made her hate the siofra more because she knew that she would never be able to convince her mother or father of who she was. She didn't want to upset them, and yet because she looked identical to their daughter, it would be hard getting closer to them.

They won't see me. Only Deirdre, she thought.

That night she went to the waves to scream out her anguish again, fantasizing about tearing Deirdre limb from limb. Taking her head.

A few nights later, Maggie went to the caves and called the Cailleach. It was cold. She could hear the waves crashing against the rocks outside the cave. She didn't know if it would work, but eventually, at midnight, when Maggie was almost asleep, the long-limbed hag appeared out of the darkness of one of the tunnels. She heard the invisible sprites whispering too: *Cailleach! Cailleach! Cailleach!*

"Why have you summoned me so early without the siofra, child?"

"I-I come to ask a favor. Me real blood parents see me as some copy of their daughter, Deirdre. It hurts them, and I can't have this, so I was hoping that... you would help me change their seein' of me. Until I can remove her and take her place, I need to look different enough to them that I do not remind them of her."

The Cailleach didn't say anything. She moved around her, gazing over her. Though she was a giant, she moved as though she were not there. Her silence was almost haunting in its effect.

"Cailleach. *Please*."

The hag grinned, showing her gruesome rows of sharp teeth and the rot caught between them. "I can place a glamour on you, child, so that your parents do not see her in you. Do you wish to keep your red hair and your eyes?"

Maggie thought about it for a moment. Yes, she thought. They were a part of her.

"I do."

"Then I will change your face enough. Move your cheekbones a bit. Upsize that small nose of yours."

Maggie suddenly worried about Cuán and Oona. How would they see her? Would the change in her face disturb them? She couldn't have that...

"Only to Colum and Mona? I want to look the same to everyone else. I want them to know the true me."

"Yes, I can do this for you."

Maggie felt tears fall down her cheeks. "Thank you."

The Cailleach drew in the palm of her giant hand and blew her sigils onto her. The wretched odor from her mouth made Maggie sick, but she stood tall and waited for her hair to stop flapping in the wind of it before opening her eyes.

The nightmarish hag looked upon her, and it upset Maggie's soul. But Maggie wondered why the Fomorians had not yet found her and couldn't stop herself from asking.

"One more thing. I swear," Maggie said.

The Cailleach only grinned.

"Yes?"

"Why do the Fomorians wait?"

The Cailleach withdrew back into the darkness of the cave a little, the shadows almost covering the whole of her face.

"I made you dark in the Hollow. The Eagla will fade someday, but it is still strong for now. But do not forget, Maggie, that you owe me compensation for your freedom. Do not forget me on your eighteenth birthday, or I will make you shine like a beacon in the Hollow."

Maggie went down to her knees, only wanting the crone to see her deep respect. She tried to not to show her fear, but she knew there wasn't much you could hide from the Cailleach. Maggie bowed her head, smelling the earth below her, and when she looked up, the whispering was gone, and so was the Cailleach.

And over the years, Colum and Deirdre never mentioned how similar she looked to their daughter. Instead of meeting her with tears, they met her gladly as a friendly village face. Even if it did break Maggie's heart.

II.

When Deirdre went to Dublin, a man named Doran Dunn hooked her up with an apartment downtown, overlooking the city. She was able to watch the busy streets below as horses and carriages, bicycles, and pedestrians made their way throughout each day.

On the days she had to herself, Deirdre went to the pubs or spent her time socializing with the other women she met at the parks, or around her apartment building. She quickly found that she didn't like the communal kitchen. Some of the women there were gossips and cheaters, but when she thought she found someone fun to have a good craic, she took up the chance. Occasionally, she'd miss home, and remember how she used to go to *Gilroy's* for lemon drops with Cuán. She found a small shop nearby that sold them and would go to purchase them. Sucking on them always comforted her.

On the days she worked, artists would have her sit for long hours, for multiple days in a row as they painted away. Sometimes they had beautiful dresses for her, or she was requested to bring one of her own. They would go to parks, or near the castles for majestic backgrounds.

A few of the artists were photographers. One of which was Toal Mullins, who had seen her photos from another photographer in Galway, and who had requested her. Doran Dunn was a major contributor to the arts, and Toal was one of Dunn's favorites. It wasn't hard to figure out, as Deirdre quickly learned, that Dunn often requested Toal to hire her. Dunn showed up to some of the shooting sessions and watched them work.

He never spoke to her. Not at first. Over time, however, Dunn came up to her and said, "You have been with us for how long? Two or three years? And look at you! So beautiful, as if you never age!"

Deirdre blushed. "Thank you, Mister Dunn. It's quite a pleasure working for you and Toal here. I can't think of doing anything else."

Dunn nodded at her with a wide grin. Deirdre was smitten, but there was something about Dunn that she didn't like. She couldn't put a finger on it at first.

"Are you still living in the apartment I found for you?" he asked.

Deirdre sighed. "Yes, but I am getting tired of it." She didn't know why she said that. It just came out, and she hoped that it in no way made it sound like she wasn't grateful.

"Oh? Well, I have plenty of room at my estate, if you don't want the burden of the apartments. It does seem so classless! You'd have the same privacy, perhaps more, and we'd hardly see each other. As long as you continue to work for me, I don't even see why you'd have to pay rent."

Would he really let her do that?

Deirdre grinned at him, overjoyed. "I would be very pleased and thankful!"

"Then move in! I'll tell my butler, Felim, to make you a room and to expect you," Dunn said.

A mansion... She was swooning with the idea playing in her mind.

It wasn't long until Deirdre started to begin to hear rumors from the other women. Whispers about Doran Dunn seducing women and selling them to brothels. Deirdre didn't believe them until she began to know some of the women that disappeared. When Deirdre asked Dunn about them, his answers were always a retort—that the women returned to their families, or he didn't know himself, and he didn't care.

"Why worry about these things? People come and go in your life all the time. If I questioned every person's coming and goings, I'd have no life!" he said.

Deirdre started worrying about the women she became friends with. She warned them, but it never stopped them from falling into Dunn's seductions, and eventually his trap. While Dunn felt dangerous to her, she wasn't sure why, but she started to like the thrill of it. What if he caught her trying to help one of her friends? What if one of his thugs tried to hurt her?

Deirdre loved the idea, unable to ignore the fantasy.

Dunn was dangerous, and she liked it. She craved it.

I'm sick, she thought many times over the years. *Sick, and I need to be committed.*

And that idea intrigued her.

But there were some nights that still left her feeling uneasy. The fantasy and thrill of her life was deluged by the weight of her nightmares. Sometimes she would dream of the *monstrous self* that came from the waters, trying to drown her in the sea's immense depths. The red hair floating in ethereal tendrils under the water, the black eyes and spiky fins, and the jagged, sharp, bone-white teeth that were revealed when her monstrous doppelgänger peeled back her lips.

When Deirdre sometimes saw her, she could feel what it was thinking. It hated her. It wanted to kill her. It called itself Seagrass Maggie.

Frightened of the creature, Deirdre started suspecting that she was real. Maybe the monster was coming for her. And it was a very terrifying notion, so every day, she convinced herself that her dreams weren't real. Her doppelgänger wasn't real.

She couldn't be. Could she?

After four years of working together, Toal Mullins showed Deirdre a photographic plate one day over lunch in his studio. The day was bright, shining in through all the windows. Drapes of every color laid around them in piles or hanging over stands for backdrops. Deirdre took the photographic plate and noticed that it was of a young blond-haired woman, the light almost making her hair seem as though it were an angel's halo around her head. She had a coy smile, and surprisingly, she was nude, sitting in a chair with her legs crossed so that one couldn't see her lady bits. Her breasts were round and creamy. Her nipples were hard. The pose in the chair—the turn of her body and the way she sat—accentuated her soft, female curves. The whole thing seemed divine.

"This, my dear, is a form of higher art. Instead of merely painting humanity on the canvas, we can light and feature the reality of it itself! Do you care to be my muse? Do you dare show others your most intimate form? To lay yourself bare for the light like a goddess while still so young and appealing?"

Deirdre laughed at Toal, but she did love the photograph. It was thrilling, wasn't it? To expose oneself and to be captured in this state, perhaps being made immortal? Again, though she didn't understand why she was drawn towards Dunn's dangerous habits, the thought of having people experience her nakedness was joyfully enticing.

It aroused her.

I'm sick, she thought. Why did she like this so much?

She didn't think she'd ever understand it. Despite the social norms and pressure to withhold these sinful urges, Deirdre wanted only to express her sexual energy and live her life fully. She didn't want her life to be stiff and dull... but *vibrant* and... *sublime*.

"It's rather bold, if I do say so. Might have to be bolloxed my first time," she said, though she didn't know if that were true or not. Could she expose herself like this? For Toal Mullins, after all?

The faint, tiny voice in the back of her head spoke up, saying, *I can feel how much you want him, but don't do it. I see dark things in him.*

Dark things? Deirdre stood up from her chair and turned away from Toal, whispering back, "What do you mean?"

As usual, the voice never answered her. When she looked back at Toal, he was standing there, looking curious.

Deirdre smiled at him.

Toal grinned, stood up from his chair, and pulled out a night-gown. "Perhaps let's start with this. Let's have it high on your legs, like you're washing your thighs. We'll start slow, and see how it goes, aye?"

Deirdre shrugged and grabbed the gown. "Aye. That sounds fine."

But did they have to take it so slow though?

III.

A.D. 1851
Kilkee, Ireland

The waves of the sea undulated, crashing against the rocks and crags in a white froth, as if the sea was delirious for the land. Cuán woke early to go to the cliffs to watch Seagrass Maggie stand at the edge, in a trance, as if she were being called back. He did this often over the years, once he realized that Maggie had to see it almost every day. He never bothered her, though. This was her time to be at peace with something that flowed through her spirit. Cuán would never think to break this moment for her.

He stuck a lemon drop in his mouth, sucking on it and reflected.

Seeing her like this was bittersweet. When she grew into herself, her body changing into that of a young woman, he noticed how much he cherished her, the deep fondness that grew naturally from their time together.

He desired her. Sometimes he found himself short of words around her, short of breath, or he caught his own eyes skimming over her soft pale skin and the contours of her womanhood: her soft, round breasts. Her long legs. Her small neck. It made him feel as if he were losing control of himself, and Cuán didn't like that at all. Yet, at the same time, he rejoiced in the desire and fantasized gleefully about her from time to time.

Horrible male needs, he thought.

Cuán thought about these things as she stood at the edge of the cliff, watching the sea. He watched the wind play with her simple, lightly ruffled dress at her calves, and her long, curly red hair. All sensual, beautiful... *Desirable.*

It left him somber at times. Seeing her like this reminded him of the tales of mermaids and the selkies—those who shed their skin, having their freedom stripped from them, and in bitter longing, stealing back their skins to return once again to their real home. Would Seagrass Maggie leave him? The thought shot an arrow through his heart. Was her love for the sea more powerful than her love for him?

Cuán felt tears coming and took a deep breath of the fresh sea air. It helped cool him off, helped him reset the sadness in these meanderings.

Maggie turned around, looking back at him. Her big blue eyes were now on him, and she gave a short wave. Cuán stood there, raised a hand to her and smiled at her. He would always smile at her. It was how he told her that being with her made him happy. It was the only expression he truly admitted to her on a daily basis, and hopefully, what she needed to stay with him for as long as she could.

Maggie walked over to him and put her hands on his chest. They looked at each other's eyes.

"I do love you, Cuán."

Cuán kissed her lips. She kissed back, pushing her tongue inside his mouth. He returned the favor, and Maggie pulled her mouth away, giggling.

"One day, you will have to give in to me, Cuán. One day you've got to stop being such a dryshite."

Cuán suddenly laughed. His Maggie returned.

IV.

Cailleach! Cailleach! Cailleach! Terrible whispers. Maggie had woken, crying, bed wet with so much sweat, it sickened her. It didn't wake Oona, luckily.

Her right hand felt strangely thick. Maggie held it out in front of her. She had long claws, and her skin looked dark, rough, and leathery. She went to run her other hand over it, but both of her hands had the claws, and the coarse skin.

What the feck was going on 'ere?

Almost in tears, she tried wiping 'it' away, but the skin remained rough.

What was all over her body?

She tore the front of her blouse open with her claws and saw that the skin over her whole chest was a dark green, rugged texture. Her nipples felt like hard pebbles. It was inhuman.

And there were scars written all over her body. Some of them were spirals. Others were triangular knots and other various ancient symbols that were written on stones before the Gaels arrived in Ireland.

Was she going back to the Deep Dens? Was this it? Was this a sign the Fomorians were coming for her?

She glanced out her window.

Ponc was there: Cuán's old wolfhound, who passed away a couple of years ago. Maggie was sure that the Cailleach, the Queen of Winter and the crone that saved her from the Deep Dens, sent the spirit of her most loved dog. Ponc was always comforting. She would often wrap her arms around him, and cry into his fur when she was upset with Cuán or anyone else.

Of course, Ponc drew her outside the house.

Ponc barked and took her down to the caves. She didn't go in, knowing that the Cailleach was there, in the darkness of the caves, watching her. Ponc sat at her feet.

Cailleach! Cailleach! Cailleach!

"Listen... to me, *chisler*. You must find and bring to me the siofra by the end of Imbolc. You have debts unpaid, so if you fail me, I will pluck you again, and send you back to the Deep Dens. Do... you... understand?"

Maggie nodded. "I will. But why by Imbolc?"

"I am the Queen of Winter, and Imbolc marks the time of Brigid."

It started to get cold, and Maggie looked at her hands. They were normal, pale hands with the light sprinkling of freckles. She opened her torn blouse and saw the soft, pale human skin underneath.

Maggie sighed in relief, understanding now why she lost control of her own body. She hoped it wouldn't continue to be a problem.

Cailleach! Cailleach! Cailleach!

The whisperings died away, leaving Maggie standing in the cold, listening to the ocean waves. Ponc barked, and she ran her fingers through his soft blue-gray fur, before Ponc ran out into the ocean and disappeared. She wished Cuán was here to see him.

The morning after Maggie met the Cailleach in the caves as she had promised when she was a child, Maggie found Cuán behind her, watching her as she listened to the ocean. Sometimes if she stood there for long enough, she could hear the sea sprites whispering in their strange tongue. It was oddly hypnotizing, making her feel as if she were not only one with them, but somewhere beyond all the troubles of her life.

Seeing Cuán there, watching her like some guardian or... (dare she think it?)... boyfriend, made her chest fill with delightful twitters. Her cheeks grew hot, and her body felt like exquisite chaos. Trying to forget the nightmare about her dark green skin and clawed hands, she quickly went to him.

He looked rather downhearted, so she cheered him up by giving him a kiss. She always loved his kisses. His mouth tasted like lemons. His tongue was warm, soft, and playful.

She took his hand and told him that she wanted to see her ma and da for a few moments.

It was always like this. 'Ma' meant Oona. 'Ma and da' meant Mona and Colum.

Cuán always went with her when she felt like going. It was an hour by carriage to the Ó Fionnáin's farm. Maybe Colum and Mona didn't know who she was, but Maggie tried not to think about it much anymore. It only mattered that she could be close to them, even if they couldn't express to each other the love between parent and child. Between blood. Otherwise, it would just upset her again, and sometimes she found that she could be ferocious and enjoy the dark things she dreamed up.

It's too easy to hate the siofra, she thought. *Think of Ma and Da.*

Maggie knew her closeness to Colum and Mona gave Colum the confidence he needed to come to them for help. He'd heard they had made plans to go to Dublin, and so wanted to speak with them. The Sunday before, once morning mass had finished and people gathered to socialize outside the church, Maggie took the opportunity to tell Colum and Mona that they were off to Dublin soon.

"Cuán wants to look at the colleges. He finally got the bollocks up to tell his folks that college was the only place for him," Maggie said, watching Cuán kicking the ball with other boys in the field across from the church.

Mona smiled, looking happy for them. "And why are you going, Maggie?"

Maggie's first answer was *'to be with Cuán,'* but they were not married, and Maggie thought they might take it wrong. (Perhaps they may think that they both forgot themselves 'on the daily,' or they'd make with the occasional 'hands-on' at the very least.)

There's killing the siofra—*the false Deirdre,* Maggie thought. Though she didn't know if she could go through with it, a part of her desired it more than anything. Maggie wanted to be 'Deirdre' again. To be her *real* self, remotely different from what the fomori had made of her, even if it all seemed impossible.

"I want to see the city. Dublin, I mean, can you imagine all the carriages, people and all those buildings? I hear they are reaching further and further into the sky. The buildings, I mean. Can you imagine? How could I not want to see that?"

Mona nodded. "I completely understand. Hopefully, the city doesn't take all you youngsters away. What would become of Kilkee?"

A bit later, Colum approached her when she was sitting on the steps, Cuán still messing about with the boys and the football in the field across the road.

"Could we talk? I sort of have a favor while you're in Dublin?"

Her da wanted something from her?

"Aye. Of course." She did her best to hide her excitement. She loved it when her ma and da needed her.

Colum sat next to her, sighing. "It's just we haven't truly heard from Deirdre in a while..."

At Deirdre's name—*her* name... something *stolen* from her—Maggie's hands curled into fists so that her knuckles were tender.

"...and she sent this letter, but it's just... not... like her. I don't know..."

After leaving the cliffs at the seaside after kissing, as Maggie and Cuán watched Colum and Mona working in their small garden, Maggie shoved that day at the church into the back of her mind and took Cuán's hand again. She looked up at his big brown seal eyes and said, "Will you come with me?"

Cuán nodded and squeezed her hand. Maggie led him across the road to them.

"We're off today," Maggie said as they approached.

Colum and Mona looked up, and both smiled. Mona came over and gave her a hug. "Take care in Dublin. Be safe. I heard that cities can be rough at times."

Maggie nodded at her. Maggie looked at Colum, who held out his arms. She fell into them, and he squeezed her tight.

"You know, Maggie, I know you're Oona's niece, and everything, but you're like a daughter to us. Take care, a'right?"

Maggie melted at that, and tears escaped. "Thanks d—uh, Mister Ó Fionnáin. I really appreciate that."

She watched as Cuán shook Colum's hand and gave Mona a hug.

"You take care of her. She's a great little missy," Mona told him.

Cuán nodded. "I will."

"And Maggie. Good luck," Colum said.

Later, Maggie filled with tears and warmth again and kissed her foster mam on the cheek. Oona had been there for her these ten years, raised her since she had found her in her attic, and Maggie felt healthy and happy. Oona would always be her true mam, and her heart hurt to know that today, they would have to part.

"Maggie, my little aos sí," she said, "I will miss you."

Aos sí—a term of endearment that Oona had been calling her since she'd offered her a faerie cake in the attic. On her birthday, Oona would make the same cake for her, knowing that it was special between them. Maggie loved the endearment.

"And I, you," Maggie said.

"You will never forget that I am your mam, will you?"

"No. Never."

They wiped their tears and laughed at how foolish they felt for opening up this way in public. Cuán stood by with his backpack, watching with solemn eyes.

"Ladies, we really must be going," Cuán said.

Maggie could actually see that Cuán was trying not to tear up himself. Maggie gave Oona another kiss, and they were out the door, where a carriage awaited them, their luggage already stored. From there, they took a couple of hours to get to Galway, and, from there, about eight hours by train to Dublin.

In Dublin, Maggie followed Cuán through the crowded streets to their apartments, paid for by the Foleys, feeling exhausted and paradoxically wired at the same time. They checked in, received the keys, and got a tour through their small rooms. The kitchen was a shared kitchen downstairs, but there was a cook who left out lunch and a supper at the appropriate times. Maggie didn't say much to Cuán about it, but she told him about apartments, certain about where she wanted to go. Deirdre had stayed there, she said. Maggie had seen it a few times when she went through Deirdre's doorway: the rippling *Fall* within the Hollow. Cuán expressed that he thought it was a bit creepy that Maggie wanted to stay there, but he wanted to make her happy. And she was glad that he complied with her wishes, wondering herself why she thought it was so important.

Once they unpacked, they met each other in the parlor to not garner any undue attention since they were not married.

Maggie and Cuan opened the last letter Deirdre sent her parents.

> *Dear Ma & Da,*
>
> *How is everyone? My career is going wonderfully in Dublin. MacKay & Dunn are treating me well. I have seen so many sites around Ireland and Scotland. There's word I might be able to do some jobs in London as my work picks up. The last few years have been amazing.*
>
> *I'm sorry I have not had the chance to visit. I will find the time. I promise.*
>
> *All my love and best,*
> *Deirdre*

Colum had given Maggie and Cuán the letter after first approaching them, saying, "I figured since the two of you were planning a trip to Dublin, perhaps you could drop by and see her? Make sure she is doing alright? Her letters... they get shorter and shorter. She used to spend so much time telling us all these details. And now look at this? Something you would write a total stranger."

Of course, Colum didn't know that Maggie was going to Dublin to face Deirdre. Maggie knew it wasn't a good idea to tell him either.

Maggie folded the letter and said, "Of course we will. I'm sure Cuán will be excited to see her again."

Cuán nodded agreement, giving Colum a half-smile in solidarity. "I would love to sit down and have a chat with 'er."

Colum nodded. "Be sure to give her a little shame for not seeing her folks in so long."

"Will do, sir," Maggie said.

Now, in Dublin, they weren't sure how to approach this. Cuán told Maggie that Deirdre mostly kept to herself. She loved books and never went to church. (Neither of them asked Colum why this never became an issue, since Colum and Mona were regular churchgoers, but Maggie had the impression that Colum or Mona didn't know the answer either.)

"I had a crush on her fer a long while," he admitted once. Maggie forgave him for it. She knew that she and Deirdre looked exactly alike. And there was a reason why Cuán was drawn to Maggie. Maggie liked to think of it as 'lover's fate.' Most of Kilkee joked around with them that they were destined to marry, and neither of them rejected this. In fact, Maggie wanted nothing else.

"Well, I think we need to be straight with her. It's not like we're being fishy or anything,'" Maggie said, waving the letter in front of him. "People are not beyond sending messengers when they themselves cannot travel."

Maggie watched Cuán smile, popping a lemon drop into his mouth. "Clever. I knew I brought you fer some reason."

Maggie laughed. "Right, yeh did."

She wondered about Cuán, though. She really did. Maggie wasn't completely honest with him either. She told him multiple times she wanted to face Deirdre, but she never could tell him that *ending Deirdre* was the only thing on her mind, that it was the only option.

How would he take it?

Maggie didn't know. She hoped he would understand, but she knew her only chance of that was if she came clean before it happened. She would have to make sure her timing was right.

There was a nice castle-modeled mansion on Black Horse Lane, on the northwest side of Dublin. This is where the carriage took them when they gave the coachman the address on Deirdre's letter the next day. The estate was surrounded by wrought-iron fencing and had an immaculate gate in front of it. The coachman said he would stay while they checked things out, so Cuán and Maggie opened the gate and walked up the drive. They walked around a large fountain with a statue of nymphs bathing in the water as it fell around them.

The mansion was three stories tall and looked to have two wings that spread out on either side of the main hall. Maggie felt overwhelmed and in awe of it, not knowing what to suspect. They went up the steps, and Cuán pounded on the door. Both of them were in quiet anticipation.

After a few moments, a stout butler answered, hair greased to the side and with a very bushy mustache and chops. He was well dressed and trimmed, though he looked confused.

"Deirdre? What are you wearing? I thought—"

Maggie understood his bewilderment after a moment. She had not been confused with Deirdre before, since she had moved on before Maggie got to know the people of Kilkee. More often, she had been compared, but only loosely.

"I'm sorry. I'm Maggie."

The butler's face changed, seemed frozen in mild annoyance to everything around him. She started to become wary of him. Something about him wasn't right, and she decided she didn't like him at all.

Maggie showed the bushy man the letter. *Come on*, she thought. *Just let us in.*

"We're actually 'ere to see Deirdre, though," Maggie said. "This is hers. Her father sent us to visit with her. You know how families are. They want us to check in on her. Make sure she's doing okay."

The butler glanced over the letter and looked at Maggie and Cuán. "Hm, yes. Why won't you come in? Very interesting indeed."

They walked into the foyer, and the butler closed the door behind them. There were tapestries of Dublin history and Dunn lineage, and depictions of horses and old wars. Dunn's family must go back a long time.

The butler took them through the foyer to a parlor, where another couple sat. A gentleman was smoking a cigar as he made his way through the paper. A woman wearing a wool wide brim derby hat sat stiffly, quietly, and stared at them. She smelled of bergamot. Maggie knew that some women would spray their clothing or gloves with perfumes, should they have the money for such things.

The butler gestured at a couch across from the other couple.

"I will see if Deirdre is here. If not, maybe the Master can help you," the butler said. With that, he left them, and Maggie found herself awkwardly walking over to the couch with Cuán, feeling agitated. The other lady in the room held her nose up and followed her with her eyes. Maggie wasn't sure why.

Why so much waiting? Maggie was aggravated by all of it. Why couldn't they go up and see Deirdre?

Let me pop her in the face now, she thought.

Maggie started whispering to Cuán, letting him know how upset she was, but the gentleman smoking a cigar cleared his throat, interrupting her.

"Never mind whispering and secrets," the man said from behind his paper. "You could hear a maid's silent fart from the other side of this echo chamber."

Maggie was disgusted, though she'd heard men talk at the Kilkee pub in a similar way many times. Perhaps it upset her so much because he was a complete stranger.

The woman next to him giggled. "Finnian. Stop the vulgarities."

Finnian gave her a look, puffing his cigar, and returned to his paper.

"Are you a... prospect?" the lady asked Maggie.

"Prospect?" Maggie said, confused.

The man—Finnian—brought his paper down, his eyes looked Maggie up and down with more consideration.

"Why she could be, couldn't she?" the man asked the woman.

The woman smiled back at him. "Absolutely delicious, my Luv."

Maggie became petrified when she realized how they were both titillated by her, and so she leaned in close to Cuán, putting her head on his shoulder. She was embarrassed and didn't know how to respond to it. Was she that much of a chicken?

Cuán changed the subject. "What does this... master—What does he do fer a living? Is he a noble?"

The gentleman smirked. "Oh no. Mister Dunn made his fortune in banking. Or, rather, his father did back during the Industrial Revolution. Now MacKay & Dunn are one of the biggest banks in Dublin. They have a branch in Scotland and London."

Jaysus, how did Deirdre get involved with him? Maggie was shocked and curious now. Maggie looked at Cuán and (despite what the strange man had said earlier) whispered, "Why would Deirdre be staying with a banker?"

Cuán shrugged.

Maggie, bored now, wondered what she ought to do when she saw Deirdre. Perhaps bite her face clean off? No, that would horrify Cuán. She was sure of that. Besides, she still needed to convince Cuán that Deirdre needed to die first.

What else could she do then? Maybe portray friendship, ask her out for drinks, and then bite her face off the first chance she got.

Maggie knew she was fantasizing, but it did make her smile.

A few moments later, the butler returned for the strange couple. The gentleman dashed his cigar in a bin, and the woman straightened out her gaudy outfit as the butler led them off into the mansion.

"Come along, Myrna. I don't want to go in there alone. God forbid he asks me to suck his dick."

What a hideous man...

Myrna laughed. "You're such a gobdaw. Me being there won't stop him from anything."

...with such a hideous woman.

Maggie felt as if the mansion itself was made to make people nervous. Part of it might be how the couple treated them and spoke so lewdly, or perhaps it was the mansion affecting her in ways she didn't understand yet. It was as if the mansion was a monster's den, and they were now inside its belly, salacious and predatory things hiding around corners in every crack and crevice. The house was now eating the strange people, and Maggie was biting her cheek, trying not to remember how the couple had looked at her as if she were candy.

"Cuán. I am getting a bad feelin' about this place. I think something is wrong 'ere."

Cuán nodded. "I feel the same way. This place is... I don't know... too quiet or something."

The butler returned, making Maggie feel a little more relieved. She couldn't wait to get out of here.

"Miss Deirdre is not here at the moment. I believe she is at one of the studios. Master Dunn doesn't have the time to meet with you now, but he'd be happy to speak with you if you'd like to set up an appointment."

Seriously? Of course, she wasn't 'ere! Maggie thought sarcastically. She was angry now. All this wasted time... And now Maggie wasn't going to bite anyone's face off today.

"Well bloody hell," Maggie said. "Mister—?"

"What Miss Maggie is trying to say," Cuán said, stepping half in front of her, "is that we don't have much time in Dublin, and we'd like to make connections with Deirdre as soon as we can. Is there a way to locate her now?"

Did Cuán have to get in her way?

The butler thought for a moment and shrugged. "Even if I did, I don't know you."

To hell with that, Maggie thought. All this man did was increase her frustrations with him.

Maggie pushed past Cuán this time, feeling sick that she was going to say this. "Look, we have the feelin' that Deirdre may not be safe. We showed yeh the letter that came from her father with her *handwritin'* on it. *Her* signature. I would love nothin' more to see that she is okay. Otherwise, we will have no choice but to involve the police. You must understand, Sir, that this letter is most unlike Deirdre. And if anyone is harmin' her, they will be held responsible."

The butler's left brow popped up and he cleared his throat. "Nevertheless, lass, I must ask you to leave."

After being ushered out, walking toward the front gates across the yard, Maggie kicked at the ground, and Cuán gave her room on the road to do it.

"They could be lying to us," Maggie said. "I didn't like that couple, and that butler was rather dodgy." *And I really wanted to bite Deirdre's face off.*

Cuán nodded. "I agree.

"I bet she's in there," Maggie said, biting her lip hard.

When they reached the gates, they found that the coachman had driven off with their carriage.

Cuán sighed. "That figures. I suppose we're walking."

Maggie frowned at him. "We'll be fine, right. Maybe we can find a place for tea on the way."

"Or brandy," Cuán quipped. "I don't know if yeh know this, Maggie, but authority figures don't take to yeh very easily."

"I know, Cuán. You remind me of this almost every week."
"Well, yeh keep forgetting."
"I do not!"

V.

On one of the tallest buildings in Dublin, there was a flat at the very top with an entry to the roof, owned by the photographer, Toal Mullins. Toal had his camera out in the light on the roof with a beach towel, balls, and sand all over the place. Deirdre was used to fabricated scenes, but she had never seen a beach on a roof before. It was exciting.

Deirdre was standing beside him, wearing nothing but a robe that had fallen open. One breast was hanging out, and he could see the red hair between her legs. Deirdre knew he could see it, because she left it that way on purpose. Men were so easy to draw in, if you only had the courage. And she loved the thrill of days like this. It felt a little dangerous and exotic at the same time. The Christians called it a sin, but she found it delicious.

"Can you believe how much sand they were able to get up here?" he was saying. "Look at this. Day at the beach. Wonderful."

In the past few years, she had not seemed to age much. Here she was: twenty-eight, and she still looked like she'd just been sent to college. They called it a miracle that she still looked so sweet and young. People loved painting her and wanted her in their photographs. She didn't mind. They gazed, joyfully. And if they tried to touch her, she'd break their fingers. Many had tried too, but there was something about Deirdre Ó Fionnáin. She was not easy to hurt. Or break.

"Why don't you take off that robe and let's see what the camera captures," Toal said. "I think you're exceptional. The light is perfect. The clouds are perfect. You're a bricky girl with a nice, soft form. It will all come together, merging into pure delight."

"Where would these naughty bits sell, Toal? Hm?" Deirdre shed her robe, letting it fall to the ground, and stood naked in the sand. She put one foot on a ball, stretched her chest out forward, and put another hand on her hip.

Toal took the exposure: one, two, three, four, five...

"Men in their private clubs love 'em. They're starting to sell for a good penny," Toal said. "Men love to envisage the fantastical, be titillated, aroused, and shown all the possibilities. Images are reminders of all the possibilities of pleasure that exist for them."

He covered the lens and started changing plates. Deirdre loved shooting out-of-doors. The exposures were over a couple of minutes with all the light, whereas with interior shoots, she would have to hold a pose for almost thirty minutes at times.

"Find another pose, Luv. Maybe, if you don't mind, show a little more meat. Something that will make a man really blush."

"Toal?"

"You know what I mean. Why don't you climb on that chair facing that-a-way and give us a look? Maybe look over your back shoulder with a sexy smile?"

Deirdre smiled, feeling the heat rise up around her neck and cheeks. Toal had never asked her to do something like this before. Not this exploitative. The prospects, though, were thrilling. It made her blood race, and she liked it. She didn't know why she was the way she was. It almost felt like there was ancient longing in her veins that needed quenched—a sexual craving that twitched in agony at her very core.

She climbed on the chair and raised her backside up to the camera. Toal stopped to look, taking it all in, and closed the camera's gate. Deirdre could feel the slight wind on her body, making her body hair move, tickling her. There was a part of her that wished Toal was man enough to take her and solve her more sultry needs.

Toal stayed professional, though. He always did. Maybe because Toal knew Dunn would break his fingers.

"Arch your back a little more and get that butt up there, Luv," he said. "Exposing. One, two, three, four, five..."

Deirdre waited the time out by imagining a hard-langered man taking advantage of her position; *roughly*. Hungry themselves to release their seed in her. Quivering.

Their jip in the gee, the other voice in her head said.

Feeling happily perverse, she wondered if the camera could see her heat rising up from her, and she reminded herself of all the possibilities of pleasure in the world that existed for her.

After three more exposures, Deirdre threw the robe over herself and went to take a warm bath. While she was fixing herself up and climbing into a casual dress, she heard Toal speaking with another gentleman in the room next to her. While they lowered their voices, they failed to keep her from hearing.

"Dunn sent me," the gentleman said. "He said that a couple of folks from Deirdre's hometown came for a visit, and he was pretty upset about it. He doesn't want them making contact and wants them gone. He wants you to have a word with them. Get rid of them as quickly as possible."

"Why? I'm a photographer, Finnian. I'm not some thug for Dunn to push around. Doesn't he have enough of those?"

"I wouldn't question him," Finnian said. "You know how Dunn can be."

"Okay, yes, yes. Okay. But what am I supposed to say to them?"

"Why don't you just send Shay and Casey? They have helped you before."

"Yeah, but they're not cheap."

Deirdre wondered who they could be referring to. Surely her parents weren't here in Dublin looking for her? If Dunn thought he was going to hurt them, he had another thing coming.

I told you, the voice in the back of her head said. *Dunn is darkness. I feel a lot of darkness around here. Why can't you go?*

"Darkness doesn't scare me," she told the voice. Of course, it didn't respond. Though she hardly ever heard the voice in the back of her head, it usually annoyed her when it did speak up.

She was lying, of course, thinking about the nightmares of the sea-creature that sometimes haunted her. *Seagrass Maggie.* Clawing at her, pulling her down into the cold, unbreathable darkness.

VI.

That evening Cuán and Maggie had supper in the dining hall of their apartment and decided to go out for drinks. A few blocks down, they found a smokey pub and went into it. They always had a saying that a pub in Ireland was always loud and boisterous, but they had never been to a pub in Dublin. Men played darts and cards at tables. Couples danced drunkenly about the room, while others sat up against walls or slumped in chairs at the bar.

They played some cards and drank a few pints before they decided to head back. The walk was sobering and allowed them to think.

"Maybe we should tell the garda that we're worried for her," Cuán said. "Maybe they'd force information out of Mister Dunn."

Maggie shrugged, putting a hand on Cuán's shoulder to steady herself. The drink obviously affected him a shy more. The lucky bastard.

"Maybe... Maybe we... we should, um, watch the place," she said. "Yeh know. From afar. If we see 'er come out, we then go speak with 'er, tell 'er that 'er father is feck-all mad with 'er shite, and she needs to go home."

"Okay. You are bloody drunk."

They laughed.

"Though yeh do make a good point," Cuán said. "We could watch the place. See if we can catch her coming out."

Maggie's mind cleared a little then. She wrapped her arms around Cuán's. "Oh, but it will be very boring."

"Boring indeed."

"Who wants to spend all day watching some tedious place like that?"

"Yes, well, do we have another choice?"

Maggie shook her head. No, they didn't. She smiled up at him, and he leaned and placed his warm lips against hers. They stopped. Their kiss lingered. Their tongues played a little. His arms took her in, warming her in the cool night. She held him tight, feeling his arousal below, against her stomach.

She pulled back, looking at him, finding that her mouth was open, and her tongue was resting on her bottom lip. She wanted to unzip his trousers and get his langer out, and yet she was unsure of how he'd react.

It surely wasn't proper, was it?

"We'll have this moment one day, won't we?" she said.

Cuán nodded. "One day, I hope. Sorry. Yes, one day."

Maggie put her hands on his face and pushed her mouth back onto his. She wanted this so bad she didn't want it to stop. It was almost impossible to hold herself back from him. She imagined throwing their clothes off, riding him, melting together with him into one. In the deep, she remembered, once a male angler fish finds a mate, he bites into her stomach and latches on until their flesh and blood vessels meld together, so they would never lose each other in all that darkness. She didn't know why, but this was very romantic to her. And erotic.

Maggie licked his lip and pulled away again. She took a deep breath of the cool night air.

"Well, if Jesus and Mary saw us, they'd go red, yea?"

Cuán laughed. "I think we should retire?"

"Aye—" Maggie stopped when she saw the men come out of the alley behind Cuán. One had a metal bar, and the other reached out for—

"Cuán!"

It was too late. One thug grabbed Cuán's arms behind his back and threw him aside, where he crashed against the alley wall. The other grabbed her arm and shouted for her to get down, holding the bar up above his head, ready to thump her scalp with it.

She envisioned that club coming up with matted hair and blood, and something inside her kicked in. The spinning world slammed into a stop, and the darkness grew less resolute around her. Maggie reached for the man's arms, seeing that her own skin had become somewhat blue...

Cuán hit the brick wall of the alley hard, though it wasn't enough to hurt him as much as he would have thought. He looked up and saw the thug pull a dagger from the back of his pants, possibly from his belt, and he raised it to attack Cuán.

Cuán, on the other hand, glanced in time to see Maggie's change. Her skin suffused a light green-blue, her eyes went darker and yet glimmered like a rainbow, and she moved faster than he'd ever seen someone move before. She reached for the man's arms and twisted them around in an impossible way. Cuán could hear the shoulders pop free and the arm bones cracking. The thug began to scream and dropped to his knees, all before the thug in front of Cuán realized what was happening.

Cuán had never seen this before.

This was Seagrass Maggie. Not the human part. The part of her that was touched by the Otherworld. And Cuán stopped fearing for himself so much as the thug that was going for him with the dagger.

Cuán rolled aside, able to get his feet under himself as the thug tried to close the distance. He swung the dagger, and Cuán barely missed it.

However, the miscreant who attacked Maggie was already down, and she was moving behind the man who was trying to cut Cuán. He seemed to notice at the last minute and started to turn, but Maggie jumped up on his back and twisted his head. His neck cracked, and they both fell together onto the ground.

Only Seagrass Maggie was on top, crouching on the man's back, her beige dress sprawled around her. Her sharp, black claws stuck out from the ends of her webbed fingers and were digging into the man's bloody shoulders. The thug, his head turned too far around, was obviously dead.

The dagger was a few feet away from his hand, having dropped it when he landed on the ground.

Cuán looked at Maggie and saw the watery teal tint of her skin, the black rainbow-sheen eyes on an angry face, and her small, heaving body at the ready. He reached out a hand and whispered. "We have to go, Maggie."

Maggie's mouth snapped at him. He saw the long sharp teeth. A lavender tongue wriggled behind them... teeth opening and closing and swiftly clenching shut. If she had a few more inches, she would have bitten him.

"Maggie?"

Would she kill him? He had never seen this state before, and he realized he didn't know her like this.

He reached out his hand again and her black eyes watched it.

Maggie's face fell, and she closed her eyes for a moment. She looked up and took his hand. Cuán started walking her away from the alley. He looked about them, seeing no one around. The last thing they needed was a problem with the police.

Maggie started to sob. Cuán put a finger to her chin, lifted it up so he could look at her eyes. They were blue again, full of tears.

"I'm so sorry, Cuán! Maggie said. "I-I didn't know that could happen!"

"I know," Cuán said. "Let's get yeh to bed before anyone sees this mess."

Maggie nodded, and Cuán pulled her close so that she knew he was always there.

This was the first time someone had tried to kill them, and Cuán didn't think it would be the last time. Whatever Deirdre had gotten herself into, it was going to be far more dangerous than they'd first realized.

By the time they returned to the apartments, Maggie was pale again. All signs of her *other self* were gone. The eyes. The webbed fingers and claws.

Cuán drew her a bath, heating water in a pot from the well, knowing that it was one of the things that relaxed her the most. The whole time he wondered what he had gotten himself into. And what would happen if Maggie turned like this when she was around Deirdre?

VII.

Deirdre watched from across the street. She recognized Cuán, but barely. The last time she'd seen him was when he was... (what?)... twelve? He was a young man now. And the girl he was with was awfully familiar. Deirdre wondered why they were here, and wondered what the hell they were thinking, going to Dunn's mansion?

She saw the thugs attempt to grab the two of them. And then, in a complete surprise to her, the girl broke the one man's arms, and jumped on the other's back, breaking his neck. Cuán helped the girl up, and as they came out of the alley, Deirdre rolled around the corner of the building she was hiding beside. Deirdre didn't want them to see her yet. She watched as Cuán helped the girl down the sidewalk, leaving the broken men behind.

The girl had changed. Her skin had turned to teal. Her eyes looked black from where Deirdre could see her.

She understood why the girl was so familiar. Deirdre was looking at the spitting image of herself. The girl looked like her sister! (Of course, not now, how she changed into this creature-looking thing, but before...) That couldn't be, could it? Her parents never mentioned any other child? Deirdre briefly thought that she was a distant relation. A cousin, perhaps.

Except when she saw that girl's face, she knew she was looking into her own as sure as she knew her own reflection.

Like in her dreams with her monstrous self... The monster who would pull her down under, trying to drown her. *Seagrass Maggie*, she thought, and her heart seemed to twist in her chest.

Could that be the monster who was coming for her?

Deirdre followed them as distantly as she could without losing them, sticking to the shadows of the streets, and watched them going into apartments. She noted the street and almost decided to confront them there, but she became worried that Dunn had other men watching her. Dunn almost always had a backup plan in case something went wrong. That's why he was as wealthy as he was.

There was no chance in hell Cuán was going to ruin this life for her. If not tonight, she was going to face them and drive them off as far away as she could. She needed to think about how she was going to do this. Did she face them privately, or out in the open?

And what if the girl with him was Seagrass Maggie?

Deirdre was terrified. She didn't know what to do.

VIII.

Two nude women were wrapped together, cooing, licking, and writhing together on Doran's bed. They filled the air with their heat and musky sex. Doran Dunn was watching from a chair in one corner of the room, hard as hell, getting ready to join them when his butler, Felim, had come in, leaving the door open.

"Master Dunn. I have some bad news for you," he said.

They walked out into the hall, one of the girls begging him to come to them as he left. He bit his hand and shut the door.

"What is it?"

"The police found a body this morning. Toal discovered that he was one of the two men he knew. He hired them to scare those two off who came looking for Deirdre."

Doran sighed. He knew this day would come. Her parents were sending for her, wanting to know where she was. He should have had them killed, but he didn't want the word getting back to Deirdre. Neither solved his problem. He waited a long time for her to come into his life, and he was going to keep her if he had to kill someone to do it.

This was the end game he knew he had to weather with all he had.

"What about the other?"

"I sent Finnian to find him. Turns out the other man is in a hospital with a broken arm. Finnian says that the girl looks like Deirdre. Just as I told you, but last night she became like a monster. Black eyes. Claws. More strength than they've ever dealt with."

Yes, Doran thought. The other girl was special, wasn't she? A problem...

Doran turned back to Felim. "Well, it's obvious they know something is wrong now. We need Deirdre to take a little trip."

Because Deirdre is mine, and I'm going to keep her, he thought.

The butler nodded. "That can be arranged, Sir."

Doran grinned and opened his door. The girls had their faces buried between each other's legs, enjoying each other, and his desire to join them returned. Felim left him as he crawled into bed, grabbing at the flesh that writhed there.

After exhausting himself, both of the women now sleeping deeply, Doran went to his bar without bothering to get dressed and rolled out a font with a gold bowl. It had clean freshwater in it. Doran grabbed the needle from the rim and poked his finger, dropping blood in the font. He stirred it into a whirl.

It cleared and in the reflection against the gold, he saw the cadaverous women with the black hair—the *maighdean uaimh*—swimming around their cages in the Feast Pit, baring their vampyric fangs. They feasted on sea life, blood dripping down their fingers, their chins, and glistening pale bodies. He saw Muirgen there, stroking one of her vampyre-sister's hair as her head laid into her lap.

Above them was a fog, which was thick and covered the whole village. Doran could see that Muirgen had made an *arrachtaigh*. It was running the village under the Devil's Breath for the vampyric creatures, drawing its essences from his body.

Doran covered the scry with a hand towel and went over to a dresser, pulling out a vial of blue liquid. He called it the *homunculus alteration*. It was time to test the philter on someone. It may soon come in handy.

The vampyres, he thought. This would be Elieris, the King of the Fomorians, making a play using the Commination. Doran grinned. Things were moving along faster than he thought they would. He didn't think Ri Elieris would wake so early. Yes, this did change his plans... But he was not going to let his prize go so easily.

Doran went back to the bed with his women. He kissed one on the mouth, pushing his tongue deep down her throat. His mind went into hers.

Her name was Delma, and she wanted nothing more than to be rich. She was dreaming about having sex with him. They came together, and while they listened to each other's beating hearts, she dreamed that Doran was speaking with her, telling her that he loved her and that they should be married. They should have kids together.

Delma's heart raced more, knowing she would be rich and happy. All her dreams were coming true. Excited and assured, she leaned down and took his member into her mouth, sucking on it with all she had left. He was moaning and she wanted him to feel how he made her feel.

Doran balked. She didn't understand that she meant nothing to him. Couldn't conceive of it. She was flesh for his pleasure and nothing else. But this was good. She was making it easier for him. One's mind was easily manipulated when their heart was completely open to you.

Doran slipped into her dream of him and enjoyed her mouth. At the same time, he reached deeper into her psyche and made her mind anchor on what he was about to say. He put the vial of blue fluid to her lips...

"Delma, Delma, that is so wonderful. I'm coming. I'm coming, my dear—"

Delma swallowed what she thought she was getting and looked up to see him beaming down on her.

"Since you agree to marry me, I have an engagement present for you. It's not here, though. You have to go and get it."

"Where is it?" Her gray eyes opened wide.

"I'm going to whisper it to you. You won't remember this when you wake, though you will know it deeply when you need to. It will be in your heart, though your mind can't reach it easily," he said. He whispered into her ear.

Delma stretched out her arms, rolling around, and she awoke.

Doran watched Delma climb naked out of the bed and stumble out of the room, saying, "I have to piss."

Doran looked at the other girl. He didn't know her name. It wasn't important. His butler, Felim, would get rid of her in the morning. In the meantime, he looked at her young flesh draped over her young bones and knew that everything she was, sat only a few inches away from his eyes. Unlike the gods and monsters, he'd seen with his own eyes, she was but a candle flame destined to burn quickly away. He would feel sorry for her, or the other mortals, if it weren't for all the cruel things the Primordials had shown him.

Death was but a fine gift for mortals.

IX.

The next day it was raining. The road was muddy, though coaches made their way adequately. Not as many people were in the streets. Cuán made his way to a shop nearby, since Maggie had mentioned that she would be happier if they had a few apples around to eat between meals. Perhaps some of their own tea so that they could enjoy some without going out. The apartments had a few pots, and the oven was usually open. Why not use it?

The bell rang when he went in. He only had a few quid, but he was sure it was enough for what Maggie wanted. Shortly the bell rang again while he was looking over the apples. It was Maggie. She must have come following along, bored or something, so he went around to speak with her—

Only it wasn't Maggie. The sweet violet perfume. The expensive dress and jewelry around her neck. This was Maggie if she were overindulged with money.

"Deirdre," Cuán said.

"You shouldn't have come," Deirdre said.

"Well, you have yer bloody folks sick with worry fer you," Cuán said. "You haven't written them a proper letter fer the last couple of years."

Deirdre looked worried. "I do care about them, Cuán, but my life is much different now. It's not a small fisherman's village anymore. You know what I mean. It's the hustle and bustle."

"And money," Cuán said. "I know. Yet how does that have anything to do with leaving yer family behind?"

Deirdre bit her bottom lip and said, "It's too dangerous for them here."

Cuán chuckled, but it wasn't funny to him at all. "I've noticed. I ran into some of that trouble, Deirdre. No thanks to Mister Dunn, I'm sure."

Deirdre touched his hair. "You must go and never come back. I am sorry."

"Yeah, fer what? Bailing on yer folks, or for me getting hurt?"

Deirdre's shoulders dropped. "For both, you bloody eejit."

There was a moment of silence where Cuán didn't know what to say, but Deirdre softly broke this spell: "Who is the girl you're with? I've noticed that she looks very much like me."

Cuán nodded. "Noticed that, have you? Her name is Maggie. Oona Connell raised her."

"I don't like the looks of her. I would watch her, if I were you."

"I didn't think you'd even remember me," Cuán said. "You weren't exactly nice to me growing up."

"How could I not know Cuán Foley in such a small town? Come on now."

They smiled at each other. It was nice to see her again. Feel her next to him again.

"You and this Maggie a thing?"

Cuán nodded. "Aye, well, I think I love her. She's a bit odd sometimes, but yes."

Deirdre turned and looked out the shop windows. When she turned back, she said, "How does she look exactly like me, Cuán?"

Cuán didn't know what to say. The more he was around Deirdre, the more human she seemed. How could she be some fairy construct or changeling creature? Would she really be this human with only twenty-eight years of mortal life?

Maybe. Maybe not. The Otherworld played so many tricks on the mind. Cuán couldn't be sure of anything anymore. He only knew that both girls seemed very real to him.

But if she weren't a changeling, what was she? Who was she?

Deirdre wrapped her arms around him. She whispered into his ear: "Dunn is a very dangerous man, and if you stay in Dublin, he will find you and he will kill you. And... this *Maggie*... think of what he could do to her. He doesn't just kill. He takes women and destroys them. Once their spirits are broken, and he's made as much money from them as he can, he lets them die all alone on the streets. Or he makes them disappear."

Cuán's flesh prickled.

"What about you?"

Deirdre shrugged, and he saw something dangerous in her eyes.

"He has pretty much learned not to fuck with me," she said. "Go home, Cuán. Take Maggie with you and leave Dublin before the boogeyman gets you. I mean it."

With that, Deirdre left him alone in the shop, holding an apple he forgot he picked up.

Cuán shared everything with Maggie once he returned while she chomped on one of the apples. When he told her what she whispered, Maggie's eyes opened wide. Her freckled nose wrinkled and she shot for the door.

"I'm goin' to strangle her..."

Cuán caught her arm and shook his head. "She's gone now, Maggie. You won't find her by just walking out that door."

"So maybe she knows she's different somehow," Maggie said, giving in to him. "Maybe she knows she's a siofra?"

"I think she's noticed something, though she acts just as human as everyone else," Cuán said. "Sometimes, I doubt our theory. Maybe she isn't a siofra."

Maggie looked at him, leaned in, and said, "They are as sentient as any human or spirit. These creatures. They know us very well. They can be very convincing. The fomori—I mean, yes, they are monsters—but there's an intelligence behind their eyes. They watch and learn—they can mimic things ungodly well."

Cuán took her apple from her and took a bite out of the other side. "That's what you get for disagreeing with me."

Maggie smiled, taking the apple back. "Sorry to disappoint yeh, but I'm not afraid of yer spit."

Cuán started his pacing routine. "If she is a siofra, then maybe she doesn't know it. Maybe she's convinced that she's completely human because it's the only thing she knows."

"Maybe," Maggie said. "Either way, we need to confront her about this. If I were 'er, I'd want to know the truth."

Cuán nodded and took a seat beside Maggie. He wrapped an arm around her and kissed her on the cheek.

"We'll figure this out."

"Back to the 'watching the mansion' plan?"

"Yep."

"What a revolting plan."

X.

In the beginning, there is always darkness. The womb of everything surrounding everything else, and there is always a light. She rushed toward the light, and her watery form solidified and became flesh. Breaching the surface, the mother has given birth to new life. There are memories in the organized chaos that ultimately leads to death and darkness. Again, it reoccurs. There is light. She rushes to the light. A mother gives birth.

It was like a nightmare, repeating, and yet somehow, it was beautiful. A dream of life and death.

Like reincarnation.

But was it a dream? Or was it life?

In one dream, there's a misty bog somewhere in the Otherworld. She and her sisters were looking for someone to help them find one of their own—a Lost Sister. They had gone deep into the bog, and there was an ogre there that hungered for their meat. A giant with lots of flat, broken teeth and warts all over his body. So many warts that parts of him looked like fleshy cauliflower. Fooling with magic there, they caused the ogre's hut to start sinking into the muddy bog to kill him, but one of her sisters held the ogre down so that the rest of them could escape onto a tree limb. They all screamed as the mud poured over their sister as she held back the ogre. They could not help her without being dragged down as well, and the ogre had to die. It was the creature, or them.

It was her second sister that they had lost on their journey. Each loss was a significant sorrow that she would never forget.

She mourned her sister with tears and song.

Near the Standing Stones of Dromberg, there was a woman with raven wings and black hair. Eyes like silver. She seethed at her: "You have failed them all. You are the last, and the Seven Springs have all but dried up. It will all be gone soon. The Tuatha sent me to exact retribution for your defeat..."

"No," she cried. "There must be some way to redeem myself. Some way I—"

The Morrígan cawed—a cry of anger and disgust. She looked at her.

"By the Tuatha Dé Danann, I summon upon you a sea of tribulations... By Danu, by Brígid, Lugh, Nuada and Manannán, I bind thee *leaganacha de chineál*..."

Things get a little blurry after that. Once she can see again, she is in a cavern as a giant bearded man with white hair sits back, legs open with his manhood in vulgar display across his right thigh. His flesh has swollen blue, and purple veins push to the surface of his skin. Bulging. He has three eyes, but the eye in the center of his forehead is huge and pulsating over the others. It looked damaged, turning milky around the bloody hole where Lugh shot a sling-stone.

The tales spoke of his death, but Balor was still breathing as she suspected. He looked up when he noticed her presence.

She knew she would find him here, exiled from the Fomorians for his failure in the Second Battle of Mag Tuired. Though she thought he had crawled here to die.

"I have heard legends of you. Have you come to please me?" She held up her black cudgel-staff with the golden head. Ancient symbols were written down its shaft. The Bod Mór.

"I have come to finish the job Lugh should have finished long ago," she said. "The Morrígan has sent me."

Balor suddenly sat up, his mighty body casting an ominous shadow over her. He flared: "I AM DEATH TO ALL. I AM... *eternal fire*. I may not have my soul-burning eye, but I am still Balor!"

Balor began reaching for her—

But she was crying now, screaming as the men hovered over her. They had tied her down in a strange, old house, turned her face up, and one of them held up a dagger. He had black robes with different arcane symbols written upon them.

She was a child?

He cried: *"Cuirim leis an gcruth seo thú! Cuirim leis an gcruth seo thú! Cuirim leis an gcruth SEO THÚ!"*

No..., she thought. *No, please, no... Please, God, don't let these men hurt me.*

While the man who kidnapped her (Felim?) held her down, the robed one (Doran Dunn?) slammed the dagger down into her chest... She could feel it break through her ribs and puncture into her heart.

Deirdre screamed, waking up with Keela's name on her lips. She was drenched in sweat. It was still dark, so she peeled herself out of bed, walked to the window and opened it. The cool night air rushed in, bathing her sweetly, refreshing her. She had similar dreams before, but not so many rushing in so fast or so clearly.

Maggie. That's what Cuán had called the girl who had her face. The girl had those black eyes and spiny dorsal fins. Her flesh was dark sea-green, and her fins and strange symbols glowed in the darkness. When she spoke, she hissed and bleated demonic things, all unnatural from her human throat.

That girl wasn't natural. She was a monster. Cuán was under her influence somehow. Seagrass Maggie was a demon. She was sure of it. How could Cuán not see it?

Cuán was in danger, and he didn't know it.

Relax, she told herself. *You're letting your nightmares get the best of you. Cuán may not be in danger. Maybe you should try to sleep on it?* In the morning, she may feel clearer and see her dreams for what they really were.

Or perhaps Seagrass Maggie was like Mister Dunn. Maybe they came from the same dark depths, wanting to prey on those around them.

Deirdre went down to the well out back, pumping fresh water into a wooden bucket. She splashed some water on her face. Her heart was racing. Her mind was tripping over its own thoughts. There were so many strange images and flashes of other surreal and unreal moments. It was as if her mind were traveling through time, leaping from one mind into another, experiencing many lives. And all of them found themselves in terrifying situations. All of them were surrounded by strange horrors.

Breathe in, Deirdre. One, two, three… Breathe out. One, two, three, four…

Distinctly, Maggie's face—*her* face—came back with the big black eyes.

You are not real. You are a fabrication, Maggie said. *And as the Commination broils up, you will feed the monsters in it. Do you hear me, Deirdre? You are nothing but feed for the demons.*

Deirdre opened her eyes in shock. Nothing was there. She could hear the wind blowing through her window.

Nothing there, she told herself. It's her imagination.

She said aloud to herself: "I am not scared of the darkness."

Yes, you are, came the tiny, faint voice in the back of her mind. The voice that she knew very well that wasn't hers.

III. Doran's Play

I.

There was a park across the street from Dunn's mansion, where Maggie and Cuán sat in the grass. Maggie had her head in his lap, napping from boredom and fatigue, so Cuán decided it was up to him to keep an eye out for Deirdre.

Earlier that morning, they had gone to see Trinity College, allowing Cuán the chance to speak with some of the professors within the biology department. After asking him what he would be most interested in, Cuan blurted out marine biology without thinking too much about it. They sounded excited enough to have him, and so he asked if he could work as their assistant for letters of recommendation. One of them happily agreed, giving Cuán renewed hope in his scholastic efforts. It was agreed that in the next year, they would find room for him. In the meantime, one professor gave him a book, *Historia Fucorum* by Samuel Gottlieb Gmelin, which was now lying on his bed back at the apartment, waiting for him. He sort of wished he'd brought it, but then he wouldn't be keeping an eye out, would he?

Now all he had to do was tell his da about what he learned and accomplished. If... he'd hear it.

Cuán rolled his eyes. *That* was going to be fun.

Since they arrived at the park from the college tour, they had been waiting around, both exhausted from the tour and all the walking around Dublin.

So, while he watched the mansion, he reminisced about Maggie as she slept in his lap.

About a year after Maggie had been living with Oona, Cuán didn't think too much about some of the mysterious abilities that Maggie seemed to display so far. Her imperviousness to the cold, or her ability to swim in raging waters without being dashed against the rocks. That is, until he'd seen her run. She was faster than the other kids. Over the years Maggie spent in Kilkee, she and Cuán would go down to the caves to explore what she could and could not do. It was obvious that though she was born mortal, the place where she'd been all these years had changed her.

When she remembered things, she would reveal some of the information to him.

"These creatures and others like them... the *fae*... they have this belief in this powerful force of creation. It binds our souls to both the natural world and the supernatural worlds. They call it the Primordial. They believe most mortals have three essences: their vitality or life-force, their spirit, and their psyche. These essences make up the soul. But the fae, they do not have a life-force such as we do. They have a *fata* essence. It's an essence that gets its energies from fate and destiny, binding the fae closer to the ever-changing nature of the Primordial itself," Maggie had said. "I don't think I have this *fata*, but me blood has been changed by it. It makes me closer to the Primordial, and it gives me strengths that I would otherwise never have."

Of course, her powers frightened him. He had seen how the other kids were noticing something different about her.

"I want you to be careful, Maggie. The other kids can't do what yeh do. But if they see how special you are, they may treat yeh differently."

"So, what do ye expect?"

"Ah, Maggie, I just want you to mind yer abilities around them, a'right?"

Maggie nodded and wrapped her arms around him. Even then, they were getting close. Even though neither had said anything, they both were already in love.

Cuán remembered all this fondly while his mind flashed back several times to what she had done to those thugs that attacked them. What *Seagrass Maggie* had done. It was the first time she had killed anyone. Of course, Cuán felt that the miscreants had it coming. It was obvious they weren't going to treat them nicely if they had gotten the upper hand. Why should they be so nice in return?

But how Maggie was able to use her power so suddenly and coldly, and how afterward she snapped at his hand like a rabid dog, it was frightening. She lost herself for a moment, and Cuán was still trying to work it all out.

Though he knew her enough by now to know that it was haunting her. If he'd lost control like that, he'd feel a little insane about all of it, too.

It was lucky that the day was nice and dry. There were a few clouds, but the sun was a nice change and made this watch so much easier than it would otherwise be.

Beside them was a bag of apples. He was sucking on a lemon drop, but his stomach was starting to growl. It didn't seem to rouse Maggie until she shifted enough while he grabbed an apple from the bag. Her eyes opened and she leaned up from his lap, stretching. Cuán saw that she was holding the pocket watch in her hand that he gave her the first night they met.

"Anythin'?"

Cuán shook his head. "No. Not yet. I'm sure it's afternoon, though. Hungry?"

Maggie smiled at him and took his apple.

"That was certainly fer my mouth," Cuán said, reaching into the bag for his own.

It was then that he saw a familiar man exiting from the mansion's front gate. No carriage awaited him, so he took to the side of the road and began his walk. It was the vulgar man they had met a couple of days before that was with that odd woman, the man who joked that you couldn't fart in the mansion without everyone hearing it. Cuán was sure of it when he saw the man light a roach as he went along.

Finnian. That was his name.

Cuán shook Maggie's shoulder and pointed at him.

"That's the guy from the day before yesterday? Finnian."

"Yes, the pervert who was ogling me," Maggie said. "What of him?"

"Well, he seemed to know quite a bit about Mister Dunn…"

"Aye."

"…And he seemed to know some of his business ventures. When Deirdre confronted me in the store, she whispered that Mister Dunn abused women until he destroyed them. Deirdre seemed to know about it because she was using Mister Dunn to get whatever she wants."

"Probably money," Maggie said, nodding.

"But remember what they had said when we were in the parlor? The lady asked you if you were a prospect. And then he looked at yeh and said something like—"

"It was 'delicious', if I recall. Gross… *fecker*."

Cuán got up and held out his hand to Maggie to help her to her feet. "I think we should follow him and confront him. You can use some of that extra physical prowess of yours. Scare him."

"Aye. If ye are game, I am."

Cuán held Maggie's hand as they followed Finnian down Dark Horse Lane, popping a lemon drop into his mouth.

They stayed far enough behind to blend in with others who were walking in the same direction. Cuán was pretty sure that Finnian had no idea he was being followed, which was good.

After walking a good half an hour, Finnian went up to a home and knocked on the door. The door opened, and he went in without either Maggie or Cuán able to see who had let him in. They waited a while, but Finnian didn't come back out.

"I want to get a closer look," Maggie said. "Stay 'ere."

Cuán put his hand on her shoulder. "What are yeh going to do?"

"I'm going to check out the windows."

Cuán looked over the two-story building. It was made of brick and didn't have much to climb on. However, before he was able to say anything, he realized that Maggie was already running across the street. Cuán followed quickly. He watched as she tossed off her shoes and waved him over.

"Help me up so I can see."

He kneeled down, and she climbed onto his back, carefully balancing her bare feet on his shoulders, and he lifted up so that she could look into the windows. Looking around, he imagined someone walking around the corner, catching them like this. They'd be in big trouble.

"No looking up me dress," Maggie warned.

"I always wondered what sort of colors your knickers were," Cuán said, meaning it sarcastically. Though his head was covered by the beige skirt, blinding him either way.

"There seems to be only two of them inside," Maggie whispered. "I say we go in now."

"What's yer plan?"

"To scare the bloody gobshite out of them," Maggie said, hopping off from his shoulders. She grabbed her shoes from him and led the way around back.

"Scare them, right?" Cuán warned.

"That's what I said, Cuán. I promise."

"No more than that." He couldn't have her hurting someone too bad. Not again.

Maggie stopped for a moment and looked at him, seriously.

"Right," she said.

There was a back door. Cuán looked at Maggie, waiting to see what she would do. She didn't surprise him: she went up to the door and kicked it open. Cuán ran up behind her as she went in, and Cuán closed the broken door behind them.

They were in a sizable kitchen with yellow wallpaper up all around them.

The man who lived there came in from the dining room with a gun raised. Maggie grabbed the gun and pushed it up, and chopped the stranger in the neck. The guy dropped the gun and fell down onto his knees as he gripped his throat, gagging.

Cuán punched him and he fell over, unconscious.

"What the bloody hell?" It was the man who they were following, a cigar stuck between his teeth. He was once again looking Maggie up and down as he came into the room, standing over the man they knocked out, the dining room door behind him. Cuán stepped in front of her, wanting to punch him too, and at the same time, worried that he'd run deeper into the house by going back through the door, slamming it in their face.

Finnian backed down, holding up his hands. "I'm not going to hurt anyone."

Maggie went to Cuán's side. "We have questions for yeh."

"Yeah. Well, that's not a surprise. Everyone knows that working with Dunn has its consequences." He chuckled and took out his cigar. "I'm an open book. I have no loyalties to anyone."

"Okay," Cuán said, nodding, "then tell us about Deirdre and the other girls."

"Not all girls are innocent, if you know what I mean. They like to make money, and guys at the clubs like the pictures. Sometimes girls want more money, and Dunn hooks them up with certain gentlemen to make a few extra quid. Breaking no laws, mind, but Dunn's men can get rough if a girl gets out of line." Finnian puffed on his cigar a few more times.

"Do you know Deirdre? Does she do this?"

The man shook his head, pulled the cigar out of his mouth again. "Ah, naw. Deirdre is a special girl. Nobody is allowed to touch her. Not even the punters."

"Why?" Cuán wasn't sure if Dunn knew something about Deirdre, or if he could sense how different she was. *He has pretty much learned not to fuck with me,* she told him. But was this true? Or was he playing her for some other reason?

"I don't know. She's special to Dunn somehow. I heard once that she broke this guy's arm. He was a powerful man too.

Nobody knows how she did it. But ever since, everyone knows something is wrong with her. Dunn says that Toal Mullins can take her picture. She gets paid. We watch her. But that's it. I don't really know why."

Finnian kept looking down at the unconscious man at his feet. Dunn does know something. *How much?* was the question.

"The photographer is Toal Mullins?" Maggie said.

"Yes. She goes to him once a week. They take the pictures. I have a guy that follows her, making sure she doesn't get into trouble in the meantime," Finnian said.

Wait. Deirdre is followed? Cuán thought, but it was too late. There was a metal clicking metal behind his head.

There was a third man.

Cuán wanted to slap his own forehead. *Why am I such a meater?*

"Oh, don't turn around, or else the gun might go off, painting blood all over my friend's place here," Finnian said, sticking the cigar back in his up-turned mouth.

Unable to move, they watched helplessly as Finnian picked up his unconscious friend's gun and pointed it at them. The guy behind them didn't move. He was waiting for them to do something that they weren't supposed to do.

"Dunn will love you guys. Really. And don't worry about it. Deirdre won't know anything. We'll keep it our little secret."

Cuán hated this guy.

They dragged Cuán and Maggie down into the basement. They tied Cuán to a chair first, and then tied Maggie down. Cigar Man (*Finnian?*) stood by, letting the gun drift back and forth to each of their heads. The basement was dank and lit only with the lamp that Finnian had placed on a chair in one corner.

Maggie looked for a way to escape.

"Don't bother screaming. Nobody will hear you. Dunn ordered a doctor to drop by, and we'll make sure you get some sleep," Cigar Man said, smirking.

"Swell. Thanks, yeh prick," Maggie said.

The two men climbed the stairs. They were talking about the guy Maggie and Cuán had knocked out, worrying about whether or not to wake him. The door was closed, and neither of them could hear them anymore.

"Well, I'm poked up. It wasn't supposed to work this way," Cuán said. "How did we not see this coming? I mean, God, how did we not figure Deirdre was being followed?"

Maggie shook her head, thinking that she would never have guessed. Did that make her ignorant? Maybe. The more important thing was getting out of here before the doctor came.

Maggie summoned as much strength as she could and started pushing her arms out against the rope. The rope was strong. Stronger than someone's neck, or the muscles in their arms. She felt it beginning to give, but it was slow and painful.

"Are yeh going to be able to get us out of here?" Cuán said.

Maggie sighed. She could tell Cuán was upset with her by his tone, which was the last thing she wanted right now. Taking a slow breath, she pushed her arms against the ropes again. After a dozen times of doing this, however, the ropes had barely any more give.

"We may be in trouble."

"Figures. You know, now that I think about it, I'm sort of upset that I thought yer way would work out," Cuán said. "It's not like we've done anything like this before, and you can get us into some doozies sometimes."

Maggie felt insulted. "Really now?"

"You can't just break down doors and demand things all the time. Sometimes yeh have to think before you act," Cuán added.

"Ah feck off," Maggie said. "It's not like yeh had a plan. Hell, yeh didn't really try to stop me."

"That's because I never had time to come up with one. You wanted to act, and you drove forward without giving me some time to think," Cuán said.

Maggie sort of wanted to slap him right then.

"If we always waited around for yer head to work, we'd get nowhere."

"*Psh!*"

"Ah feck off, will yeh?"

There are only a few times they got into fights, and Maggie never liked it when they did. It made her sadder than angry in the end. They sat in silence, Maggie giving up on the ropes.

All she could think about was if this was the end, she would never get to resolve things with Deirdre, and that made her angrier. It wasn't fair. That bitch had taken her life, and now she would never be able to punish that *siofra* for it.

It wasn't Cigar Man who came down the stairs for them. It was the guy Maggie originally throat-punched. He was grinning as he escorted another man into the room. This guy had a heavy bar-mustache and white jacket. He wore gloves and carried a white cloth, and a vial of some clear liquid. He poured some of the liquid onto the cloth and went to Cuán.

No!

She couldn't lose Cuán. "Get the feck off him! I'll kill all of ye!"

When she looked over at Cuán again, the doc was removing the cloth from his face, and Cuán's head fell, hanging, as if lifeless.

Lifeless.

The doc was pouring more fluid on the cloth.

"Don't worry. Sleep comes pretty quickly," the doc said.

"Fuck you! Fuck Dunn! Fuck ye, I'll kill you! Prick."

The doc covered her mouth. There was no way to fight his grip, and she found it hard to stay awake. She barely understood what was happening before the darkness overcame her.

II.

Below the cold, dark waters in the Deep Dens, Maggie was shaped into something resembling a hybrid eel-shark. She had her arms and her face, but her lower half was a long, spotted tail with a spiked dorsal fin running along her back. Her lavender tongue was longer, tendril-like, and her eyes were big and black. Her hands were webbed and had long, sharp claws. There were gills running along her upper, paler torso around the ribs. They took their claws, and they carved glowing symbols into her flesh as well. Wherever their claws tore, it lit up and shined an aqua blue. Each year they'd add another symbol until her whole body was covered in these bioluminescent patterns.

If a human had seen her, they would see a monster.

The fomori would get into her mind and drive her to watch and protect the eggs. When they hatched, they would snap and sometimes get ahold of her with their teeth, rending and tearing flesh. One creature tried eating her, though she was able to break free and hide between the rocks until she was commanded back to the eggs.

There were others like her, sure. Many others from other places, all twisted and formed for differing reasons that only the fomori understood. The Altered Ones. She was certain they shaped you for whatever purpose they desired. Once primordial beings, shapes and shapelessness were their specialties.

Maggie was remembering this as she woke. Never before had her dreams and memories been so vivid. It was more than enough to make her heart ache and her eyes dampen. She hated the Fomorians for what they did to her, but she feared them with every inch of bone in her body. They represented a life of cold slavery and isolation that drained her soul.

How had she lived through that? How could she have been so foolish to have found something so good like Cuán and Oona to risk it all for this now?

Cuán. He was who she wanted. He was the life she wanted. Once she was finished with Deirdre, there'd only be the two of them. Living life together.

How could she do this to them?

She tried looking around. Her eyes wouldn't focus easily. Partially because of the tears, she was sure, but because whatever had drugged her messed with her eyes. Her mind. Maggie blinked, held her eyes closed, and shook her head. After a while, her vision became clearer, and she saw that she was in a fancy room. Probably inside Dunn's mansion. The window was suggesting it was late, or very early in the morning.

Instead of being tied to a chair, she was lying on a bed. A new rope was tied around her arms, holding her arms down.

There was no sign of Cuán. She didn't like it at all.

There was a raven-haired lady in the room with her. She was watching her like a mad, hungry woman.

"Where am I?"

The woman sighed. "You're supposed to keep your mouth shut."

Maggie focused on the gun the woman was holding.

"Feck that. Who are yeh?"

The woman grinned. "Dunn's fiancé."

"Where's Cuán?"

"Is that the man who accompanied you? Ah, well, I'm sure Dunn has him somewhere around here. Don't know, don't care."

Maggie's head hurt as if a baton had pummeled it a few good times. She put her hand to her forehead, but it did little to relieve the pain. When she looked down at her feet, she realized that there was a chain around her right ankle above her shoe.

"Yeah, that's Dunn's idea. People say you're a dangerous girl. I don't see it. You're so little. No trouble at all, I'm sure."

Maggie didn't care about this woman's condescension. Rather she worried about Cuán and where he was. Hopefully, he was still alive. If he wasn't, she would never forgive herself. Or Dunn.

The door opened and Dunn walked in with two other audacious thugs behind him. He was dressed in an expensive suite and his dark hair was combed stylishly to the side. She could see how women seemed to let him get away with more than he should. "Thank you, Delma. Watching her carefully?"

The thugs dragged Maggie to a chair and sat her in it, the chains dragging on the floor, still attached to her right ankle. Once they were done, they moved to the back of the room, giving Dunn his space.

Maggie noticed that Dunn didn't glance at his fiancé too long, only to see the gun in her hand. Satisfied, his eyes fell on her instead and grinned. He was shaking his head as if he could not believe it. Dunn attempted to touch her face, but she snapped at his hand with her teeth. He whipped it back just in time.

"Don't touch me!" she said. "Where's Cuán?"

Delma laughed, but she did as Dunn asked and kept her eyes peeled, keeping the gun trained on her.

"Nasty, nasty," Dunn said. "I bet you are an animal."

"Where's Cuán? Tell me, or I'll rip yer heart out."

Dunn ignored her. "This is rather wonderful, you know. Very few are taken by the fae and actually escape them. Bravo! Spending time with the Primordial Beings changes you though, yes? A part of it touches you forever?"

Maggie went cold, unable to believe what she was hearing. "You know of the fomori? Yeh know of me?"

Dunn nodded. "Aye. That's why I keep Deirdre close to me. She's the changeling—the one they replaced you with when they stole you away. You're the *real* Deirdre, aren't you? Tell me, how did you escape the Fomorians and their Nead Domhain?"

Maggie thought about not telling him. He didn't deserve to know anything, but she didn't see how it mattered. In fact, it may just make him fear her a little bit more, which could be useful. "The Cailleach."

Dunn's eyes opened wider. "Well. That crone is still around, eh?"

"She is forever," Maggie said.

Dunn spat angrily back: "She is dying, returning to the Primordial like many of the others. This world is slowly destroying itself, and there's nothing she can do about it. We have already fallen over the edge of the Great Balance, and we've set their paths of fate... as well as our own. The Commination reigns now."

Again, Maggie didn't understand any of this. She understood that the Fomorians and other fae had *fata essences*, making them a part of the Primordial, but she didn't understand what the Great Balance was or what this Commination was. Whatever Dunn believed, it didn't sound good. Did this maniac support some terrible thing that she didn't herself know of? It was possible, she thought. She was but a child in the grand scheme of things, wasn't she?

One thing Maggie did know, though: he was Deirdre's gatekeeper. He didn't want Deirdre to get too far from him, wanting to know where she was at all times. Maybe if Maggie could prove to him that she wasn't afraid of him, he'd listen to her.

"I'll tell you what. Yeh let me go and give me Deirdre, and I'll forget all of this," she said.

"Why do you want Deirdre so badly?" Dunn said, cocking his head.

Maggie didn't want to tell him, but the way he looked at her, she realized he was beginning to understand.

"You want to kill her, don't you? She took your life, and you want it back. Do you really think that killing her will fix all your problems?"

"I want her head," Maggie said. "I know it won't fix me problems, but it'll be some form of justice, methinks. I might even be able to... forget."

Dunn laughed. "Forget? Oh, you will never forget, my dear."

Dunn seemed to calm down. He grabbed a box, and he sat down in a chair opposite her, taking out a pipe, stuffed it with tobacco, and lit it. Once he was done, puffing away at the black bit of the pipe, he placed the cigar box at his feet. He didn't say anything for a while. Instead, he regarded her, as if he were thinking.

"If anything has happened to... *to Cuán*, you will regret it, Dunn," Maggie said.

If Delma didn't have the gun trained on her or she wasn't tied up, Maggie would strangle him now until he gave her Cuán's whereabouts. Maybe Deirdre's. And she would break his neck and hunt that bitch down.

"Did you know, Maggie, that I was once communed with the Cailleach? There was this fae. The others called her Cherry Fox—'*Sionnach Silín,*' in the old tongue. The tale I heard was that she was once one of the maidens of the Seven Virgin Springs until the Fomorians raped and abducted one of her sisters. She and her other sisters went to the gods, but none would help, except Manannán mac Lir—the god of the sea. He helped them discover Tor Mór, where the fomori were held up before they were exiled after the Battle of Mag Tuired. One by one, the sisters died, even the one they meant to rescue, save one: the one who would become Cherry Fox. And because she did not die in battle or succeed in her task, she was cursed by the Morrígan and changed. Legends grew up about her, so I knew of them. I knew of her. Eventually, our paths crossed.

"The fae, you see, they gathered because they wanted to see the child of the Cailleach. She was to be a changeling in the court of Nicholas Netterville and Elizabeth Fitzgerald. Only Cherry Fox didn't want this to happen... So she came to me and took her from me. It didn't go well for either of us, I'm afraid. The Cailleach can be a ruthless bitch, even to her consorts."

Maggie struggled with her ropes as Doran Dunn sat in front of her, smirking at her futile attempt. Maggie finally gave up, sighing. *Feck me,* she thought.

"If yer that old, how are yeh still alive then? 'Ere? Before me?" Maggie said. She looked for lying in his eyes.

Doran shrugged and laughed. "The Cailleach cursed me soon after for failing her, of course."

He stopped, and she saw his lips tremble for a moment. The Cailleach truly hurt him.

"With immortality?"

"Did she punish Cherry Fox for murdering me and ruining her plans? No. That crone punished me for my failure! All I did was live for the love of Nicholas and Elizabeth. I worship the old gods in dangerous times, and how am I rewarded? With this long life, so that she can haunt me forever?"

Doran spat again. This time the spit was yellowed from the tobacco smoke in his mouth. He tapped the pipe into a tray, the smoke dying quickly.

"But it's okay, isn't it? It means that I have plenty of time to get what I want."

Maggie tried moving in the chair as the ropes bit into her arms. Delma held the gun higher, making sure she remembered that she was not supposed to move at all.

"The ropes are pinching me," she told her.

Delma smiled again after a long yawn. "I don't care."

Maggie looked at Doran Dunn. "We're not friends and we aren't working together. I don't care anything about yeh, or this fae pup, Cherry Fox. I only want Deirdre and Cuán. Let us go. Now."

Doran sighed, looking disappointed with her.

"Really? You think you can demand things from me?"

Maggie sighed. She didn't understand why Doran wanted Deirdre anyway. Was it because he knew she was a siofra?

"What is a siofra, anyway? A changeling, yeah? I don't understand how it could take my life like this. How could it look so much like me?"

Doran sat back, mulling it over for a moment. "A siofra is a special kind of fetus, beget by the High Erus like Danu, Brigid, etcetera. So, yes, they are changelings. These gelatinous creatures, born in a divine womb, can be born early without form. When done this way, the siofra are highly adaptable, soaking up information on both a physical level and a psychic one. Once they have time to absorb information from a nearby host, they have the ability to use the information and transform themselves into perfect doppelgänger. Usually, once the process is complete, the fae takes the original baby... like you, leaving the siofra in their place.

"They're hard to kill, too. For if the siofra's corporeal body is killed, its gelatinous form can free itself from the dead carcass and produce a whole new body for itself. It's quite remarkable. And if that's not frightening, it can hide inside other hosts. It has the capability to assimilate through an interblending process with any living animal. Yes, it's quite beautiful."

Maggie couldn't believe it. "So why do you need Deirdre so badly? You wish to remake her?"

"The real question," Doran said, ignoring her, "is what shall we do with you? I could kill you. After all, the changeling has taken over your life, hasn't she? She aged in time with your life, and your age has moved much slower. How can you prove that you are the real Deirdre? You cannot. Nobody would believe you. Nobody would bat an eye if you were gone."

What an arselick, Maggie thought. They were getting somewhere, weren't they? There was something Dunn wasn't saying about the *siofra*. He was hiding something more nefarious than he even wanted to admit.

"Before yeh think that over, I would like to say I'm happy being Maggie. I made me own life," Maggie said. She thought of Oona and Cuán, specifically. They were her life now and she felt their loyalty and their love. Yes, she sometimes longed for her lost life with Colum and Mona, for them to see her as their beloved daughter, but Maggie was okay for now with loving them from afar, knowing they were okay.

It was better than nothing.

Deirdre would always be a different story, and Maggie was going to have her head.

Doran seemed to consider this and nodded. "I could have you work with some of my ladies... But you are *piocadh*, a Maris Demidian. You have been touched and it has made you stronger."

He got up and went over to a shelf full of books. There was another box. He grabbed this and snapped his fingers a couple of times. Delma stood up as the two other large men moved in on Maggie.

Doran opened the box and took out a black anklet. He put the box back on the shelf as Maggie looked at Doran's men.

"What are yeh doin', Mister Dunn?"

He walked over as the men moved closer.

"I thought I asked you to call me Doran," he said, smiling. He showed her the black anklet. "The men are merely here to make sure that when I put this on you, you won't struggle."

"What is it?" Her heart raced.

"It's cold iron," Doran said, and smiled again. "You see, all that extra prowess you get from being *piocadh* is subdued when you are in close proximity to cold iron. If I were to make a weapon with this, and if I damaged some of your internal organs, it would poison you and kill you pretty quickly."

Definitely an arselick, Maggie thought. Not wanting the device on her, she started to struggle in her shackles. It was all useless. No matter how hard she tried, Dunn had her good.

One of the large men kneeled and removed Maggie's shoes, baring her feet.

"I had this one specially made. The lock is much like how they make handcuffs. You see here how it slides over this pawl, holding it in place? It makes it very difficult to get off. I'm thinking, if we put this on you, then you can very easily work with my ladies without issue, correct?"

Doran kneeled and snapped it onto her left ankle. The iron felt cold, a little uncomfortable. She realized—at least for the fae—the 'cold' was literal.

"Yeh can't do this," Maggie said, trying not to panic.

The men stood up, and Doran said, "Let's give this a try."

One of his strong-arms went behind her and was pulling at the knots. She felt the ropes loosen, and when she was free, she got up. Then she realized the blur in front of her face was Doran sucker punching her. Her vision shot to blackness and the pain vibrated in her head. Already unbalanced, she lost her footing and landed on her ass beside the chair.

When her eyesight came back, she was holding her hands in front of her face for protection and saw a blurry vision of him standing over her.

"Come on, lass. Show me what you got," he said.

Anger suddenly burned through her, and she tried grabbing him. The pain in her head throbbed through her, making it more difficult, but she growled and lunged with all her strength.

Doran grabbed her hands, pulled them to the side easily, and he smacked her across the face. The hot sting made her cry out, and she started to sob. He did it again and again, each slap getting harder and harder until she could barely feel her face at all. Just the blows.

There was nothing she could do to stop him.

Out of the corner of her eye, she saw Doran Dunn gesture to one of his men. They grabbed her and lifted her to her feet, and one dropped to remove the chains from her right leg. Doran walked back up to her, getting into her face, the hot stink of the pipe tobacco washing over her.

"You a bloody virgin? I wonder how high your bidding will go? Pretty high, I suspect," Doran spat, still breathing heavily from slapping her.

The men laughed. She could hear Delma laugh too.

She wished Cuán was here. That's all she wanted right now.

III.

Deirdre awoke. She touched her face, where the sting was now beginning to dissipate as if it never existed. There were many times in her life when she thought she felt as if she was connected with somebody else. When she was younger, she chalked it up to living in Kilkee, but she would dream about swimming in the deep depths of the cold sea. If she woke up from nightmares, it was only because she had nightmares of monsters that lived down there, like Seagrass Maggie. It was one of the main reasons why the sea always scared her. Not just because of drowning—though that would be horrible—but because of what she knew lived in it.

Not just a dream, the tiny voice said in the back of her head. *No, not at all...*

Now she was starting to understand that while her dreams were always fragmented and didn't make much sense, Deirdre was sure that she was actually getting glimpses in her dreams about what Maggie was seeing. They were connected, though she didn't understand how or why exactly.

She could feel the truth of it deep inside herself.

Was Maggie the same as Seagrass Maggie? Was Maggie really as much of a threat as she dreamed?

Maggie wasn't just in her nightmares. There was more between them than that, wasn't there?

And because this 'Maggie' knew Cuán was in trouble, so did she. For the first time, both of their feelings were in sync. If Cuán was in trouble, they both cared enough that they were going to do their best to help him.

Calm down, she thought. What if you're imagining things? Or going insane, for God's sake?

She still had to find out.

Deirdre climbed out of bed, threw on a shawl, and stepped out of her room. Unable to see anyone, she made her way around to the left-wing smoking room. It had windows that overlooked the front yard and driveway.

Over the many years, she knew that Dunn was trouble. Friends of her disappeared, and she was sure that many of them ended up in the brothels, or crossed him, earning an early grave. All along, she loved the danger. It thrilled her. Made her feel alive, but she didn't want anyone she loved harmed. That was where she drew the line. It was why she didn't write to her folks often, and it was why she tried getting Cuán to go home.

She couldn't penetrate the darkness inside herself to understand why she craved peril or why she felt so lascivious all the time. It was like a deep primal code was written into her blood, and it made her this way, and she didn't know exactly how to control it.

From the window, she watched as two of Doran Dunn's men shoved Maggie into a carriage in the driveway. The way she looked, she was too weak to fight.

Deirdre didn't know whether to be glad, or worried that Maggie couldn't help Cuán.

Where *was* Cuán?

Dunn better have not killed him.

Deirdre went back to her room, had a quick wash, and got into a simple powder blue dress and her brown shoes, hanging a silver chatelaine on her skirt last. Making her way around to the rooms Dunn frequented (all but one... the one at the end of the hall, where he told her she was not to go), she found him in his study, pouring over papers.

"Doran," she said, walking in, realizing that a tall brunette was standing in a corner, sipping from a teacup. The woman had been around for several days, following Dunn like a puppy. The woman sneered at her. Deirdre rolled her eyes and looked at Dunn, who was now regarding her. Deirdre didn't care if the woman saw her as a threat, whatever was between her and Dunn at the moment.

"I want to make an arrangement to speak with the boy from Kilkee who came looking for me. A short one. I think I know what to say to get him to go home and leave us be."

Of course, this was all a lie. She wanted to pressure Dunn into admitting that he was containing Cuán. After all, she cared for him. He was like a little brother once, and though they'd grown apart, it wasn't right what Dunn was doing to him. Hopefully, Dunn hadn't hurt him yet.

"Oh, well, I have heard reports that he got on the train this morning," Dunn said. "I think we solved the problem."

That was a problem. Cuán could very well be dead. She knew that Doran Dunn was a ruthless man, and she was sure that he had murdered people behind her back. She thought back to a couple of her women friends that mysteriously disappeared over the last few years.

Deirdre noticed that his right hand was red, the knuckles bright white.

She wanted to press him, but with the slender guard dog in the corner, she decided not to try.

A part of her began to wonder why Doran Dunn was doing this at all. Sure, she saw how he liked to own people, but attacking people that popped up out of her past? Why? What was he so worried about? Was there some strange reason why he really wanted her around, something she wasn't aware of? Why had she survived so long under his employ without him tiring of her as he did with the other women?

This was disturbing.

Deirdre smiled. "Well, I suppose we have no problem then. You two have a wonderful day."

They watched her leave, and she started wondering how much danger she could be in. After all, if Dunn was this audacious to keep her, she had to consider why. For a long time, she knew that Dunn was dangerous. It was thrilling and sometimes disturbing, and she didn't know why an inner part of her craved the uncertainty so much, but she only craved it when she thought *she alone* was in danger. Now that Cuán was in trouble, Deirdre didn't like it at all. It wasn't right.

She knew that if she crossed Dunn, he would take everything he gave her away: the money, the career, and possibly the city itself. Deirdre wanted to keep all that she had. It was hers. She earned it all. She deserved it all.

To hell with it, she thought. Cuán's life was more important than her career. It hurt her to say that, but it was true. Dunn didn't get to hurt Cuán. As much as she loved her life, she would lose everything to make sure they weren't hurt.

Deirdre went back to her room and found the dagger she bought for personal safety around Dunn's men. Today she might need it.

Why did she have to care so much? She sort of hated herself for it.

Finnian spat in Cuán's face. When he opened his eyes, he saw that he was still in that dank basement. Finnian was holding up a picture of Deirdre. She was standing nude in the woods somewhere, looking off into the distance, looking like a goddess. Hair like cotton strands, wavy and long. Milky flesh. Big eyes.

"You can buy these for a pound," Finnian said, "in Dunn's gentleman clubs. These nudes are quite the new thing, really. Most erotic material gets illustrated, but with these photographic technologies getting better and better, it becomes cheaper to get street trash to show us the real goods. Deirdre's a popular feel, you know?

"It's like you can smell that fishy Kilkee pussy right through the print," Finnian said, taking a deep sniff of the photograph. "If only Dunn wasn't such a meater. I would have shown her what a real man can do."

Finnian laughed.

Cuán wasn't impressed, and if he could, he'd knock the bloke's jaw off-kilter.

Cuán groaned. They gave that drug-shite to him twice, knocking him out cold each time. And the effects left him with the worst headache of his life. His head throbbed like it was on the edge of erupting out his eyes, nose and mouth.

"Can I get water?" he said.

Finnian eventually nodded and got up from his chair.

"Don't try anything," he said. "I'll be back."

Cuán watched the arsehole go, thinking about Maggie. All his life, he'd been keen on higher learning, escaping Kilkee, and now all he could think about was his girl—the only thing that mattered. Had he really expressed that to her?

Cuán knew that he could probably die for her... and he was okay with that.

He was here for her, wasn't he?

Without knocking, Deirdre walked into Toal's apartments, and heard a woman whimpering. She followed the noise into Toal's bedroom, walking in on Toal, thrusting between a woman's open legs. Deirdre got a good lewd view of the back of his manhood as he worked, unaware of her presence. While it gave her an idea, she could only think about how much danger Cuán was in, and how important it was to get to him as quickly as possible. When she saw Toal, she saw Dunn, and she went red.

"Bloody fuck, Toal!" she shouted, and Toal jumped, covering himself with a sheet as the strange woman used the blanket. Deirdre laughed, but bitterly.

"Oh, bloody hell, Deirdre," Toal said. "This isn't funny."

Deirdre abruptly stopped laughing and glared at him, clenching her teeth as she withdrew a dagger. "I'm going to cut your fucking balls off, Toal. How does that sound?"

"Fuck off," Toal said. "Can't you see I'm busy here?"

Was he not taking her seriously? Deirdre became head-burning furious, tightning her fists at her side.

Deirdre flipped the dagger's blade facing down in her fist with a snap, and stabbed Toal's leg. It slid in between the muscles, and blood oozed up as he screamed out the full of his lungs.

When the other woman realized what was happening, she screamed along with him.

Deirdre removed the bloody dagger and stabbed the air in front of the screaming woman.

Both stopped screaming, but they were sobbing, as they watched her wide-eyed.

Good. They were all serious now.

"Now, how about them balls, Toal?"

IV.

Two men came back down the stairs into the basement. Cuán knew it was daylight as he saw it flare behind the men before they closed the door. Finnian had a canteen and he put it to his lips, letting him drink some water.

"Hey, I have to tell you. I'm not usually the kind of guy that does this. Usually, Dunn uses his browbeats, you know? I wouldn't have gotten into this if it weren't for you and your lady following me. So, I'm not exactly thankful for what you've done here."

He poured more water down Cuán's throat. Cuán drank steadily, wanting all that he could get.

"Yeah, so this gives me no pleasure, but we got the word from the boss. This little water here is the last nice thing we get to do," Finnian added.

Cuán wanted to sob. This was it. They were going to kill him.

"Where is Maggie? Where did they take her?" he said, worrying more for her.

"Ah, boy, I don't know. All I know is Mister Dunn wanted to speak with her. He wasn't sure what to do with her or you. I guess he's made his decision, though, eh?"

Finnian handed the other man the canteen.

Keep him talking, Cuán thought. *The more he talks, the longer it takes for him to kill you.*

"Maggie is the only thing that means anything to me," Cuán said. "I love her."

"Yeah, well, that's a horrible twist of fate. But that's life. It's not always nice. People get chewed up and spat out like they're nothing all the time."

"How can you be so horrible? What have I done to you?"

He felt snot dripping down his nose over his upper lip.

Finnian chuckled at this. "Don't pretend you're better than me, boy. I had a rough life too. My father died before I was born because he was a miserable drunk, and my mother used to beat me with a stick. One time she broke all my knuckles when she was wailing on them. I ran away, had some street thug fuck me in the ass, got pissed on by another guy who expected me to steal wallets. Nobody ever fucking cared for me. Be lucky you came from some nice fishing village with a mammy and da. I had to work out of it, and I worked hard to do it. And believe me, I had to step on people to get where I am today."

Cuán remembered one man in Kilkee claiming that man's only hope of good living was getting atop the other man.

"Conquer without mercy," Cuán said. "Sounds cheap and ruinous to me."

Finnian laughed. "Maybe. But it is a fact of life."

Finnian took a knife out of his boot. It looked like it was only three inches, but it would do the trick. Cuán shuddered.

"If you're going to do it, do it," Cuán said. "I just want it to be over."

Finnian nodded, grinning, and handed the knife to the other man in the room. "I'd rather not. I don't want to mess up my suit."

He started up the stairs while the other man stepped closer to Cuán.

"Don't worry," the new guy said. "I've done this lots of times. I like to think I make it quick."

Nothing like a cold-hearted man to pass an execution along to an even crueler man.

The stranger placed his large palm on Cuán's forehead, pushing back his head to expose his neck. Cuán closed his eyes tight and waited for the blade to slash it.

"Help me, God my Savior, for the glory of Your name, deliver me and forgive me for my sins for Your name's sake. Lord, I pray that You remove my guilt and wipe away my sins so that I can draw closer to You. With You, there is forgiveness so that I can, with reverence, serve You.

"*In nomine Patris, et fillii, et Spiritus Sancti.* Amen."

The bastard, Cuán thought. *Praying for forgiveness for my murder? You should go to Hell for this.*

So Toal was good for two things. One, he knew where they were keeping Cuán. Two, he had a gun and bullets. Leaving him sobbing in bed with his tart, Deirdre loaded the gun and stuck it in her bag, signaling down a carriage once she was outside. She asked the teamster to get her to the address as quickly as possible, but she still worried that she was too late. Dunn had no reason to keep Cuán, so he was as good as dead if she was too late.

However, as they went, she realized that the carriage wasn't going in the direction she asked.

"Where are you going?"

The teamster turned around and shouted back, "I'm sorry, Miss, but Mister Dunn expects you at the estate forthwith."

"Have you been following me?" Deirdre said. She thought a few times that maybe she'd been watched, but apparently, she wasn't doing a great job trying to dodge her shadow.

"I do as Mister Dunn requests of me, Miss," the teamster said. "Save your spit and fire. We're almost to the mansion."

Bloody fucking hell, she thought. A sudden panic washed through her. If she had any hope of saving Cuán, it was gone now.

Until she remembered the gun.

She took it out and crawled up to push it against the back of the teamster's head. If it wasn't too late, she was going to save Cuán's life. And when this was all done, she was maybe going to London, she thought. Take the money and leave as soon as she could. Because after this, she knew Dunn was going to shun her, or come after her himself.

Crossing this line terrified her. She'd have to start a whole new life now.

But what else could she do?

Time seemed like forever, as if it slowed down. There was darkness behind his closed eyelids, but Cuán could still smell the dank stink of the basement that he was trapped in. He could feel the killer's fingers in his hair, holding his head back to expose Cuán's neck, and Cuán felt his aching heart banging in his chest.

A loud shot rang out. The man who was holding his forehead let go, saying, "What the bloody 'ell?"

The door to the basement opened, and a light flared from above. Two more loud shots went off. Cuán watched the man beside him fall back, unmoving on the ground.

"What the *fecking fuck*?" His ears were ringing loud enough that he couldn't hear anything else.

That's when he saw that it was Deirdre coming down the stairs, holding a smoking gun.

"Oh, Cuán," she said. "I'm sorry."

She went to him and started untying him.

He was never so thankful in his life, and he giggled, not knowing how else to react.

Maggie, he thought, sobering. She was still in trouble.

"Where's Maggie?"

"I think I know. She's safe for now. Let's get you out of here, get you some food and work out how we can do this," Deirdre said. "We'll get the two of you home."

IV. The Key & The Hollow

I.

Doran Dunn's goons put a bag over Maggie's head, and they transported her in a carriage to another house. She didn't know where she was being taken, but eventually, she was pushed into another chair, and the hood was removed from her head.

She had to admit—she was frightened enough that she couldn't stop shaking. She didn't know what they were going to do to her and had no idea what to expect next from any of them.

"Bloody hell," Maggie said, her eyes starting out all blurry as she tried to focus.

Someone slapped her. Maggie could see movement, and so she shook her head until her eyes cleared.

"Stand up," a slightly overweight yet tall woman said. Maggie saw that she had one milky eye that wandered off.

Maggie didn't move, but the milky-eyed woman ordered two men to lift her up, and they ripped and tore Maggie's clothes off so that she stood naked in front of them. She was too weak to do anything about it, and when the woman's men were done, the only thing she wore was the black iron anklet that still clung to her left ankle.

Humiliated, Maggie teared up, sniffing as her nose threatened to run.

"Oh, don'na be crying in 'ere," the woman said, her milky eye flipping back and forth. "My name is Madam Granya. I run this brothel for Mister Dunn, and we won't be havin' any of these cries in 'ere. I don't have the patience for it."

A young man came in, looked her over with a smile, and whispered into Madam Granya's ear, interrupting her. Despite the iron anklet affecting her abilities, Maggie could still make out what he was saying—"Dunn said Finnian is dead. I don't think you should tell Myrna yet. It won't be good for her."

Madam Granya nodded at the boy, and he nodded back. He looked Maggie over one more time, giving her a perverted grin, and left.

Maggie looked hard at Madame Granya, only because she didn't want to get hit again.

Granya walked around her and looked her up and down. Every once in a while, she'd grab her breast, her thigh, or her ass. Her hands were cold and rough. Maggie tried to ignore the molestation by looking at the walls. There was a theater bill with swirling red lines and the words:

COME SEE THE GREAT KÁRPÁTI!

HYPNOTISM AND MESMERISM!

YOUR MIND IN TRANCE DOES MANY WONDROUS THINGS!

REMEMBER THINGS YOU HAVE FORGOTTEN!

KNOW YOUR OWN TRUTHS!

That's what she wanted. A trance state… To leave these groping hands and the prying eyes.

"Think you'd pass a virgin test?" Granya said with a grin.

"I don't know what that is, Miss," Maggie said.

"'Madam,' you slag," Granya said, staring her down.

Maggie looked away.

"It's when we open that little bunny between your legs and make sure you still got your cherry," Granya said.

Everyone in the room laughed as Maggie looked revolted.

"It doesn't matter anyway," Granya said. "No man ever knows the difference. You're new. They'll think you're a virgin, and you'll act like one, and they'll be happy with what they pay."

Granya rubbed Maggie's belly and gestured to one of her men to come over. "Take her to the girls."

The man grabbed her arms quickly and started pulling her out of the office.

Maggie looked back, unable to look away from Granya's milky eye as she said, "You'll have a bath. You'll rest. When you're healed, we'll put you in one of the rooms."

Maggie wanted to spit in her face.

The man dragged her naked down the hall into another room, where several women lounged around. The man swung her so that she'd lose her balance, and she fell to the floor. She collapsed hard. Every bone in her skeleton felt as if it was rattling.

"Madam Granya said to clean her up," the thug said, and he left the women alone.

Women swarmed Maggie, helping her up. Some laughed while others asked her if she was okay. Maggie didn't want to speak with any of them and only let herself sob. Despite this, women poured cold water into a bath, put her in it, and they started scrubbing her down. Some of them were too rough and her skin burned.

"What's this?" one woman asked, grabbing her left foot and holding it up to show the others the anklet.

"Is it worth anything?" another woman asked.

They tried to tug it off, which hurt. No matter how hard Maggie fought back, the girls were stronger together. They pulled and tugged until they decided that they wouldn't be able to remove it. This left the top of her foot and ankle sore.

"Seems worthless anyway," another girl said.

They forced her up and dried her with a towel and showed her to a room with several cots. Another woman brought her a gown. It was ragged and full of small holes, but it covered her and warmed her a little. She crawled onto her cot. *I hope you're okay, Cuán. You are everything to me. Please be okay. If we can both find each other, we'll go away. We'll go far away from all of this.* And then fell asleep.

She awoke a few hours later and saw through one window that it was dark out. Many women were sleeping on their cots. Through the walls, she heard men and women moaning, making their bed frames and floors creak. One was crying out somewhere after each loud clap of flesh, a sound Maggie recalled once when she got caught lying to Oona and got a whooping.

Maggie hated all of it.

Of course, her mind went back to finding Deirdre, too. If she didn't leave this place, she'd never get to the siofra, and Maggie couldn't have that. Maggie would have her revenge, and the Cailleach would have her prize. It was a sworn promise to both of them.

She wanted to check the time, realizing that she'd lost the pocket watch Cuán had given her. Upset, Maggie wanted to cry again.

She *had* to get out of here.

Maggie went to the window and found that it was a direct drop. Normally she thought she could make the jump, though the ground looked like cobblestone. With the iron anklet weakening her, she was afraid she'd break her ankles or something worse.

"I wouldn't try it," a woman behind her said.

Maggie looked back and saw a woman in the shadows in one corner. A bergamot perfume wafted from her, not altogether unpleasant. Maggie tried to remember where she smelled it before.

"I'm the night watch," the woman said. "I make sure you don't go doin' something stupid like that. I get along great with the others. We can too, but you can't be causing me any trouble."

The sound of her voice was familiar, but Maggie didn't care why.

Maggie looked out at the Dublin night. Not many lights were on, so Maggie was guessing it was past midnight, sometime after the pubs had closed.

"My name is Myrna. What's yours?"

"Maggie." She tried to smile, thinking about Cuán, but it wouldn't come. "He calls me Seagrass Maggie from time to time."

Myrna came over, nodding, and sat in the window next to her as Maggie looked out into the night.

"Haven't we met before?"

Maggie didn't look at the woman, but she knew who she was. This was the woman who was with Finnian at Dunn's manor.

"Perhaps."

"It's going to be okay. Sometimes the men can get rough, but Madam Granya punishes every one of them that step out of line. She doesn't like it when the women are hurt because nobody wants to fuck an ugly duck if they can help it. It's work. It's often hard work. Gross, too, really. But it's better than starving on the streets. And when you're with Madam Granya long enough, she pays a farthing every week so you can buy candy. Better than the fucking factories anyway."

Maggie looked at the older, stalwart woman beside her and said: "They made a mistake. I have friends and they're looking fer me. They'll come, and they'll help me get this anklet off me leg. And when they do, I will show them what a mistake they've made."

Myrna looked sadly back at her with her gray eyes. "I wish I could say that I haven't heard that before. But it's better just to accept what's happened and move on. Life is short, and you have to enjoy the good moments when they come because they only come in small measures."

Maggie looked away from her. Myrna was wrong. She wasn't going to let this woman break her down. It's what Myrna wanted. That's what they all wanted. They wanted to take away her strength, break her spirit, make her pliable for their perverse and selfish whims.

No. She would not be broken.

Maggie left the window and crawled back into her cot, throwing the blanket over her head without another word.

I could have you work with some of my ladies... But you are piocadh, *a Maris Demidian.* You have been touched, and it has made you stronger, Doran Dunn had said.

Maggie had no idea what a Maris Demidian was. In the Deep Dens, they referred to themselves as the Altered Ones—or *athraithe*. Those who had been changed by Elieris and the shape-shifting properties of the Otherworld seas. Was a Demidian the same thing? And what did Maris mean?

Would any of this help her escape her prison?

Probably not. Not with the cold iron around her ankle.

Doran woke up the next morning.

Delma was beside him, still sleeping. He briefly wondered why he allowed her to stay in his room. At this point, she'd sleep wherever he liked without pouting because she didn't want to ruin the 'rest of her life'. It was exciting, if he was going to be honest with himself. He wanted to see what happened to her when she opened up the blackness he put into her heart.

Doran hoped he'd be there for it.

He took a deep breath and rolled away from her, throwing his feet onto the floor. Without dressing, he went out in his gown and made his way to his study when he realized that Toal Mullin was standing outside his door, one leg wrapped and bleeding, holding his crumbled bowler hat in his hands.

What did he bloody want?

"What on earth are you doing here? And why do you look like a wounded dog?" Doran scowled.

Toal was rubbing his fingers into his felt hat, possibly ruining it. "Deirdre came by and asked me about that fisher's son. And she, uh, she... She took my bloody gun, Mister Dunn."

Doran frowned and quickly made his way toward Deirdre's room. He pushed open the doors and found that her bed was not slept in, and her closets were not disturbed.

She was supposed to be there. How was he going to concentrate on his Great Work—that is, sacrificing Deirdre for his *apotheosis*—

if she was going to cause so many problems? Perhaps he needed to think about detaining her in some fashion. Maybe in a cellar. Doran was certain that if he didn't expand his power, ancient forces were going to come back to get him. And he was done with their games—being their pawn.

Doran kicked the door hard, which drove pain straight through his foot and up through his leg. He cursed and hobbled back to his study. "Felim! Felim! FELIM!"

In a few moments, his butler came rushing into his study. "You were calling for me, Sir?"

"I need you to do a couple of things for me," Doran said. He watched as Delma walked in, holding her loose gown closed. "And one of them is getting her a *fecking* room down the hall!"

II.

Deirdre was really pretty. Her red locks. Her blue eyes. If he didn't know any better, he would easily mistake her for Maggie. Looking at her, he wanted to kiss her and hold her close. Only he knew it wasn't Maggie and this made his heart ache. No matter how beautiful and alike they seemed, Deirdre would never be Maggie.

Cuán sighed, subtly conscious of the incense of benzoin, frankincense, and myrrh. "I've rested. Now, where do we find Maggie?"

Deirdre looked at him and looked around the church that they found refuge in. She seemed disturbed to be here: St. Peter's church in the north of Dublin. The largest parish church in Dublin, Cuán learned only a few minutes before.

"I swear, the foul stench in the air!" she said. "It nauseates me."

They'd gone through a wrought iron fence and went into the church nave to find seats in the back, out of the ears of anyone there with them. Many of the patrons were sitting in the pew or on their knees praying in clusters here and there, most seated in front.

Cuán's arms were sore from the tight ropes that were once wrapped around his torso. He rubbed them every so often while he rolled Maggie's pocket watch around in his hand, the one he gave her at the caves after they had first met. Once Deirdre had saved him from the goons, he saw that they'd taken it from Maggie and laid it on the supper table before they escaped the cursed house.

"I'm scared of her, Cuán. I don't know why, but something in me tells me she's dangerous," Deirdre said. "Is she dangerous? If I help her escape Dunn, will she come after me?"

Cuán sighed and scratched his head. He wanted a lemon drop, but Finnian and his goons took them from him, and he couldn't find where they had put them back at the house.

"Cuán?"

"Aye."

He thought about Maggie's sharp teeth. The night in the alleyway. How much should he tell her? All of it?

"I'm not going to lie. She's upset with you. She thinks you stole her life."

Deirdre moaned and planted her face in her hands. "I don't understand any of this. It's all so confusing. What are you even bloody on about? Stealing her life?"

Cuán sometimes worried about Maggie's obsession with Deirdre. He understood it to a point, but what if Deirdre didn't know she was taking someone else's life? Until Cuán saw Maggie's more monstrous form—and he hated using that word, 'monstrous' to describe her, but what other word was there?—he did worry a little that Maggie would kill Deirdre. On the other hand, he thought he knew Maggie pretty well, and he saw her warm heart everywhere they went. Perhaps that heart was in a deep chasm now, but he knew Maggie could escape it if the 'monster' in her didn't take control of her.

"I think it's something the two of you can work out. I don't know what yeh think of her, but she's only protected me and other people in the village. She's a good soul, if a little weird."

Disregarding her other *form*, he thought. The one that made his blood cold.

There was a moment of silence between them after that. Cuán let her consider what he said. Finally, she sighed...

"The hard part, Cuán," Deirdre said, "is that I know, generally, where she is at. Doran Dunn has brothels, but he has more than one. The worse part: he has brothels in Scotland and even owns one in London."

"So, she could be at any one of them, or being sent afar?"

"Aye. It makes it much more difficult," Deirdre said. "I have been thinking about it, though, and I may have come up with a few good ideas as to where to look first."

"Yea?"

Deirdre leaned back in the pew and twirled her red locks. "One idea is that Doran sent her far away, which would be Scotland or London. I thought that maybe he'd want to get her as far away from you as possible. That doesn't make sense, though—"

"Actually, it does if he knows about *you*."

Deirdre looked at him, head cocked. "Why?"

"Well, back in the shop, if we'd have more time, we were going to tell you something that we have no real proof of, except that maybe you'd know about it anyway on some level."

"You're speaking riddles, Cuán."

"Aye, I know. This is hard, okay? I'm going to say it straight. We have a feeling you're not the... the, uh, *real* Deirdre Ó Fionnáin."

There was a moment where Deirdre soaked this in.

"What the fuck are you on about?"

"Maggie isn't yer twin or a cousin. There's a really... *absurd* reason the two of yeh look alike, and yet there's a strong truth to its... uh, possibility. Maggie. She's the real Deirdre Ó Fionnáin. We think you're a changeling."

Deirdre started laughing.

"I'm serious," Cuán said. "She has—somehow—the memories of being taken from her mother and father when she was a baby. *You* were put in her place."

"Are you calling me artificial, Cuán? An imposter? How dare you say all this to me? Why... Why—That girl is younger than you. What is she now? Eighteen, maybe?"

"Deirdre. Look at me."

"I'm twenty-eight fucking years ol' Cuán. It don'na make sense."

They looked into each other's eyes. Deirdre's brows were partially furrowed.

"Deirdre. I wouldn't believe it myself. But I'm the one who found Maggie on the shoreline. I have been with her this whole time, and I have seen proof that she is fae-touched. She even tells me stories where she sometimes feels you or sees things that you see. That shop where we met. The apartment we rented. Think of those."

Deirdre's eyes widened.

"Aye. Maggie knew that it was the first shop you walked into after getting to Dublin when you wanted to purchase lemon drops. Remember when we were younger, going down to Gilroy's for lemon drops? You were away from home, and yeh remembered Gilroy's. You remembered me and yer ma and da. It made you homesick, so yeh went into that shop and bought a small bag. And what about the apartment? Isn't that where Mister Dunn first set you up? You hated how you shared the kitchen, though. Eventually, Dunn offered for you to stay with him. Don't you remember all of that?

"That's Maggie. She sees into you sometimes. And we came and we wanted to let you know that we knew too. We figured that if Maggie was connected to you, you were connected with her? Maybe you could feel and see her as much as she can see you?"

Deirdre's eyes never left him, but then she blinked, and her eyes fell.

"It's how I knew the two of you were in danger," Deirdre said. "But how do you know that she isn't the changeling? The imposter? Maybe she has been tricking you this whole time?"

Cuán sighed. When he was with Maggie, he never felt more loved, though sometimes she did feel wild and dangerous because of it. He sometimes wondered about his safety or felt as though her love for the ocean was greater than her love for him, but his only real sense of her was that she was very much like himself. Anchored to the natural world. He couldn't explain it any other way and had no idea of how to describe this to Deirdre either.

On the other hand, Deirdre glowed.

No, Maggie was the real deal. Fae-touched, but very real.

Deirdre was divinity.

With Deirdre, there was something magical about her. Her hair glowed a little more than human hair. Her blue eyes shone a little brighter, glassier than human eyes. Her body wasn't subjected to gravity as much as a human. Hell, if Cuán didn't know better, he'd think she was a real goddess made incarnate. He could feel her like a warm sun on a cool day.

Deirdre may look like Maggie, but Maggie didn't have that same lambent aura.

"In the stories, the siofra were put in place of a stolen child. I found Maggie wrapped in seaweed near the cliffs.

"Deirdre, why didn't yer parents take you to church?"

Deirdre looked around. "I hate those places. It's uncomfortable."

"Why? Don't you like the windows? The candles? The gold and silver lights that play over the stones? Or the bible or the cross?"

Deirdre sat back in the pew, letting herself relax. "No. It's not that they burn me, for feck sakes. It's not like I'm some demon if that's what you're referring to."

"Then?"

Deirdre's eyes wandered around the church, and she sighed again. "It's just another power, and it has nothing to do with me," she said.

And she looked at Cuán. Cuán, himself, couldn't believe what she'd said.

"Maggie says that there are different forces in the world. Places like this are filled with *empyrean* essences. Yours' is—"

"Primordial," Deirdre said, as if seeing it herself for the first time.

"The *fata*. The essence of the Primordial. Yes. At least, that's what Maggie has come to understand," Cuán said. "She knows more about this stuff than I do. She's been to the Deep Dens Beyond the Ninth Wave and was a prisoner of the Fomorians for eighteen long years. When she escaped, she continued to grow and age because time moved strangely in the Otherworld. She didn't start aging the way a normal human would until a few days before I found her on the shore."

Cuán looked at Deirdre, who looked lost in her own thoughts. "You okay?"

"I don't know. But if I'm not human... What does that make me? What is a changeling? A siofra?"

Cuán watched a tear escape her eyes, thread down her cheek. It surprised him. He hadn't seen her cry like this since they were much younger.

He put a hand on her shoulder and gave it a short squeeze. "I'm going to be here for you no matter what. I'm sure Maggie would be as invested in helping you as I am. We'll figure this out. Who knows, maybe you are a human... but a different sort of human or something. I don't know. A lot of the information we gathered comes from legends, sewn together with Maggie's patchwork memory married with other stuff we dug up from old books. There could be something we don't understand—"

Deirdre wiped her tears away and looked up at Cuán through her red locks.

"It doesn't matter right now," she said. "We need to get Maggie back."

"Yes, sorry. Before, you were saying yeh had a few ideas where she might be?"

Deirdre nodded. "Yes. If Dunn didn't want her anywhere near me, because he knows this, then he might have sent her far away. That's what I was going to say—"

She stopped and thought for a moment. "However, if he thought to keep me in line, or thought she might be useful, he'd want to keep her close."

Cuán could see either-or. "So, how do we know?"

Deirdre's eyes seemed to glaze over.

"Deirdre?"

"Sorry. Aye. Um, let's assume we don't have to go to London for now. If he wanted to keep her close because he thought she'd be useful, he'd want to place her with somebody he trusted. That can only be Madam Granya. They were lovers a long time ago, I heard. Though they both moved on, she's still very loyal to him. He responds by taking only thirty percent of the take, so she's the wealthiest of the madams."

Cuán looked at the crucifix where Jesus was hanging by his nailed palms, the loincloth barely hanging onto his emaciated waist. There was blood dripping from his crown of thorns, his hands and his feet. A gruesome image that drove men to pray in grace and gratefulness. He understood the sacrifice. You do so for those who you love. And he would sacrifice everything for Maggie.

"So we'll try there first. How do we get in?" Cuán said.

"Getting in will be easy if we act quickly. You go in as a punter. If you're lucky, you'll see her amongst the other girls. Getting out is the tough part. There's also another problem."

"Which is?"

"Doran will be enraged. He's probably acting right now to get me back and kill you. It'll be a trap. They'll know we're coming."

When Cuán told Deirdre how she was the siofra, she wanted to deny it. How could it be? Yet, she remembered the dreams of all those past lives. Whose lives were they? A part of her thought that maybe they were somehow hers. Or they could be all the lives she has stolen over the centuries. And what about her carnal needs? The rush she got from being around Doran Dunn? How many times had she told herself that she was sick and needed help? Could all of this be because she wasn't human? It was all disturbing. All the information she was getting was starting to make some sort of mad logical sense, and she didn't know what to do with it. How do you process something like that?

Her sadness was so deep, she thought she'd never find normal again. Her whole life: a lie. Of course, she learns this at the most inopportune time, with Maggie's life hanging in the balance. In a moment where she wanted to crawl into herself, she must force herself to bury this feeling as far as she could and concentrate on their current problems.

It was very hard to do.

A part of her still didn't trust Maggie. A part of her still wanted to hate that little bitch.

Seagrass Maggie. What a horrible name, really. The name of a monster.

Sighing, she laid back on the pew with Cuán sitting beside her head, closing her eyes and trying to feel Maggie. She reached out with her mind, trying to reach that same space that she sometimes found in her dreams where Maggie was.

Truthfully, Deirdre wanted to do it not just to find Maggie for Cuán, but maybe she could use the Hollow to find out more about her as well. Perhaps finding her in the Hollow would reveal how dangerous Seagrass Maggie really was.

She felt like she slipped—she dove down deep like plunging into deep waters—and fell and fell and...

She fell into a state of deepness and quiet. Deirdre first sensed a little more weight on her head. Raising her hands to her head, she felt the three-pointed horns that slicked back from aside her forehead. Her fingers went to her ears and found them much longer and pointed. Wanting to know more, she conjured a reflection and found that she was fae with red locks and strange, star-shaped pupils over silver eyes.

This isn't what I want, she told herself. *I need Seagrass Maggie.* Her reflection disappeared and now she was feeling around in blackness. She felt like she was floating. When she felt Maggie near, she tried putting them together. She thought of it like combining hot and cold water. They met and moved together, harmonizing together to be in the same place.

Her face started hurting. Her eye burned and felt swollen.

Deirdre was inside Maggie's memories of what had happened to her at Dunn's manse on Black Horse Lane. She felt how scared Maggie was. She didn't know where she was at first and when she realized it, her mind broke a little.

Deirdre felt Maggie's body, feeling the cold anklet around her left ankle. Touching it, it burned her skin, and she whipped her fingers back in surprise. Instinctively, she understood why Doran would use this anklet on her.

Cold iron.

Deirdre woke herself up and Cuán was looking down at her. Maggie was very human, and she was more than a monster. While Deirdre could feel her anger, she also knew that Maggie loved Cuán more than anything in the world.

It's why Cuán was fighting to save her.

Deirdre sat up, twisting her body around to face him. "I couldn't feel where she was exactly, though I feel that she is still close. I think Madam Granya's brothel is still probably the best place to look for her. Also, I have never done this so consciously before. It surprised me in a lot of ways. I think—"

Cuán grabbed her hand and saw her strawberry red fingers. They were peeling.

"Are you hurt?"

Deirdre nodded. She would tell him later about her reflection in the dream world. Instead, she concentrated on the important parts. While she had hoped to get Cuán out of Dublin for his own safety, it now looked like getting him and Maggie out would be the best idea. They needed to go together. Once she got them out, she would leave Dunn for London as planned. She would once again have the life she wanted: the excitement, the adventure. Maybe far more sex.

"Aye, this happened because I touched iron."

"Iron? That doesn't make any—"

Deirdre nodded. "But it does, Cuán. If I am fae, cold iron weakens me. I touched it through my connection with Maggie, so it burnt me. It's more dangerous there. She's wearing it like police handcuffs around her ankle. An anklet, I think."

"So, if cold iron weakens the fae...?"

"Doran Dunn put it on her leg, so she has no connection with her fae-touched powers. The only thing that survives—and it's very weak, I may add—is my connection with her. So, I have an idea, though it may be just as dangerous. You will go to the brothel and see if you can find her. I'm going to go to the mansion and get the key. If I can get it to you, we can work together to get out of there together."

"What if we run into Doran?"

Deirdre opened her bag and pointed at the gun inside it. "You'll have this."

III.

Why couldn't Delma remember if she ate? She felt hungry. She felt full. She felt as though she couldn't put two and two together. She tried very hard, though, didn't she? She always did. Otherwise, her father would get out the stick and beat her ass until it bled.

Her first thought was of Doran Dunn. She was going in for a morning kiss, but he placed his hand on her face, and her mind reeled. Her eyes went dark.

Well, her brain, too, actually. It was *sooooooo* hard to think.

Why was she trying to think? Wasn't she coming down for some cock? Who needs to think when you want cock?

No, no Delma, damn it. There was something you were supposed to remember. Remember? Doran Dunn put it in your head, wanted you to think of it at the right time.

Was it the right time?

Yes, Doran said. *Yes, it is. It's time to go deep into that darkness and bring back that little thing I gave you.*

Delma wanted to prove herself to him. Think of what you could do with all his money? Yes, yes, all that money... Boats. Houses around the world. Jewels.

You're a scamp, Delma, and will always be nothing but trash, dying somewhere in some city gutter. Childhood bullies hating her. Pulling her hair. Calling her names. Spitting on her.

Finally! All the pretentious slags would be jealous of her!

Dig deeper, Delma. Go down into that darkness all the way. You don't have much farther to go. You're almost there. It will be worth it. I promise.

Delma dove deeper and she found that spot that was blacker than black. Delma assumed everyone had this dark, roiling spot inside themselves.

Naw, Delma, that's the secret that Doran Dunn gave you. This was his gift to you!

Delma reached for the black spot and it was the coldest thing she ever touched.

She screamed as it consumed her hand, her arm... it worked up her shoulder and her neck, crawling down and consuming her whole body.

Very, very strange, she thought. *This is horrible.* It was like being an infant. As if you were learning about where your body parts were supposed to be. The feel of your hands and feet. Your legs and arms. Your breasts, buttocks and stomach. All of these things, you feel where they are. You KNOW WHERE THEY ARE.

This is the thing that scared her. She didn't know why she felt these parts of her shift. They WERE MOVING in the inky darkness of her new body. Shifting. Changing.

Delma didn't know what was happening, but it was *very, very wrong*.

She screamed and screamed, wanting to escape it, but once Dunn's darkness had you, there was no place to go.

Doran lifted Delma up off his study floor and carried her up the long stairs and down the hall to an empty bedroom. She thrashed a little. Seized a little. He didn't let it deter him from getting to the room, throwing her on the bed, and walking out to lock the room behind her.

If he couldn't be there, Delma would be. While he didn't think before that she might be a good guard dog, it was as good a time as any to see what happened. At the moment, he didn't have a better idea.

Felim's stalky form was crossing him in the hall as he made his way back to his study.

"Felim. Room eight down the hall. Ignore the screaming, will you?"

Felim nodded. "Yes, Sir."

"Is my carriage ready?"

"It's coming around now, Sir."

"Good."

IV.

Outside St. Peter's Church, a patron had left a bike outside the fence. While Cuán felt a little off about taking it in front of a church (or at all, really), they had no other good choice. Deirdre was reticent about carriages. She sat on the handlebars and Cuán stood up as he pedaled them down the road. Deirdre gave him directions as they wound through the Dublin streets, eventually stopping outside the brothel.

While nobody approached them, Cuán could see and feel the glares from people who looked like they were measuring you up to see if you were worth mugging. The buildings were run down. People were in rags. Someone's cries echoed down the street. The stench was unbelievable. It was a bad part of town.

Deirdre hopped off the bike and grabbed the handlebars. Cuán hopped off himself, legs aching a bit, and looked up at the brothel.

"It's too early to call," Deirdre said. "You might want to find a pub nearby and wait it out. Maybe about seven go on in. They'll take you to a room full of women. You'll be able to pick one, though some may approach you to get your attention. See if Maggie is with them."

Cuán nodded, once again thankfulness swelling within him. He pulled out Maggie's watch to look at it before returning it to his pocket. Deirdre got on the bike, splitting the skirt of her dress so that it wouldn't tangle with the pedals on either side. He checked the gun that he had stuck in the back of his pants, shifted it to make sure that it wouldn't fall out.

"Be safe."

Deirdre gave him a smile and leaned over to kiss him on the cheek. "You too."

Deirdre pedaled off on the bike and Cuán surveyed the street again. He took one last look at the brothel and decided to look around for a spot to watch the building. Maybe he'd find a pub later, but he felt more comfortable actually having his eye on the place.

If there was ever a chance to see Maggie, he wanted to take it.

I'm here for you, Maggie.

Maggie looked out the window again. Her face was still sore, and her face was a little puffed up, but it felt much better than the day before. She didn't see Cuán, or anyone she knew. The streets were filling up with people.

Deirdre was out there somewhere, living Maggie's stolen life.

Myrna walked over and put a hand on her shoulder. Maggie resisted the urge to swipe her hand away.

"You're on the cleaning crew," Myrna said. "Let's get you a bucket and a sponge."

They walked down to a large utility room, which had scrubbing tubs, mops and other cleaning equipment. Myrna marched a few women there and got them mops or brooms, giving a bucket and a sponge to Maggie. Maggie filled the bucket with water and they were taken to a bedroom.

She found they all stank like man sweat and some of them urine.

"Pull the sheets and blankets," Myrna said. "Careful, you don't want to get your hand in any punter puddin'. Maggie, hit those floors. Make them nice and clean."

They worked half the day and they had sandwiches for lunch. Just a bologna and bread, but it was better than nothing. Maggie gulped down her glass of water and ignored it when the other women tried to talk to her.

All she thought about was Cuán and getting out of here. Was he still alive? Was he dead? She wouldn't forgive herself if he wasn't. But she knew for certain that if he was alive, he was going to find her. Cuán would never give up on her.

As she worked, she looked for opportunities to escape without being noticed. There were so many women, though, she realized that there was never going to be time to slip out without being seen.

This was going to be challenging.

After lunch, Myrna took Maggie to Madam Granya's office. The bigger woman had her sit down, and she took her old, rough fingers and spread Maggie's swollen eye. It hurt and Maggie groaned until Granya finally let go of her eyelids.

"It looks like two or three days. Then you'll be good enough for the customers," Granya said. "Then you'll be able to earn your keep around here, girl."

Maggie hated her. She wished the milky-eyed old sow would punch her. Without thinking, she spat in Granya's face.

"Maggie! Christ!" Myrna shouted.

Maggie winced, expecting another hard fist to the eye.

Nothing.

She waited and opened her eyes slowly. Granya was taking a handkerchief from Myrna, who was scolding her with her eyes. Once she wiped away the spit, Granya's milky eye flitted on Maggie. "That was stupid. You think I'm going to hit you, keep you from the punters a bit longer? You're mistaken. If I hit every girl in here for being a little sow, I'd make no money."

Granya gestured for Myrna to remove her, telling Myrna, "There is to be no bloody supper tonight and no breakfast in the morning. If she breaks the smallest of rules, she loses dinner for another entire day."

"Aye, Madam Granya," Myrna said, grabbing Maggie's arm and forcing her from Granya's office.

Myrna's fingers were so tight Maggie eventually cried out. "Let go!"

Myrna stuck a finger in Maggie's face. "You want to mess around? Have you ever heard of my brown snake, Mister *Pungere*? Trust me. You don't want to know. He hurts, and he doesn't leave any wounds for the punters to bitch about. Mark my words, you keep up this behavior and you'll find out what I mean!"

Myrna grabbed her arm again, dragged her angrily through the halls to another room to clean and pushed her.

The women who watched Maggie fall laughed at her.

Maggie shifted onto her buttocks and reached down to the anklet. She tried to twist and pull it, but it was too strong. She took one barefoot and tried to push it off her ankle, around her heel, but it was too tight. All she did was tear more skin and bruise her ankle further.

The women continued to laugh, thinking the whole thing funny. Eventually, all Maggie could do was shout, "Feck off, ye horrid tarts!"

This made them laugh even harder.

Horrid *slags*, all of them.

Deirdre threw the bike down near some trees on the other side of the gate and made her way by foot up to the mansion on Black Horse Lane. She saw that the carriage house was empty. This was good and bad. Dunn had left, but he was probably on his way to see Madam Granya.

She had to worry about Felim. The older man seemed like a simple butler, but that man was very loyal to Doran for reasons she didn't understand, and he was as nasty in his own way.

When she passed the fountain, she looked up at the water nymphs. For a moment, she remembered being water and wading through it in the form of a young woman. She thought, *I was once one of the Seven Sisters of the Seven Springs.* Deirdre didn't know why she thought that. Saying this aloud saddened her. The springs were all dead now. Gone, and it was all her fault.

Was the memory hers? Or one of those past heads she bounced in and out of through time?

Deirdre slapped herself, breaking her mind from her fragile and murky memories. She reminded herself that there were more important things to do right now.

Instead of going through the front entrance, she made her way around to the west side servant's door, which took her in through a pantry and kitchen. The help paid her no mind as they worked.

Her blood was pumping hard. Her chest ached a little. Deirdre grinned. It felt exceptional, a rush unlike anything else. Though it was a fight within herself, she knew she really wanted to be caught.

The feck you thinking? she thought.

But it was true.

On tiptoes and with the softest movements, she made her way up the stairs and down the hall to the room across from Dunn's study. Felim was nowhere to be seen, but the doors across from his study were still open.

When she took a step into the room, however, she felt something behind her. Deirdre turned and looked, seeing a shadow going into Dunn's room. Was it that Delma woman? Had she seen her?

Deirdre had to check, so she peaked into Doran's office and briefly saw an old woman grabbing a gold locket off a bookshelf, letting it drop onto the floor. Deirdre had never seen the old woman before—or she didn't think she had—and was stunned when the woman disappeared before her eyes. The locket was still on the floor, and trying to piece it all together, she walked over and reached for the locket, picking it up.

The gold-leaf locket casing was engraved on the outside with a spiral. Once she picked it up, she felt the old woman with her, and something whispered around her: *Cailleach!*

Was it some sort of talisman? A *déantán*? She remembered her third-class teacher, Mrs. Donoghue, who once mentioned fetish objects made to symbolize the power of a god or goddess.

Deirdre opened the locket. Instead of a hair or tooth, she found a piece of paper with a small ink sigil for winter written upon it. She didn't know why, but it comforted her. And she didn't know why she wanted it, but she hung it on her chatelaine.

She looked around the study again, not seeing anyone there. Unsure if the old woman had been there, Deirdre realized that if she didn't get moving, she would be caught. Looking out into the hallway, Deirdre saw that no one was there and tempted fate again, rushing across the hall into the room she'd intended to reach, to begin with.

Deirdre went in and closed them, hoping that this would make it harder for someone to catch her there.

This was the room where Dunn did some of his nasty business when he had to bring it home. Deirdre took a seat and closed her eyes, reaching out to Maggie. Again, she found it easy to slip off into the dreamlike Hollow. Feeling Maggie was another story. This other psychic space that Deirdre thought of as the Hollow was surreal. You didn't know up from down, or which way was which. You had to feel your way or know your way. So, when Maggie felt so far away, Deirdre knew that the Hollow wasn't going to let her see her without already knowing how.

Deirdre opened her eyes and looked at another chair. She was certain that in her last visitation, Maggie was sitting in that chair when they placed the anklet on her.

She moved to that chair and closed her eyes. Again, she slipped into the Hollow to reach out for Maggie. The girl felt equally as far, but it was much easier to see the memory of Maggie in the chair, Dunn on the floor putting the iron cuff around her left ankle. Deirdre pushed her mind deeper into that moment, trying to get into Maggie's memories and go back through them.

Doran Dunn was smoking a pipe in the chair Deirdre was just sitting in. He taps the pipe out and goes over to his bookshelf for a box. He opens the box in front of Maggie and shows her the anklet.

Deirdre felt excited and opened her eyes. Over on the shelf, as Maggie had remembered it, the box was still sitting there. She smiled, went to it, and opened it. Inside was a key with a wagon wheel-shaped bow. Deirdre touched the key. It didn't burn her, but it felt like ice to her. Instead of picking it up, she dumped the key into her small coin purse on her silver chatelaine, hung on the waist of her skirt.

This was easier than she thought. If she could escape the manor without Felim seeing her—or one of Dunn's other thugs—she should be back before Cuán walks into the brothel.

She went to the doors and slowly opened them again. She peeked either way down the hall, and seeing no one, she started to make her way to the stairs.

As she went, a grumbling moan came up behind her, raising the hairs on the back of her neck. Deirdre turned around, hearing another throaty moan coming from one of the rooms further down the hallway.

There was no way that sound was natural.

Get out, she told herself. *You don't want to see whatever IT is.*

There was another moan. Then a throaty voice. It sounded like slimy, viscous flesh sucking and slipping across more slimy material: *"Deirdre!"* A deep sigh. *"I can smell that it's you, Deirdre. Come on back here and see me."*

Deirdre shook her head.

"Deirdre. I need your help. It's Delma. Dunn locked me in here, and... I can't get out."

Deirdre knew she had heard something of the voice that was familiar. Delma. Why had her voice changed so much?

"Deirdre. Please. Mister Dunn has done something to me, and I need help. Please don't leave me. I'm so afraid!"

Deirdre went up to the door. She could hear Delma breathing harshly on the other side.

"You were always a bitch," Deirdre said. "Why should I trust you?"

Even in saying this, Deirdre tried the door. Delma was right. It was locked.

"If you get me out of here, Deirdre, I'll never be a bitch again. Please. From one frightened woman to another—Please save me."

Deirdre closed her eyes and mustered that urge she needed to pull up her power.

Strength filled her like a cool wind washing over her. Tightening her grip and turning that strength into a quick twist of the wrist, the wood splintered, and the mechanics of the knob fell apart. Deirdre opened the door wide and looked in.

Delma was naked on the floor. It looked like her back was twisted. Her bones looked as if they'd grown, pushing out against her taut skin. Blood vessels had broken all over her aching body.

Her body heaved and deflated as she breathed rhythmically.

"Dear God," Deirdre said.

Delma's body seemed to fold, and her face turned up. There were no eyes. No nose. Only a massive maw filled with sharp, shark-like teeth. It snapped and chomped, a black tongue rolling inside its cavernous mouth.

Deirdre knew it was too late for Delma and started backing up. She didn't expect it to use its flesh-like tendrils to grasp the doorframe, and to slingshot its twisted body through the air at her. The maw opened, and Deirdre thought it was going to bite her face as it came at her, but part of Deirdre's power slipped into movement, and she was able to shift to the floor, rolling backward once to her feet.

Crouching, she saw the Delma-thing reach for her with its tendrils, wrapping around her body. A panic set in and she tried to hold her breathing back.

She didn't know how she was going to escape this thing.

The maw opened again, its teeth latched onto her shoulder, and Deirdre screamed as the teeth drove agonizingly deep.

That's when Deirdre realized she had enough reach to grab its mouth with both her hands. Grabbing its skull and jaw, she started pulling them apart until she heard the jaw crack, and blood spurted forth from its mouth and ears.

Deirdre let go, thinking to escape it now, but to her surprise, it turned out to be a bad idea.

The tendrils whipped around her tighter, and its head bounced up. As it came springing back into her face, its long, pointed teeth grazed her cheek, scaring the hell out of her. She cried out, and once again struggled against the tendrils to get at the resiling face.

Her hands once again got a hold of the head, and she twisted it with all her might. The neck snapped and crackled while the tongue shot out, dripping thick bloody strands, and it wagged about a moment. The thing hissed, though it was going slack around her.

Deirdre didn't wait. She pulled herself free from Delma's twisted cadaver and started to make her way back around through the kitchen, savoring the rush within her.

Unfortunately, when she opened the kitchen door, Felim was coming out the same door at the same time. They both looked surprised, and Felim smiled.

"Oh, look. Deirdre. You know, Master Dunn was hoping you'd drop by."

Deirdre made to push by him, saying, "Naw, I don't have time—"

But she felt the hard muzzle of a gun push into the right side of her rib.

"Please stay. It would be much better if you make this easy on the both of us."

"Felim. You're a fucking bastard."

Felim grinned in her face, his yellowed, knotty teeth and vinegary breath making her nauseous. "Ah, really, Deirdre. I thought I heard you were getting comfortable with guns."

Cuán found a crowded pub later that afternoon and grabbed a pint. He drank it down, waited until the time was closer to seven. When he couldn't take it any longer, he adjusted the gun in his pants out of sight and made his way down the street toward the brothel. The walk was only a few minutes. A couple of men were coming out. He followed another one in.

He hoped Maggie was okay. Hoped some punter didn't force himself on her. (The idea sickened him and made him angry.) Cuán tried to focus and not worry about it, but it was always on the back of his mind.

The place was lit up and comfy looking, couches and pillows and velvet curtains. The place was dressed cheaply, but specifically to make one feel safe and excited. They were greeted by a middle-aged woman who called herself Myrna. Cuán found her familiar but didn't think too hard about it.

"Come on in, boys. It's a shilling for a quarter of an hour. Find a girl, and she'll escort you to a room. You have to pay upfront with me."

Myrna held her hand out to Cuán, and Cuán dug in his pants for the coins Deirdre had given him. He gave her three shillings (each for each quarter-hour), trying to buy enough time to find Maggie and somehow get them out of there. If need be, he had three last shillings to spend.

"Bugger all. Haven't emptied the balls awhile, aye?" Myrna grinned at him with her yellow teeth.

She didn't seem to recognize him. That was good.

Myrna gestured toward a larger parlor where there were several women standing or sitting around on the couches. There were women of every type. Brunettes, blondes, redheads, short, tall, skinny and obese. A veritable candy shop for needy men. Some of them asked him for his name or told him that they'd be happy to find them a room. Cuán barely noticed any of them as his eyes flitted from face to face to face.

Cuán had to pull his arm free from women actually trying to gather him out of the parlor to be sure that Maggie wasn't there.

She wasn't, and his heart sank.

This was going to be more difficult than he thought, though he could find solace that the brothel wasn't advertising her yet. After a while, he let a short little brunette drag him off.

"Forty-five, darlin'," Myrna called to the young lady hauling him away by the arm.

"Don't worry. I'm going to make sure you get every penny's worth, my boy," the brunette said.

Cuán looked her over. She wasn't unattractive. She had big brown eyes that made her seem pretty—if only her makeup wasn't so hurried and thick. It made her a little clownish.

"What's your name?" he asked.

"Róis," she said. "And yours?"

Cuán thought it might be dumb to say his real name, so he said, "Brian."

Róis took both his hands with a big smile on her face and pulled him into an empty room. "Well, Brian, come on in and take your pants off."

She closed the door as he looked around. It was a cheap room with a bed in it. It was obvious it had only one purpose.

Róis came up and ran her hand up between his legs, getting a good feel for his excitement. His body reacted, but Cuán felt awful about it. He grabbed her hand and removed it from his groin as she frowned at him. He held the hand and patted it, saying, "I'm sorry. Could we slow down a bit? Perhaps have a short craic?"

Róis's smile returned. "Yes. Sure. Sorry. You know we don't have to be in a hurry. Just, you know, once your time is up, it's up. 'Forty-five,' remember?"

"Okay." Cuán sat on the bed, looking around, trying to think about how he should do this.

Róis sat beside him.

"You like girls, don't you?"

"Aye. Very much."

Róis looked at his groin and bit her bottom lip. "I could suck on it while you think?"

Her hands went to his pants to undo them, but he grabbed them again, shaking his head. If he didn't get to the point, he realized she was going to jump him anyway.

"I have to admit something," he said. "I'm not here for... fer a ride or a jag or whatever."

Róis frowned again. She looked very disappointed. "Then... Why? Aren't I pretty?"

"You are. Oh God, aye, you are pretty," he said, not wanting to offend her at all.

"You're sort of a dream fuck," Róis said, chuckling. "It figures, right? You're my type and everything, my first punter of the evening, and you don't want a ride? It's ironically disappointing. Okay, that being said, I am done ranting. Go on. Why are you frustrating me this way?"

Cuán smiled and laughed a little.

"What's so funny?"

"Just, aye, I know what you mean. I'm sorry."

"It's not funny. You think I don't have a type?"

"Naw, I'm bloody sorry as hell. I am. Please accept my apology."

Róis's frown disappeared, and she sat up. She took another look at his groin and shook her head. "Stop apologizing. It's appalling. What is it?"

Cuán sighed. "Do you know anything about a redhead girl coming in here last night or sometime this morning? Goes by the name of Maggie."

Róis thought about it.

"I suppose there was a girl that fits that description. She got an awful brown shiner, so the Madam isn't putting her in the parlor until the face looks a bit better. I don't remember her name, though."

Good, Cuán thought. That's a good start.

"She would have been wearing this light beige dress. Brown shoes."

Róis shrugged her shoulders. "I didn't see her until this morning. All I've seen her in is the gowns the Madam throws you when you come in with very little to nothing. They're boring rags, really."

Cuán nodded. "She was taken from me, Róis. I would like to try to get her out of here. She belongs with me. Do you understand?"

He hated making it sound like Maggie could belong to anyone.

Róis licked her lips and looked at Cuán again. "I could maybe go fetch her. I could sneak her in, though I don't know how that would help. You would get the chance to see if it were her, though."

Cuán snapped both his fingers and clapped his hands together in excitement. "That is a brilliant idea."

Róis smiled. "I'll get her." She walked to the door and looked back with a silly grin on her face. She turned and softly grabbed his member again. "You sure you don't want anything before I go? She wouldn't have to know."

Cuán didn't have to grab her hand again. She removed it herself.

"Ah, that's alright. It was worth one last thought anyway," Róis said.

V.

Maggie's stomach ached and now she was regretting spitting in Madam Granya's face. She was trying to imagine Cuán spooning her from behind, holding her while she sobbed in her cot. He would be comforting her if he were here, and it hurt her more to know it.

She hoped with her whole heart that Cuán was okay, wherever he was. Alive. Dear God, please be *alive*... Maggie couldn't bear his death.

It was better to think of Cuán, even if it hurt. The alternative was Deirdre and that only made her angrier. By the gods, if only Maggie could get her hands on that woman, she would bite her throat until she won her head. It was the least the slag could do for what she'd done to her.

Maggie wondered where Deirdre was. Was she in her mansion? Was she sleeping with Doran Dunn? Could she be laughing at Maggie's failed attempt to capture her?

Maggie had tried to connect with the Hollow whenever she had time to close her eyes and relax, but the iron on her ankle kept her from connecting. She couldn't look for Deirdre, let alone torment the woman through her dreams.

She felt someone come into the room, but she didn't come out of her blanket, not even to look.

"You going to cry yourself out all night?"

It was Myrna.

Maggie hated her. Pretended to be friendly but was really a bloody hoor trying to manipulate her into giving into this horrid life. She decided she was going to ignore her.

"I mean, you can sit in here all night and cry and mewl and moan. You can do it every night all you want. It's going to change nothing. You hear me? Nothing. Soon you'll run out of tears, and you'll need to laugh and have a craic, and you'll find this place isn't so bad after all."

Feck off, Maggie thought. *I'm not listening to this.*

"Try to keep it down. Don't need to hear no punter complaining about the sad girl warbling terribly in the room over."

She heard Myrna move back toward the stairs. There was some mumbling. She half-heard Myrna ask someone why she wasn't with her customer. The girl replied that the customer wanted her to wear earrings, and that she had a pair under her pillow.

"Okay. Get them and get back. I don't want any customer complaining that his time wasn't of fair duration."

"Aye, ma'am."

A few moments later, she heard a *pssst*. "Maggie?" It was the same girl, whispering.

Maggie ignored her.

"Is it Maggie? I, uh, I have a gentleman. He's a customer, but he says he's not here for me. He says he's here for you, and he wants to take you with him."

Maggie's eyes widened and she sat up, shoving the blanket aside. The short brunette with big brown eyes. Thick makeup.

"You're lyin'?"

The girl shook her head. "No. He says his name is Brian."

Maggie stood up, excited. Could this be real? Brian was Cuán's da.

Code, she thought.

"If we go now, I think we can get you into the room without anyone seeing. Myrna went downstairs. Madam Granya is speaking with a gentleman in her office. The other girls are busy, or down in the parlor."

Maggie nodded. She wished she had shoes.

"Come on," the girl snapped. "We'll get caught if we stall. Let's go."

The girl escorted her down the stairs. They quickly moved down the main hall, and the girl opened a door to one of the rooms, Maggie wondering if this could be true. Was she getting out of here?

The girl followed Maggie into the room and shut the door behind them.

When Maggie saw Cuán and his big brown seal eyes she couldn't help but grin and throw her arms around him. They held each other tight, and their lips touched, and their tongues touched a little. She was so glad he was alive! Somehow, she doubted herself and it had always been on the back of her mind, knowing full well what Doran Dunn was capable of. She could feel how awful that man was.

She wanted nothing more than to hold Cuán tight. It was a strange, wonderful rush, holding him.

Maggie only pushed back from the kiss for a breath, and to say, "I knew yeh would come for me."

Cuán was examining her face. "Your face. I'm so sorry—"

Maggie shook her head and put a finger to his lips. "No, no. Do not blame yerself for this."

"It was yer mouth, wasn't it?" Cuán said.

The girl who brought them together was watching them, trying not to smile.

Maggie felt a little humiliated and swatted Cuán's arm. "Really? Ye joke now?"

Cuán's smile disappeared. "You're right. We have to get yeh out of here. Like now."

He went to the window and Maggie followed him. Just as with the room above, it was a straight shot onto the cobblestone road. If they jumped, they'd get hurt.

Cuán went to the brunette behind them. "A'right, Róis. Do we have another way out of here?"

"I'm afraid not."

Only it wasn't Róis who spoke.

Myrna was walking through the door into the room.

Cuán, shocked by the sudden entrance, stepped back and pulled a gun from the back of his pants. He pulled the gun's hammer in Myrna's face, making that distinct click, and she stepped back, holding up her hands: "Whoa boyo! Ye don't wan'na be messin' with that thing."

Róis screamed but covered her mouth.

Maggie, herself, was terribly surprised by Cuán's bravado and the heavy gun.

Maggie didn't know what to do. She watched all of this and realized that this could be very bad. She grabbed Myrna's hand, twisting it back, and forced her to the ground. With Myrna on her knees, crying out, Cuán kept the gun on her.

Róis closed the door. "Just so you know, I do not know why I'm helping you, but I'm really bloody *fucking* myself here, aye?"

Maggie realized that if they escaped and left Róis behind, Myrna would punish her severely.

"When I get a hold of you again Mister Pung—!"

"Myrna. Yer going to stay 'ere," Maggie said, and she punched her hard in the back of the head.

Myrna fell over sideways, unconscious. Her hair and skirts sprawled all over the floor. It was very satisfying, and Maggie let it swell within her for a moment as everyone looked at her.

"We make a break for the door," Cuán said as he hid the gun under his shirt, sticking it back into his pants.

As they rushed through the hall and down through the parlor, Maggie asked, "Where did yeh get the gun?"

"Deirdre gave it to me," Cuán said and smiled at Maggie.

Maggie grabbed Róis's hand and pulled her along with her.

The women in the halls and the parlor parted, not wanting to get hurt as Maggie and her company rushed through. A couple of goons—who were standing guard by the door—saw them and started to move in front of them, so Cuán was forced to bring the gun out again.

"Move aside, or I'll shoot," he said. Some of the women saw the gun and screamed. The goons retreated, letting them go out the door.

Trying to run, Maggie cried out. "Me feet! I've no shoes!"

She was trying to hold onto Róis's hand, but the pain in her feet made it difficult.

Cuán lifted her up in his arms, and she wrapped her arms around his neck.

They ran down the road, finding a dark alleyway and ducked into its shadows. Róis was right behind them.

Maggie, trying to catch her breath, patted Cuán on the leg as he sat her down.

"Now... what?"

Róis started crying. "What... the... *fuck*... ha-have... I... done?"

Women came pouring into Madam Granya's office and Doran stood up, surprised. They were talking over each other, but Doran caught "...had a gun..." "...Myrna got hit..." and "...they went down the street..." And he knew that he hadn't been fast enough. He didn't expect them to move so quickly or boldly.

How did they even know Maggie was here?

These people didn't know who they were messing with, which actually armed them with some balls and urgency that he didn't expect.

It was time he stopped underestimating them, or they were going to ruin everything. It was obvious they were familiar with the Hollow and were using it. There was no other way they could have found Maggie so quickly.

"I'm sorry," Madam Granya said as he started for the door.

Doran looked back at her, gazed at her one cloudy eye, and shrugged. "Send your men out. Try to find them. If not, well, you did your best, didn't you?"

"You don't surely blame me?"

When the woman was much younger, she was an outstanding beauty. As with many mortals, however, the years hadn't been kind. However, Granya always had a special place in his heart.

Doran blew her a kiss. "Never."

Once outside her office, he stomped his foot and kicked the wall, letting the fire in his head and chest explode out of him. Spontaneous combustion.

He was tired of letting them play their bloody games.

VI.

Felim kept pushing the end of his revolver into Deirdre's ribs, bruising them. She wanted to rip the gun out of his hand and smack him with it.

"You know, in the beginning of all of this, I thought Doran Dunn was on opium, or absolutely mad. He tells me about all this superstitious nonsense, and I grew up most of my life as a skeptic. Then I started seeing things. Shadows moving. Things happening around him without any logical explanation," he said, pointing at the room where Deirdre had found the key for Maggie's anklet.

Deirdre was scared, yes, but she was also determined. She knew that if she let them hurt Cuán, she'd never be able to forgive herself. *And I only have myself*, she thought. There had to be a way out of this. She wasn't going to give up so easily.

Her eyes skimmed over the room, looking for something to help her.

"And then there's this girl. Doran tells me to kidnap her. So, she's standing outside a shoe shop, her parents inside, and I snatch her and carry her away. Doran tells me that this girl is no ordinary girl. She lives multiple lives, reincarnating over centuries, and if we can stop her cycle, he can make himself into a god. I don't believe him, of course, even with the uncanny happening around him from time to time."

Inside the room, Felim gestured to the chair with his gun.

"But you still work for him," Deirdre said, taking a seat in the chair.

Felim nodded. "Aye, well, he did pay me very well, and he is a good source of income for me, yes?

"Anyway, yes, I kidnapped the girl. What was her name at the time? Keela! That's it. I swore I'd never forget that name. She was the first person I ever helped murder. It was shocking. All the blood. The dying light in her little blue eyes."

Deirdre remembered being in that girl's head: being yanked along with a sore arm, being tied down, and being thrown on the dirty floor of some abandoned house. There was a man wearing a robe... he had a dagger... and he plunged it into her chest.

"You helped him murder her," Deirdre said. "And you're proud of it?"

Felim rolled his eyes... and that's when she made her move. Deirdre rushed him, driving her shoulder into his gut. They toppled together to the floor, the gun going off and sliding away from both of them.

Furious, it was easy to find her strength, and she straddled him, grabbed his head, and started pounding it into the floor. Thud. *Thud.* THUD. When she checked his face, he looked as if he was knocked cold out. Trying to catch her breath, she got off of him and grabbed his gun, tossing it out the window.

I see inside you, Deirdre. I see waaaay back, and I see you, the tiny voice said in the back of her head. That eejit voice that came and went, saying eejit shite that she didn't understand. *You can be just as dark as any other. Maybe even darker.*

Not now, she thought. *Go away.*

Deirdre made her escape as fast as she could, leaving the manor for the bike she left beyond the fence. Riding it down the road, she thought back on what Felim was telling her. Though he was unable to finish his story, she knew where it was all heading. When Keela died, he somehow bound her with the old language. She didn't know how or why, or how it even related to her, but she was sure Dunn was planning to use her somehow.

Deirdre didn't want to be used by anyone.

"Calm down," Maggie said, trying to catch her breath. Róis's face was wet with tears and her makeup was running. It did her no good to freak out and Maggie was wholeheartedly behind helping the girl out any way they could. The poor thing saved them, even if she didn't know what she was getting herself into.

While Róis looked around the corner of the building, looking out for anyone following them, Cuán grabbed Maggie's shoulder. He looked serious. "There's something I have to tell you."

"Well, what is it?"

"Deirdre is helping us out."

Maggie was enraged by hearing that woman's name. "Why would she help us? That *siofra* bitch! Where is she?"

Cuán started shaking his head. "Maggie! Listen to me. She's not what you're expecting. She's not a bad person."

"Cuán. Shut yer mouth. Ye don't know anythin' about her! She took me life from me! She took me parents! She took everythin'!"

Cuán looked at her. "Maggie. Please."

Maggie grabbed Cuán's face with both her hands and saw that her skin was already turning bluer. It was time to tell him.

"I'm gon'na kill 'er, Cuán. I'm goin' to tear out 'er throat with me teeth and I'm going to win 'er head. And when I'm done with 'er, I'll give the Cailleach the siofra as her prize. It's what Deirdre deserves fer what she did to me."

Cuán grabbed her hands and pulled them off his face, looking at her with horror. "You would do that? I thought you were the girl I found on the beach. *Are* you the monster, Maggie? The one in the alleyway? The one who breaks someone's neck with no remorse?"

She *had* compassion. Guilt. Maggie didn't want to harm those two men. She had to. They would have hurt them if she'd given them the chance...

"Cuán—," she said...

"No. Maggie. Deirdre has a good heart."

"She's manipulatin' you! She isn't as she seems! I felt it when I went through 'er doorway in the Hollow. She's *not* right!"

Cuán shook his head again, looking disgusted at her. It hurt her and yet she didn't know what else to say.

"You say that, but I'll prove it to you, Maggie. Yeh need to trust me."

Maggie reached for him, and he pulled away.

"Don't touch me," he said.

Cuán started walking down the alleyway. Róis looked at her as she walked by, following Cuán. Maggie looked down at the iron around her bruised ankle.

Was he leaving her?

"Come on, Maggie. We have to get that thing off you."

Maggie followed him. They went a few roads over to a pub, which was filled with patrons. When Cuán opened the door, heavy smoke rolled out.

"She didn't trust you. Luckily, she didn't listen to me, and she asked for a public meeting," Cuán said. He gestured for Róis and Maggie to go in.

Was Deirdre inside? The thought hurt her more. She was enraged, but she feared Cuán's reaction more. How could he not understand her? Why couldn't he see that Deirdre was the monster?

God, she wanted to tear that woman's head off... This is what she was waiting for... for a long time.

Cuán suddenly grabbed her shoulder, whispering into her ear: "Don't hurt her. Do yeh understand? Don't mess this up. Be the Maggie I know you can be."

Maggie wanted to bite his hand. The urge swept through her, and she remembered the disgust Cuán had on his face a few moments before. The pang of it cramped heavily in her chest again.

The pub was small, but it was filled with forty or more men and women all crowded together around the bar, or around the tables along the long wall toward the back. There was only a single tender, and he was working diligently to fill drinks and collect his coins. A woman wearing a simple cream dress in one corner was singing an old Irish folksong, *Cockles and Mussels*:

She died of a fever
And no one could save her
And that was the end of sweet Molly Malone
But her ghost wheels her barrow
Through streets broad and narrow
Crying, 'Cockles and mussels, alive, alive, oh!'

At the back table, in a beautiful, lacy blue and white dress, Maggie's doppelgänger sat, her curly red hair tied back in a bow. The smoke of the pub was hazy around her. Maggie could see her whitish aura, her beautiful magnetism and understood right away why Cuán could be so smitten with her. If Maggie were an angel, this would be Deirdre.

Alive, alive, oh
Alive, alive, oh
Crying, 'Cockles and mussels, alive, alive, oh.'

"Any troubles?" Cuán said.

The other woman smiled up at Cuán and frowned when she looked at Maggie. Seeing the woman's face change twisted something in Maggie, making her want to grab her throat.

I want to bite your head off, she thought. How easy would it be to slip now into the Hollow and dive into her subconscious, putting her into a coma for the rest of her miserable life?

But Cuán was looking at Maggie. His face as solid as stone. She remembered that pang in her chest again—that hurt when she saw his face—and Maggie shrank.

Now what was she going to do? Her whole life, she wanted to get back at this woman. Make her return what she had taken. Hell, the woman didn't respect or care enough about the parents she took from her. She was a despicable beast.

Yet, Cuán was now watching her and expected her to conduct herself in a friendly manner with her. And Maggie was beginning to suspect he meant 'or else'.

As in, *Or* else... *it would change everything.*

Maggie couldn't bear it. She couldn't lose Cuán. Could she? Would she sacrifice Cuán for the need to punish Deirdre?

"Plenty of trouble, actually," Deirdre said, gesturing toward the other seats. "You three joining me?"

Maggie sat opposite her. Róis, who Deirdre largely ignored, sat on Maggie's right-hand side, and Cuán sat on her left. Deirdre's eyes never left Maggie's. Neither of them seemed to want to blink either.

"You're the monster in my dreams," Deirdre said, not expressing much more than thinning her lips.

Maggie bared her teeth. Cold washed over her.

How *dare* she?

Maggie nodded. "A monster, eh?"

"That ugly fucking face with the teeth..." Deirdre said. "Isn't that what the Fomorians made of you?"

Maggie stood up, her seat falling backward.

"How *dare* ye!"

Cuán grabbed her arm and she yanked it free, looking at him. She saw his glassy brown eyes and the tightness inside her released. She was hurting him, and she didn't like it at all.

Cuán moved to pick up her chair, so he could gesture for her to retake her seat.

Maggie sat down. The tug-a-war of anger and guilt was exhausting her, but she didn't want to back down to *this* woman. A deep part of her wanted to let Cuán make of it as he will, so long as she had Deirdre's head. The other part couldn't lose him. He was the only person in her whole life that truly understood who she was, even if now, he was startled by her raw hatred.

"Ye stole me life," Maggie said, biting her bottom lip painfully hard. "It's only fair, isn't it?"

"However the two of you feel about each other," Cuán said, "remember that we have someone in common that is looking for us right now."

True, Maggie thought. But wouldn't 'taking care' of Deirdre end all their problems? Deirdre dies. They go back to Kilkee, leaving Dunn to piss the rest of his life away?

No. That wasn't right. Maggie knew very well that Dunn would come looking for him. She never thought about it until now, but Dunn wanted Deirdre more than anything else for reasons unknown. If Maggie ended her doppelgänger's life, Dunn would go to the ends of the earth to find them and take his revenge. What Maggie already knew of him, he was both mad enough and capable enough to do it, too.

Deirdre sighed, looking at Maggie still.

"I know you want to kill me," Deirdre said. "I have experienced the nightmares myself. But I do not wish you harm. I don't wish Cuán or anybody else harm either. Whatever you make of me, I can only promise you that the only danger I see here for any of us, is Dunn and his thugs.

"I can only hope you believe me and that you can forgive me for anything you feel that I have done. I only want to live my own life, which is why I came here to the city."

With that, Deirdre leaned over Cuán and grabbed Maggie's bare foot, putting it on her lap between them. Maggie yanked it back, but Deirdre grabbed it again and gave her a stern look before running her soft hands over her bruised ankle around the iron anklet. The light touch stung a little, but the fingers felt good pressing into the meat of her foot.

"Trust me," she said.

Maggie stopped struggling, letting the woman have her foot. Surely, she wouldn't hurt her in front of Cuán, would she?

Deirdre dug into her cleavage and pulled out a familiar key. She stuck it into the anklet and twisted it, and the pawl clicked back, opening it. Deirdre placed it on the table between them, placing the key beside it.

Maggie took her foot back, laying it over her other knee, and rubbed the bruise on her ankle.

"You should get your strength back soon," Deirdre said. "I hope you know I'm trusting you 'ere."

Róis's eyes bounced to each of them and looked at Maggie.

"I'm a little confused about this conversation, but I dare say, we should be going. Madam Granya will be coming through here anytime. She's not stupid. If you guys have a better place to be, shouldn't we get there?"

Maggie looked at Cuán, who was watching her every move. He looked upset and she hated it. She reached over and grabbed Cuán's hand, expecting him almost to whip it away. He didn't.

Maggie looked at Deirdre again.

"A contract then. If yeh swear, *we're* in no danger... I swear, I won't harm yeh either."

When Maggie swallowed, it felt like the biggest lump ever. Saying that—letting this go—didn't feel right at all, but maybe she was giving too much into her own dark habits. Perhaps the Fomorians rubbed off on her more than she knew, making her this angry, hateful monster. And the last thing she ever wanted was to be like them.

For Cuán. For herself. She would never ever be like the fomori. It was time to prove it to Cuán. She was the woman he knew.

Maggie's thoughts changed as her mind bounced from Madam Granya...

Madam Granya will be coming through here anytime. She's not stupid.

...to Doran Dunn.

That's why I keep Deirdre close to me. She's the changeling— the one they replaced you with when they stole you away.

Doran Dunn wanted to stop them from reaching Deirdre, but he was consumed with his hatred for the Cailleach. Why? And why did Dunn tell her about the fae girl—Cherry Fox? What did that story have to do with Maggie or Deirdre? Was she once someone they knew?

Either way... Doran Dunn was an arrogant bastard and was the real enemy now. He'd be hunting them all down.

Panic filled her. This was getting worse.

"Aye. Róis's right. Whether it's Madam Granya or Doran Dunn, we have to go," Maggie said. She looked at Cuán. "We all go together."

Maggie grabbed Róis's hand and pulled her from the table.

V. The Great Kárpáti!

I.

Felim had cleaned up the mess that Deirdre had left of Delma, all the while nursing a gin and tonic for his head, and Doran stayed in his study, pacing as he tried to think of a way to catch Deirdre and kill those other, impossible children. He wouldn't have Felim do anything this time. The man wasn't young and stalwart enough for this type of job anymore.

Doran started thinking about replacing him. It was too bad Finnian was killed.

The whole point was to hold Deirdre close until he was ready to sacrifice her, so that her soul could be destroyed, and transformed for his own apotheosis. But he wasn't ready. Nowhere in history had he ever come across a case with a similar formula, so he was responsible for testing and thinking through the alchemical perplexities on his own. It was difficult, and her running away wasn't making it any easier on him.

It pissed him off.

Later that night, while lying in bed, something pulled Doran's mind into the psychic schism of the Hollow—he projected as an astral being in the realm that linked the minds of the whole universe together from the past, present and future. The Hollow was a realm of doorways, but the doorways were always hidden and could only be found by the cleverest of people. The coldness and the flickering, rolling caustic lights around him made him realize this was part of the Hollow nearest the Deep Dens. He was being summoned. It was a magical summons—his soul being called by the Fomorian King. His astral being obeyed with little fight.

Doran's astral projection floated to a cavern mouth, the entrance to the Deep Dens, and went into its darkness, somewhat afraid. The Fomorian King was known for stirring up minds into mad leanings, reigning over a frenzied army of creatures, and besting many of the other gods. This King wasn't any horrid thing that hid in the dark. It was the god of these dark things. Doran was sure he was one of the greatest dangers of the known world.

Doran was psychically directed to the back of the cavern. He could sense the Fomorians watching him, saw one or two, half in the shadows. Horrid, twisted things with rubbery skin, nodules, monstrous mouths filled with sharp teeth, and spiked fins all over their massive forms.

The fomori would have torn him limb from limb if he were present and not a psychic projection.

He first saw the massive crustaceous creature with octopoid arms and tentacles billowing out through the waters. Swimming closer to the logarithmic spirals at its heart, Doran could see Elieris' face and crown—both of which one couldn't tell where one ended and the other began.

While Doran was sure he wasn't seeing him in his fullest, he was sure that in that darkness, deeper into the caverns, Ri Elieris was more ominous and terrible. He was the den of monsters.

The one thing Doran knew was that gods always stood amongst the giants. And they frightened him more than anything. He tried working outside their vision, but he realized over the centuries that at least one of them still had their eyes locked on him.

Doran Dunn. You can be a god. It is within your grasp, Ri Elieris said, his voice booming inside his head.

Doran thought his brain was going to be torn apart by the voice ricocheting around in his skull—it felt so awful. He couldn't move until this sound tapered off, which took a moment or two.

Once he recovered, Doran looked into the face of the Fomorian king. "Why would you help me?"

She is slipping through your fingers. The Cailleach works now to return her to the Cycle. If you do not act now, then you will lose her.

Doran held his head, squeezing his eyes shut, trying to suffer through the agony.

He was sure the Cycle Elieris was speaking of was Deirdre's reincarnation cycle—the curse Doran was able to gap with his magic, merging Deirde's soul with the siofra. If Deirdre were to die, she would return to that Cycle and her true power.

When the voice stopped psychically echoing through his head, Doran looked up again, showing this monster that he was willing to suffer it. He was not afraid. (Though he truly was...)

"How?"

Suddenly Doran was no longer in the Deep Dens but floating over a village covered in fog. He had seen this before when he first felt the maighdean uaimh awaken and crawl to the surface. He had felt Ri Elieris' mind flow onto the land, raising the mists of the sea (the *féth fíada* or Devil's Breath, he was not sure, though they were nearly the same thing), calling the vampyric sisters of the brine forth.

Séala Bán was now a cursed village.

Then it hit him. Séala Bán was a small village on the bay north of Kilkee, where Deirdre and the others would want to return. Ri Elieris was putting them all into play from the very beginning. This monster knew that Doran would fail in Dublin, so he was setting a trap.

The Fomorian King was plenteous with *fata* essence, and like the gravity of things with much more mass, it pulled the threads of all their fates together, intersecting everything to his advantage.

"Still. Why would you help me?" he asked the Ri Elieris.

And he replied: *You are not the only one who wants to take Deirdre out of the Cycle completely.*

The voice was too much in his head. He woke in his office, screaming, his head feeling as if it were splitting open. Blood gushed from his ears, nose and mouth. He choked and coughed, dropping onto his knees.

It was all too much to take, and Doran Dunn passed out on the floor of his study.

The ebb and flow of the tides. The darkness of the caverns and the depths of the seas. In this darkness, half shadowed, was the weathered and wrinkled face of the Cailleach. Her elder skin seemed to drape her skeleton. Her flesh was thin enough that it was tearing where you could see the blood and bone beneath. With her insides all shriveled up and her arm impossibly long, she looked more like a monster than a human.

"The ebb and flow of the tides are greatest on the full moon nights," she said. *"Imbolc is closing in, and we must be ready."*

Seagrass Maggie woke up, noticing that Cuán's arm was around her. It was the first time in her life that she had woken this way, feeling Cuán so close, wrapped around her. She could feel that he was hard as he rested behind her, and his warm breath washed over her neck. It was exhilarating and it all but evaporated her nightmare.

She had her pocket watch back. Cuán had found it, giving it to her once they reached the apartment after their escape from Madam Granya's brothel.

Maggie rubbed her ankle with the toe of her other foot, glad to have the iron gone. Ever since Deirdre removed and tossed the anklet aside, she felt her strength returning little by little.

It had been two days since they had escaped. Deirdre went to the bank and withdrew most of her money before Dunn thought to freeze her accounts, and they got another apartment near the south end of Dublin with fabricated names. They planned to hold up here until they were able to get a train out of Dublin.

It was still the four of them. Róis slept beside Deirdre. It was the least they could do for her since she was now homeless. And though they weren't married, Maggie slept in the other bedroom with Cuán. They put a pillow between them, though they both still struggled with keeping their hands to themselves. And the pillow had a habit of being moved somewhere in the middle of the night.

One day she'll have the courage to nudge Cuán into something more, something she wanted so desperately. Married or not. Find the happy pleasure in each other, for themselves. Their relationship.

And despite the fact that she promised herself that she would kill the siofra to take back her life, the whole fantasy started to feel ruthless to her now. Here, Deirdre was close enough that Maggie could wrap her fingers around her neck or shoot her with the gun, but Maggie couldn't do it anymore. She could no more kill her than any other innocent person. Cuán was right. Deirdre didn't deserve her scorn or her malice.

Cuán had saved her, really. He was the only one who could get through to her, and it made Maggie feel ashamed of herself, but she tried not to think about it anymore. He seemed to be giving her a second chance after that scene at the pub, and she didn't want to ruin it. She wanted to forget it. Take the piss where she had to, but move on to the forgetting.

Maggie carefully rolled out from under Cuán's arm, and he responded with a sleepy sigh and rolled over the other way. She looked at him. The dashing brown hair, the nice jaw, and dimples. And when he opened his eyes, they were like a seal's, dark brown and gorgeous. *One day,* she thought, *I hope he gets over whatever he needs to and asks me to marry him.*

As usual, though, her thoughts turned to their biggest problem: getting out of Dublin. They had scouted out the train station, but Deirdre recognized some of Dunn's goons before they recognized them in return. While he didn't think to close Deirdre's accounts quickly enough, he did think about many of their escape options. They decided to lay low and yet Maggie knew that Dunn wouldn't give up. He wanted his prize back.

"Good morning," Cuán softly said behind her.

She turned, watching him stretch. He gave her those big seal eyes. She smiled back at him. "Good morning, Luv. Want some breakfast?"

Cuán grinned. "Aye, please."

"Then get up and get your butt to the shop. It would be wonderful if you brought back some tea and some rolls."

Cuán laughed. "You're such a princess."

"Come now. You know I have a worrisome mash on you, and food makes it all feel better."

Cuán sighed. "Me too. Or agreed. Whatever it is I'm supposed to say at this point."

They found Deirdre already up and sitting at the table, gazing out the window at Dublin. Róis was sitting next to her, drinking a glass of water.

"Cuán is going for some rolls," Maggie said.

Róis grinned. "Oh, that would be swell."

Deirdre didn't say anything. Maggie sat down.

"Actually, Róis, do you mind going with Cuán?"

Róis shrugged her small shoulders.

"Sure, Maggie."

A few minutes later, both dressed and were out the door. For the first time, Maggie and Deirdre were alone. Maggie now had the habit of putting one leg over another, so she could rub her ankle where the iron anklet had been. Maggie was overjoyed when they'd removed the damn thing. She was grateful for it still.

"Have I thanked you for the key and removing this damn thing?"

Deirdre only glanced at her and continued spacing off outside. "No worries about that. It's awful what he did to you. But don't think I trust you. I feel danger in you, Maggie. Something dark.

Something beastly. When I'm near you, I feel how hungry you really are."

Maggie was stunned. "You call me a beast—?" She stopped herself. She could show Deirdre the beast inside her, and yet, what would that do? The more she thought about it, Maggie knew what was inside of her, and could feel the same dangerous side of her lurking below the surface. No, she was not going to be mad at Deirdre for being right. Besides, Maggie did have a lot of pent-up anger about her losing her family to this *uncanny duality*, to being enslaved by the fomori and abused by them. Only it wasn't Deirdre that took it all away from her, as she had originally thought. It was Doran Dunn.

"Deirdre—"

"Don't worry, Maggie. Cuán told me everything and I think I can see it all. It makes sense, doesn't it?"

Maggie shrugged. She didn't know if it made sense—

"We grew up listening to fairy stories from Mrs. Donoghue. I remember the story about the siofra. I mean, it makes sense. Look at us? We're more doppelgängers than identical twins," Deirdre said, looking at Maggie finally. "I knew something was different about me. The strength. The confidence. The *knowing* that some places glimmered with different energies..."

Deirdre started playing with her red locks.

"Um, well... I thought maybe if we talked—"

"About what? Cuán told me enough. I'm not human. I'm something else pretending to be human."

"Could yeh please stop interrupting me? We don't know what a siofra is. We don't. And what if you are not human? Maybe you are some fae creature? Doesn't that mean that you are closer to the gods? That's not a bad thing, having their blood in yer veins."

Deirdre rolled her eyes. "I am in Ireland, and Ireland is in me. Praise Danu."

Maggie laughed a little. "I'm being serious. And aside, part of it is in me. At first, I felt as if I had been spoiled or ruined by this *altered being*. Luckily, I had Cuán, who showed me that it didn't matter and that I was still someone. You're still someone, too. Even if yeh don't feel it. You're not pretending. You're being who yeh are."

"You're being corny, Maggie."

Maggie smiled. "I know."

"So, what is this altered being?" Deirdre said.

Maggie leaned back, sighing. "The way Dunn described it, it sounds like it's what the fae call those that were born at least half-human but have fae blood."

"So, we join forces to bring down Doran Dunn then?"

"It's the only way, isn't it? Him or us?"

Deirdre returned her gaze to the window. To the city. "I think so."

Maggie thought to tell her about the Cailleach but didn't know if the right time was now. Deirdre looked as if she were somewhat at peace with herself. Maggie didn't want to ruin it. In any case, Maggie did wonder about who Deirdre really was, and what being a siofra meant. Her mind went over this a few times, and she had an idea.

"Have you ever heard of mesmerism?" Maggie said.

Deirdre shook her head. "Can't say that I have."

"I saw a bill at the brothel fer a hypnotist. The Great Kárpáti! He says that he can find things hidden deep in yer mind by putting yeh into this trance state. What if we went to him? Maybe there's something in yeh that we can learn about the siofra? Perhaps something we can use against Doran Dunn?"

"What do we have to lose?"

Maggie thought of one thing: her mind. What sorts of dangerous things may come up in the trance? What if it turned her, made her lose her humanity? Maggie shuddered to think.

Róis had placed the rolls into the basket they brought with them while Cuán paid for them. Once they had finished with the small shop, they began walking back. Cuán was watchful of the streets around them, making sure they wouldn't be followed.

"Brian—I, uh, I mean Cuán. I just wanted to say that Maggie is a wonderful person," Róis said.

Cuán smiled. "She is, isn't she?"

Róis nodded. "And I'm sorry for coming on so hard with you. It wasn't right, me grabbing you like that. It was disrespectful to her and especially to you."

"Apology accepted, Róis." He smiled at her, so she knew he meant it.

After a brief silence, Róis sighed, and said, "I should probably be moving on, eh? I mean, your friends will get tired of me sooner or later."

"You can stay with us as long as you need. The way you helped us, maybe yeh saved our lives, and we owe you the same amount of gratitude. You're protected if yeh stay with us."

"But I've no money."

Cuán shook his head. "We'll figure it out. Deirdre seems to have enough for now. Let's not worry about it, aye?"

"Okay."

"Okay."

Near the apartments, Cuán saw the elder landlord giving a few pennies to a homeless man. "The Lord be with you," he said.

"Thank you, Mister. The Lord shines on you, Sir," the homeless man replied with a crooked-toothed grin.

Surprising Cuán, Róis grabbed his hand and pulled him aside a building.

"What is it?"

"I saw Myrna. She's with a goon. I think they're actually looking street by street."

Cuán peeked around the corner and recognized the woman who walked in on them, who Maggie punched unconscious.

"Bloody hell," he said, looking back at Róis. "We'll stay here. Watch them. See where they go. As soon as we can get into the apartments, we grab our stuff and go."

"But where?"

Cuán shook his head. "I don't have a clue."

They watched Myrna and the goons get into a black and red basket phaeton with the hood up. Once they were out of sight, Cuán and Róis made their way to the apartments without turning around.

Deirdre and Maggie were still sitting at the table when they walked in. There was a silence between the two women. Cuán could tell both of the women had had a serious talk, and neither of them seemed dead, so that was a good sign. He was a little proud of Maggie right now.

Róis started passing out rolls, reminding him.

"We saw Myrna, and Madam Granya's goons," Cuán said. "We should probably move."

Deirdre pulled the curtains, the sun flaring in, and looked down at the roads. "Where did you see them?"

"They got on one of those expensive carriages and moved on. A phaeton. At least Myrna and the other two we saw," Róis said.

Deirdre looked at Maggie and said, "But where do we go? Dunn does have the manpower to check almost all of these apartments in a few weeks' time. People will talk. I'm sure it's just a matter of a few days, and he'll catch up with us."

"Well, I don't have my anklet anymore. They'll have a fight on their hands. That's fer sure."

Cuán rolled his eyes. "Maggie. We're not going to win just throwing our fists about."

"Why not?"

Deirdre and Róis laughed.

Róis threw her hands out, shaking them. "I'm sorry. You two fight like an old married couple."

Maggie gave her a once over. "Damnit, fine. Cuán. Fine."

An idea popped into Cuán's mind. "We stay."

"What?" It was everybody, looking at him gobsmacked.

"We pay off the landlord. Pay him double rent to keep his saucebox shut. We hold up, don't go anywhere unless it's vital."

Nobody said anything, and Cuán thought they might all think he's mad.

"What if the landlord takes the money and still blabs off?" Deirdre said.

"He won't," Cuán said. "He's a man of grace, as they say. Give me the cash. I'll handle it."

Deirdre looked at his outstretched hand and sighed. She took the money out of her bag, counted out enough, and placed it in Cuán's hand. "You better be right about this."

Cuán nodded. "Aye, I'm with you there."

Cuán left them in the apartment and went down to the landlord's door and rapped. The older, bonier man opened the door. His face always dropped as if it was always morose. Around his neck was a silver cross. Cuán had on more than one occasion seen him kiss it or cross himself. He saw the man fix a child's bike when the chain came off outside on the road the day before. Always the helping hand.

"Sir, may we have a talk?"

"Sure, boy. Come on in."

Cuán walked in, and the landlord shut the door behind him and gestured for him to have a seat. "How can I help you? It's not about a late payment, is it?"

Cuán shook his head. "No, Sir. Actually, I have to ask you a different favor, I'm ashamed to say." He put down the money in front of the landlord. "This is double the rent. We need yeh to not let anyone know we're here."

The landlord took a seat but sat up. "What do you mean? Not in trouble with the police, are we?"

Cuán crossed himself and said, "No, no police problems. Look, I'm hoping you're a man of grace, and that you're a servant of the Lord as I am."

"I do my best, son."

Cuán told him about rescuing Róis and Maggie from the brothels. He told them how they were stolen from their families. He left out the part about Dunn and the supernatural pieces that were already hard for Cuán to believe himself, but he told the landlord that the thugs were out searching for them, and they were dangerous men 'claiming to work for Mister Dunn.' Cuán told him that these were lies. They were using his name to scare people into outing them.

"...but rest assured, if they catch us, we will all be killed. Now we aren't asking much. Only that if others ask about us that you say that we aren't here. I know this to be a lie, but one made for the greater good. God willing."

The landlord listened and looked at the money.

"Now understand, I'm not offering the money as a bribe. Only as a tithe to the good I've seen you do, and should yeh want, your church," Cuán said.

"Those poor girls. Many men manipulate and abuse the woman's meek bodies for their perversions. The daughters of Eve," the landlord surmised.

"Aye. We have little money, and I am working on getting them out of Dublin very soon. We need a little more time, is all. Do you think this is too much a bother?"

The landlord slammed his fist down, showing his gnashing teeth. "Hell naw. You are safe here, my boy. They won't lay one finger on any of you, so long as I'm alive to do anything about it."

Cuán nodded. "Thank you, Sir. Thank you. Yeh don't know how appreciative we all are. May God shine upon you."

"And may he shine upon you, son."

Once Cuán stepped out, shutting the door quietly, he felt a bit bad lying to a man who could be putting himself into danger for them. It was selfish and wrong, but he had to think about his own right now. It was the only way they were going to make it.

II.

The next couple of days, none of them saw Dunn's men that they were aware of. They were taking every precaution. Someone was always watching for anything unusual. They didn't leave unless they had to. They stocked up on canned food and they hung blankets over the curtains to hide from prying eyes.

In the meantime, the landlord became more helpful when he learned of their plight. He had a brother who brought farm-fresh vegetables to town for the street markets. They hatched a plan where they'd go to the market, hide in the wagon, and get escorted out of town to the man's farm. They would be safe there while they figured out how to get onto a train for Galway, and Kilkee.

The day before the plan was to commence, Maggie sat with Cuán on their bed. "Deirdre and I are going out tonight. There's this mesmerist or hypnotist or whatever. His name is Ambrus Kárpáti. He's from London. He's only here for a couple of days, and since we won't have time tomorrow, we want to go see him tonight."

At first, Cuán wasn't listening as he was looking at her eye, the swelling all gone and the bruise now a yellowish color. Maggie asked him if he was listening, and Cuán laughed and said no.

A might frustrated with him, she repeated herself.

Cuán looked flabbergasted. "A show? Our lives are in danger and you two want to—"

Maggie shook her head. "No, no. We don't want to go see the show. We want to see him afterward and see if we can get a private session. See, Deirdre and I think that if we can put Deirdre into a trance, Kárpáti can unlock memories of who she really is as a siofra. I mean, yes, it could go wrong, but think of what she may learn of herself? The powers she might know? She could keep us safe and put the final stopper in Doran Dunn's plans."

It occurred to Maggie that they still didn't know why Deirdre was so important to Dunn, but if she had to guess at the moment, she thought it might be that he wanted her power, and still didn't know how to unlock it. In any case, escaping Dunn might be a top priority now, but if they didn't *handle* him, he'd ruin all their lives. This, she had no doubt.

Cuán sighed, and his shoulders dropped. "I don't like it, but if it's that important—"

"It is, Luv."

Maggie leaned and kissed Cuán on the lips. She kept it there for a long moment, not wanting to be away from him. Wanting, instead, to remember this connection they had forever. When she did finally pull back, Cuán brushed a curl away from her cheek and slid his soft fingers over her jaw.

"Have I told yeh that I love yeh?"

Maggie grinned and rolled her eyes. "Aye. Like six billion times!"

They laughed, and Cuán tickled her until she lost her balance and fell to the floor.

"That's what ye get messing with me," he said.

The neighbor below them pounded on the ceiling. There was some yelling. Cuán, with a big grin on his face still, put his finger in front of his lips and hushed her.

Later, Maggie and Deirdre left, wearing bonnets and shawls to cover themselves. They tried to time their arrival for the ending of Kárpáti's show. They waited at the back door for a long time and snow started to fall. It was rare to see snow in Ireland unless you lived in the hills or mountains. They huddled to keep warm, but eventually, the door opened, and the stage crew began coming out to make their way. Shortly after that, a blond man in his fifties came out, wearing a long, dark jacket over a tan suit and black shoes, walking with a cane though it was obvious he did not need one.

At first, the man bowed his head and moved to pass them, but Deirdre walked up behind him, saying, "Excuse me. Mister Kárpáti?"

The man turned and nodded. "Indeed. Have a good night, ladies."

Maggie noticed that the head of the man's cane was a silver skull.

"No, please," Maggie said, rushing to catch up behind him. "We have a request, but it does come with a monetary reward. We'll pay ye."

Ambrus Kárpáti turned to look at them and slowly smiled. "Twins, is it? Alright then. Spit it out."

Deirdre looked around. There were still crew coming out of the theater.

"If you don't mind, Sir, it's quite private. Would yeh mind if we went somewhere else?"

Ambrus nodded and Maggie gave him a large grin. "That's good. Come with us. We know a good spot."

Deirdre looked at Maggie. "We do?"

Maggie rolled her eyes at Deirdre and gave Ambrus a smile. "A good walk down the road will do, wouldn't it?"

Ambrus laughed a little. "Sure, ladies."

Maggie took his arm and led him down the road, Deirdre following. "Friends call me Seagrass Maggie. I'm from Kilkee. This is Deirdre. She's also from Kilkee, um... but they just call her Deirdre. In fact, I don't think she likes nicknames."

"Bloody hell, Maggie. Try to be straight with him. You're all tied in knots."

"I'm being straight. Anyway, here's the thing. We believe in the spirit world, too. They're everywhere, aren't they? Ghosts of people who haven't moved on and all. But some secrets are inside of us. Some magic is inside of us. Don't yeh think so?"

Ambrus Kárpáti nodded. "Actually, I'm familiar with the supernatural world. I mean, what I do on stage is counterfeit magic. Illusion. Performance. It is only for the shows. Privately, I do practice the arcane and occult."

Maggie nodded. "And in yer shows, you hypnotize people and make them act like chickens?"

"Well, yes. But with a longer session, theoretically, you could unlock past lives. There's an Eastern theory that when we all die, we all get recycled back into the world somehow. In a past life, for example—before you were born—you could have been a tree or a... a squirrel! And in this life, you are you. In the next, who knows? You could be a brand-new star in the sky."

Only gods became stars, Maggie thought.

This is what Maggie was hoping to hear. In the papers Maggie had read—that came all the way from Dublin—she loved the articles that spoke about spirit journeys and the subconscious worlds, how they open doorways to the past and future.

"If we paid yeh, would yeh mind putting my friend under and seeing if you can unlock her past lives?"

Maggie knew that Deirdre had no past life. At least, according to Mrs. Donoghue, the fae were immortal. They were here at the beginning of time and would be here long after mortals departed the earth. What Maggie hoped was that they unlocked what Deirdre could do before she was implanted as a siofra.

Her theory could be wrong, Mrs. Donoghue could be wrong, but that's what they needed to find out.

Deirdre came up beside Maggie and looked Ambrus Kárpáti in the eyes. She was playing with a golden locket that she had around her neck. "Please. I'm afraid that something might be haunting me from this other life. Something bad. I've had small visions about things I can barely make sense of. I'm afraid that if I don't know how to put the pieces together, I may end up mad."

"I'm sorry, ladies, but I don't know any of you. I don't do private shows. There's hardly enough money in it for me," Ambrus Kárpáti said.

Maggie wanted to hit him over the head and throw him over her shoulder, make him go whether he wanted to or not. Except, it wouldn't really get them anywhere.

Ambrus turned to go, but Maggie couldn't let him. She reached out and grabbed his hand.

"Please!"

What else could she do?

Ambrus pulled his hand away, sounding disgusted with her. "If *you* please!"

And Deirdre closed her eyes, slipping her golden locket into her blouse. Ambrus Kárpáti looked at her, and for a moment, the two looked into each other's eyes. Maggie looked at both of them, confused as to what was happening, but she felt its psychic vibrations in her skin and in her mind.

Deirdre was reaching out to his mind through the Hollow. She was letting him see they meant no harm and showed him the psychic walls that were blocking her memories. Maggie was conscious of *The Falls*—Deirdre's doorway—opening up.

Oddly enough, Maggie thought she felt some erotic suggestion in the vibrations, but she wasn't sure. When she looked at Deirdre, it was confirmed. Deirdre's face had softened, and her eyes glazed with playfulness and hunger.

Deirdre looked at Maggie, breaking the psychic reach. "What?"

Maggie must have been making a face, so she shrugged.

Ambrus touched his head and shook it.

"We really mean ye no harm, Mister Kárpáti," Maggie said. "We're desperate."

Ambrus Kárpáti nodded, shaking it off. "I may need some of what you Irish call the black stuff. Might help."

Maggie patted the man on the back. "Thank you, good sir! I happen to know a perfectly good pub nearby."

In a smoky pub down the road, Deirdre ordered them all a pint and Maggie showed Ambrus to a table. It didn't take Maggie long to realize that it was the same pub where Cuán had drawn a line in what he was going to accept from her when it came to how she treated Deirdre or anyone. It reminded her how ashamed she was of herself.

Putting all that aside, Maggie reminded herself to focus on what was at hand here. If Ambrus could help them unlock Deirdre's potential power, they would be able to face Doran Dunn and end this.

Maggie saw that Deirdre couldn't keep her eyes off the stage magician. The man didn't look like he noticed, but you never knew. Something about him made Maggie think he could be a sly one.

"How did you become a magician, Mister Kárpáti?" Deirdre said, taking a sip from her mug, eyes still glued on the man.

Ambrus didn't seem to mind the question, as forward as it was.

"Truthfully, I went to the university in Oxford to learn advanced engineering and science, but I was bored with it by the time I graduated with my doctorate. I have always been a bit of a showman, you understand. The engineering has helped me build my boxes, like the 'Decollation of John Baptist' illusion. I actually make some of the internal components out of bicycle parts."

"Decollation?" Deirdre said.

Ambrus nodded, running a finger across his throat. "Beheading."

Maggie grinned. She liked that.

"Truthfully, my uncle was into magic when I was a child. He raised me after my parents departed this world. Once he was gone, all I could do was put myself into my studies for a while, but you can't keep yourself from what you're truly meant to do for long, if you're to be happy," Ambrus said.

That had never occurred to Maggie before. She realized that some things people were just meant for, which made her think of Cuán and the sea. Both somehow called for her, but they couldn't be more incompatible.

"And what of the real magic, Mister Kárpáti? Do you know anything of that?" Maggie said.

Ambrus was looking into Deirdre's eyes before he found Maggie. He sighed and smiled.

"Magicians never give away all of their tricks," he said.

Maggie watched him finish his pint, realizing that she hardly touched hers.

Maggie took another big drink of her Guinness, her eyes falling on Deirdre. The woman had turned toward the door. She was watching for Dunn's men.

Yeah, they should be going.

After their drinks, they made their way back to the apartments. Deirdre introduced Róis and Cuán. Ambrus shook their hands. Maggie thought the man seemed friendly enough.

"What do we need?" Maggie said. "Anything special?"

Ambrus looked around, taking off his jacket. "This couch will work. I will need Deirdre to lay upon it. The rest of you may want to stay back and stay very quiet. Any sudden noise will ruin the trance."

Cuán took his coat, and Róis got Ambrus a chair, setting it next to the couch. Once Deirdre was lying down, Ambrus took the seat, pulling out a necklace with a silver pendant that looked like a teardrop.

Maggie stayed close so that Deirdre could see her. Her intention was to comfort her as much as she could. The rest did as Ambrus Kárpáti asked and stayed back: Cuán against the wall, arms crossed. Róis sat at a chair at the table, having turned to see from across the apartment.

"Now," Ambrus said, "this is a special pendant. It's silver. See how it gleams, Deirdre?"

"Aye."

"I will be swinging it back and forth very slowly. I want you to follow it with your eyes. Only your eyes. Do you understand?"

Maggie watched as Deirdre crossed her arms on her chest.

"Aye," Deirdre said.

Ambrus nodded and held the pendant over Deirdre's face. Maggie could feel herself getting tense, not knowing what to expect. Deirdre, though, she looked calm. Maybe that was a good thing?

Ambrus, however, seemed a learned man and expressed himself with a confidence Maggie liked.

He started letting the pendant swing back and forth. Deirdre's eyes started rolling back and forth, following it.

"Deirdre. I want you to listen to my voice."

Maggie realized that Ambrus did have a wonderfully soft voice, too. His tone was handsome and full, seemingly wiser than how he looked. She remembered the erotic tone of some of Deirdre's vibrations when she connected with Ambrus near the theater. She understood now why Deirdre liked him so much, despite the man being much older.

"I'm going to count backward from thirty. I want you to follow the pendant, okay?"

"Aye." Deirdre's voice had softened. It was little more than a whisper.

"Thirty…"

"Twenty-nine…"

"Twenty-eight…"

"Twenty-seven…"

Maggie looked at Ambrus as he watched Deirdre. He was slow and deliberate with each count.

"Twenty-one…"

"Twenty…"

"Nineteen…"

Maggie looked at Cuán and Róis, but they were all watching the pendant, watching Deirdre. The pendant flared silvery yellow as it caught the lantern light, swinging back and forth, back and forth, slipping and sliding through the air as if it were the air itself, slipping and sliding like a pulse within and through the ethereal.

"Four…"

"Three…"

"Two…"

"One."

Ambrus flipped the pendant up and caught it in his palm. Deirdre remained staring off into some other place.

"Deirdre?"

"Aye."

"You feel tired?"

"Aye."

"Go ahead and close your eyes."

Deirdre closed her eyes slowly.

"You seem to stand in a void. Are you standing in a void?"

"Aye. It's blackness, going on ferever."

"You're in the trance state now. If I snap my fingers, you will wake up from the trance. Do you understand?"

"Aye."

"While you're looking ahead, you see an oakwood door in front of you. It has a brass doorknob. This door takes you to when you were a baby. Go through the door and tell me what you see."

Deirdre is quiet for a moment. She suddenly begins to open her eyes, still staring off, but her eyes begin to shift.

"It's the cliffs of Kilkee. I'm being carried in someone's arms. It's lightly raining. They pass me to a young woman. I see her and her black eyes. Only… Only—she has long pointed ears, and her skin has a purple tinge, and it's sometimes shiny. She has tall, twirling horns. She takes me and she puts me in a basket. She smells of the Spring Squill."

Maggie looked at Cuán, who did finally look up at her. Was this strange woman the one who swapped her for Deirdre? Was this fae her abductor?

"Where are you now?" Ambrus asked.

"I'm in the basket. I can't see. I'm so tired. When I wake, I—I'm in a crib. I will never see that strange woman again. I'm excited, though."

"Why are you excited?"

Deirdre begins to smile. "I have hands and feet again. I'm kicking my feet in the air, laughing. This strange man comes to me, and he laughs and tickles my new feet. He gives me a raspberry on the tummy, and it tickles. I can't stop laughing. He's my new father."

"New father?" Ambrus looked at Maggie, perplexed. Then he asks, "What do you mean you have new feet and hands?"

Deirdre, still smiling, says, "Because I used to have hands and feet long before. I remember that. I used to walk and speak, but something happened. I remember a great agony and a period of blackness. When I woke up, I didn't have hands or feet."

There was a short silence again, and Ambrus started asking another question, only Deirdre interrupted him: "*Cuirim leis an gcruth seo thú! Cuirim leis an gcruth seo thú! Cuirim leis an gcruth SEO THÚ!*"

Ambrus leaned toward Maggie, whispering, "What is she saying?"

Maggie whispered back: "It's Irish Gaelic. She's saying something like 'I'm binding you to this form.'"

Ambrus nodded and looked at Deirdre. "Deirdre. Why are you saying that?"

"I'm not," Deirdre said. "It's what I hear in the blackness. Before I was put in the basket, I hear it in the back of my head sometimes. Sometimes I still do to this day."

Maggie forgot who was running the hypnotism. She had so many questions. "Deirdre. What is happening to you?"

"My name was Keela. I was reborn, but Doran and Felim found me. They took me to this abandoned house, and they killed me. They had the siofra and they bound me to the siofra. The next thing I know... I'm Deirdre. I'm now part of the siofra!"

Maggie whispered into Ambrus' ear, "Can we ask her about Doran Dunn?"

Ambrus gave her a nod and looked back at Deirdre.

"Okay, Deirdre. We want to know the first time you ever came across Doran Dunn, and what he means to you."

There was another long moment of silence. Ambrus was about to speak again, but Deirdre's eyes flashed wide. "I'm angry when

I see him. He's carrying a basket and I know in the basket is a siofra. It is meant to take the place of Nicholas and Elizabeth Netterville's firstborn. We're outside his castle and it's storming, and we're covered in fog. I can't let this happen. I move among the other fae that have come to the cliffs of Kilkee. Doran sees me and knows who I am. He stinks of the Cailleach. The siofra stinks of the Cailleach. Like chlorine.

"I move quickly. I move between the rocks of the shores and confront him. He begs me to let him go, but I know that if I do, I will let the Cailleach succeed in her task."

Ambrus looked at Maggie again, and he whispered, "I don't understand any of this. What does it mean?"

Maggie shook her head. "Ask her about the siofra."

But before he could, Deirdre was continuing her story: "So I stabbed him with my dagger."

Deirdre could no longer hear Ambrus Kárpáti. She could only see the standing stones where she looked for a way to the Hollow and watched as the men in armor surrounded her on their horses and started jabbing her with their javelins and spears, piercing vital organs.

She cried, unable to stop them. But she was *Sionnach Silín*—Cherry Fox. As she lay dying, and as they cut off her horns, she knew that this body was not the end. The Morrígan had cursed her as punishment for the lack of victory or death in battle.

So, her name was not originally Deirdre. Maggie and Cuán had been right after all. She was the Sionnach Silín. And in the blackness between, before she was born Deirdre, it was Doran's voice that bound her to the form of a siofra, taking her out of her reincarnation cycle in order to trap her.

Cuirim leis an gcruth seo thú!

Doran Dunn was trying to punish her in return for the dagger in his chest (like when she was Keela, yes?) and stealing away his destiny that was driven by the Cailleach herself.

Finally, the armed guard severed her head, and he snatched her by her curly red hair, holding her high into the air, crying out a victory in the name of Nicholas Netterville.

"The fae-bitch is dead!"

Reliving it made her forget herself as Deirdre. It was all too real.

Deirdre woke screaming, feeling most of the psychic walls of her past lives breaking away. She was remembering again. Remembering everything, even if most of it still felt disjointed and confusing to her.

III.

"Are you okay?" Maggie said.

They had all watched as Deirdre snapped out of the trance, screaming. Maggie, worried about Deirdre's condition, dropped to her knees and threw her arms around Deirdre. She didn't know why she did it. Instinct. Was she beginning to care for Deirdre?

Maggie let it go and hugged her close.

Ambrus sat back, watching them.

"What happened?" Maggie said, looking at Ambrus.

Ambrus shook his head. "I have never had anyone break themselves out of a trance like this before."

Deirdre's chest was heaving in panic. Maggie could feel her heart racing.

"It's okay," Maggie told her. "We're all 'ere. It's okay. You're safe."

Deirdre looked around and nodded and wrapped her arms around Maggie. After a moment, Maggie gave her some space.

Deirdre swung her legs around and put her feet on the floor, sighing.

"Doran Dunn is a sorcerer," Deirdre said. "God, it's getting so hard to keep things straight in my head. But Doran Dunn used to worship the old gods when Christianity had already swept over Ireland. For his, uh... piety, the Cailleach, a goddess queen of winter, tasked him to exchange a child and siofra. Only on the night of the Netterville child's birth, I... I was there because I could feel the Queen's presence rise up from the Otherworld, and I... I felt the Cailleach breached this contract. More happened. God, it's so foggy."

"Doran told me that he was killed by Cherry Fox," Maggie said, remembering the story he told her when she was tied down in one of his many rooms. "You're actually—You're Cherry Fox."

Deirdre nodded her head, adding: "I would never have been reborn as a siofra. He used his power to make me be reborn in this false form so that he could use me. I heard him chanting the binding spell in the old *Gàidhlig* between lives. About eight or nine years later, once I was born as Keela, he had me kidnapped from my family, and he murdered me, and when I was between reincarnations, binding me before I came to realize who I really was. I think he's after revenge for what I did to him while he was under the service of the Cailleach.

"Partly, anyway. He told his assistant Felim that he wanted me for apotheosis so that he could escape the Cailleach's curse."

"I don't understand," Maggie said. "I thought that the fae were immortal? Why are you cycling through lives?"

Deirdre looked at Maggie, tears running down her cheeks now. Once the psychic walls broke during Ambrus' mesmerism, most of her memories came flooding back. Flooding her head. While it seemed as though it was all there, it was a confusing mess as well. An avalanche of information, burying her in more experiences than she could almost handle. She grabbed her head, running her fingers through her thick red hair, grasping her skull hard. With her eyes closed, she started peeling the information away, looking for some sense to all of it.

It was as if her dreams were made into reality. Or what she thought were mere dreams, were actually true memories.

She remembered the Morrigan, coming to her as a young woman with black corvid wings on her back. The Morrigan reminded her of how she failed her sisters—the other six of the Seven Virgin Springs—and how the gods decided to punish her for it.

You have failed them all. You are the last and the Seven Springs have all but dried up. It will all be gone soon. The Tuatha Dé sent me to exact retribution for your defeat. You will make up for your failures in your life cycles a thousand-fold, Morrigan said. That is the sentence you will take up, and if you succeed, only then will you be summoned to the glory of Tír na nÓg.

"I once was. But Doran Dunn was not the only one who upset the gods. They made me a *Leagan*—cursed to walk in human skin. I'm only immortal in that I have a reincarnation cycle once I die."

Deirdre had a lot to sort through, but she could see her many past lives. Many of them were very foggy, but the longer she thought about them, the easier it was to see them. When she was cursed by the Morrigan, her soul was filled with an excitable spirit. A need for battle and danger. The rush it gave her was immense, and it became a part of her. It was her fate—her *cinniúint*—to tempt it.

That's why I crave being around Dunn, she thought. I need the danger.

The Morrigan gave her a harsh geas, ironically snatched from her life. She was once a sprite, a daemon of the Seven Virgin Springs—*Siúracha Seacht dTobar*. For her failure in saving her sisters and the springs, Morrigan's cruel joke was to curse her into a Cycle of Reincarnate Life *and* abstinence from one of the greatest pleasures that life offers. Sexual gratification.

It's why she craved sex. She was subconsciously living out her sexual fantasies that she had never before been able to experience. Deirdre had multiple lives and she had been afraid to lay with someone in every one of them. It was the one thing she had always desired most—to find a lover and give into herself.

She thought about that voice in the back of her head that spoke up to her from time to time. Deirdre had seen the voice floating around in her dreams and memories like a little ball of white light. She knew that whatever it was, it was stuck in her head, and it *was definitely* the faint voice that often spoke vaguely and sometimes didn't express itself well.

"Are you the siofra?"

For the first time, the faint voice answered her: *Yes.*

What did that mean?

"I thought I was the siofra?"

Yes. And... no, the voice said.

"How can this be?"

I am the unborn. You are the infiltrator. Put inside me like a black spot by Doran Dunn.

"What does that mean? Why didn't you tell me this before?"

Would you have heard me?

"What do you mean?"

The voice stopped answering her.

Deirdre sighed. This was impossible to understand. Frustrated, she relaxed into Maggie's arms.

"LEH-gon," Maggie enunciated. She had never heard this term before.

Ambrus Kárpáti stood up and started rubbing his hands together. "You guys must fill me in on what is happening here. I'm afraid my Irish lore is a bit rusty."

Nobody spoke. Maggie didn't know what to say. Could they trust him? He seemed to be trustworthy, but Maggie had a hard time trusting anyone thanks to the abuses she endured amongst the fomori.

Cuán sighed and stepped forward. "I know that this must all sound strange and... well, weird... but I want to thank yeh fer helping us out—"

Ambrus chuckled and shook his head. "No, no, no. You don't get to bring me here and just bloody push me away after revealing all of this. Listen. Despite my stage performance—of which I enjoy very much—I take the occult world very seriously. I belong to the Lodge of Hermetic Magick in London. My life's work is the occult world, and though I don't know much about Irish lore, I do have a well of arcane knowledge that may be very useful to you."

Cuán nodded. "We appreciate that, Sir, but you have to understand—this Dunn is a very dangerous man. He is not only a sorcerer—which is scary news unto itself—but he's the co-owner of MacKay & Dunn banks. He's a very powerful man in his own right. He's got goons sweeping the city for us, and if he catches us, he's going to kill us. I'm sorry, Mister, but yeh do not want to follow us anywhere."

Ambrus looked at Maggie and at Deirdre, who were only looking back at him. Maggie thought that the help would be useful, but in the end, Cuán was right. She didn't know what else to say.

"I'm not letting you get rid of me so easily. I have a show tomorrow. I would like to know where to find you afterward," Ambrus said. "If you don't allow me to help you, you'll find it a big mistake."

Cuán looked at Maggie, and Maggie reached out for his hand. He stepped closer, giving it to her, and she held it against her cheek, and gave it a kiss above the knuckles.

"I'll leave you to think about it. You know where to find me," Ambrus said. With that, he took his leave.

Early the next morning, Maggie laid beside Cuán in bed, laying on her back and stared at the ceiling. She reached out her mind into the Hollow. Like a ghost, she left the apartment and she walked down the near-empty and quiet streets of Dublin. That evening they were planning on meeting with the landlord's brother so that once he was broken down in the market, they could ride in his wagon out of town, so Maggie wanted to know if she could look in on Dunn to see if she could use any information to keep them safe.

She wanted to think about what Deirdre had said—that Deirdre was not a siofra in her many past lives, but something else. Maggie wondered if that meant she could no longer access who she was until her next cycle. Would she have power to access while she lived as Deirdre?

Maggie was frustrated by the whole thing. If only they had one more day to try to access her powers. Maybe it was a good idea that Ambrus Kárpáti came with them after all. Perhaps they'd get another chance to figure all of this out.

Another thought: once they escaped, none of them had any idea how they were going to get at Doran Dunn. They were escaping Dublin because of him. They couldn't go home. Dunn would have people in Kilkee watching for them.

Maggie found her hands shaking and took a deep breath, willing herself to calm down. She focused on her projection, going like a specter through wrought iron gates, but they stopped her. The iron vibrated back against her astral form, so she had to lift her projection into the air to cross over, before floating past the fountain of nymphs, and into Dunn's mansion.

She saw Felim coming out of his room early. He made his way to the servant's quarters, where they woke to get ready for the day. Felim spoke with them, none of them knowing she was there. Felim focused on the oldest woman in the kitchen, who looked comfortably plump.

Maggie was a little surprised. None of them shimmered like the doorways she was used to seeing. At least not in the mansion.

Doran Dunn was a sorcerer. He would protect himself and make sure that his staff were not open for her to manipulate or read in any way. It wasn't difficult to figure out.

Was all of this useless? She didn't know...

"Master Dunn will be gone for a few days," Felim was saying to the head chef. "We'll want his breakfast to be special this morning, so I'd make his favorites morning cakes."

"Aye, Felim. It'll be done," the woman said. "We'll get started right away."

Where was Dunn going? Why wouldn't he want to be in Dublin, personally looking for them? Maggie decided to follow Felim. The oily-haired man with the chops climbed the stairs from the main foyer onto the second hall, where he peeked into a study. Maggie went through the wall, looking around herself.

Dunn was not there.

Felim knew this, too, and he shut the door.

She passed through the wall back into the hallway and followed Felim to the end of it, where a large redwood door stood. Felim knocked. Though he didn't get an answer, he took out a key from his pocket and unlocked it anyway, peeking in.

Maggie went in. It was a large room with tables, chairs and several shelves with odd things on them. There was an ambix puffing out steam with a small burner under it, a cucurbit dripping blue fluid into a small jar, and retort passing steam from one jar to another. A red stone oven had a pipe that went out through the wall, ejecting its smoke outdoors.

Dunn had his white sleeves rolled up, wearing only a woolen vest as he worked around the tables.

This is where he must manufacture his magic, Maggie thought. She went to his desk and looked down at his open notebooks and papers. There were sketches of bottles and formulae. A description in hasty ink was written across the top of one page: the *homunculus alteration*.

Another open book was open to a chapter entitled *Apotheosis Through the Chemical Processes of Angels*.

Maggie didn't understand any of it and she wished Cuán was here to see this.

"They'll have breakfast ready on the hour," Felim said. "Are your bags ready?"

Doran looked at him, looking slightly annoyed at the interruption.

"Aye. They're next to my bedroom door."

"Thank you. I'll have them on the carriage, and you'll be gone as soon as breakfast is done," Felim said. Felim added a long sigh afterward.

Doran stopped messing with one of the jars for a moment and looked at Felim.

"What is it?"

"Are you... sure that calling the Fomorians is a good idea? I know you want to get Deirdre back, but... traveling to the western sea and summoning such... vile creatures, it seems very dangerous. Is she really worth you risking your life, Sir?"

Doran chuckled.

"What life do I have, Felim? *This?!* THIS?! I'm bored and the only way I can have the life I want is by introducing her essences to my formula! Something as grand as this should be dangerous, Felim!

"Besides, I can't wait to see the look on that Maris' face when she sees them coming for her. She'll know what a mistake it was to *fuck* with me."

Maggie was glad he couldn't see her now. She was in shock. *In horror.* If Dunn called the Fomorians, they'd come for all too happily. Her world would be over.

No—

Felim nodded. "I didn't mean to upset you. I'm trying—"

"To look out for me. Yes, Felim," Doran said, smiling, "I appreciate it. But I must do what I must do."

"The driver will have your train ticket. From Galway, I've wired to have a carriage ready for the rest of your trip to Séala Bán."

"Good. Leave me. I'll be in for breakfast in a moment."

Felim left them as Maggie walked to Doran's face and looked at him as he returned to his jars and chemicals and papers. It was too bad he locked his psychic doorway, otherwise, she would have gone into his head and sussed out as much information as she could, leaving only nightmares and madness in her wake.

"If you think you can harm my friends, I will show you pain," Maggie seethed.

Maggie returned to her body and woke herself up. Her hands wouldn't stop shaking as she went over and over it through her head: Dunn was going to call the fomori. He was going to *destroy* her. Her mind flashed memories of the swarms and swarms of monsters that swam around their titan King in the Deep Dens.

The Cailleach made her invisible to magic, but that didn't mean that Dunn couldn't lead them right to her door.

They had to stop Dunn at all costs. And they had to get out of London as quickly as possible. The landlord's brother couldn't take them to his farm for them to hide. Hiding was no longer an option, because, with Dunn's assistance, they'd find her where she went.

Maggie reached for the handkerchief of lemon drops on their nightstand and turned onto her side, facing Cuán and shook him awake. He noticed the fear in her eyes right away, and he got up quickly. "What is it?"

Maggie handed him his lemon drops, saying, "Have a roll in the kitchen and one of these. Your breath stinks, Luv." He popped it into his mouth, and she pressed her lips against his, pushing her tongue inside his warm mouth, tasting the sugary sour lemon.

She went into Deirdre's room. Maggie realized Róis was in the bed alone, curled up in a fetal position. She shook Róis awake.

"Where's Deirdre?"

Róis looked around. After she finished yawning and stretching out one arm, she said, "I don't know. She was right here when I fell asleep."

Maggie gave her a roll.

Great, she thought. *Bloody great.*

Cuán was behind her when Maggie turned around.

"You want to tell us what's going on? You look white as a ghost when they walk in on their widowed husband getting their bang on."

Maggie sighed in frustration. "It's no time to joke, Cuán. I projected myself through the Hollow... to Dunn."

"You... Wha-What?" Róis sat up. "What does that mean?"

"I can leave my body sometimes in an astral form. I learned it a long time ago while I was trapped in the Deep Dens. I haven't used it since the last time I used Deirdre's doorway to get into her mind. I thought I could do it with Dunn, but he was using magic to block out everyone's psychic doorways, including his own.

"But that's not as important as this. No, Dunn is leavin' Dublin. He's going to this village on the west coast, um... uh, Jaysus... Séala Bán!"

"What's he planning to do there?" Cuán was confused.

Maggie told them what she saw and heard: the lab, the chemicals, the arcane parchments, adding that Dunn himself was leaving for Séala Bán to call the Fomorians.

"If they find me," Maggie said in horror, "it will be worse than Hell. I don't know how we're goin' to do it, but we cannot leave with the farmer. We have to stop Dunn. We have to go to Séala Bán now. We have to stop him. God, we have to stop him, Cuán."

Cuán nodded. "The fastest way is by train. But how are we going to get to it?"

"I don't know, but assuming he gets there by tonight, he will have until the high tides come in the next morning. If he leaves a call on the tides for the Fomorians, they will take it upon the low tides of the evening after. That's if he makes it."

"But what if he uses the Hollow?"

"I don't think he himself knows how to use it," Maggie said. "Otherwise, he would have sensed me, or tried to stop me while I was there. He would know that we know what his plans are."

That's when Cuán noticed that Deirdre was missing.

"Where did she go?" Now he was in a panic.

IV.

Deirdre found the address Ambrus Kárpáti left for her and knocked on the door. After a moment, he answered, pants still on but shirtless. She glanced at his body, enjoying the muscular chest, the hard stomach. The hairs that seemed to lead her eyes to the rim of his pants, teasing a pathway to his manhood. For a man in his early fifties, he looked good.

"Maggie? Deirdre? I'm sorry... I'm yet unfamiliar..."

"Deirdre," she said. "I'm sorry. People usually can see the difference. I have a better taste in clothes."

Ambrus nodded, grinning, gesturing for her to come in.

Deirdre stepped in, saying, "I know you have a show tonight. I know you probably didn't get much sleep either."

Ambrus showed her to a chair, and he went to a pot, steaming on his stove.

"Tea?"

"Yes, please. One sugar."

Ambrus poured her a cup of tea, stirred in one cube of sugar, took it to her, and set it before her. She thanked him again and took a sip.

"How can I help you?" Ambrus said. "Would you like another hypnosis session?"

Deirdre nodded. "But first, I have to have something, and I was wondering if you would do the honors."

"What do you mean?"

"The fae have what is called a *geas*. Have you heard of this term?"

Ambrus nodded. "Yes. It's a sort of divine law or prohibition that you must follow, or there's a punishment for not doing so. As I said, I'm not overly familiar with Irish lore, but wasn't there a hero that could never eat dog meat, or deny food offered by a woman? A hag tricks him into eating dog meat and this leads to his death. It's a popular story."

"Yes." Deirdre was excited, nodding. "Exactly, Cú Chulainn." She sat up in her chair, took another sip of tea, and sat it on his table. "I, too, have a ban. Only in this siofra form, I don't think the ban applies. I'm stuck outside my Cycle until I die. I think when Dunn bound me to the siofra, he pulled me from the curse for a single life. I don't feel the pull of my geas."

Her divine self—the fae being inside her—Cherry Fox, was caught up in the Morrigan's curse. A Reincarnation Cycle. Doran Dunn had plucked her soul from the Cycle with his magic and bound her to the siofra. That little voice in the back of her head meant the siofra's own consciousness was still alive inside her as well. While she was in this body, they were one. While she could access her ancient past life memories, she could feel that she was now outside this Cycle, free from the curse until she died and was returned to it. Dunn had found a magical loophole and was using it to trap her.

Deirdre almost had to laugh. Free from the curse? Sure! Only to be trapped in Dunn's witchcraft, which weakened her, kept her from her true self, her true power. Though she wasn't completely certain—and she knew she was ready to die for it anyways; it excited her, deep inside herself: in her mind, her chest, and between her thighs—Deirdre hoped that she could be more than a servant warrior, to do something she wanted to do since her very First Life.

"That's good, isn't it?"

Deirdre sighed. She took a deep breath and closed her eyes for a moment. When she opened them, Ambrus was still there, looking at her. He was confused, but his beautiful blue eyes drew her in.

"I know we don't know each other. I also know that I may die before this is all over…"

Ambrus shook his head. "You shouldn't speak that way. It's so… defeatist."

"Aye, but at the same time… I want this chance that I may never have again in any of my Cycles," she said. "At least this once."

Ambrus still looked confused, so she decided to waste no more time. She stood up, having already made this easy for herself. She untied the loose straps on her dress and let it drop to the floor. She wore nothing underneath.

Ambrus sat up, gazing at her, looking shocked and yet pleased at the same time. He stood and walked to her, and she wrapped her arms around him, pulling him in. He was already hard, pushing it against her stomach as their mouths met and their tongues played hungrily. She grabbed his excited organ through his pants and rubbed it, feeling his balls as he pushed against her hand with his own sudden needs.

When they had his rigid member out, she sat on it, letting it plunge inside her. Deirdre held her breath. There was that feeling of vulnerability and the electric rush that heightened her senses, now blending with her hunger to fuck him. Was she going to die? Would she live? How could this feeling make her not give a fuck either way?

God, he felt so good inside her.

Deirdre waited. Scared. Thrilled. In heat.

Death must have forgotten her. Smiling in relief, she pressed her mouth against Ambrus', playing with his tongue in her sudden greed.

After a few wonderful minutes together, the two of them exploded together, her arms wrapped around his head, holding him against her bare, soft breasts.

She felt Ambrus Kárpáti's body relax under her. Still holding his organ inside her, she laid her chest against his, to feel them breathing together—to feel both of them glow and come down from the highest of highs together.

Inwardly, she still waited for death. To see if she was truly outside her cursed Cycle. But it never came, and it let her relax into this moment with Ambrus.

They cleaned themselves up and held each other for the longest time. It was incredible being in the comfort of his arms.

Wanting to know more about him, she asked in a whisper, "How does one become a sorcerer? How do you seem so aware of the supernatural world? Surely you have a reason to believe in all of this besides me."

There was a long, silent moment.

"I know you don't know me—" Deirdre began to apologize, but Ambrus kissed her lips, quieting her.

When he pulled back, he looked into her eyes.

"My uncle belonged to the Lodge of Hermetic Magick in London. He left me this tome of magic called the *Archidoxis Magica*, which was my ticket in. Well... he led me to it after he was dead. I was maybe seventeen. There was blood on the walls. I followed them up to the attic and he was waiting there for me. I could see through him. He was cold. He gestured to this chest that had some of his effects: tobacco, reading spectacles, and the *Archidoxis Magica*. I never saw him again, but I knew that he was guiding me toward this life. It was a little while before I embraced it," Ambrus said.

"He was a ghost?"

"Yes. Since then, I have seen a manner of things that a normal person finds allusive. Unseen things. Many of them have been nightmarish and terrible. They have taken things from me."

"Like what things?"

Ambrus shrugged, and then his face changed, becoming melancholy.

"Like Annabelle.

"I'm sorry. We're here to entertain ourselves. Find a little happiness in all this pain," he said.

"To learn about one another, if I'm honest," Deirdre said, taking his face gently in one hand. "Tell me about her. What happened?"

There was another silence between them, but Ambrus was prompt with it this time: "She was probably my first love. My first lover. She was only partly human, though, and she was hunted by this creature called a vampyre. He was a Captain of this sea-going vessel called the *Madeline Leigh*. Somehow, she could leave trace copies of herself behind, and the Captain had killed many of them, trying to get to her.

"Imagine that, will you? A woman who could make a physical copy out of her own flesh and then move on, leaving some of her essence and personality in it to fool anyone who tried to track her down. I'm not sure what the vampyre wanted of her, but he was relentless. And while one of my companions—a woman named Miss Underhill—was able to drive him away, we always feared that the creature would return for her. Eventually… Annabelle feared my death over hers and moved on to protect me. That's what her letter said anyway."

"And you won't stop looking for her, will you?"

Ambrus sighed and shook his head. "Never."

"So, is the Lodge in London? Is that where you live?"

Ambrus nodded. "I work at the Gog-Magog Theatre in London most of the time. I came here to see if some rumors were true—if Annabelle was indeed here. My employer doesn't know this. But it was the only way I could find money to get here in time."

"And—?"

Ambrus shook his head.

"A dead end, eh? I'm sorry, Ambrus. But I am glad we are here together, right now."

Eventually, Ambrus dared the subject: "So… I have never heard of a geas prohibiting… coitus. Sounds bloody horrible."

Deirdre kissed his chest and his neck. "It is. Way back in the beginning, though I've forgotten most of that time, I do remember one thing: we were creatures of the Seven Virgin Springs."

"I have never heard of it," Ambrus said.

Deirdre almost wanted to cry. "When my sisters were murdered, each spring dried up. It doesn't exist anymore. Not for centuries. When I was the last sister left, the battlecrow goddess, Morrígan, punished me, and part of it was the geas that I would remain a virgin forever. If I broke my geas, I would die again."

Ambrus sighed. "Well, you're not dead, so I'm assuming that you're right. In this siofra form, you're out of your Cycle and free from your curse for the time being. But I don't think that means that your power is gone."

"What do you mean?"

"Well, out of Cycle means that you are free from the curse by also trapping you as a siofra. I mean, you were not technically reborn on the Cycle. That will happen once your soul is released from the siofra. You're still you...in a different form. Your power is still inside you somewhere. You can tap into your own true essence."

"So, I could learn to use my power again?"

Ambrus shrugged. "I really don't see why not. The only problem is, while Dunn bound you to this form, he did obfuscate the memories to make this a very difficult task."

"But it can be overcome?"

"It can be overcome. It may not be overnight, however."

Ambrus checked his pocket watch and looked her in the eyes. "Let me go with you. Let me help you, Deirdre."

"Call me Sionnach Silín—Cherry Fox."

"Cherry Fox."

He kissed her deeply, and she felt herself tingling for more of him again.

"I suppose you could be very handy," she said and reached for his swollen organ again, finding that he was ready for her.

V.

Cuán and Róis had them packed in no time, though they didn't have much to take. Róis made sure they had a basket of food that would hold them for a couple of days. The one thing Cuán was concerned about—besides Deirdre having left them—was that if Myrna was in the neighborhood, the goons could be there any moment, or were already watching the apartment.

Maggie was on the roof. Once they learned that there was roof access, she decided to keep watch while they got ready. Cuán let her know when they were ready, and they moved.

Maggie seemed worried as she looked down the street.

"Where do you think Deirdre is?"

Cuán shrugged. "I'm not sure, Maggie. I don't think she would ditch us or face Dunn alone. She's not stupid, but we don't know everything she saw when she was in that trance, do we?"

Maggie snapped her fingers, her pretty blue eyes widening. "Maybe she felt like she needed more. What if she went to where Ambrus Kárpáti is staying while his show is in town? She might be having him hypnotize her again. If I were her, I'd keep pushing to learn more. I mean, it feels right to me."

Cuán shrugged again. "Well, aye, I suppose that makes sense. Should we try fer the train station, or should we go find Kárpáti?"

Róis spoke up. "I vote to get out of Dublin myself."

Maggie gave her a severe look. "We're not leaving Deirdre."

"Then that decides it," Cuán said. "Let's go. Keep yer bonnets on."

Maggie had enough coin to get them a coach, which was good. It was harder for others to see who was inside. As long as they weren't randomly stopped by Dunn's goons, they should have no problem getting to Ambrus Kárpáti.

Cuán sat on the same side as Maggie and he grabbed her thigh to let her know that he was there, and that he wanted to comfort her. She put a hand on his. Róis saw the hands, but looked away, giving her attention to their surroundings as they moved along.

"Don't worry. We may not have a plan yet, but all is not lost. We may stop Dunn yet. I highly doubt getting a message to the Fomorians is as easy as sending a telegram," Cuán said.

Maggie gave him a small smile. The first he'd seen today. She frowned again.

"But if they find me, Cuán, I won't be able to stop them. They can do whatever they want to me, but I don't want them to get to you, Róis or Deirdre. It's not fair. I couldn't live with myself. And I wouldn't be able to stop them. Hell, even if Deirdre did access her powers, the Fomorians are large, hideous monsters, and they come in swarms. There are so many."

Cuán wished she would stop thinking she was alone. It was one of the reasons why he wondered if she would stay with him forever. She sometimes spoke like her life was its own and it always would be.

Cuán wanted their lives to be one. Both of them, always together.

Cuán squeezed her thigh. "Don't give up hope yet."

Was he being a romantic fool?

They knocked on the door and Ambrus answered, letting them in. Deirdre was at the table eating a sandwich with some tea, making Cuán breathe easier.

"Deirdre. You're lucky we figured out where yeh were," Cuán said. "Maggie learned some terrible news."

Deirdre put her sandwich down. "What news? How?"

Maggie pushed in front of Cuán. "Through the Hollow. I was trying to see if I could find his subconscious. Learn some of his secrets. Deirdre, I found out that Dunn is on his way to the western shore to call the Fomorians. Dunn is going to lead them straight to me."

Deirdre stood up. "Then we have to get out of Dublin as soon as we can." She walked over to Ambrus, who was putting on his jacket. "If we can get a train for early tomorrow morning, will you be there?"

Ambrus nodded. "You won't be able to stop me."

Cuán thought he felt an intimacy between the way they looked at each other.

"So, we are letting him come with us?" Cuán said.

Deirdre nodded. "If anyone can help me unlock my true self through this siofra form, it's him."

Cuán couldn't believe Deirdre would be this selfish. It was a fleeting thought, though, as his mind reeled on the real problem at hand now: how were they going to get out of Dublin? And swiftly?

Maggie sighed, obviously thinking along the same lines. "Dunn has men at the train station. How are we supposed to get by them? Come on. We've got to figure this out."

"Maggie. If what you say is true, we don't have time to mess about," Deirdre said.

Róis went to Deirdre's plate. "Mind if I have the rest of your sandwich?"

Ambrus thought quickly and told them an idea that he had. They all listened until he was done. Not everyone was in agreement on whether it would work. Róis thought it sounded very uncomfortable, which Cuán thought Deirdre would have said, if she had the chance.

Once a plan was made, Ambrus and Cuán left together.

VI.

Myrna sat down in the chair in the study and crossed her legs, placing her hat in the chair beside her. She didn't want to be here, dealing with Dunn, but he had her money. She'd rather be out looking for her lover—Finnian—who has been ditching her for the last few weeks. Myrna was worried about him, and this soured her mood more than she wanted to admit.

The greasy butler with the chops attempted to take her hat from the chair, but she shook her index finger at him.

"Naw. This stays with me."

She looked at Doran Dunn sitting behind his desk, as the butler held up his hands in defeat and stepped behind her. On Dunn's desk was a bag of money.

"This mine?"

Dunn grinned. "Of course."

Myrna matched his grin. "Good. I love a man who keeps his promises."

Dunn stood up and placed both hands on his desk, leaning over it toward her. "This is only half of it, though."

"That's not what we agreed on."

"I need a face she already knows. She trusts you more than anyone else right now."

"I don't think so. Barely measurable, if any," Myrna said.

"This money here," Dunn said, holding his hand over the bag, "is what I said I'd pay, but it's half of what you can make. I've decided that if you go all the way, you're worth spending double."

Myrna laughed. "Suddenly I'm worth something."

Dunn nodded. "For the time being."

This man was a riot.

"Well then, Mister Dunn. What may I do for you?"

Dunn shrugged, came around his desk and sat back onto it. "I have this side project. You won't understand all of it, but the gist is this: the alchemists reported coming up with a manner in which sentience can be resembled through magical energies in objects. Their results were called *homunculi*. I have been working with these formulas, modifying them so that I can use the same approach to human beings. I call it the *homunculus alteration*."

"You're right. I follow none of this," Myrna said.

"Well, you see, I find that human beings are very fragile. For example, I could reach over and break your neck right now. All I have to do is take your head with both hands and twist it around until the spine, at its weakest point, snaps. By introducing this formula into your system, effectively reforming your body to work as a homunculus object, you surpass this weakness."

Myrna imagined this all too well, and it made her upset that this man would threaten her like this. But she held her tongue. He still had her money.

"I tried it first on this woman named Delma, but there were mistakes in the *homunculus alteration*. Her body became like putty, and I discovered that she was easily broken. I went back to work, and I think I found out what I did wrong. (It's in the magnetism process, but that's all the science bits that go way beyond you. Trust me.) Anyway, I fixed the formula with this."

Dunn held up a vial of blue, transparent liquid. It had a silver screw-on cap.

Myrna didn't like this at all.

"Why would you think I'd be some lab rat for your experimentation?"

Dunn's eyes darted from the vial to her.

"I promise you; it won't kill you. You'll still be able to enjoy all the money here. It will, frankly, change your life for the better."

Myrna shook her head. "Look. I like money, but the amount we agreed on is enough."

Dunn nodded. "Oh, damn, I was hoping greed would win the day. Felim!"

Myrna jumped when he shouted. Before she could turn to see what was happening, the stalky butler was reaching around her chair, grabbing her forehead to hold her head back along with her jaw, squeezing fingers between her cheeks that she couldn't bite down.

Her eyes locked on Doran Dunn as he unscrewed the cap on the vial, kneeling before her on one leg, and put it to her lips. The potion smelled like black licorice and cleaner. It tasted no better. She tried to spit it out, but the butler was quick. He popped a hand over her mouth, pulled the chair back, and grabbed her neck so that she involuntarily swallowed it.

Like vodka, it started burning the pit of her stomach.

The butler held her down and she screamed into his hand. Dunn leaned in closer, his lips moving close to her ear, and he began whispering.

At first, all she could hear was the rapid thumping of her heart and the whispering. Somewhere along the way, she couldn't see, saw only darkness, and smelled Dunn's cologne. He was telling her not to be afraid, to embrace what he puts into her, and he added another secret. The secret, she was sure, was a little black spot that he could use to change her at his whim.

When she opened her eyes, Dunn was once again behind his desk. The butler was no longer with them.

How long had she been out?

She was merely laying back in the chair, her head hanging so that her neck had stiffened.

Myrna rubbed her neck as she sat up. A part of her wanted to rush the bastard and kill him for what he'd done to her, but she knew this would be a dangerous choice. It was very difficult for her, yet she withheld her anger.

"You better give me the other half of the money," she said.

Dunn looked up at her and pushed the money bag toward her.

"Felim is downstairs. He has my notes on what you are to do. If you follow it carefully, you shouldn't have any problems. Of course, if Plan A doesn't work, we always have Séala Bán," Dunn said. And his eyes returned to his work as he grabbed a pen and started writing. Before she turned, he added: "And if you ever need what I have put in you, I want you to sing 'Mary Had a Little Lamb.'"

Myrna still wanted to punch him.

"I forgot to tell you one more thing. Something that might help motivate you a little more. Finnian is dead. They killed him. Shot him in cold blood."

Myrna ground her teeth, feeling anger rise in her like pressurized gas ready to combust. Finnian was dead? Oh, she hated when people thought they got the best of her. How smug were they that they could fool Madam Granya and kill her lover and get away with it? She wanted to break their necks. All of them.

She grabbed the money and walked out, turning her mind to Maggie and Róis. She grinned. Myrna was going to teach them about Mister Pungere. And when she was done with that, she was going to cut their throats.

There. All settled then.

That night two of Dunn's goons—Anraí and Tavish—knocked on Myrna's door. She kissed her husband, telling him that she had a late knitting party with her friends, and left with them in a carriage. He would get worried when she didn't come home, but she decided that she was ready to move on anyway. Her husband didn't know about her money, and he was completely useless to her now. Bastard couldn't even keep it up anymore.

As Dunn mentioned in his notes, Tavish had been following Maggie and the others around for the last couple of days. Myrna knew him because he worked for Madam Granya. He was, in fact, one of the guards at the door when Maggie's boyfriend put a gun in his face.

Now she was in charge. And now, she was enraged. Finnian's death was going to be avenged. Maggie, Róis and the others... every one of them. *Dead. Fuck*-all *dead.*

Tavish showed her his gun, a Colt Walker Revolver. "I bought this yesterday. I figured if they had one, we should too. It's a point forty-four ball. Should do the trick."

Myrna nodded. "Appropriate. When we get to the show, I want you to find all the exits and keep yourself down. We want this to be a surprise."

"What if they recognize you?" Tavish said.

"Fair question. They won't. At least, not until it's too late."

"What I don't understand," Anraí chimed in, "is why are they going to this show? Why aren't they trying to get on the train?"

"They know Mister Dunn has men waiting for them there. They have another means of escape. It doesn't matter, however. We're going to try to catch them before they implement it," Myrna said.

While the carriage rolled on, she opened her bag to see the large, mushroom-shaped piece of wood.

Your time is coming, Mister Pungere, she thought.

The show was filling up. Lights were beamed at every wall. The whole theater was filled with people, chatting away about their day, gossiping or bantering away, laughing. Larger bills were posted on the doors and walls: THE GREAT KÁRPÁTI! TONIGHT IS THE LAST NIGHT. A MAGIC SHOW YOU WON'T BELIEVE!

Myrna hugged a wall, lowering her face so that her brim covered it. She scanned the room carefully, going from face to face to face. Anraí stayed by the front door while Tavish made his way around to the backstage door.

Were Deirdre and her companions planning on watching the show, or were they going to wait outside for Ambrus to finish it? It could go either way. On one hand, the show was over two hours long. Fearing boredom, she could see them trying to watch the show, laying as low as they could. However, if they really feared Dunn, they'd play it safe and remain close by, appearing when the show was over.

When they had to.

VII.

Earlier, Ambrus put one of his crew members on standby. Cuán felt bad about it, but there was no other way. Ambrus 'hired' Cuán right away, saying, "This guy can run lights B and C." Nobody questioned him, though some grumbled under their breaths. Ambrus had another light operator show him the ropes, and after practicing it a few times (Cuán gumming it up a time or two), Ambrus said it was good enough, and that the show was ready.

Before Ambrus was to take the stage, Cuán overheard Ambrus telling one of the crew members that his 'Decollation of John Baptist' box was at *Byrne's Bicycle Shop*.

"We won't be including it in tonight's show. It will be a repeat of last night," Ambrus said. "Make sure you go to get it before midnight, though. It needs to go back to London with us."

Cuán hated being separated from Maggie and the others. Especially Maggie. He wanted to be outside with her, but the plan wouldn't work that way.

Worse, it could be dangerous. If they were caught before they got into the building, Maggie would have to fight for herself. And though Cuán thought she was capable enough, he hated it. Things could always go wrong.

When the lights came up, Cuán pointed light B on center stage and put C into position. He couldn't believe the show's turnout and realized that Ambrus was indeed a celebrity in his trade as many filed to their seats or gathered along the side and back walls.

There were drums and Ambrus came out, wearing what he usually wore, only this time he had on a black cape with a scarlet inner-lining.

"Ladies and Gentlemen! Hello and welcome to my show: *The Great Kárpáti!* Tonight, I have five magical tricks that will surprise you... nay, stun you... nay—SHOCK you to your very soul! Are we all ready for a grand show tonight?"

Everyone clapped and cheered. There were a few emphatic whistlers.

"Very well. But before we go on, be warned. What you may see is not for the faint of heart. Some of it is damn right gruesome. Are we going to fear the mysteries?"

"Nooooooo!" many cried.

"Then yes! We. Are. Ready!"

Ambrus, commanding everyone's eyes, threw his cape back, throwing out his hand to point off stage, and said: "Then let us welcome my assistant, *Adelynne Parish*, Ladies and Gentlemen!"

A sexy young blond came out, wearing a short, black velvet skirt—something you'd only see at shows. She wore a red blouse, ending above her navel, with a black velvet vest and a black top hat. Her black boots ended just below her knees.

Cuán had a little trouble keeping his eyes off her long, thin legs. He started picturing Maggie wearing the outfit and that wasn't a good idea either. His body uncomfortably reacted.

Adelynne rolled out the first contraption. It seemed like a simple box about ten feet tall. Red on white, the lettering read: THE GREAT KÁRPÁTI! There were what looked like occult symbols along the edges of the box.

"I designed this box, ladies and gentlemen, but the original design comes from an ancient Celestial origin."

Adelynne opened the box.

"As you can see, inside, it seems like an ordinary box. There is nothing inside. But do you see this?"

Ambrus pointed at the symbols along the edges of the box with his cane. "These are Celestial symbols! Here are the true mechanics of this box. Yes, yes, we are going into the arcane realms to make magic happen tonight, folks! Adelynne, my love, will you please step into the box?"

Adelynne smiled at the crowd and waves. She turns to Ambrus: "Yes, Master!" She furrows her brow. "It is safe, isn't it?"

Someone laughs in the crowd.

"Of course, it's safe, Adelynne! We have talked about this." He winked at the audience.

More laughter.

Adelynne nods her head, getting into the box. She still looks a little worried.

"Yes," she says.

Cuán can't help but to chuckle a little. Adelynne was funnier in front of people than she was at practice.

While the show went on, Cuán started scanning the crowd from the high walkway he was on, where the lights were fixed. He didn't know if he'd recognize any of Dunn's goons, but he thought it was worth a shot.

Looking over all the faces so far away was harder than he thought. There were a lot of faces.

Maggie and Róis waited in a pub a few blocks away before they sat out for the theater, both feeling nervous about the plan and about their chances. After all, if they failed to get out of Dublin tonight, they were all as good as dead as the Fomorians would surface for them, happy to punish them all for her recreancy.

It was well after dark, but the gas lamps made the roads feel a little safer. When they got to the theater, they went around to the alleyway. They were about to round a corner that put them in sight of the backstage door, but Maggie saw the goon and pushed Róis back before she stepped out into sight, her heart thumping hard in her chest.

Maggie recognized the goon at the backstage door. He was the one at the brothel the night they escaped. She whispered that back to Róis, who was behind her, looking around the corner of the next building over.

"Tavish. So, what do you think we should do?" Róis said.

Maggie looked back at the goon, this Tavish. Cuán had left them his gun. Since the goon was alone, Maggie could hold him up, and they could hide him behind the building they were standing behind now. It was unlikely he'd be found for a while.

Maggie looked at Róis and said, "I think you should stay here. Just in case. If something happens, then you can get the information to Deirdre."

"So, you have a plan?"

Maggie pulled Cuán's gun from her bag and gave Róis her bag. "If I make it back, we'll have to tie him down somehow. Keep your eyes peeled."

Maggie stepped out and held the gun up, walking toward the goon.

Tavish looked up and immediately put his hands in his jacket, pulling out his own gun.

Maggie didn't expect this. Her stomach turned. She had never shot anyone before.

"Hold it!" he cried. "I don't want to have to shoot you! I will though, goddamn it!"

Maggie was too scared to put down her own gun. She thought back to the goons that jumped her and Cuán before, how easy it was to break them. But Cuán had been in danger. She had motivation and rage behind her.

None of that was in her now. She was scared. Maybe because thinking about the Fomorians coming for her made her too vulnerable.

"Put the gun down now!" the goon growled. "Or I swear, I will put a bullet right in that pretty forehead of yours."

"Forehead? Maggie! Shoot him in the dick!" Róis called behind her. "That's much better."

Maggie groaned. Didn't she remember to tell her that she wasn't supposed to be seen or heard either?

Maggie pointed the gun at his crotch.

"I'm not putting this down," Maggie said. "You will... or I'll— I'll shoot you in the dick." Good a thing as anything, she thought.

"You won't shoot me in the dick," Tavish said. "You wouldn't do that. You're just a fucking scared little gi—"

Maggie tossed the gun at him as hard as she could, straining her shoulder. The goon saw the gun leave her hand but didn't understand what was happening until the weight of the cold steel slammed right into his crotch. She watched him drop his gun as he collapsed onto his knees, holding his groin. After a slow groan, Tavish cried out in agony.

Maggie rushed to grab his gun and kicked Cuán's away. Róis went up and grabbed it, so that they both had a gun pointed at the goon.

They watched the goon writhe on the ground, holding himself, cursing for a bit.

"What the bloody fuck? Who the bloody hell throws a fucking gun?" he groaned.

"Well, I mean, I can't have anyone *hear the gun go off*, can I?" Maggie said with a growl.

"Now, what do we do with him?" Róis said.

Maggie kneeled down and hit Tavish in the head with the gun. The weight of the metal made a swift thwacking sound on his head, and the goon went right out. A part of her wanted to hit him repeatedly until his head caved in, but she remembered Cuán's rejection to murder, and she knew that it would be wrong of her.

"Help me drag him behind that building over there."

"What do we do with the guns? I don't have pants to stick it in?"

Maggie laughed. "I suppose I don't either."

She gave Róis the other gun and grabbed the goon's arms, and started pulling him along on her own. He was heavy, but some of that extra strength she had kicked in, and it was far easier than it normally would be. Once he was lying in the dark shadows of the alley, up against the wall, she started gathering trash and covered him.

"If he wakes up?" Róis said, following her closely and watching her.

"Hopefully, we should be in our places," Maggie said. "I don't want to kill him unless we have to."

Deirdre was in the theater's parlor before she saw a goon take the front door. It was Anraí. Dunn's favorite hitman. She knew right away that Anraí would recognize her, so she turned her face away, turning her bonnet in such a way that he wouldn't be able to see her very easily.

She walked through the crowded theater and saw Myrna trying to hide against the wall. While she hadn't been at the brothel when Maggie, Róis and Cuán had escaped, she knew Madam Granya's main staff. Myrna was probably more malicious than the Madam. There were stories of her wicked perversions and sexual abuse of other women. A nasty piece of work.

Deirdre slipped back into the crowd, knowing where both of them were. Now all she needed to do was watch them until the show was over.

She couldn't help but watch Ambrus as well. It made her think back to earlier in the day and it brought a lot of joy to her. It being such a special thing, Deirdre wished that when she returned to the Cycle that she would never forget it.

Only she knew that's not how the Cycle worked. It was a curse for a reason.

Really, though, it was time to focus. This wasn't about her next Cycle. It was about getting Cuán and the rest of them out of Dublin so she could get away to London. Get her life back that she worked so hard to make here in Dublin, only across the Irish sea to Britain.

If she survived, that is.

Through the show, Myrna moved down the wall and walked down the back to the other side. Anraí, meanwhile, remained at the front exit. When Ambrus and Adelynne bowed and the curtains started closing, people got up from their seats to clap and cheer again.

That's when Deirdre struck. She quickly moved in on Anraí. He saw her coming and his hands became fists. Deirdre backed up suddenly and started back into the crowd. When she looked back over her shoulder, Anraí was following her, pushing people aside.

It worked.

She went behind the red vinyl entrance curtains, disappearing as people moved about her, and as Anraí came around looking for her. When she saw his legs, she summoned her strength, and she kicked his kneecap as hard as she could. Besides the hard thump of her shoe hitting him, there was a loud pop, and Anraí began to scream. Out from around the curtain, she picked up her skirt and started pushing toward the door.

All this, so Myrna would see her too.

She watched Myrna's face turn red, and she started pushing through people toward Deirdre. Deirdre, as planned, made her way out the exits to the front of the theater.

She crossed the street, staying between the gas lamps to make it harder to be seen. She waited, hoping they'd take the bait. Eventually, Myrna and Anraí emerged from the theater and saw her.

Anraí pointed at her, and Myrna called out, "Stop, Deirdre! Dunn gave us orders to kill you if you *don't* stop!"

Deirdre ran as fast as she could into the night.

As people started funneling out of the theater, Cuán watched Deirdre slip through the crowd, chased by the goon who found her. But there was no time for Cuán to wait, and there was nothing he could do for Deirdre while standing up in the rafters with the lights. He climbed off the walkway and went down the ladder to get backstage as swiftly as he could.

He didn't know why, but he worried more about Maggie.

Maggie and Róis huddled in the dark of the alleyway to keep warm. Maggie watched the junk pile where they hid the goon, hoping he'd stay out long enough for them to get away.

"You think everything is going to be, okay?" Róis said. "Do you think this will work?"

Maggie put her forehead against Róis's and looked up into her eyes. "I'm trying not to think about it, really."

Sometimes Maggie wondered why she had such a bleeding heart for other people. Róis wasn't a stranger any longer. A friend, maybe. But Maggie adored her. The Fomorians would see this as a weakness, and she'd take the piss, and she didn't care anymore. Screw the half-wits.

Suddenly the backstage door sprang open and Cuán was there, holding it open for them.

"Thank God! I was getting nervous," Róis said. They went in and Cuán led them around to the backstage, where Ambrus kept his props.

Ambrus appeared, removing his cape, tossing it aside, and grabbed his cane. Maggie was happy to see the both of them.

"That was a wonderful show, even if I have to say it myself," he said.

Cuán grabbed and squeezed his shoulder. "You are a good man for doing this."

Ambrus looked at him seriously and poked him in the chest with a stiff index finger: "I am *not* a good man. Remember that Mister Foley!"

Maggie wasn't sure what he meant by that, as he seemed a good man to her.

Ambrus turned to Maggie and Róis. "The crew are having a quick meeting about the changes. They thought they were loading this stuff up on a boat tonight, but they need to deliver it to the train station instead. It's time to get you in the boxes before they get back."

Ambrus opened a cabinet up, though nobody moved right away. "Well. Get in."

Maggie sighed. This idea seemed very uncomfortable—though riding in a wagon didn't either—she was sure this was much worse. After looking at everyone, she decided she'd be first. She climbed in and Cuán followed behind her. Ambrus closed the lid on them and was placing a lock.

They heard him say, "Now it's your turn, Róis."

"Wasn't this the one where you saw through Adelynne's body? In half?"

"Indeed."

"Do I have to get in this one? Is there blood?"

"Just get in, Róis. No real choices here, I'm afraid."

Maggie, in the dark of the cabinet, wrapped her arms around Cuán, found his lips, and kissed him deeply, feeling her love for him soar. Their chests were pressed together, and she delighted in feeling his body against hers, comforted in the rhythm of his breathing and his heart. They had cuddled before, but each time seemed new with him. And with this cuddle, she found his member hard against her hip.

"Um..."

"Sorry," he whispered.

She didn't want him to feel awkward about it and was delighted to know that in these strange circumstances, she affected him this way. It was sweet, really.

Maggie brushed her lips against his. "Never be sorry, Mister Foley."

His lips slightly touched her.

There was that electricity between them again.

He pressed his lips into her more, giving her another deep and hungry mouth. The tongue made her giggle, and she whispered, "Stop. We can't get too bothered in here. I'm afraid we might forget ourselves."

Cuán whispered back: "Of course we'll forget ourselves."

Maggie closed her eyes and hoped Deirdre was okay.

VIII.

Myrna gasped, rage like lava pooling up in her skull. She pushed through the crowd outside the theater and looked around. Anraí slapped her on the arm and pointed Deirdre out across the street. She was trying to hide in the shadows between the streetlamps.

"Stop, Deirdre! Dunn gave us orders to kill you if you don't stop!" Myrna shouted at her, but Deirdre started running. "You will pay for killing Finnian, *you feck*ing *bitch!*"

Of course, she was running. Myrna looked at Anraí and pointed at her. "Run after her, you bloody idiot!"

Anraí pointed at his hurt leg but grumbled and started hobbling after the girl as fast as he could. Myrna sighed and went around back, looking for Tavish. When she got around to the back door, she realized that he wasn't there.

Was he hiding in the alley? "Tavish! Are you here?" she called.

No answer. It looked like he was not going to help either.

The backstage door opened, and a few theater crew members came out to smoke pipes. Myrna looked at them as they stared her down.

"You haven't seen a redhead and blond wandering around here, have you?"

They shook their heads.

That figures, Myrna thought. She took one last look around and went after Anraí and Deirdre.

Deirdre heard them coming for her. She knew that Anraí wouldn't stop until he caught her, and she couldn't run forever. She was hoping that when she hurt Anraí that it slowed him down enough for her to sneak into a shop.

She tried the door and it opened. The bell rang and she reached up and silenced it as fast as she could. She went inside and held the bell so it wouldn't go off again. Once the door was shut, she twisted the lock in place, and backed up into the darkness of the shop. Crouching there, she watched the road until she saw Anraí stagger by as quickly as he could.

Eventually, he would think she was doubling back. He wasn't stupid. Besides, Myrna would probably be right behind him. She waited there for a long moment.

The stillness was almost palpable.

That's why she almost screamed out when a man opened a door behind the counter. She clapped a hand over her mouth and the man looked down at her.

"Are you the lady? Deirdre?" he whispered.

She nodded.

He reached a hand out to her while keeping a watch out for the front of his shop. "Come with me."

Deirdre took his hand and he led her to the back room. This room was lit by a single lantern, keeping most of the workshop in the dark. In what unsettling, being in a strange, dark place. The man closed the door between them and the front of the store. Meanwhile, Deirdre looked at all the bicycles and bicycle parts. In the center of the room was another one of Ambrus Kárpáti's magic boxes. The hidden moving parts inside, he'd told her, used bicycle parts. When he was in Dublin, this man helped fix his machines.

The man smiled warmly and opened the magic box.

"Thank you for this," Deirdre said, though she wasn't sure about it.

She had to remind herself that she did trust Ambrus, even for the short time she knew him.

The man nodded. "Ambrus has always been good business when he's in town. He's good people. I'm happy to help out. You may want to hurry, though. Ambrus told me to expect one of his crew to pick up the box almost right away."

Deirdre got into the box and the man closed it down, clicking a lock in place.

She hated being locked up in such a small area, but this plan was all they had. Taking a deep breath, she laid back and tried relaxing.

This was going to be a long ride.

VI. The Devil's Breath

I.

The first stop for the train was in Kildare.
The journey was terrible. They had to lay in their boxes the whole night, get bounced around when they were put into storage, and had to wait another forty-five minutes for the train ride before they finally came to a stop.
Maggie and Cuán held each other in their box. The noises of the train were loud enough that they found themselves whispering directly into each other's ears to speak. Maggie felt Cuán getting hard again—their bodies pressed so tightly together. Wanting to pass the time and hungry for Cuán, she thought about having her first ride on him, but she didn't want it like this. Cuán's member was so hard though that she wanted to ease his discomfort, and so she grabbed it and squeezed it, rubbing him firmly. Liking how it felt in her hand.
"What are you doing?" he whispered into her ear. His breath tickled her neck.
"Shut up and enjoy it," she whispered back into his.
There wasn't much room to move. She was able to roll her hips sideways to free a little space between them, allowing her to undo his pants, pull his hardness out. The skin was the softest

she'd ever known, and it felt pulpous with a hardness underneath. He gasped, and she started rubbing it, skidding the soft skin back and forth over it. Cuán's body tightened up and he let out a soft moan into her ear. This made her smile, knowing it was making him feel so good. If only she could move to put it into her mouth, or inside her.

She licked his ear, and he rewarded her with a deep moan.

His breathing increased, and she pushed her mouth into his, nudging her flicking tongue as deep as she could. His body stiffened and he whimpered into her mouth. As he shook, she continued to massage the erection, and she felt her hand getting sprinkled with his warm, glutinous climax. *His puddin'*, Myrna would call it, Maggie thought.

"Was that good fer you?" she said, feeling his body jerk and his breath huff in bursts. Disappointed he wasn't inside her, she was nevertheless happy for him.

He breathed heavily onto her neck. "Thank you."

Maggie buttoned him up again and laid back onto him, kissing his neck and cheeks.

"I want more, Cuán. I want more of yeh," she said. Maggie would have never realized before that pleasing him would have its own warm reward. His happiness meant everything to her.

"Same," Cuán said. "Why haven't we already done this?"

"Because you're afraid of me."

It was a truth, and he didn't deny it.

"I'm also afraid *for* you," he said. "I don't want anything bad happening to yeh. I don't want you to leave me."

"Cuán, I'd never. Not on purpose. Nothing will make me leave."

"Are you certain of this?"

"Cuán. Yes."

He kissed her again and she realized that his right hand had found the right spot between her legs. She opened her legs for more room, and his hand slid back and forth until she was grinding back against it, wanting more. Maggie felt very juicy and when the waves of pleasure rocked through her body, she thought she moaned a little loud and took a small bite into Cuán's neck to quiet herself.

"Fuck," she said, trying to catch her breath. "We've got to get locked up in boxes more often."

Cuán chuckled a little. "Indeed."

While passengers got on and off and the minimum maintenance was being done, Adelynne and Ambrus released them from their boxes and gave them tickets. Once rescued, they were all sore and hungry.

With the rest of the trip promising to be more comfortable and knowing they were away from Dublin, Maggie attempted to be pleasant, despite the terror she felt inside. If they didn't stop Dunn from getting to the Fomorians in Séala Bán, they'd all be in danger. And it would be her fault. A part of her already thought it was all over, but she knew she couldn't keep thinking that way.

Ambrus treated them to a large lunch in the dining car as the train started rolling again. Chicken drums, oranges, grapes and wine. When they had their fill, the conductor was making his way around. They showed their tickets and then found seats. Cuán let Maggie have the window and she hung her arms on its edge. She rested her head there so that she could see the countryside go by, feel the sun warm her hair, her face. The window was half down, giving her some air and making her feel as though everything was going to be okay.

Sort of.

Róis and Deirdre sat opposite and facing them. They looked like they were in great spirits.

Róis was excitedly ticking off their stops: "...Kildare, Athlone, and Galway. But we have to travel south, correct?"

Deirdre nodded. "Yes, Séala Bán bay is a small bay south of Galway. According to the itinerary, it should take about two and a half hours altogether."

"We'll have to purchase transport. It'll probably be by wagon. But the trip should only take a couple more hours," Cuán said. "We'll be in Séala Bán before dark."

Róis started gazing out her window. "I've never been out of Dublin. The countryside is beautiful."

Maggie agreed. In many ways, she wished the train ride would last forever. At the other end of this line was a danger she wasn't ready to face, and despite knowing this, she tried to keep her mind off of it for now.

Eventually, she decided that Cuán would be more comfortable. She put her head on his chest, and he put an arm around her. She fell asleep.

Cuán didn't wake her until they stopped in Galway. Maggie sat up, rubbed her eyes, and asked where they were, and Cuán grinned and said, "We're getting off here."

Maggie smiled at him, her hair a bit of a cute mess, and he gave into putting his lips on hers. That made her smile bigger, and he so loved her smile.

"I don't deserve you, Cuán," she said.

Cuán rolled his eyes. "Just remember that when I'm in trouble."

She laughed a little. "I'll try."

They got up and followed Deirdre and Róis to the exits. They met Ambrus and Adelynne there and all walked together from the platform. On the western shore, the day was overcast, dulling colors and casting large shadows across town.

Ambrus had to talk to his crew, giving them the news that the magic props needed to be returned to London. He put his team lead in charge. They were a little upset they made the trip to Galway, but none of them made too much of a stink. They were mostly glad to be returning home. He kissed Adelynne's hand and sincerely thanked her for her help.

"Come back safe, Ambrus. There are more shows that lay before us."

Ambrus grinned. "And the bloody show must go on?"

Adelynne smiled, waved, and went off with the crew.

With business taken care of, Cuán started asking locals if they knew someone who would take them to Séala Bán. Several minutes later, they found a man who was willing to give them a ride for a pretty cheap price. He had a wagon and some blankets, and they all sat close to keep each other warm as they started out.

The closer they got, Cuán felt Maggie getting stiffer beside him.

"My father and I would go out on the dogger nearly every day when I was first starting out learning the ropes, even over the weekends. I hated it mostly because whenever we went out to sea, it was like leaving the rest of my life ashore. Whatever happened on land, I had no control over. So, I'd fret and get worked up about situations, thinking things could go bad, and I wouldn't be there to stop them. So, it became an excuse I'd give my da every day. 'Da, no, I don't want to go out on the dogger. Ponc is sick.' Or, 'Da, no, what if my friends visited early and left without saying goodbye'.

"My da, being a clever man, got tired of this and said, 'For god sakes Cuán, what's the point of worryin' when it might not happen. Imagine all these anxious fits you have, shaking and frettin', and what happens when you realize that everything is fine? Can you go back in time and stop yourself from wasting your time worryin' and frettin'? No. Why would you do that to yourself? Never ever let yourself fret about such things. Frettin' is for afterward, when the bad thing already happened, and there's not a damn thing you can do. And even then, life is about picking yourself up and pushing forward no matter what."

Cuán shrugged. "Of course, I'm paraphrasing a little here. He was a bit fermented when he said all this."

Maggie rubbed his stomach under the blanket. "Thank you for that, Cuán. Not sure if it helps…"

By wagon, it took about two hours to reach Séala Bán. The closer they got, the mistier the day became. So much so, they were totally enveloped by a thick fog as they rolled into the village.

Cuán could hear the sea in the distance, and he could smell it. It had a welcoming feeling. The village itself was a different matter. All the fog made the village feel forlorn and empty, and there were very few people about them. Cuán did see the beam of a nearby lighthouse, something he searched for out of habit that his father probably pounded into him since before he could walk.

Aye, he thought, a marine biologist. That's what he needed to be. They hopped off the wagon and they all looked around.

"I was only here once when I was like eight," Cuán said. "But I'm sure we'll be able to find someone who wouldn't mind taking us in for a few quid."

Deirdre stepped beside Cuán and looked at him. "Do you think we should split up? Maybe we'll find something sooner that way."

"I don't see why not," Cuán said.

Most of those ashore, before the doggers came in, were women with their aprons and woolen petticoats, all working at the unloading houses, preparing for the men to return. There was a stocky old-timer with a long white beard wearing a heavy raincoat, supervising and helping where he could. He looked like someone who might help them, so Maggie approached him, "Sir?"

He turned, seeing her and Cuán, and frowned. "Strangers, eh?"

"Yes, Sir. We're travelers and are in need of lodging for a few days. Do yeh know where we can find any? There are five of us total."

"Five of yeh, aye?"

"I'm Maggie. This is Cuán. We split up, so the other three aren't here. Deirdre. Róis. Ambrus."

The old-timer nodded. "Name is Declan. Nice to meet yeh."

"Nice to meet you, Sir," Maggie said.

The man threw down a rope and scratched his head. "There are only a couple places that could hold you up. I would only suggest one of them. Come on. I'll take you to the Hearns."

The old-timer walked them up a winding road through the village to a larger manor house at the top of the hill. They went through the gate and stepped up to the door. The man knocked, and the door was opened by a woman in her late thirties or early forties.

"Declan. How may I help you?"

"Eireen. There's some travelers here. This lady says there's five of them. They need a place to stay while they're in town. They were wondering if yeh could accommodate them?"

Eireen looked the two of them down, frowning.

Maggie stepped forward, hoping she would not dismiss them right off. "We have money, and we don't plan to stay long." She looked at Cuán, who looked at Maggie, and suddenly realized why she was looking at him. She recognized Cuán. This was good. Hopefully.

He reached out a hand. "I'm Cuán. Maggie and I are actually from Kilkee, but we have little business here in town. Just for a few days, ma'am."

Eireen slowly nodded and opened the door wider so that they could come in.

"I'll get the others," Cuán said. "I'll be back soon."

Maggie nodded and went in alone, Cuán backing down the sidewalk and into the night.

The manor house was not as large as Dunn's mansion, but for a home in the area, it was extravagant. Two stories with decks and patios, and the small acreage around them were lavishly landscaped with paths, bushes and miniature trees. Inside, the house was immaculate and well-lit with the latest gas pipe lighting. In the large foyer, there were portraits of fishermen and their wives, ships of rough seas and sea-monsters.

"This is poor timing," Eireen said. "But we can have you if you can afford a pound per person per day."

"I think we can manage that."

Maggie hadn't dealt with many of the 'elite society' or 'snobby' women before, but she figured that she could handle quite a bit next to the idea of facing the Fomorians.

On the second floor, past the banister, Maggie caught glimpses of a pale girl with dark hair looking down at them. She looked fourteen or so, but she was thin and had dark rings around her deep eyes.

"However, it's my husband that makes the final decision, so we won't know fer sure until he returns home. I suspect the ships will be in within the hour."

Maggie nodded. "We'd be happy to help in any way that we can."

Eireen shook her head, sighing. "This really is a bad time to have visitors. Because of the fog that perpetually haunts us, we have a stiff curfew. Doors must be locked at eleven fifty-five just to be sure that they are locked before midnight. There is no going in or out. Supper is six-thirty sharp, breakfast at seven, dinner at noon. If you can't make it at these times, you'll have to find your food elsewhere."

"No problem, ma'am."

The girl behind the banister started coughing, and Eireen whipped around. "Nola! Nola dear, you must get back into your bed."

Nola stood up. "Ah, Mam..."

Eireen snapped at her: "I believe I told you to go back to bed."

Nola coughed hard and started making her way back to her room.

Maggie felt for the little girl.

"Is she okay?"

Eireen looked at her and Maggie realized that her frown wasn't because of some disapproval with taking them in. She was deeply sad... and, perhaps, frightened.

"The girl suffers a weakness. The doctor from Kilkee checks on her once a week. He is not sure what is wrong with her. I would not bother her. Being so frail, visits seem to worsen her condition."

Maggie turned, surprised to see an old woman, wearing a dark brown shawl, standing next to Eireen. Her hair was white as cotton. Maggie nodded at her as the old woman regarded them. Maggie didn't understand how visitations would weaken someone, but she nodded. They needed a place to stay for a day or so. It was important that she didn't upset their only chance of having a roof over their head.

Maggie grinned at the old woman. "I'm Maggie."

The old woman smiled back. "I am Eireen's mother. Nice to meet you. Do not let my daughter scare you away. We love to help those who are in need."

"We have three spare rooms," Eireen said. "You can split them up as you see fit between the five of you so long as it's appropriate. The beds are big enough to be shared. Though, I must say, this household is a house of grace and piety. There should be no amorous congress under this roof."

Maggie shook her head. "Of course not."

Eireen looked her over one more time. "Alright. Follow me."

As they climbed the stairs, Maggie noticed the copper-framed calendar hanging on the wall, seeing that it was January 31st. Tomorrow was Imbolc—the day the Cailleach demanded Maggie return to the siofra to her. How could she forget? Of all her problems, why did everything have to converge on one single day?

Because, she thought, *it's fata.*

Cuán walked alongside Declan, only now noticing that the old-timer kept his left hand tucked in his jacket. In a glimpse, he saw that he had a wooden hand. He once knew a man who had lost a leg out fishing, and Cuán wondered if that would be his fate if he stayed on to help his father.

But there were more important things right now. He quickly started to put together a lie.

"Declan. I was wondering if... uh, there were any other strangers in town. You know, people visiting the village for a very brief time."

Declan looked at him, looking somewhat concerned. "Why do you ask?"

"Well, to be honest, we're looking fer someone who was working for our boss in Dublin. Our boss is a huge banker named Mister Dunn. Out here, yeh might not have heard of him, but he's looking to buy some farmland nearby. I was hoping to help persuade Mister Dunn by speaking with someone he trusted. It's all business venture stuff, I should say, but if we can locate them, it would really be helping us out."

Declan seemed to think about it, and he said, "No, no. You're the only outsiders I have seen for a very long time."

Figures, Cuán thought. Nothing could ever be that easy.

"A'right then."

There was only one shop and a church in town. Cuán found that Deirdre and the others had visited the shop and were directed to the church. He found them there as they waited for the priest to finish speaking with a woman in his office.

They were all sitting in a back pew, bringing back memories of his conversation with Deirdre at St. Peter's Church in Dublin. It already seemed so long ago.

"Maggie and I found lodgings," Cuán said.

The group almost sighed together.

"Thank God," Róis said. "I could use a good bed right now. Thought we were stuck sleeping in these bloody pews. Ugh."

They parted Declan's company when Cuán insisted that he knew how to get back to the Hearn's residence. As they walked, Cuán told them that, according to Declan, there were no other outsiders in town.

Ambrus shrugged. "Then we have four possibilities, as I see it. One, Dunn is someone that the village wouldn't consider an outsider. Two, we somehow got here before Dunn got here, though it seems unlikely. Three, Declan's lying. Or four, Dunn is hiding."

"I think two is hard to swallow. He had at least a day on us," Deirdre said.

"Four sounds off as well. There's nowhere in a small village to bloody hide," Ambrus said.

"I don't know," Róis said. "And I don't think one is great either. I mean, what are the chances Dunn knows someone in this village, trusts them enough to hide him? Sounds far-fetched to me."

Cuán nodded, biting his lip. "So... either Declan is lying, or one of you is wrong."

Róis grinned. "You're a wise arse, Cuán."

"But he's not wrong," Ambrus told her.

After supper, most everyone went off to sleep, appreciating the large luxury beds and coverlets—especially because of their travels. Maggie and Róis in one room, Ambrus and Cuán in another, and Deirdre in her own room. Of course, Cuán decided to hit the sheets when the others crawled into theirs, leaving Maggie to sit by the fireplace alone for the time being.

Eireen was knitting in her rocker. Once her husband, Aran, grumbled a bit about them staying, he agreed with the wife to keep them on for a few short days. After that, he went down to the local pub to sit with his crew and drink a few beers. Their oldest son, Clancy, went up to read to his sick sister. As Maggie understood it, Clancy felt guilty for his sister's condition, and when he was home, he was there for her as much as his parents allowed. It was all sad and sweet.

A grandfather clock started chiming. Their clock was set ten minutes early so that the midnight toll started early, giving Eireen time to make sure the windows and doors were locked down.

Maggie helped her.

"What about yer husband?" Maggie said.

Eireen shook her head. "If he's out this late, he usually passes out at the pub. They'll lock their doors. He'll be fine."

Despite her acceptance of this, Maggie could sense her holding back a little bitterness about it. Maggie didn't know if she could do anything like this to Cuán. Though, she supposed, she may do quite a bit to protect her children, wouldn't she? It was hard to imagine when there was only one in the picture who she could dream about ever living with.

"I know this may be none of my business—I'm not from around here—but why the curfew? Why the locked doors?"

Maggie was wondering about what Cuán and Deirdre had told her—how Declan said there were no other outsiders besides them. Could the Fomorians already be here, or could Dunn have been a message *and* an offering to these creatures?

The last thought was wishful thinking, really.

"It has been a few years now," Eireen said. "The fog came, and it refuses to leave. Nobody knows for sure what is out there, but people end up dead from time to time."

A few years? Maybe this had nothing to do with Doran Dunn. But then, Maggie didn't know how Dunn decided on this village. He chose it for a reason, and it could be because he had a history here.

And that got her thinking... What if this was a trap?

Eireen scoffed air out her throat in disgust. "If you ask me, it has something to do with the commissioner, Eamon Macrae, and his family. Nola—she didn't get sick until a few months ago. She says something came at her in the fog. Women with black hair. Skeletons draped in pallid skins. I think the fog poisoned her. I think maybe God has condemned us because of our mortal sins."

Maggie didn't know what to say. She was thinking about the fog. Perhaps it was demons, but so close to Kilkee and the place where she'd escaped the fomori? No. This was an ethereal mist from Beyond the Ninth Wave—*An Naoú Tonn*. It was a curse, but not at all biblical.

"Do you think this 'Eamon' would know more about the fog?"

Eireen shook her head. "I have no evidence. Only a gut feeling. Eamon is a bad man. If I were you, I would stay clear of him."

She went back to knitting in her rocker, leaving Maggie to gaze into the fire.

Going up to bed, Maggie saw Nola in her white gown, peering out her door at her. The poor child had dark rings around her eyes, and her complexion was ashen.

"Hello," Maggie said as softly as possible. She didn't want to scare her.

"They are women. Like sirens, they come in from the sea—only they don't sing. They wail. Muirgen is their queen," Nola said. Her voice was weak, and she sounded so young, but kids did that sometimes, didn't they? Sound younger when they felt ill. "They lay in wait, taking sacrifices until they catch the Seagrass Girl."

Muirgen... That name sounded so familiar. Where had Maggie heard this name before? When it hit her, it made her dizzy. Maggie remembered protecting Crab Eye from the newborn vampyric creature that came out of the egg when the Egg Keepers tapped it for a trophy head. To protect the young Altered One, she bit through the newborn's neck, making it easy for Maggie to tear the head clean off the rest of the body. It was Muirgen's daughter.

That was a long, long time ago.

Now she was beginning to understand why Doran Dunn brought her here. He knew more about her than she thought he really knew. But how?

Unless he was already in communication with Ri Elieris, the Fomorian King.

"How do you know all of this?"

The girl's eyes looked intensely into hers.

"When Muirgen fed on my blood, she whispered this to me. They said I should be their eyes, and they would come when the Seagrass Girl entered the fog."

"How would you know this Seagrass Girl?"

Nola licked her lips. "She said there would be a sign—a time when she came and moved the time of the tides."

Maggie furrowed her brow and shook her head. "That sounds scary."

Nola nodded. "If I don't find her, she will kill me. Are you the Seagrass Girl, Maggie? Are you the one to move the time of the tides?"

Maggie forced a smile. "Of course not. I'm just a normal girl."

Could Muirgen be seeing through the girl? Could she be in astral form, hovering near, watching her?

Nola nodded solemnly. "I have to go to bed. I'm marked, yeh know. My mother won't admit it, but the arrachtaigh will come for me and take me to the Feast Pit soon."

Arrachtaigh?

Nola closed the door, leaving Maggie standing there, thinking, *Monster?*

Maggie crawled into bed beside Róis, trying not to wake her. She spooned her and put an arm around her. She buried her head into her back and closed her eyes, trying not to think about how angry Muirgen would be with her.

Her vengeance would be bloody.

As when she was younger, she heard the wailing. It echoed and then became soft in the fog. She remembered that wailing, realizing it was all around them now. And it was much louder, crawling over her flesh. This whole time, Muirgen was calling for her.

When had she first heard them? Possibly before Oona caught her trying to stay in her attic?

Maggie tried to cover her ears. How much of this did Dunn plan? What did he expect to accomplish by all of this?

Oh, Jaysus—

Maggie had murdered Muirgen's daughter.

She began to tremble nervously. Maggie was terrified.

II.

Near the cliffs of Séala Bán, overlooking the bay, the Macrae estates stands. Bedelia Macrae was at the gate when she heard the wailing. Sometimes she dared come out into the night and listened to the crashing waves, and the dark sirens that had been haunting them for many years now.

Like now, she always felt on the fence between two impossible dangers. Out here: the sirens that haunted the cliffs and shoreline. And her home: the estate she found herself living, where Eamon Macrae awaited her.

Eamon would take her and leave her sore on the bed before falling into his fitful sleep. And like almost every night, she would try to remember how to weep, and it would escape her.

Hope had left when the fog came. There were now only the vampyric sisters of the brine, and the monster she called her husband. In many ways, she wished that her father hadn't been a coward, but at the same time, she knew she couldn't totally blame him. When the fog came, and Eamon's first wife fled, never to be seen again, people looked for any way possible to save themselves from being a sacrifice to these sea vampyres.

No, she couldn't blame them at all. Life was what it was. And for Bedelia, a few months past the age of seventeen, it was Hell on earth.

Bedelia thought that she was lucky in some respects. Eamon was much like the vampyres. He had to lay low during the day because the light bothered him. He hated company, and so Bedelia didn't have to look the part of the fancy housewife. She could drink some of her painful ruminations away with the whiskey in Eamon's bar.

That sounds nice right about now, she thought.

As she turned around to go back inside, she glanced at a beam of light. When she looked back, she realized someone was coming up the path with a lantern. It was a woman with two men. The men were climbing down from a carriage behind her, the teamster taking off, leaving them there. One of the men seemed to be hobbling.

She decided to wait for them to come up.

"Who may you be?" she asked once they were in hearing range.

The woman nodded. "The commissioner—your husband—has something in common with our boss. We thought we should talk."

"My husband doesn't take meetings this late," Bedelia said.

The two men finally caught up with the woman. She gestured to the two men. "This is Tavish and Anraí. My name is Myrna. Trust me. He'll want to have this meeting. Tell him Doran Dunn, on behalf of Muirgen, wants a word."

None of these names were familiar, or even mattered to her. Bedelia looked up at the estate. She realized that if this was important, he would be too occupied to think about laying with her. It would be something she could look forward to.

Bedelia opened the gate. "Come on in."

She led them up to the house, let them in, and went up to Eamon's study. She knocked at the door and told him that special guests were waiting for him downstairs. Bedelia never went into his study. It was off-limits, and she would get a beating if she went in without permission.

Suddenly his rough voice broke the silence. "What guests, Bedelia? I thought I told you—"

"The woman, Myrna, mentioned someone named Doran Dunn. And, um, Muirgen?"

There was a deep sigh.

"Tell them I'll be down in a moment."

"I—I—I will," Bedelia said. "Afterwards, I'll go to bed."

Don't be mad, she thought.

There was no answer, so she left him alone to return to the guests. Bedelia escorted them into a parlor and said that Eamon would be with them shortly. They took a seat.

As Bedelia left them, she noticed the one called Anraí was looking her over. He was the one who seemed to have hurt his leg. Not wanting to give him hope, she looked away.

She didn't let herself ponder how he would judge her in disgust if he knew, knowing how she was Eamon's trash.

Bedelia went to the bar in the den, poured herself some whiskey, and went up to her bedroom. She downed her drink before she opened her door. She put the glass clumsily on her nightstand. As the alcohol hit her, she blew out her lantern, slipped her legs into the covers, and pulled them to just under her breasts as she laid back. She closed her eyes and listened as the keening rose again.

Myrna's hair rose on the back of her neck when she heard the wailing again.

In the carriage, when they first heard it, they were going through the fog. They could not see a thing, but they heard the women's somber aria reverberate through the air around them.

Myrna was thinking about Finnian—the many secret visits they made for each other, to be together, wrapped in each other's arms, gasping in pleasure. He was always such a prince compared to her bumbling, useless husband.

"Sirens?" Anraí guessed.

"We don't have sirens in Ireland," Tavish said. "It's the banshee. If you hear her cries, someone is about to die."

They listened to the wailing around them. Eventually, it drifted off and they were left in silence as the village began to appear in the curtain of the ocean mists.

"It sounded like there were more than one," Anraí said. "Maybe five? Six?"

"Maybe there's a banshee for each of us," Myrna said.

Tavish shook his head. "It's the echoes. There are so many cave systems in the rocks and cliffs around here."

"How do you know?" Anraí said, looking as if he didn't believe him.

"I read books on occasion."

Now they were sitting in the commissioner's parlor, listening to it rise and fall again. Banshees? Myrna didn't think so. She was sure that Doran Dunn's occult leanings made him bedfellows with monsters right out of people's nightmares. If they survived this, she'd be surprised.

She watched Anraí, who she had started to realize was much softer than Tavish. As Tavish confidently moved about the parlor, looking at things, Anraí was holding himself and looking around as if he were expecting ghosts. Myrna suspected that he was softer than he was letting on, which may be a problem. She needed both men to perform their jobs well, especially if they wanted to survive.

Footsteps broke her out of her head. She looked up and saw that a tall, handsome man was walking down the stairs. His hair was jet black. He had a strong jaw and deep brown eyes.

She was enamored.

Myrna stood and approached him, almost bungling it.

"What can I do for you?" Eamon said.

Myrna introduced them and said, "Doran Dunn sent us to inform you that the Seagrass Girl is here. We're supposed to help you return her to the sea."

Eamon didn't smile. "Really? Why should I believe you?"

Myrna snapped her fingers, and Anraí brought her the black shell, staggering some as he walked. She put it in his hand. Eamon looked disgusted at it, and saw the black sea snail come out, bleeding red blood. This was a sign of the presence of Ri Elieris.

Eamon closed and squeezed his fingers around the shell, and the creature was made into a crumbling gooey pulp in his palm. He swiped his hands together and gestured for them to follow him. Myrna told Anraí and Tavish to remain there, and they went up to his study, leaving the two goons behind.

He closed the double doors to his study after Myrna was inside, saying, "I knew this day would come. Muirgen hasn't lied to me yet. A drink?"

Myrna grinned. "'I'd love one."

Eamon went to his bar and poured her a brandy. He took it over to her as she sat in a seat near the large fireplace.

"Comfy home you have here, Mister Macrae."

Eamon took a chair opposite her and threw his foot over his other knee, relaxing back.

"I've not heard of Doran Dunn."

Myrna took a sip of her brandy before she answered. "Mister Dunn is one of two owners of a large bank in Dublin. MacKay & Dunn Banks. They have one location in Edinburgh and one in London as well. He's also a magus."

Eamon laughed. "A magus? You assume too much, I'm afraid. Am I supposed to know what that means?"

Myrna shook her head and took another sip of her drink. "No, no. I didn't know what it meant until I looked it up either. I think the real term is sorcerer."

Eamon frowned. "Is this how he knows of Muirgen and her... *sisters?*" The word 'sisters' was said with considerable disgust.

Myrna placed her glass on her knee, the dark maple liquid sloshing around inside, and leaned forward. "Doran says that if you want to command Muirgen and her sisters, then you need to be more than a monstrous minion of the maighdean uaimh, a slave of the brine vampyres. You are a thing to them, so to rise up and *command* them, you need to be more than what you are now."

Eamon's face went ugly with anger, arching his brows and baring clenched yellow teeth. "I am no one's slave!"

Myrna sat back, and with one gulp, finished her drink. "In order for you to become more powerful, you must get over your ego and embrace Mister Dunn's offer. The only way to make those vampyric bitches heel is through sheer power."

Eamon stood. "This is over. You may stay the night, but I do not want to see you or your men again. Tell Mister Dunn I will not be manipulated."

He is truly afraid of them, she thought. Or he dared not hope to be free from the vampyres' clutches.

Myrna rolled her eyes. "Aye. Fine. I will let you think on it." She stood up. "You really don't want to lose this opportunity. It will be the only one you have."

Myrna left him to stew in his study and returned to Tavish and Anraí. They asked her how it went, and she shushed them for now. Soon a servant attended them and escorted them to their rooms.

When Myrna was alone in her room, she opened her bag and ran her fingers over Mister Pungere. She looked it over, imagining Róis or Maggie begging her to stop. Tears. Blood. They would deserve what was coming to them for what they did to Finnian. No doubt about it.

She placed it back and opened Dunn's note. She reread what he asked of her and played through the moment when he put the black stuff in her mind, making her drink the vile potion. Though she was still angry about what Dunn had done to her, she was experiencing a secret world that very few knew of. She was a part of something special here. Myrna felt... *proud* to be Dunn's assistant now, though she would never admit to this aloud. This was all more than she ever was, and the more she thought about it, it seemed it was all the more worth it.

Myrna built a fire in the fireplace in her chamber, and she tossed the note into it. Once this was done, she crawled into bed, dreaming that Maggie was begging her to stop. "It *hurts. Please!*" She slept with a grin on her face. Pain is what Maggie deserved. It's what they all fucking deserved.

Myrna slept, and the fire died in the middle of the night.

III.

In her own bed in her white nightgown, Deirdre thought of Doran Dunn and wondered why her memories felt too fragmentary. Why was it so hard to put together? If she could figure out what had started all of this, maybe she could figure out how to fix it.

Would Dunn know? Could she get him to tell her what happened? If so, why did he hide it fom her?

Doran Dunn had always been secretive and had lied to her too many times to count. She didn't believe it. Doran would continue lying to her. So, how was she going to find out the truth? Put her memories in order?

Could Ambrus help her do it?

She didn't know. Deirdre unconsciously grabbed the locket she had around her neck with the spiral carving engraved on the outside, and an inked sigil drawn on the inside.

An idea came to her, but she wondered how dangerous it would be since Doran was a sorcerer. And an arsehole, at that. Maggie told her that she tried looking for Dunn through the Hollow, but she wasn't successful. Why shouldn't she try as well? Was she really that scared?

Dangerous situations never scared you before, Deirdre told herself.

True.

Deirdre closed her eyes and reached out into the Hollow.

The Hollow was like floating through the natural world—only the mind could attune itself to vibrations that came from different directions. These vibrations manifested themselves in different ways inside her mind. It could be a chill. The scent of fresh bread. The taste of a sharp red wine in the air.

Deirdre had never used the Hollow to look for Dunn before, but she imagined the scent of his rich cologne mixed with the musky scent of sex and blood. Unfortunately, this led her to Dunn conversing with Felim in a laboratory. Since Maggie had already seen this, Deirdre suspected it at once and waited until it looped.

    And it did loop. Replayed itself out before her eyes.

    It was a trick. It was what Dunn wanted them to see.

    But why? And if this was a trick, how could she find him?

    Deirdre closed herself off from all of the vibrations in the Hollow and only let her ideas float about her. It didn't take long for everything to sort itself out and she had her idea. Deirdre grasped the *déantán* around her neck. The locket with the ancient sigil of the Cailleach inside it that she'd found in Dunn's study when she was looking for the key to the anklet Dunn had placed on Maggie's leg. In the Hollow, it was more than the simple, strange locket she'd found. The locket was now haloed with a cold blue and dark light. It not only looked cold; it was cold. These were the vibrations of the Cailleach, but when Deirdre tried harder to focus on the déantán, she realized that she could sense Dunn's vibrations as well. His stink was on it.

    The déantán was a fetish—a talisman dedicated to a god, holding within it a faint amount of power. If Dunn knew she had it, he would be able to use it to find her. But Deirdre was willing to bet it worked both ways.

    Following Dunn's vibrations from the locket, Deirdre reached out and found herself closer to Kilkee. There were purple Spring Squill beds and a wooden doorway that could only be seen in the Hollow. Deirdre opened it and went in.

    Deirdre was in shock when she realized that she could not see herself. She stepped back out through the door, and her body reappeared. She had never seen her body become invisible this way, and she didn't like it, but she knew that she had to go through the door.

    So, she tried it again. She had no hands, arms, legs or feet. She was invisible, and it was terrifying, but she could breathe, and she still felt alive, so she went on.

Up on a hill, she could see a castle, and she went inside, following the déantán to where Dunn could be found. They were in a hallway outside the royal bedroom. Deirdre instinctively found herself moving into Dunn's body as he went to the window and looked out at the storm. Lady Netterville was crying out in birthing pains and Lord Netterville was pacing back and forth, looking like he'd seen a ghost.

Inside Dunn's mind, she could read him as though she was living through him.

A.D. 1304, Kildare

A woman cried out in pain, which resounded through the keep. Doran watched as the maidservants rushed through the castle halls to gather extra linen and more water as the midwife made her way into Elizabeth's chambers while he and Nicholas waited outside, Nicholas pacing in worry.

"It sounds so awful," Nicholas said. "I cannot believe that something so important must be made in such agony."

Doran felt for him. "Thus is life. For there to be something new, there must be sacrifices made—a price."

"And the women must pay for it while all we can do is watch."

"And be there," Doran said. "You are doing everything you can. I'm sure it will all end well."

Elizabeth cried out again, and Doran heard the midwife ask an attendant to help her be still. He could no longer bear watching Nicholas in such a state, so he made his way to the window and looked out at the rainy night. There was no lightning, but the sea was stirring. It was reacting to something else, an opening between worlds. Doran had foreseen it and helped guide it to this very night. If only he could tell Nicholas and Elizabeth how important this night would be, help them understand what was about to happen.

Doran grasped a locket that he had around his neck. The locket had a spiral carved into it.

(And Deirdre noticed with some surprise that it was the déantán she'd found.)

No... this must remain a secret for it to work properly, he told himself. It was important. It was for the betterment of the people.

Lightning flashed. One, two, three... and it resounded thickly in the night air. It was time.

The midwife cried, "Push!" Elizabeth cried and heaved behind the door. Nicholas bit his fist.

"I must check on something, my Lord," Doran said. "I will be back soon."

Nicholas barely heard him. Giving a short nod, Doran excused himself to the stairs, down to the main hall, and through the front walls. He reluctantly left the protection of the small castle, wound down through the rocks of the cliffs, through the wild, purplish Spring Squill flower beds, holding his hood over my head to defend himself from the rain.

"*Lover?*" A whisper nearby him, but nothing more. *Aisling.* It was not time to be with the Squill, so he ignored it and continued on toward the cliffs.

As he made his way, Doran saw the storm light up the green fields. There were other creatures over the nearby hills. People with horns, fangs and claws—those things that slithered and moved more like animals than the very humanoid forms they essentially beheld.

The fae. They had come to watch.

One such was a girl with dark red hair with three-pointed horns, holding a staff. The others called her *Sionnach Silín*—the Cherry Fox. She was amongst the creatures yet standing apart from them as if she were their leader.

As soon as another lightening flashed, Doran could no longer see any of them.

The barriers were opening and closing. He had to hurry.

The sea roiled and dashed frothy white at the rocks. Spirits were under the dark waters. Doran could see their forms turning and twisting beneath the surface. As he approached, the spirits began to fan out, making space in the waters for her. Doran wiped his face, drew in the deep scents of the salty waters as he grasped the déantán around his neck, and spoke loudly: "*Lean ort, tá mé anseo! Tá me anseo!*"

And *she* crawled from the waters as if the waters were almost lifting her above itself. First, a coil of long, dark hair, and black robes, dripping with the sea, algae and fishbones. She was bent over, crawling onto the rocks with a weave basket slung over her shoulder.

Doran stepped back in fright, not trusting this creature. He knew what he'd seen in his visions, but he knew that the Cailleach could not be fully trusted. She extended her long, twisted fingers, and Doran was beside himself with horror. Some legends say that if you kissed the Cailleach, you would instantly die at the touch. She commanded respect.

Of course, she did, Doran told himself. He reached for her bony hand, his own shaking as he touched it, and felt the cold depths of her being. Doran lightly kissed it, making the moment as brief as possible.

The Cailleach grinned broadly, a smile impossibly big for her small head. She reached into the hooded basket she had slung over her shoulder and held it out to him.

She spoke in the ancient Irish tongue: "*Roimh an maidin. Roimh an... maidin.*"

Doran held the basket to his chest and bowed as the Cailleach returned to the sea waters. Once she was gone, he could feel the hosts watching. He looked up at the cliffs and saw Sionnach Silín. She was watching him amongst the rocks with the others with her silver eyes but disappeared behind them.

Doran nodded and started up the rocks, holding the basket tight. He could feel the creatures leaving. They had all seen what they came to see and returned to their own matters. Doran started to feel as if he worried for nothing and that all would go according to his vision.

He smiled. According to the Cailleach, Nicholas Netterville and his wife, a Fitzgerald, would begin a dynasty that would lead to the birth of the Viscount Netterville, who would become close friends with James I, the King of England. Many good things would come from this union, and all because of—

Doran stopped, hearing the clattering of smaller rocks above bounce off each other. One rolled down to his feet. He looked around, his pulse thumping away in his neck, and wondered if one of the creatures dared move close to see Cailleach's *pacáiste*.

"I am Doran, son of Deoradhán, guardian of Netterville. Who goes there? I command you to speak!" he shouted. Maybe he could scare the person or creature off.

Only no one answered him.

Doran continued on, trying to watch all around for any surprises. Eventually, he made it to the top of the cliffs and saw the castle. He made his way, noticing the storm had quit, and now the land was filling with a thick fog. Doran tried hurrying, thinking that he heard things moving behind him. He tried to think of any spells that may help me in this situation, thinking of only one.

Doran whispered: "*Cuir an ceo ag imeacht.*"

Once uttered, Doran swept his hand before him, and the fog acted as if he had taken an impossible breath and blew it back several feet. He watched the fog rush away from him and the Spring Squill at his feet, and in so doing, uncovering the horned redhead, Cherry Fox. She was standing there with her staff, her skirt blowing in the wind. Her red hair drenched with the rain.

"Sionnach Silín," he said. "I have heard of you. I am no danger to you."

Cherry Fox smiled. Her tongue traced her lips and her silver eyes fell on the basket.

"*Tá tú i mbaol,*" she said, "*agus níl a fhios agat é.*" You are a danger, even if you don't know it.

Doran held out his hand in defense. He was trying to keep his breath steady, but his nerves were all shook up. Part of him felt as though fate would save him from her, and another part expected this to be his mortal end. Doran knew how dangerous her kind was, and one's fate was always mysterious.

Doran was not ready to die, though. He thought of Nicholas. He had been there for that boy since he was very young. Doran was like a father to him. What would the boy do without him in a world this dangerous?

Somehow, he had to finish this.

"*Geasa fola...*," Doran said, incanting yet another spell, hoping that he would be quick enough.

Cherry Fox could see the blood spell coming and had already moved. He couldn't believe how fast she was, but before the blood spell could even manifest, she had closed the distance, unsheathed a knife, and buried it cruelly into his heart.

Doran stumbled back and fell to his knees, the knife still sticking out from his chest. His heart exploded with agony and his body seized. Cherry Fox removed the knife and re-sheathed it on her belt. And she wrenched the basket from his gasp.

As darkness descended upon him, as he laid in the purple Spring Squill bed, Cherry Fox began removing the contents of the basket, and he wasn't able to do anything about it.

Deirdre remembered being the horned Cherry Fox, shoving the blade of the dagger into Doran Dunn's heart before he managed to spit out the whole of his incantation in the fog near King Netterville's castle. Whatever he was planning to do, he stopped, and his eyes began to bulge as the agony of his death began.

Cherry Fox watched his life slip from his eyes as she took the basket he was carrying, opening it and finding the caul-like siofra inside. It was gelatinous and wet, and it jumped upon her face.

Cherry Fox screamed to get it off, feeling it trying to meld with her flesh, trying to become a part of her. She felt her powers dying as the gelatinous thing broke up and mixed with her blood, but she closed her eyes, dipped into the Hollow, and found the siofra inside her, and started forcing it out.

Once she had the gelatinous creature in her hands, she dropped it onto Doran Dunn's body, and it began melding with him. She came out of the Hollow, trying to catch her breath and watched the siofra disappear into Dunn's dead flesh.

Still hurting, Cherry Fox staggered through the woods to the standing stones. They were laid out in three circles, one inside the other, with the largest dead center. The central stone stood for the Dagda. She supplicated him with tears. The pain inside her was unforgiving. The Dagda did not come. By the time she woke, Netterville's men were there, standing over her, drawing swords and spears.

"You heinous devil!" the warrior spat. "You will pay today for your crime! And let your death be known to all others of your kin."

The man swung at Cherry Fox with his sword and her heart felt as though it exploded in her chest at the same time, combusting like black powder out of its barrel.

She screamed, sweating, and withdrew from Dunn's psychic doorway, finding herself in the Spring Squill. Dunn was at a desk as if he had moved his study to the flower bed, though Deirdre knew this was another psychic trick.

Only Doran looked up from his work, raising his pen from the book he was writing in, and looked around.

He sensed her!

When he did, everything began getting dark, except the two of them and the desk.

Felim went to bed around nine, leaving the mansion quiet for the last few hours. Doran Dunn found himself in his study, thinking about how the Fomorian King's voice had almost given him an aneurism. Thinking about the vampyre sisters and how Ri Elieris promised that his trap would work, Doran tried working on all the paperwork for the bank that was left on his desk.

Doran needed the Fomorians to be successful. If he could get the *homunculus alteration* to work correctly, he would be able to sacrifice Cherry Fox's body into pure *croí*—Primordial energy that could reweave the fabric of the universe and reconstruct Doran Dunn into a god. With the *homunculus alteration*, he could make himself pliable to his magic that would allow him to control how the croí recreated his new form.

And once he had his new strength, he would face the Cailleach and have his curse removed.

Freedom, he thought. *I'd have all my freedom back!*

He was certain it would work. But if he lost Deirdre, it was all for nothing. He hated being so far away, relying on Myrna and the fomori. He preferred to be in the thick of it, but he knew that Maggie—the Maris Demidian—was dangerous. Deirdre, having learned who she was, would not be happy with him.

No, being in the thick of it would only put him in a perilous predicament that he didn't want to be in. Even if he lost Deirdre—Cherry Fox's soul—he would be alive to think of other ways to escape his curse.

No, it was safer right here in his office.

Except, Doran looked up from his paperwork because the air in the room shifted. It became warmer and started smelling like the sea. The wood in the walls groaned as the weight in the room shifted.

Yes, there was a presence here.

"Who is there?" he demanded.

A vague blue illuminance appeared in the center of his study. It was partially transparent and formed in the shape of a woman. After examining it for a moment, he saw that it was Deirdre. She was projecting herself through the Hollow to find him.

"Deirdre! I see you have learned some tricks!"

"I'm not just 'Deirdre,' am I Doran Dunn? I am Cherry Fox."

She did know. He figured as much.

"Sionnach Silín," Doran said. "The once-child of the Seven Virgin Springs. Aye. That's right."

Deirdre smiled. "Yes. I know what you've done. You have used the siofra and bound me to it so that I would slip out of the Cycle that I was bound to by the Morrigan."

Deirdre looked around the room.

"All I see is darkness around you," Deirdre said. "Are you using magic to hide yourself?"

Doran grinned at her. "I'm no fool, Deirdre."

Deirdre's luminant form came at him, stopping before his face. Both of their noses almost touching. It surprised him and he found himself falling back over his chair onto the floor. She hovered down toward him.

"I was not truly reborn, was I?" Deirdre said. "You trapped me in this body the siofra made for us. I'm still dead in a way... living inside the siofra."

"Exactly. The siofra is a sponge. It adapted first to Maggie so that you would appear like her. It allowed you to take her life. But as you spent time in the siofra, it adapted to your soul as well. As a siofra, you are something new now. It's in you, reformed. And you belong to me," Doran said.

"Reformed? So, I can direct it to leave me."

Doran shrugged. "Perhaps. But you wouldn't live long in this life without it. You have a symbiosis with it."

"But can it live without me?"

Doran laughed. "Of course. The siofra always awaits its next birth. It's hungry for birth, you see. That's the wonderful horror of it all. Aye?"

Doran started to slowly rise as Deirdre's astral projection backed away from him, floating over his desk to hover by the door.

"You're a right fecker, Dunn. Consider our relationship over."

Dunn attempted another smile to show her that he wasn't scared, wanting to hide the reality of it from her. "We'll see."

With that, Deirdre seemed to evaporate before him, leaving him alone once again. At the last moment, he noticed that she was wearing the fetish of the Cailleach, the totem ealaín.

That's why she was able to get this close to him through the Hollow.

Did she see where he was? Hopefully the veiling magic didn't allow her to see that he never left Dublin. They would be looking for him. Wanting to capture him.

And they'd fall into his trap.

It would work out, he told himself. It had to.

Not wanting to think about what she'd done, Deirdre got up and slipped out of the room, and went down the hall to the room where Ambrus and Cuán slept. Ambrus was peacefully out, looking handsome even with his disheveled hair and light snore. A part of her would like to stay with him, and yet she knew very well that he had a different path. He needed to find his lover, Annabelle, and go wherever that led him. It was her place to let him go and follow her own path, whatever that was after all this was over.

If it ever ended.

Don't think about it. *Be with him while you can.*

She crawled into bed with him, shifted under the covers, and put his sex into her mouth. His arousal was almost immediate as he started to wake.

Deirdre crawled up to meet his sleepy eyes.

"Deirdre?"

Deirdre kissed him deeply and pulled him out of bed, holding his organ firmly, dragging him through the hallway and into her room. She threw him down on the bed and climbed onto him. Ambrus was pleasantly surprised, and it was written all over his smiling face. Once he was inside her, she quietly took them both to a pleasurable climax. In each other's arms afterward, she told him that she found Dunn in the Hollow and she remembered what had happened. Stopping Dunn from exchanging the siofra for Netterville's son so many centuries ago.

"After I was able to get the siofra out of me, I let it merge with Dunn before I tried escaping to the Stones of the Dagda. If I had only killed the siofra, we wouldn't be here today."

"But the siofra belonged to the Cailleach?"

Deirdre nodded. "It would have made one of the strongest gods mark me for an eternity."

"I wish there was something I could really do for you to end all this," Ambrus said.

It warmed her to hear him say that. He was a sweet man.

"You can help me find the part of myself where my power hides. I need to help Cuán, Maggie and Róis. They wouldn't be in this mess either, if it weren't for me," she said. "Can you do that for me?"

Ambrus sighed. "I don't know. But we will try in the morning. What will you do after Cuán and Maggie are safe?"

Deirdre remembered her dream of moving to London, rebuilding her fevered life that she had in Dublin until Doran Dunn's plan was revealed. Now she wasn't so sure. That was Deirdre's old dream. Now she was Cherry Fox.

And Cherry Fox was going to appeal herself to the gods. They would lead her to this life's fate, whatever it was. She was sure of it.

She shrugged and kissed him on the cheek, beside the mouth.

"By the way, I have been thinking about this fog. I may not know how it was conjured, but I might know what it is," Ambrus said.

"Oh?"

"Many call it the Devil's Breath. Several medieval texts I've read refer to it as Ostium. And if it is Ostium, these creatures have been possibly tainted by the Commination."

"What does that mean?"

"It means that they have bound themselves to an evil that existed before man was even dreamed," Ambrus said. "That's all I know about it. But... *still*—it's enough for me to understand what is happening here. Think of the Ostium as a reaction to two worlds colliding. If you stick a red-hot poker into a bucket of water, the water boils and steams. Imagine the hot poker is one world and the bucket of water is the other. The Ostium is the result. It is a doorway. And if it's a doorway—"

Deirdre grinned. "...We can close it."

Ambrus smiled at her. "Exactly. Or... theoretically. I'm not absolutely sure how yet. I mean, something like this would need energy. A font of energy. There's a source that feeds it."

"Essence," Deirdre thought aloud.

"Energy. Essence. Yes. Some vital force."

Deirdre gave him another kiss on the forehead. "You better return to your room. I wouldn't want the lady of the house thinking we were breaking her rules."

Ambrus pulled the blankets across the bed, covering Deirdre up as he got out and got to his feet.

"I'll see you in the morning. Perhaps after breakfast, we can attempt another session... of hypnosis," he said.

Deirdre nodded, grinning wide. "Good night, Ambrus."

Once he left her, Deirdre was finally tired enough, and sleep came gently.

IV.

February 1st—Imbolc

After breakfast the next morning, Cuán went with Maggie to ask if it was okay for them to use the Hearn library in private. Eireen allowed it on the condition that they didn't ruin anything in the room. They thanked her, and the five of them gathered in the library, closing the doors so that they would not be interrupted.

Ambrus told them all about the Ostium—the Devil's Breath—and how he thought that he and Deirdre would try hypnotism again. Maybe they could unlock her past identity and her past identity could tap into something they could use against Doran Dunn.

Maggie told everyone what Eireen and Nola mentioned the night before. About Eamon and the Devil. The vampyric sisters. Muirgen. Though Cuán realized she didn't tell them who Muirgen was to her. She only mentioned that Muirgen owed fealty to Ri Elieris, the King of the Fomorians.

"If Cuán goes with me, I'd like to go to the shoreline and check out the rocks," Maggie said. "Those wails... I want to see if we can find evidence of what is making those noises. It's better to go by day."

"But why?" Róis said. "What do they have to do with Doran?"

Maggie shrugged. "If Doran did come 'ere to summon the fomori, and if Muirgen is truly 'ere too, Doran Dunn will be with them or somewhere nearby. It's all connected."

Everyone agreed, so Cuán and Maggie left the library and stepped out of the manor house. Behind them, Cuán noticed that Róis was following shortly behind.

"Róis?"

Róis smiled at him but took Maggie's hand. "One moment, Cuán. I need to speak with Maggie."

Cuán nodded and let them step off together. Róis was whispering in Maggie's ear, and Maggie nodded and smiled at Róis. She reached into her handbag and gave some coins to Róis. It looked like Róis thanked her and waved at Cuán before rushing off down the hill through town.

Maggie joined him.

"I don't want to know?"

Maggie smiled at him, taking his arm and patting his pec. "Female matters, Cuán."

Cuán shrugged and thought about everything that they've heard since getting to this village. "I have been thinking."

He almost expected a wisecrack here, but Maggie said nothing.

"What if Declan didn't lie," Cuán said. "What if this is a trap?"

Maggie looked curiously at him. "Oh, it's a trap. Doran Dunn is 'ere."

"I find it strange that up until now, Doran has had thugs trying to catch us, but hasn't done any of it in person. Don't yeh find that weird?"

"He's a coward, Cuán. Plain and simple, really."

"But what if he didn't call the Fomorians?"

Maggie looked confused, so Cuán sighed and added: "What if this is a trap? Maybe he didn't have to summon the Fomorians here. Perhaps the Fomorians are already here, and the creatures that brought all this fog are here because of the Fomorians? Maggie... We should leave and get as far away from here as possible."

Maggie looked down, frowning. After they let this sit in silence for a while, Maggie said, "I thought about that. Muirgen, after all, is one of Elieris' mercenaries. These people are in danger, Cuán. If what you're thinkin' pans out to be true, I don't think escapin' would be that easy. I think we need to see this through. Even if this... kills me... I think we need to stay and stop all of it. It's the only way anyone 'ere will be safe. It's the only way *we'll* be safe."

Cuán looked at her, feeling pressure in his eyes. He thought he'd lose a tear. Maggie saw his face and stopped, turning in front of him.

"Nothing will happen to you or the others. I won't allow it," Maggie said. "I will die fer you."

Cuán wiped his eyes. "That's what I'm afraid of, Maggie. I don't want to lose yeh. I'm standing here right now for you. I won't endure anything happening to you."

"Then let's do this smart, a'right? Let's figure this out, find the advantage, and thump 'em all straight to hell. Take their heads as trophies."

Cuán nodded. He still wasn't sure, but he wasn't going to leave Maggie alone. Not ever again.

Ambrus closed the curtains as Deirdre laid back on the couch with a floral threaded pillow under her head. He lit a single lamp and put it on the end table so that when he started letting his necklace pendulum back and forth, it reflected light into Deirdre's eyes. He soothed her, told her to relax as deeply as she could and to clear her mind. He counted back from thirty.

"Five...

"Four...

"Three...

"Two...

"One."

Deirdre found herself in darkness.

"Can you hear my voice, Deirdre?"

"Yes."

"I want you to find a memory where you felt as though you were in danger. Sometime in your past where you looked inside yourself for your power, drew it out, and used it to remove the danger."

"I... I was Cherry Fox—*Sionnach Silín*," she said.

The darkness around her began to fade into blurry light and colors. The blurriness became sharper, forming a forest around her. She sought through this forest, looking for herself.

She already knew where she was. She could feel it.

At first, she was outside herself, of course. She had to connect, *bond*, be her *old* self again.

Her fae being was bathing in a small waterfall near the rocks somewhere in the Harz Mountains in Germania.

Cherry Fox was bare-skinned, her Irish-dark red hair clinging to her pale flesh, her three-point horns glistening wet. While Cherry Fox felt that Deirdre was pretty enough, she was almost taken aback by this luminous form. She had forgotten—or perhaps never understood—the charismatic power of her own divine nature.

Cherry Fox was far from Ireland, traveling toward the Brocken, following the vibrations of the ley lines and how the sprites reacted in the Hollow. They had been disturbed as something powerful had broken through the barrier between the Quick and the Dead.

When was this? She tried to think and could only remember it was sometime in the fourteenth century.

Deirdre slipped into Cherry Fox, and it all came racing back.

She was washing herself, trying to get the human blood off her skin. There had been a couple of monks who had jumped her with their daggers. They tried to hold her down and cut her throat, but she was too strong for them. Cherry Fox had broken one's neck, took his dagger, and planted it in the skull of the other. He spurted blood, and it was running down her body when she climbed into the water.

Once cleaned, she stepped out and crouched at the water's edge to wash the blood from her clothes.

She was looking for a man named Thorsten De Vaulx. The last she had heard of him was that he was with the sorcerers of Geistencross—some sanctuary for those who were gathering the magical arts, fighting the *Immaculate War* between the Old Ways and Christianization. Later she would learn that this would lead to the Commination, but at this point in time, she had no idea where this underground war would lead. As

Cherry Fox, she was deeply concerned about it, knowing that her people were in danger. She was hoping that he would know more about the Ostium and the nightmares she had been having over the last few years.

It was getting dark, so she hung her clothes up to dry on tree branches and started a fire. Naked, she sat beside the fire and warmed herself. These mountains were getting cold. Far colder than the natural climes she was used to in Ireland.

Not too far away from her laid her blackthorn cudgel-staff, what they called a *shillelagh*. It had runes and ogham written upon it, as well as other archaic and arcane symbols. She called it her Bod Mór. It was her protector and weapon in battle.

While thinking of the distance she still had to travel through the mountains, her mind switched to the scent in the air. A large, male canine was approaching her. Strangely, it had the scent of a human on it as well.

Once Cherry Fox reached for Bod Mór, she heard the creature growling behind the bushes. She snatched Bod Mór quickly and rose in time for the large, red wolf to enter the clearing, growling at her with all its sharp teeth bared.

It definitely wasn't a normal wolf. Far more of its teeth were pointed and the front side was far more muscular. Its front legs had human-like hands with long, black claws.

It was a werewolf.

Cherry Fox had never fought a werewolf before. The thing was fast. It leapt at her, and its teeth sunk into her arm as she tried to hit it with Bod Mór. She could feel its teeth grazing the bones in her arms as blood started pouring down to her hand in rivulets. It was standing on its hind legs now, and its clawed hand grabbed her hair, pulling her head back, exposing her neck.

Frightened, she realized that when it let go of her arm, it was going to sink its teeth into her throat. Its other hand grabbed hers—her fingers clamped tight around Bod Mór.

"No!" she cried, feeling its jaw let go of her arm.

Cherry Fox brought up her right leg and kicked into its furry chest, but the monster was too strong. It held her fast, snapping at her throat, missing. She could feel its hot breath and its saliva splattered across her neck and face. The creature began to open its jaws again and she felt her arm weakening, so she had only one chance left. With all her might, she kicked again. This time, she aimed lower and felt its male organ get crushed in the ball of her foot.

The werewolf whined out and let her go. Cherry Fox, rage overcoming her, reached inside herself and found her divine power. She took some of it and put it all into her swing. Before the werewolf could recover from her kick, she was smashing through its skull with the Bod Mór. Blood and brain splattered out, and its hulking hirsute body fell to the ground in front of her.

Trying to catch her breath, she went to her clothes and her supply bag. As fast as she could, she dug through other items until she found the silver dagger and withdrew it. She went back to the body of the creature, and she stabbed it multiple times through the chest where she thought its heart might be. She stabbed and stabbed, sobbing and shouting out all the anger and terror that she felt because of the creature.

Unable to move anymore, she went back to the water.

This pool was getting a lot of blood today.

She warmed herself by the fire, letting the body of the werewolf lay where it fell. It was slowly transitioning back to human form. She would never know who it was. The head was crushed beyond recognition. And, of course, he had no clothes. No belongings.

Once she was dry, she stoked the fire again and wrapped herself in a fur blanket.

"I put on my glamour, and I went to sleep," Deirdre said.

Do you know the place where you found this divine nature?
"Yes."
Can you still feel the place where this divine nature resides?

She thought about it. "I do, but it's been locked away. I need the key to open it."
And what is the key?
"Bod Mór," she said.

"What's this?" Cuán said.

Cuán was overlooking what he could see of the cliffs and the ocean, wishing the fog would let him see the whole damn thing. It so reminded him of home, and he started to yearn for Mam, Da, and his old wolfhound, Ponc. Of course, he thought about Maggie and how she loved to gaze out to sea every morning, and how he thought every day that she would leave him. For a long time, he resisted letting their relationship get to another level, and she again proved how much more courageous she was than him, making sexual contact with him, and showing him a deeper intimacy. Was he still frightened of her leaving him? He was. But maybe not as much anymore.

He should marry her, take his chances. Shouldn't he know what to do?

He looked over to see Maggie squatting, looking down at her feet, her hand disappearing into the ground there. She was adamant that if they found this nest of vampyres, they'd find Doran Dunn so they could put him down once and for all. While he didn't agree on stopping Deirdre, he did see how Doran Dunn was far too dangerous to remain alive. If they were all going to be safe, it was the only way.

As he walked up to her, he realized that she was feeling around a dark cavernous hole about four feet in diameter.

"Jaysus," Cuán said, noticing the stained blood on the rocks around its rim.

"Nola mentioned a Feast Pit," Maggie said. "Do you think this might be what she's talking about?"

"For God's sake, why wouldn't they have this marked?" Cuán said, squatting on the other side of the pit. "People could fall right in."

The hole was dark, but when Cuán leaned his head in, he could hear the sounds of the waves crashing against the rocks far below. It was deep.

"I think the pit goes all the way down to a sea cave. It sounds like water comes in," Cuán said.

Maggie leaned her head in and they both listened.

"I think this is where Muirgen and her sisters come."

"They probably sleep at the bottom."

"So, how do we get down to them?"

Cuán thought about it. "I don't know how far it goes down. We could use rope, but that's feckin' risky. But, hey, if we hear the waters crashing in from here, maybe there's a cave entrance at the shoreline?"

Maggie nodded and reached out for his hand. "Question is: is it fully under the water?"

Cuán shrugged. He saw that her hand was shaking and decided not to say anything.

"Then let's go."

They ran hand in hand to the side of the cliff and looked down. The problem was readily apparent—there was no shoreline. It was a straight drop to the rocks and violent water below. There was a dark recess at the base of the cliff, which could be the cave entrance. They couldn't see it very well from this angle.

Maggie squeezed his hand. "I have the strength to do this, ye know. I could jump and make it."

Cuán was horrified by that idea. "Oh, no, no. Look at those rocks. You'd dash into bloody bits. And if yeh did make it, you're not doing this alone. Maybe we should go back and get the others."

Maggie shook her head. "Deirdre and Ambrus are working on closin' the gate. If Deirdre is as powerful as we think, and she can access it, she and Ambrus should be able to take care of things. This is *my* job, Cuán. This is me part. I destroy the vampyres, and I find Dunn."

Cuán sighed. "This is *our* part, Maggie. Our part. Let's go to town and see if someone will rent us a small boat. If I can get us close enough to the cave entrance, we can both go in together."

Maggie nodded. "Okay. Together."

Cuán nodded as well. "Right. Together."

Cuán took one more look around, making sure he had his bearings. He still didn't like doing this without the others, but he knew he wouldn't be able to stop Maggie. She was not only fighting to free herself of the fomori, but she was trying to save everyone's life. He got it. He wished that they had more time to prepare for the worse.

Because, Cuán thought, *whatever was down in that Feast Pit, it was going to be terrible.*

When he turned around, Maggie started screaming.

He only made out some details: the night-dark hair, the marble-white skin, and the bloody orb eyes. It was reaching for him, wrapped its arms around his legs, and he fell back onto the ground with her. Before he could reach down, the female creature was dragging him over the ground and down into the dark Feast Pit.

He saw Maggie looking back down the pit after them, and he screamed, realizing he was falling with the creature down into the darkness. He briefly saw Maggie at the pit entrance, but she disappeared above him as the strong, crushing arms of the creature seemed to climb him, holding him fast as they fell.

They were engulfed in what felt like black, liquid ice. Briefly, he saw the faint, beautiful face of the monster. She opened her sharp-toothed mouth and put it on his, sticking her tacky tongue into his throat. He tried pulling away, but his strength failed him. He could barely move as her arms remained firmly around him.

The creature's tongue was another thing. Somehow it felt viscid, and it was long and stringy. It spread in his mouth, some of it pushing into his trachea. A warmth suddenly washed through him, but he couldn't understand why.

Was she injecting him with venom?

V.

Myrna was reading in her room, waiting for Eamon to change his mind, when someone knocked on her door. When she answered it, she was surprised to see Tavish standing there with a big grin on his face.

"I went to the shop as you asked, and I purchased a bottle of brandy," Tavish said. "And while I was there, I noticed a young woman who was purchasing strips of cloth."

"Yes?"

"When she left the shop, I followed her until I was sure I wasn't seen, and I hit her over the head and carried her back here," Tavish said.

"Who?"

"That girl from the brothel. Um," he snapped his fingers a couple of times, "...Róis. Is that right?"

Myrna grinned. "Really? You brought a present for me? You shouldn't have!"

Tavish laughed.

"Anraí is watching her now," Tavish said. "Would you like me to bring her to you?"

"Yes, please. And perhaps one of those tarred pallin canvases the fisherman use, will you?"

"Yes ma'am."

Maggie almost jumped after Cuan. Crying and unsure of what to do, she thought about lowering herself along the edges. Maybe she could get a good grip, but when she started to try, she realized how slippery the surface was. If she attempted it, she would slip and fall.

Her hands were shaking, and her heart made her blood roar in her ears. What was she going to do? She couldn't leave Cuán in such danger.

He could be dead already.

No. Please.

Would they kill him outright? Would they do that so quickly? If he survived the fall?

Maggie tried to think, but it wasn't working. The urge to jump in and deal with whatever came kept growing and growing in her. She paced and stopped.

No. You can't leave Cuán here to die. If you don't do something now, the longer you wait, the more chances you have of losing him.

Truth, Maggie.

Do it now.

"Yes."

Maggie went to the edge of the Feast Pit and was about to jump feet first—

Except she saw the pale creatures with the long black hair rising from the darkness of the pit. They scurried, rising until they were bleeding over its rim. Maggie backed up, seeing that there were three of them. All naked, pale flesh. Long black hair, blowing in the wind. Most of them had milky-white or black eyes, and bared long fangs in their open mouths.

Ghouls. Vampyres. Whatever you wanted to call them.

The tallest and lankiest of these women stepped forward, her mouth covered in blood. There was a dagger sheathed in her left breast. Maggie had only seen her in astral projection a long time ago, deep in the Deep Dens, but here she was in the flesh. And Maggie had to force herself not to tremble in front of her.

"Seagrass Maggie," Muirgen hissed. Her voice was slippery and wet. "*You finally have a name… and you have come.*"

"Give him back!" Maggie cried, warm tears running down her face. "I'll destroy all of you."

Muirgen laughed.

"*We will keep him, but you can join him, eh? Aye. We would feed on you, and we will watch you die in our arms. You will be a sacrifice to the Fomorian King.*"

Maggie wasn't sure how strong these creatures were, but did she dare test them? How would dying serve to keep Cuán alive?

"I want him back!"

Muirgen laughed and reached out for her. Maggie instinctively turned and ran. She heard the sisters wailing behind her, but she ignored them. She needed to be smart, she told herself. If they killed her now, it would ruin everything. And she had to admit, she was afraid of them.

"*I remember you, Seagrass Maggie! Oh, I... remember!*"

What could be down in that pit? The brine vampyres? Was Elieris himself down in that pit, waiting for her too?

Tonight, they'd come for her. Maggie was sure of this. Though it was sometimes difficult, she could recall her promise to Muirgen and how Maggie herself murdered Muirgen's daughter to protect another child. Muirgen had a hatred for her that Maggie didn't think she could ever understand.

What was she going to do?

Deirdre woke up on the couch and found that Nola, their host's daughter, was looking down upon her. Ambrus was nowhere to be seen.

"Are you the Seagrass Girl?" Nola said.

"No. I am Sionnach Silín," she said. Deirdre reached up and put a hand to the girl's forehead. Nola's eyes rolled back into her head, and she fainted. Deirdre acted in time to lift her up in her arms and took her up to bed.

On her way, Ambrus was coming out of his room, messing with the buttons at his cuffs. She was glad to see him, and they had to catch up.

"Deirdre?"

He followed her into Nola's room as she lay the girl down.

"What happened?"

"When I woke up, I saw her sickness for what it is. The vampyres have been draining her vitality. I gave her some of mine.

That should break the link between her and the vampyres—until, that is, they come for her again," Deirdre said.

"You mean you gave her some of your *fata*?"

He wasn't sure what that meant. She always had *fata*; it was part of her soul. But as a leagan, reincarnated into a new life, her ability to unlock her connection to her fata so that she could affect the Eeries (*Eagla*, in the old tongue), she needed that key. The Bod Mór. In the past, she would begin to dream about the Bod Mór around puberty, learning of it, and she would have one crafted for her. Once she possessed the completed cudgel-staff, her consciousness would be able to draw upon her fata. She'd have her powers.

Deirdre didn't want to answer him. It would take too long to explain it to him right now. What was important was that they stopped Doran Dunn and the Fomorians, wherever they were. Once Cuán and the others were safe, she could return to the Tuatha Dé. Where she truly belonged.

"We need to go now," she said.

Ambrus stepped in front of her and put his hands on her shoulders. Looking into her eyes, he said, "So, what about this Bod Mór? We have no idea where it could be. It could be on the other side of this island."

Deirdre kissed him on the bottom lip and said, "The Bod Mór is always within me. When I go through my lives, I must retrieve the Bod Mór this way. I need to find a craftsman."

"I don't want to worry the Hearns," Ambrus said, escorting Deirdre from the room, shutting Nola's door behind them. "Let's speak with the priest. He may know somebody useful. Besides, I have a few more questions for him as well."

Deirdre nodded. "Let me grab my shawl, and we can be on our way."

VII. Into the Caverns

I.

Eireen, Nola and Nola's grandmother were the only people in the Hearn manor house. Nola was resting in her bed and Eireen was getting ready for lunch. The grandmother was knitting in her rocker in the parlor.

"You didn't see them leave?"

Eireen nodded. "They slipped out without notifying me."

Maggie sighed, trying to calm herself from all the panic gathering in her chest. She needed Deirdre and Ambrus. They had to help her. Where could they have gone?

"There aren't many places to go around here," Eireen offered. "There is the shop, the bay, and the church. If you try them, they will be sure to be at one of them."

Maggie nodded. "Good point. Thank you, Eireen."

Maggie headed back out, but as she went down the steps to the path toward the gate, she looked up and saw two familiar goons heading up the road. They locked eyes with her and started running for her. She saw the bigger guy pull a gun out of his slacks.

No, not now—

Maggie turned and ran again, only the slight slope made her slip and fall forward into the mud. Hands and knees caked with mire, she started picking herself up, and the gun rang off. For a moment, she thought she'd been shot and couldn't feel it yet.

"Stop, or we'll make the next one count!" one of the goons cried.

Maggie looked back and became conscious that they didn't have far to shoot. If she tried to run, they'd surely be able to hit her in the back. Perhaps the back of the head.

Maggie hoped Eireen heard the gunshot, looking up at the house. She did see Eireen looking out the window, but the woman didn't move to come out. She must be afraid for her life.

Maggie looked back at the goons who were now standing in front of her. Tavish poked the gun into her shoulder, and she groaned in pain.

"Feck off me, arsehole," Maggie seethed between clenched teeth. "I have to save him! I can't deal with this right now!"

"You have no one loyal to you here," the thinner goon said. He was staggering to keep up with the bigger guy. "You might as well come with us easily. The other way is much harder and much more painful."

Maggie wondered if Eireen had told them about her and her friends. It didn't matter, though. Her real concern was with Cuán. How was she going to get to him now?

God, if she survived this, she was going to take Doran's head as a trophy.

"Don't try anything," the bigger goon said. "None of that magic-shite either. I'll blow your brains out if I think you make the slightest wrong move. Don't think I forgot you throwing that gun at me bollocks."

Maggie sighed and raised her arms, but the bigger guy slapped her hands down.

"We don't need a display," he said. "Think of it this way. If you don't come with us, and you actually try to escape, we'll put a bullet in the other girl's head as well."

"Róis," the thinner guy said, chuckling.

"Yeah, that Róis bitch. We'll put her brains all over the floor while I hold her down with me boot on her back."

Róis? Good God, they must have grabbed her when she went out for some cloth. Everything was falling to shite. Where the hell was Deirdre and Ambrus when she needed them?

On the other hand, if Doran was here, then maybe Muirgen took Cuán to him, or otherwise had a way of communicating with the vampyres, so she could get Cuán back. They would take her straight to Dunn. Maybe she should make this easy for them.

"A'right," Maggie said. "I won't do anythin'. You've got my word."

They all walked together toward the cliffs near the bay, not too far from where Maggie remembered seeing the Feast Pit. There was a mansion here, bigger than the Hearn manor house, and it was fenced in. They took her through the front gate, where she spied a young blond looking out her window as they brought her in. Not Róis. Someone else.

They pushed her through the door. One closed it while the bigger one said, "I'll take her up to Myrna. You watch for Eamon."

"Tavish," the thinner one said, "don't take your eyes off her at any cost. She's dangerous."

"No shite. I'm the one who still can't feel is left bollock."

Maggie couldn't wait any longer for answers.

"You know when I see Dunn, I'm going to bite his face off," Maggie said.

Tavish laughed. "Dunn wouldn't waste his time being here. He's got more important matters. No, he sent us to make sure you're out of the way and Deirdre is returned all nice like."

"Us? It's just the two of you?"

Tavish didn't answer her.

Inside and in privacy, the big guy used the gun more confidently. He pushed it into her back and told her to climb the stairs. At the top, he gestured with the gun which way to go.

Not that she didn't know. She heard Róis crying and screaming out as loud as she could.

"What the fuck are you doin' to her?" Maggie said. The thought Dunn wasn't even there evaporated in her mind as the girl's pain echoed down the halls.

Tavish shrugged. He pushed open the doors to a room, and he grabbed Maggie by the hair.

"Ouch! You unrigged lobcock!" she said.

He pushed her into the room, which smelled of bergamot and rich blood.

They had some canvas splayed out over the bed. Róis was stripped naked and tied in a naked X, face-first into the bed. Her face was red and buried into the mattress as she screamed. Sitting on the edge of the bed, Myrna was forcing a big brown wood object up Róis's backside. It was bloody, and when she shoved it in, Róis cried out again.

"What the fuck?" Maggie said. "Stop hurting her!"

Myrna looked up at her, grinning, and withdrew the large wooden dildo. It was slick with blood and other bodily juices.

"Oh, Maggie! Wonderful! You're going to be next! Mister Pungere doesn't ever get tired!"

Disgusting woman.

"I'd rather a bullet in me head," Maggie said.

That's when she felt the cold metal of the gun tap her on the back of the head. Maggie tried not to think about it, but it terrified her, the bullet that could blot out her life just inches behind her.

"That can be arranged," Tavish said.

Myrna got up as Róis turned her red, wet face to look pleadingly at Maggie.

"I've always found it so easy to hate," Myrna said. "I hate so hard that all this rage bubbles up and explodes."

Myrna turned around and hit Róis on the back of the head with the dildo. It sent a loud crack through the room. Róis's mouth and eyes opened wide.

"No!" Maggie shouted. "Stop!"

Myrna looked at her for one minute and started beating Róis's head into a bloody pulp. "FUCK YOU, MAGGIE! FUCK ALL YOU! I. WILL. NOT. HAVE. YOU. TAKE. MINE!"

That crazy bitch!

Maggie hurried to Róis, but Tavish grabbed her hair and pulled her back, forcing her to watch as Myrna bludgeoned Róis's scalp again and again. It was bloody, and her head started looking wrong as her body jerked and twitched.

Maggie felt her knees weaken.

How could she?

She fell to the ground onto her knees and searched for the strength inside her again. Maggie closed her eyes, looked for whatever energies dwelled inside her, and saw Cuán in her mind. He was surrounded in white light, glowing. It was the Primordial in her, the image having formed from inside her. She let Cuán touch her, and she opened her eyes.

It was like slow motion. Tavish was pointing the gun at her while she twisted around, falling onto her back. Once solid on the floor, she kicked the inside of his leg, throwing him off balance, and reached for his gun. It came out of his hand easily, and at first, she didn't know why. Then she saw it: she had kicked his leg so that a bone fractured, driving right out of his flesh like a wooden spike.

Maggie turned the gun on him and fired. The gun gave off a loud pop, and Tavish's left eye socket went black as the bullet erased his eye.

There was no pain in her chest now. Only numbness, and she focused it outwards, projecting it onto her enemies.

As Tavish fell dead, Maggie turned around with the gun as Myrna began realizing what was happening. She stood up; their eyes trained on each other.

"Filthy *madge*," Maggie seethed and fired again, aiming for Myrna's face. Myrna turned her face away, trying to block the bullet with her hands, but it didn't stop—the bullet took off her fingers. She dropped Mister Pungere onto the floor, to roll away, leaving a trail of blood across the hardwood floor.

Myrna dropped to the floor and Maggie went over to her body. She saw blood pouring out somewhere beneath Myrna's arm, under her left breast. Maggie shot her in the chest two more times and went to Róis.

Róis was lying very still. Maggie tried to listen for a breath, or feel a heartbeat, but she sensed nothing. Róis was dead. Maggie untied her, tearing the rope as if it were taffy.

Maggie couldn't look at the poor girl's bloody head. She knew it was crushed.

Maggie cried, walking out of the room. The lean goon was in the hallway, having heard the commotion, and staggered toward her. He saw her, holding up his hands in defeat. At the other end of the hallway, the blond girl that had been looking out the window at her earlier, stood there, staring at her.

Maggie thought, *I should shoot you too. All of you. Make you pay for her suffering and her death.* Yet, she couldn't bring herself to do it. They both looked so frail and insignificant to her.

Maggie pointed the gun at the hobbling goon. He started to shake, eyes squeezed shut, and teeth clenching. "Do you understand that I am more than I look? I was human, but I have been changed by the serpent's blood. I am dangerous. Do you understand?"

The man nodded, starting to sob. "Aye. This is over. *All* over."

Maggie looked at the girl, who only watched with tears running down her eyes.

Maggie left, tossing the gun aside as she went down the stairs. She carried the numbness with her.

If Dunn wasn't here, there was only one thing she could do.

II.

Father Brian sat on the other side of his desk, looking them over. The church was very old, so he lit the room by opening the window shutters and placing a lamp in the window. Above his desk, over his head, was a large silver cross with the Latin, *Deus Peccata Dimittit.* God Forgives.

Deirdre had never spent much time in churches. Whenever she was within one, it was almost like putting a bad, bitter taste in your mouth... only that bitterness was a vibration that moved through you. Though uncomfortable, she pushed herself to bear it, knowing that they wouldn't be there long.

"Ambrus and I had a few questions, and we wondered if you would humor us?"

Father Brian held up the palm of his hands. "I'm here to help."

Ambrus cleared his throat and leaned forward. "You have noticed this fog. How unnatural it is."

Father Brian sighed and nodded his head. "Yes. It's one of the reasons why I find myself staying."

"Oh?"

"Yes. It's clear that God has condemned this village. I hope to be the guiding light in returning us to God's favor," Father Brian said. "One soul at a time, if I must."

Ambrus looked at Deirdre and she looked back at him. Ambrus turned to the priest and said, "I have heard it called the Devil's Breath. Are you familiar with this term?"

"I'm afraid not, but it does sound rather apropos."

"Indeed."

And here is where Deirdre knew that Ambrus was not telling the whole truth—

"I've heard tales from other priests that the Devil's Breath was the sighing of demons loosed from Hell itself, and that it opens doorways between the Quick and the Dead. Do you stand this to reason?"

Father Brian looked confused, but he nodded.

"So, if this were the Devil's Breath, a summoning of such great infernal power, would not the church be wise to exorcise it from our midst?" Ambrus said. "I mean, many of heard of exorcising demons from people, but there are cases where *places* may be exorcised as well. Am I wrong?"

Father Brian looked at him frankly, and he slowly nodded. "Yes, it would be within the power of the church—But, you understand, I believe this to be the culmination of the sinners in Séala Bán and nothing more. If I work on the sinners—"

"But you see, Father Brian, either way, this is infernal power. This is Satan's doorway. Don't you think that an exorcism may be the first big step into helping these people? If you shut the door, it will be easier for the sinners to find the grace of God, especially through an act of such powerful faith."

Deirdre had to hold herself back from smiling. Ambrus was magnificent.

Father Brian nodded again. "I can see this reasoning."

"The fog came in from the sea," Ambrus said. "I believe if we held the ritual at the cliffs, drove the fog back into the sea, then I believe that a great many people would owe you their lives and their souls. Hell, I think the pope might see this as a saintly act."

Father Brian's eyes widened.

"Well, I'm above the selfish need of recompense," Father Brian said, "but if an exorcism once again turned God's eye back on this village, I wouldn't be able to say no, could I?"

"Indeed, Father," Deirdre said.

Deirdre was sure that Ambrus was right. The fog was unnatural. With her memories as Cherry Fox, she recalled the Tuatha Dé could produce *féth fíada*, something similar to the Devil's Breath, but she was sure that this fog was produced with *vital essence*. *Féth fíada* depended on glamour.

And she didn't smell glamour in the air.

"One more thing, if you don't mind," Ambrus said. "I heard your commissioner is in a bad state. Perhaps even feeding on others."

Speaking of *vital essence*...

Father Brian looked away. "Eamon Macrae is a very important man in this town."

"Man?" Ambrus said. "Or monster?"

Father Brian didn't look up and Deirdre could see that he was terrified. She felt sorry for him as much as the others who've had to deal with this terror now for many years.

"Father Brian. Tell us about him."

Father Brian swallowed hard. "He may be in league with the devil. The light of the sun bothers him. He sees people, but very rarely. I've only talked to him a couple of times over the years myself. I don't think he likes me. His little blond wife—*sometimes*—comes and sees me, confesses her sins. Her nightmares."

"What else?" Deirdre prodded. "How does he get around if nobody sees him?"

Father Brian rolled his eyes and looked up as if he wanted to see the face of God looking back down upon him.

"Some say that he travels in the caverns below us, but it's just a monster story. I think the vampyres do most of the killing. Oh, I don't know. He is a monster. I can feel it. I just don't know how to understand it, do I?"

"Maybe these things aren't for us to understand," Deirdre said.

Deirdre looked at Ambrus, who reached out for her hand. She gave it to him, and he squeezed it. It made her feel safe and she liked it. Cherished the moment.

"Thank you, Father," Ambrus said.

Once they left the priest's office, Deirdre followed Ambrus outside. She wondered about Maggie, Cuán and Róis for a moment, hoping that they were okay. She didn't know what they were doing or where they were, and it bothered her a little.

Maybe she should reach out through the Hollow to see if she could touch Maggie?

"While the Good Father sets up his ritual, we will have one of our own," Ambrus said.

This surprised her.

"So, the exorcism—?"

"Yes, that was a lie as well," Ambrus said. "I mean, it may possibly help. But I'm more interested that someone sees a priest ridding us of the Ostium rather than a lone sorcerer on a shoreline. I need to work invisibly."

Deirdre nodded. "Good point. So, what are we going to do?"

"We're going to kill the font of the Ostium."

"Which is?"

"The arrachtaigh," Ambrus said. "See, when the brine vampyres came here, they needed a living font of vital force. A human body. If they make him the arrachtaigh and make him the font, then they do not have to expend themselves. And as an arrachtaigh, he can protect himself."

"But who do you think is the arrachtaigh?"

Ambrus pointed up at the mansion near the cliffs. "I think it's the commissioner, but we won't be sure unless we confront him."

Deirdre thought about her Bod Mór. If they were going to face some menacing creature, she wanted to be ready for them. Besides, she wasn't fond of dying. No matter how many times she'd done it before now.

"Before we do that, we need my blackthorn," she said.

Ambrus sighed. "Yes."

Deirdre thought about the Cailleach. The witch was mad at her for ruining her plans to incorporate her lifeblood (her *fata es-*

sence) into the Netterville line. She vaguely deliberated whether the Cailleach was behind all of this, forcing her hand to fix things, or if the Goddess Queen of Winter was now fast asleep in some eternal slumber. *Codladh Domhanda Eile*, perhaps.

Once they had the siofra freed, she was sure they'd find out.

"The priest said to talk to Declan, so let's... uh, talk to Declan," Deirdre said.

III.

Myrna awoke, though it was tough to see anything. She could feel the holes in her chest, felt her blood pouring all around her. She was going to shout for Tavish, who was obviously bigger, but she remembered seeing Seagrass Maggie shatter his leg, take his gun and blow his head off.

"Anraí! Anr*aí!*"

There were footsteps. She could sense him hovering above her.

"Oh my God! You're still alive, misses?" Anraí said.

"I need help to see Eamon Macrae. He's lost his chance to make a choice," Myrna said. "Help me up!"

"Aye," Anraí said. She felt his arms wrap around her, and he lifted her up. When he lifted her, she felt the holes in her flare with an agony that she had never experienced before. Eventually, he had her arm around his shoulder and his own arm wrapped around her waist.

She tried to step while he walked with her, but he did most of the work.

The little blond bitch, who they met at the gate when they first got here, was standing there in the hallway, mouth wide open.

"You there! Fetch your master! He must see me before I die," Myrna growled, spraying spittle and blood.

The girl wiped her tearing eyes and nodded. "Aye, missus."

They followed her past Eamon's study.

"Where are we going?"

The girl tried to explain: "Well, he doesn't sleep here. Ever since I moved in, he has always slept in the basement."

"In the basement?"

"Aye. He said no matter how much he blocked out the daylight, it was never enough."

Anraí tried to be careful with her as they took the stairs down to the first floor. The girl escorted them through a few doors beside the kitchen and to a back room, where they found another door. The girl took a key from around her neck and unlocked it.

Myrna's lungs felt cluttered, and she coughed out as hard as she could. She heaved and coughed until blood poured out of her mouth, partially clotted. Once she was done, they continued on through the door, stairs routing them down into the basement.

"Mary had a little lamb, little lamb, little lamb. Mary had a little lamb. Its fleece was white as snow..." Myrna sang and started another coughing fit.

The blonde's nose wrinkled with disgust.

Myrna wanted to spit in her face but concentrated on her singing.

The basement was unfinished, but in the center of the room, there was a rectangular pit of murky brine water. The girl lit several lamps around the room and kneeled before the water.

"Everywhere that Mary went, Mary went, Mary went, Everywhere that Mary went, the lamb was sure to go..."

"Eamon. Myrna and the others are here to see you," the girl said, her voice shaking in her throat.

She was afraid of him. Yes, indeed.

Myrna spat more blood. She would swear she could feel each organ dying. Whatever Dunn had done to her, he made her something more than human. It served her now, and it would serve her revenge.

"Eamon!"

The water suddenly splashed up, and Eamon's top half surfaced. Myrna could see his tallow, glistening wet flesh, almost transparent with thick veins and pulsing arteries. He had long black hair and his watery eyes rolled around in his head in such a way that Myrna thought would be impossible. From his purple lips, an impossibly long, black tongue came out like a tendril, whipped through the air, and snapped back inside his mouth.

Those watery eyes fixed on the girl as she backed away from his murky pit, never moving away from her.

Myrna was happy with what she saw. She conjured her strength, drove her weight onto her feet despite the excruciating pain, and pushed Anraí aside. She took a step, then two, toward Eamon.

"It followed her to school one day, school one day, school one day... it followed her to school one day, which was against the rules..."

"I told you I wanted nothing to do with Doran Dunn or his manipulations," Eamon said.

Myrna didn't say a word. She jumped on him, and they both fell back into the dark mire. She found the dark spot within her, willed her flesh to fuse with his, and they started to become one. The blackness in her was making them whole together.

Both screamed out what oxygen they had as they wrestled into the bond until there was total submission. The flesh of two bodies became one, the powers of both became one. Myrna died, but Eamon absorbed her and her power—the *homunculus alteration*.

Eamon never felt so good.

IV.

When Cuan first opened his eyes, he realized he was floating deep under the icy water. The vampyre was still wrapped around him, though her arms were no longer around his. She was holding him fast with her arms and legs, her mouth on the top of his. By doing this, she was feeding him oxygen through his mouth—though now she seemed to be doing so in her sleep. He breathed out, filling her lungs. The gills along her ribs fluttered. And she breathed out, filling his. It was symbiotic.

Around them was a rusty cage, holding them under, containing them. If this vampyre was not feeding him oxygen, he would be dead by now.

Maybe the rusted cage was old enough that it would break apart?

He tried swimming to the cage with the weight of the creature on him. It was slow, but it didn't seem to wake her. It made moving harder. He eventually grabbed a couple of rusty bars.

Cuán had no idea why they were keeping him alive, or how he was going to get out of this. He couldn't see in the murky depths but for a few feet, and he was sure that was only because it was daylight.

And he couldn't forget that he was in a deep black pit.

It was cold, too. Frigid as diving naked into a snowbank. The only thing he could imagine would allow this possibility is if the vampyre was giving him enough warmth or strength to endure it.

He tried to pull the bars apart or push on them. No use. No amount of human strength could break these bars, even if he were the strongest man on earth.

The sea is the beginning of life. It is the earthly representation of the Primordial itself—formless, unfathomable chaos... and boundless in its power. As Maggie climbed down the rocks to the shoreline, letting the cold waters lick at her feet, she watched as her arrival pulled the tides in, raising them as Nola had said they would. She closed her eyes and let her body and mind reach out to it. Shedding her clothes, she could feel herself changing. She let her rage out into the withdrawing waves and let the power of the sea come into her when the waters washed back over her feet.

Ponc was there. The old wolfhound barked and walked across the water as if showing her the way before it disappeared as the higher waves came rolling in. She wanted to go to him and wanted to feel the waters wash over her. Between the elemental world and the Hollow, the sprites wound and wove themselves like a great interlacing dance.

Maggie's flesh changed through the teal blue tone she recognized from before, and her skin turned a dark sea-green, thickening like leather.

She could feel fins running over her scalp under her thick red hair, down her back, and down the long tail, itself having grown from above her buttocks and almost as long as her legs. Her tongue felt her teeth lengthen to sharp points. Her ears lengthened out to points, sticking out of her curly hair like weeds. Maggie looked at her webbed hands and the claws. And in the reflection of the sea, she saw the bright blue swirling colors of the symbols on her skin, glowing with some bioluminescence deep in her dark skin where the Fomorians scratched her.

Though she looked like a monster, she felt renewed. Charged.

That ugly fucking face with the teeth... Isn't that what the Fomorians made of you? Deirdre had said.

Seagrass Maggie, Cuán called her. Poor Cuán. Taken by the vampyres. Possibly dead. She thought about Róis and how Myrna violently took her life, and she thought how she possibly failed everyone, all for the sake of her own life. How could she let this happen? Though she loved him more than anything, she should have left Cuán and dealt with her loss another way. Now she failed them, and it was only a matter of time before she failed Deirdre and Ambrus.

And don't forget you failed Muirgen, and she's doing this to hurt you, she thought.

Yes, yes... but she didn't have a choice, did she? Muirgen's daughter attacked Crab Eyes, attempting to kill the poor child. It wasn't Maggie's fault. Yes, she broke her promise, but she had to. Didn't she?

You can't feel bad for everything.

Maggie realized that if dying would save Cuán, she'd be more than happy to.

Maggie dove into the water and swam deep amongst the water sprites. It had been a long time since she embraced the sea, plunging into its depths, so it frightened her a bit, but she forced herself to open her mouth and breathe in the briny waters. Her lungs accepted it and she found herself breathing fine. Her skin grew numb to the cold. She could still sense it, but it no longer affected her.

She had always been a creature of the sea. *This is where I belong*, she thought.

Was this what Doran Dunn meant when he called her a Maris Demidian? Whatever she was, she had a Primordial energy residing within her, connecting her to the sea, and it gave her strength.

Maggie swam deeper, feeling the pressure increasing around her, and she stopped, floating in the darkness of the waters as her legs slightly curled, knees up in front of her. She closed her eyes again, stretched out her arms and legs, and again reached out to the sea with her body and mind. The dark and pale sprites rushed around her, dancing and playing.

The sea felt as though it was passing through her, and she used its ebb and flow to carry her towards the cave.

When she got closer, she stopped, recognizing underwater standing stones. She swam down to them and saw the hatched ogham lines and spirals. These were the summoning stones for the *maighdean uaimh*—the brine vampyres. It was how the vampyres were called and fettered to the bay by the Fomorians long ago. They were what gave Elieris his power over them.

Maggie grabbed a rock and she started dashing out the symbols. Hopefully, this would weaken them.

The sprites swam away, all parting to the sides beyond the stones.

Behind her, she heard a voice: *Oh Maggie. I thought you would never return. I actually recognize you better this way...*

While Ambrus was gathering components for his ritual, Deirdre found a blackthorn tree and hacked at it with a hatchet until she got a piece of it that looked about 36 inches. She took it to a man Declan knew, named Kelly, who told her that he could make her the shillelagh, though it would need a week to dry. Deirdre knew that she wouldn't be using it as a walking stick, so she only asked him to craft it for her, saying that she would take care of it while it dried.

Before he got to work, while they were both holding the blackthorn, Deirdre told Kelly, "*Glac an chuid seo díom agus saoirsigh go láidir í.*" This opened a doorway between their minds, so that Kelly could reach in and take what was there and craft the Bod Mór with all its special properties. All subconscious, he didn't even realize it happening.

Kelly sanded the blackthorn down, rubbing off the thorns, and brushed on a coat of shellac. After letting it dry a few hours, Deirdre picked it up so she could feel the Bod Mór. With it in her grasp, she could shed the siofra and return to her Cycle. Inwardly, her consciousness could gleam the sacred fata essence inside her, and she saw how easily she could spin it into the Eeries.

It was done.

"Thank you, Kelly. I'll never forget this," she said.

Kelly gave her a smile. "Making a good shillelagh is always a pleasure."

With that, Deirdre went to the bay and shouted to the sea, "*Tar chugam, a Chailleach! Tar agus labhair liom!*" In the back of her mind, she couldn't escape the idea that the Cailleach was watching her, Maggie and Cuán, waiting for them to access the siofra so that she could take it back.

And behind her she saw Eireen's mother. She was walking with a gnarled wood cane and her white hair was blowing in the breeze.

"I am the Cailleach," the old woman said.

Deirdre looked at her shadow and saw that it was of a young girl. She was the Cailleach. How could she not sense her at the Hearn manor house?

"You have found yourself, and you have come to me. Thank Maggie! She has done what I have asked of her," Cailleach said.

"I don't understand how my Cycle has come to this?" Deirdre said. "I am Cherry Fox. Daughter of Brigid and the Dagda, cursed for failing my sisters by the Morrígan. I have walked many lives trying to find my way, and here I am, still lost as ever."

Deirdre found herself sobbing, but she was ashamed in front of the Cailleach. The old woman did not move to comfort her, however, and said, "You have lost your way many times throughout your Cycle, and you will probably lose your way a great many more. You are no longer the daughter of the Seven Springs. They have all dried up many centuries ago! You are now Cherry Fox, and you are now a servant of the gods. This is your lot, and it is written into your *fata*. Your *cinniúint*."

"Why am I here?"

The Cailleach sighed and pointed out to sea. "Maggie seeks to destroy the brine vampyres, so it is your mission to return the siofra to Doran Dunn."

"But I stopped Doran from exchanging the siofra long ago! It does not belong here!"

"And it was not yours to stop. It was how you were put in the place you now find yourself," the Cailleach said. "If you wish to return to your Cycle, then you must do as I say."

"How do I shed the siofra? I don't even really understand what it is, except for what Maggie has told me."

The Cailleach looked her over. "The siofra is a sponge. It adapted first to Maggie so that you would appear like her. It took from her cells and blood and some of her mental faculties, and it gave them to you. It formed this corporeal housing—your body—and gave you all her aspects. It allowed you to take Maggie's life from her. But as you spent time in the siofra, it adapted to your soul as well. As a siofra, you are something new now. It's in you, reformed.

"And shedding the siofra? You will know what to do when the time is right. For now, you have a bigger problem. The arrachtaigh is on the hunt for your companions, and it has grown much stronger."

"What? Where is it?"

But the Cailleach was no longer there. As effortlessly as she came, she was gone. Deirdre took a deep breath and let it out slowly, holding tight to her Bod Mór.

Deirdre ground her teeth, trying not to let her anger come over her. Why didn't the Cailleach take the siofra from her now? Why wait?

"Cailleach!" she screamed. "Come back to me! *Tar ar ais chugam!*"

Ambrus had his job, Maggie was finishing whatever she started with the brine vampyres, and now it was Deirdre's turn to step it up. The arrachtaigh had to be put down for everything to come together and for them to escape this curse. If that is what she must do, Deirdre thought, then that was what she was going to do.

"*Liúdramán thú!*"

Bedelia saw the water churn and bubble, a white froth building at its surface. She looked at Anraí, who was frozen in terror, looking as confused as ever. And while she too was frightened, she kept thinking about that woman with the red hair, how she killed the large thug so quickly. Bedelia had heard the gunshot go off, ran down the hall, saw the thug dead on the floor, and the redhead was shooting into the bitch standing beside the bed.

Bedelia had backed away in fear and watched the redhead leave the room, threaten Anraí, and look at her with such power in her eyes.

Bedelia followed her as she walked down the stairs, tossing the gun aside as she went. Once the redhead had stepped out the door, Bedelia raced down the steps and got the gun, lifting her skirt and sliding it in the back of her underwear.

She felt the gun now and pulled it out. Bedelia wanted to be as powerful as that redhead. She wanted to stop her pain and take charge of her own life as she had.

Eamon Macrae deserved it.

Anraí saw the gun. "What do you think you are doing?"

"I'm taking back my own life," Bedelai said. "Go. Run as far as you can."

Anraí swallowed hard and shook his head. "No. I won't leave you. Whatever is going on, it's evil, and I'm not letting you deal with it alone."

Bedelia was charmed and smiled at him. "I don't know why you would work for such an evil woman. I wouldn't suspect you of being so kind, working for that witch."

Anraí shrugged. "I'm a lost soul, lass."

A hand came out of the pit. Strings of pale flesh were banded across darker flesh. The hands had claws and the fingers were longer than they used to be. Bedelia turned the gun back on the pit as the head came up... Myrna's taffy blond hair clinging to her skull, mouth agape as if pried wide like a hood around the second head that came up... Eamon's. Myrna's eyes were like milky orbs, but Eamon's were big and black, the lamplights flickering deeply in them.

Bedelia had never seen such a horrific betrayal of nature. Anraí gasped beside her, bringing her out of her own terror-induced torpor. She chose Eamon's ugly face and unloaded the rest of the bullets into his head.

The Eamon-creature screamed as big bloody holes appeared in its face, and it reached out one arm—an unnaturally long arm—and grabbed her leg. Without hesitation, it started pulling her toward it.

It raised a leg from the murky pit, setting its twisted foot on the floor. Bedelia saw its erection come up, and the other hand wrapped around her face. She screamed, expecting it to be over any second when she heard Anraí yell. The Eamon-creature let go of her face to swat Anraí away, who was on his back, stabbing it with a dagger.

The hand grabbed Anraí and threw him over his shoulder with such ease, Bedelia didn't understand what was happening until Anraí was already in the air. He collapsed in a pile against the wall near the stairs.

Bedelia looked back and saw the Eamon-creature's face had healed over. The bullet holes were completely gone.

And it was grinning at her.

"When I am through with you Bedelia, your blessed cunny will burn even after death," Eamon said, his voice now deeper and far throatier.

Bedelia cried and threw the gun at its heads. It missed Eamon's entirely, and the Myrna-head took the blow and moaned, but otherwise, the thing didn't seem affected. Her heart raced and her chest heaved quickly as she anticipated the end.

But Anraí was not done. He had lifted himself up, still holding tightly onto his knife. He growled and rushed the Eamon-creature again. This time he rammed the knife into its gut, thrusting it deep into its bowels.

Bedelia started kicking as much as she could, as hard as she could, and the Eamon-creature let her go to remove the dagger from itself. Anraí helped her get to her feet, pulling her back from the pit towards the stairs. Bedelia moved as quickly as she could, both hurt.

"Bedelia," the creature said.

Bedelia looked back over her shoulder.

"I always loved you." The Eamon-creature grinned with clenched teeth and tossed the dagger.

Bedelia screamed, flinching, but when she opened her eyes, she felt the blood dripping on her back. She looked over her shoulder, seeing that the dagger lodged itself straight into Anraí's forehead. He had a surprised expression on his face, which was now frozen there.

She felt his weight topple onto her, and she cried, "Anraí!"

Frightened he'd take her with him, she shrugged aside, shamefully letting the body tumble down the stairs.

The Eamon-creature laughed as she slammed the basement door between them.

"*There is no escape from me now, Bedelia. I am now a god. And you will always BE MINE!*"

Bedelia didn't know what else to do, but she knew she couldn't stay in the house. She ran for the front door, down to the estate's front gates, and threw them open. She looked back, expecting to see the monster following her, but there was no sign of it.

You have to get out of town, she told herself. *It's the only way you're going to survive this.* Bedelia had no idea what she was going to do after she left Séala Bán, but even if she lived on the streets, at least she would be alive.

And she thought: *I'll withdraw Eamon's money. I'll go to London. He won't find me there...*

That seemed as good of an idea as any.

V.

The vampyric sisters swarmed around her, the five of them all spinning around her in the dark waters like a school of large shimmering tuna. Out of this cloud of pale flesh and black hair, one would strike her from behind or one of the sides. Each time she tried to anticipate it, but she was too slow. She wanted to rake them with her claws, make them realize how dangerous she could be, but they only played with her.

Teasing her, she thought.

And they all struck at once. The five brine vampyres all reached out, taking arms and legs, holding her fast as Muirgen swam close enough to lean into her face.

We got you!

Maggie tried to fight them, but they were all incredibly strong. They started to pull her over the rocks and into the cave. Muirgen swam ahead until they came into a chamber with rusted cages. They tossed her into one and slammed the door shut, throwing the bolt.

Maggie, outraged, grabbed the bars and shook them, trying to bend them. It wasn't long before she realized that she wouldn't normally be able to see as much as she could. It was darker here, though some light came from the surface. Her eyes were much keener than they were before.

It occurred to her that the bars of the cage were made of red-rusted, wrought iron and were covered in barnacles. They were suspended in the water rather than sitting on the cave floor. A large chain rose above the surface of the water, holding them in place.

They knew she was fae-touched, and this was their trap for her.

Maggie was sure that they were below the Feast Pit. Before she could think too much about it, she saw the other cages barely visible in the underwater murk.

The brine vampyres swam around each other and her cage. Their flesh started glowing, illuminating the waters all around them. Muirgen sounded a slight sonic pulse from her lips, and the bioluminescent algae clinging to the cave walls started glowing. They lit the whole cave with caustic green and blue lights.

Could she faintly see Cuán in another cage?

One of the vampyres had wrapped her arms and legs around him and had planted her mouth on his. She seemed subdued. Cuán noticed her and was able to move to the bars of his own cage.

Cuán—She was so relieved to see him.

They were keeping him alive somehow. Feeding him oxygen and warmth enough to stop any hypothermia.

How? Why? It didn't matter... He was alive, and she could still save him if she could only get out of the cage.

Muirgen slipped through the others as they swam and grabbed hold of the bars. She looked intently at Maggie and grinned.

See your beloved? See how she embraces him? We could keep him this way forever. We could put him into a deep sleep, make him live out the rest of his life in the cage under these waters.

She was speaking with a form of telepathy through the Hollow. It was how the Fomorians spoke to each other when not using their song.

Maggie hadn't done it since she was in the Deep Dens, but she tried it now—

Muirgen, listen to me. You can keep me and return me to the Fomorians. I will make it easy for you, but only if you let Cuán free.

Muirgen laughed. *You have already made this too easy for me.*

Please, Muirgen...

Muirgen bared her teeth. *No! What makes you think I have any sympathy? Your begging is a waste of time. Did you have sympathy for my daughter? You took her life from me!*

Then what do you want? If Maggie knew of a way to help her—

Muirgen licked her lips and leaned in closer to the bars. *I want to watch your spirit be torn apart as you watch your lover die.*

With that, Muirgen turned around and screamed into the deep. This sonic cry rippled through the waters, temporarily lifting the mud from the floor into a near-impenetrable cloud, making it even darker and harder to see. The vampyre turned back to Maggie.

They're coming now, she said.

The Fomorians.

Maggie looked over at Cuán, who was still watching from his cage. Suddenly, he grabbed at the head of the vampyre who clung to him, and blood poured from their mouths. She heard his cries through the waters.

No, stop. There must be something I can do! Maggie shouted. *He did nothing to you.*

And what does that matter? Muirgen said.

They all heard another sonic cry that pounded into their ears. This time it wasn't Muirgen. Maggie covered her ears and strained to look over at Cuán once more. He was pounding the vampyre's head between the bars. The vampyre was crying out as he shoved and shoved...

None of the other vampyres moved. All watched as Cuán grabbed the vampyre's hair and pulled their mouths and heads apart. The vampyre was baring fangs, crying her sonic cry, and Cuán rammed his forehead into her face.

He won't be able to breathe, Maggie thought. She looked around, trying to figure a way out of the cage. She needed to get to him soon, or he was going to drown.

Muirgen was watching Cuán and her sister struggle, humored by the whole thing. She didn't care who won the battle, though Maggie was sure that Muirgen knew the vampyre was much stronger than Cuán.

Maggie reached between through the cage, grabbing Muirgen's arm, and pulled it back through the bars. Muirgen growled and tried to pull her arm free, but Maggie bent it back against the bars and twisted it until she heard the bone snap. Muirgen cried out, which made the sisters all stop and turn toward her.

Free me now, Maggie said.

They will never listen to you, Muirgen hissed in her head.

Maggie reached for her hair and grabbed a handful, pulling Muirgen's head back against the bars as fast as she could. With her other hand, she grabbed the hilt of the dagger in Muirgen's breast, unsheathed it from her flesh, and held it to Muirgen's exposed throat.

If you do not let us out now, she will die.

The vampyre sisters went to the cages and opened them. Maggie swam around, tossing Muirgen inside.

Tá níos mó againn fós ná atá agaibhse, one of the sisters said. *There are still more of us than you.*

And you lost your leverage, another hissed.

Maggie held out her hands to the other sisters, trying to get them to see that she didn't want to fight them. *I only want to take Cuán, and I only want to know where Doran Dunn is.*

The sisters all laughed.

Behind her Muirgen hissed. *Why would Doran Dunn come here when Elieris has us?*

Maggie's hands made fists. The vampyres were right. Dunn had tricked her. He had never come here. He didn't have to.

The vampyre wrapped around Cuán and started growling and hissing through the water. A rage of bubbles came between them. One of her hands came up and clawed at his face, and she opened her jaws wide to expose her mouthful of sharp teeth.

After the cave walls began to glow, lighting up the caves, the vampyre bit Cuán's tongue, and he fought for his life, not thinking about how he'd lose her air once he broke free from her. Cuán pounded her head into the bars, and she let go of his bleeding tongue, but her grip tightened, so he grabbed her hair and pulled his mouth free from hers.

Cuán knew she was stronger and that she was going to free herself and possibly kill him, but he fought anyway until she overpowered his arms, and fought free of him. She kicked at him under the water, hitting him hard in the chest and arm.

Trying to hold his breath, he saw that the vampyres were opening his cage and falling back. Looking over toward the redheaded sea-creature, he saw that she was twisting her body through the water, throwing Muirgen into the cage. She slammed the cage shut, and now all the vampyres were floating nearby. All still. All eyes on her.

Maggie?

Cuán swam up for air as fast as he could. His lungs burned, and several times he had to consciously remind himself not to accidentally breathe. It was like the ocean was trying to suck away what was left in his lungs. The surface always seemed so far away, but he paddled at the waters with his arms, desperate to pick up speed, not knowing how fast he was going but knowing he didn't have long.

Don't breathe, don't breathe, he told himself. *Don't let it suck away your life.*

When the surface looked within reach, he still didn't know if he'd make it. His body needed the air, and it was going to arrest control from his mind whether he liked it or not. His arms were getting too tired. The waters seemed so heavy.

When he breached the surface, he gasped until his lungs began relaxing. He thanked whatever gods he could, knowing very well that he couldn't stay in the water. The vampyres would come up for him. They could snatch him at any time.

They were in the sea cave. He could see the Feast Pit above them. The central part of the cave ceiling above ascended like a chimney flue, where a small chunk of sun penetrated the main cavern. There were chains driven into the stone ceiling of the cave around it, which must be holding the rusted cages in place beneath the waters. Cuán counted four of them.

Cuán wanted to help Maggie, but he felt like a flopping fish out of water down there. Useless. He swam to the edge of an embankment and started pulling himself out of the water. Cuán tried thinking of ways he could help Maggie, but he was very cold, shivering and he knew he couldn't go back into the water. He turned around, crawling toward the water's edge.

Water splashed up before him, and the vampyre, who had been embracing him, landed on the cave floor in front of him now. Cuán stopped and fell back onto his ass and then tried climbing to his feet in a hurry. His legs gave, however, and he fell back again. She hissed, and her white tongue sprayed out like a weblike net before recoiling back between her purple lips.

Cuán started crab-walking backward away from her.

"The fomori are coming for your sweet Maggie," she said. "You have lost her. Choose to die now and free yourself of the burden of her loss."

"Fuck you, you crazy bitch!" Cuán yelled.

The vampyre grinned.

The vampyre sisters grabbed at Maggie and took bites as they floated there somewhere in the middle of the cold cave waters. Teeth sank into her arms, her legs, and one had the audacity to bite into her breast.

Maggie knew that she wasn't going to make it. In a way, she should have known this was coming. How could a monster like her live in a world like this without an even bigger creature coming along and destroying her? Maybe it was time for her to let it all go and let it all be done.

Muirgen's cruel laughter echoed in her head, and she cried out: *Maggie's going to die. Maggie's going to die! Maggie's going to DIE!*

She felt herself weaken as they drew her vitality from her. She gazed up, seeing that Cuán was no longer there. He had escaped,

she thought. At least she hoped so because she had nothing left in her.
I'm sorry for your daughter, Muirgen. I didn't see any other way.
Fuck you, Maggie. We had a contract, and you broke it!
For Cuán's own sake... For the love she had for him... You can't let yourself die.
Maggie tried to swing her arms as the monsters drank from her. One vampyre was briefly knocked free, but the creature was able to latch onto her with her teeth in a short amount of time. All the blood that floated around them was hers.
It was no use.
Yes, Maggie, give into the darkness. Sleep. It will all be over soon.
Where did she drop that dagger? she wondered. It wasn't in her hand anymore.
Never you mind, Maggie. Sleep...

Cuán turned to move away from the vampyre, to go deeper into the cave if he had to, but the vampyre leapt above him, crawled across the cave ceiling, and dropped on the other side, blocking his way.
Behind him were the cold waters where the vampyre sisters remained and were most likely outnumbering Maggie. Killing her.
There was no escape that he could see. Just dark, winding caverns and chambers.
Cuán held up his hands in front of him. "Don't do this. Please. Maggie does not deserve this. She was taken from her family unfairly. None of this is fair!"
The vampyre nodded. "She belongs to the fomori. They chose her, and they have authority by the Contracts."
"Contracts?"
"If you take innocence, you must replace the innocents with like," the vampyre said. "It is the contract the Milesians made

with the Tuatha Dé Danann long ago. She needs to return to where she belongs. You... YOU are merely nourishment and will serve your purpose now."

Cuán connected the dots. The vampyre was talking about the mysterious people who moved to Ireland and started a war with the fae-people, the Tuatha Dé. Upon winning battles, the Tuatha Dé sat down with these Gaels—who were called Milesians in the old Irish texts—and wrote out contracts between the people. The most popular of which was that the Milesians would live on Ireland, and the Tuatha Dé would live 'beneath the mounds,' a euphemism for the Otherworld and the Irish Hollow that was hidden from their eyes.

The vampyre jumped and fell on him, hands at his shoulders and legs pinning his. She hissed, opening her fanged mouth, and the white tongue came out, spreading almost like small, viscous tendrils and mucilaginous webs.

Cuán grabbed her arms and twisted them the other way. This knocked her aside enough so that he could free a leg and kick at her. As he crawled away, she reached for him and grabbed his foot. He kicked back with his free foot again and again...

And she bit into his leg. He felt the long teeth go in deep, piercing muscles. Piercing bone.

Cuán kicked her face, and her teeth came free. With a sudden renewed strength, he pushed himself to his feet and started to run back toward the cave waters. At the edge, he grabbed a handful of mud and swung around as the vampyre made the large leap to be right in front of him.

He stuffed her face with the mud, and she cried out, and Cuán punched her face as hard as he could with his fist. She fell back, clawing the mud out of her eyes.

"You wretched shite!" she cried.

Cuán knew he was only pushing off the inevitable, but he ran past her, deeper into the cave.

VI.

Deirdre stood above the stairs in Eamon's basement, seeing one of the goons she recognized as one of Doran Dunn's men: Anraí. There was a dagger sticking gruesomely into his forehead, and his blood had pooled out around his broken body, resting at the bottom of the stairs all sprawled out. At first, seeing him shocked her. The part of her that was Deirdre was not used to death, but the part of her that was Cherry Fox, that part was able to easily move around it and focus and what she was here for.

She had reached out to the Hollow, feeling Maggie out. She felt 'closer' down here. Had Maggie been here? She wasn't sure. But she felt physical pain and heartbreak. Desperation. Maggie had lost people, and she thought they were both dead, but the cathexis she left in the manor was faint.

And maybe it wasn't in the room but wafting off the trail left behind by something else...

Deirdre slung the Bod Mór over her shoulder and slowly went down the stairs. She saw the lamps that lit the area and the muddy saltwater pit in the center of the room.

Next to the pit was a gun. She stooped over and looked at it, opening the barrel and finding it empty. She could smell the warm burnt powder. It had been fired multiple times recently.

Deirdre noticed the black, slimy blood around the edges of the pit. Some of it had spattered the unfinished basement walls. Deirdre figured that whatever was in the pit, it took fire. The wall had debris that flew free when the bullets made contact. She sighed and looked around.

The black slime was around the pit, but there was no water or slimy bits up the stairs or around on the first floor. Assuming this was the arrachtaigh, where could it have gone?

And was it the thing that wafted with Maggie's cathexis? What had it done with her?

Deirdre checked around the room and looked back at the pit. Eamon Macrae's estate was sitting near the cliffs, overlooking the sea when the Devil's Breath wasn't obscuring most of it.

What if the network of caves were under the estate as well? Maybe this is how the arrachtaigh got around while the sun was at its highest? This murky pit may lead to such tunnels, where it was hiding now.

Deirdre could smell the filth of the pit but decided this was the only way. The thrill of knowing how dangerous it was filled her body with a rush of joy. Who knew what was down there? What if she got lost in the darkness? What if the creature was waiting for her?

She took a deep breath, tightened her grip on the Bod Mór, and dove in. At first it was dark and filthy, but these were surface flotsam. The deeper she dove, the clearer the brine.

Deirdre hoped that killing the arrachtaigh would not only drive off the Ostium but destroy the curse on the village once and for all. Once that was taken care of, she could get the Cailleach off her, and she could find her way again. Even though she found herself again, a part of her still felt lost. And that was why, as she figured it. Deirdre could no longer do what 'Deirdre' wanted—the thrill of the city, the sex—but she had to follow what had been laid out before her by the Tuatha Dé Danann. Refocus herself.

Only, secretly—deep down in the very pits of her being—she knew that her fata essence had spun out a very short cinniúint—fate, or destiny, for this life. She was beginning to wonder if she'd survive the day. With one's ability to form the Eeries, the fae were able to change their fates to a certain extent. Every so often, their cinniúint was woven far more ingeniously than they could imagine.

She wasn't a particularly good swimmer, but she made her way. In her mind, she incanted, *"Soilsigh!"* A ball of ethereal light formed from her *fata croí* beside her and followed her, illuminating the watery tunnel as it floated by mysterious means.

It wasn't mysterious, though. Those who had the fata essence could exude what the fae called *croí* and form it into their Eerie. If the fata was a cloud, the croí was its rain. With the proper knowledge in what the fae called the arts, croí became effect. In this case, a floating ball of light for her to illuminate the darkness.

It was nice to have her knowledge of the arcane arts back. It made her feel more like herself.

The tunnel evened out and opened into a larger chamber, and she found that there was a surface. She broke it, and looked around, seeing a large black cavern in front of her. She climbed out of the water, shook off her shillelagh, and continued forward. Her ball of light followed her, illuminating the way.

Deirdre reminded herself about what Maggie had mentioned to her and the others earlier—about the vampyres that lurked in the village—the creatures owing fealty to the King of the Fomorians. They could be down here, too. Watching her. Waiting for her.

The cave was very quiet at first, as she suspected it would be. She heard water dripping and the occasional bat squeaking, but nothing prepared her for the screams up ahead.

The vampyre's supernatural speed shocked him. Cuán didn't see her move until she dropped in front of him again, still grinning. He would be impressed if he weren't so terrified by her.

"You think running will help you? You're already dead. Just *embrace* it! Feckin' *embrace* it!"

Cuán shook his head and prepared to turn, but large hands came out of the darkness behind the vampyre and snatched her. The vampyre cried out in surprise and Cuán backed up, taking in the form of some deformed *mutation*: two people melded together into some kind of unnatural horror. It was a mess of meat and bone and blood.

Cuán's gut retched.

The monster grinned at the vampyre.

"*You no longer control me,*" the monster said and started pulling on her arms until they broke from their ball joints. The meat and muscle tore, black blood pouring onto the ground. The creature tore her limb from limb, tossing the meat aside like she was nothing. All the while, the vampyre screamed, truly undying until it was quiet. *Gone.*

Cuán started running back toward the water.

"Maggie! *Maggie!*"

Deirdre saw the arrachtaigh tear the vampyre apart and saw Cuán run, crying Maggie's name. She couldn't believe she found them.

However, her first concern must be the arrachtaigh. It threw the vampyre's pieces in several directions and stepped on her head, crushing it into pulp. It was nightmarish. Some mutation merging a man and a woman like some bodily cancer. Myrna's head half fused to the other; one of her useless arms hanging off and broken; and its body had swollen with muscles, bursting with surface veins and rashy, peeled skin.

It was much bigger than her and she knew that even with the Bod Mór, this creature was going to hurt her.

Deirdre ran at it and shouted, "*Dóitear anois!*" as she fed the Eerie the last of the croí she could muster, reforming it with her art. The ball of illumination that hovered near her shoulder changed into a blazing green ball of fire, and it flew at the arrachtaigh's back in a fiery-tailed arc. When it hit, the ball of fire buried itself into its fleshy body—singing the massive wound and spreading fire up the creature's back, climbing violently as it went.

The arrachtaigh screamed and turned to look at her as it clawed at the singed wound that fed a dark cloud of smoke around it. It filled the air with the scent of burnt flesh. The monster bared its teeth and turned on her, the fire already dying out as it began to move toward her.

You will know what to do when the time is right, the Cailleach had said to her.

Deirdre knew this was the only way, though she hated to give up all the great things she'd had in this life. She charged, shouting her battle cry, and used her strength to drive the pointed end of the Bod Mór through its chest. The creature cried out again, attempting to grab her with its massive hand. Deirdre was able to pull back just quick enough, and she tried kicking it between the legs. She felt the genitals mush in the impact, but the arrachtaigh ignored it, shoving its palm into her chest. The blow sent her backward, and she felt the flesh on the palms of her own hands triturate on the stone, making her cry out.

Ignore the pain, she thought. *Kill the fucking thing before it kills you...*

Deirdre got up and charged it again, hoping to grab the Bod Mór that was stuck in its chest. The arrachtaigh was ahead of her. It grabbed the cudgel-staff and started to pull it free, so Deirdre ran at it, grabbed the end of the Bod Mór, and tried to shove it back in.

The cudgel-staff went in and the arrachtaigh bellowed out, swinging the Bod Mór's end to sideswipe her into the cavern's wall. Her head hit the rock with a crack and a loud ringing went off in her ears.

The arrachtaigh grabbed her shoulders with its hands, pulling her like a rag doll away from the cavern wall. He pushed down on her until her legs gave and she was forced to her knees. Deirdre, fearing that it would club her down, grabbed the Bod Mór and twisted it. The arrachtaigh screamed out again and tossed her, and Deirdre landed on the ground, rolling. Feeling like every tumble was breaking bones and tearing flesh.

"You can't kill me," it said. "I am the ascendency. Lawmaker. Judgement. Punisher. Pain. Not even the vampyres have dominion over me! I *am* Séala Bán!"

Jaysus Mary and Joseph, she thought. *How am I going to kill this thing?*

Unable to move much, Deirdre looked up at it as the arrachtaigh came over, grabbed her around her ribs, and lifted her back up in its massive hands. The womanish skull that once belonged to Myrna coughed up blood, laughing as its large hands tightened around her ribs. She felt the hands beginning to crush her, feeling her ribs snapping inside her.

The siofra is a sponge. It adapted first to Maggie so that you would appear like her. It took from her cells and blood and some of her mental faculties, and it gave them to you. It formed this corporeal housing—your body—and gave you all her aspects... But as you spent time in the siofra, it adapted to your soul as well, the Cailleach had said.

This is what the Cailleach had wanted: everything to return to where it came from. Deirdre to her Cycle. Maggie to her home. The siofra to Doran Dunn. The siofra was supposed to be independent, not merged with her. That was Doran's doing. The small voice in the back of her head was the siofra, and it was conscious. It was time to do what she should have done a while ago. Closing her eyes, putting her mind into the Hollow, she drove the siofra out of herself, charging it to find Maggie.

I am afraid, the siofra said inside Deirdre's mind. *Please don't make me go.*

You must return to your mother, and the only way back is through Maggie, Deirdre replied and shoved her out of her body through the Hollow. *You deserve your own life. Like Maggie deserves hers. I want... no, I need you to be free now.*

Deirdre wondered how long she would live without the siofra hosting her soul? Without it nurturing her current body, she was sure that it wouldn't be long.

Thank you, Deirdre. I will never forget this.

Reluctantly, the gelatinous siofra slipped from her flesh, and flew through the air, past the arrachtaigh, and into the darkness deeper into the cave. When this happened, Deirdre felt the deformed creature crush the rest of her ribs. Her lungs were pierced, and it felt like she could feel every internal wound happening all at once.

It didn't matter how long her body would last, she supposed. She was going to die here no matter what.

Still, she had the strength of Cherry Fox, and she found herself withdrawing the Bod Mór from the creature's body and replanting it into the creature's head. It went through Myrna's old skull through her gaping, lolling mouth and into Eamon's head. The black blood spurted out Myrna's mouth, splashing over her, but she didn't care. Eamon's eyes rolled around, his tongue shot out, and his teeth bit into his tongue.

They fell to the floor together, the arrachtaigh gasping out its last breath in a deep rattle.

Gotcha, you fucker, she thought.

Deirdre's heart quit then. Her mind stopped having thoughts. Just like that: her essences were returned to the Hollow.

A jellied thing with writhing tendrils flew by Cuán's shoulder. Deep in its nearly transparent core was some brain/heart amalgamation, and it had thin blue veins branching out through its entire form. The alien thing flew by him and dove into the water. He didn't know what it was, thinking that it was possibly some strange ability the arrachtaigh could exhibit. It sent chills through him, knowing that there were monsters lurking everywhere in this damnable cave.

He fell to his knees at the edge of the water, unable to take anymore. He was afraid Maggie was dead. The giant, monstrous thing behind him would be there soon and would surely kill him. Despite the caustic ripples of lights from the glowing waters splashing the cave walls, he only saw shadows moving below. He was unable to make out who was who. For all he knew, they were all vampyres.

How did he let all these things go so wrong?
Where was Deirdre? Ambrus? Róis?
How could he have expected this to go any different?
This was not his world. He was not strong enough to protect anyone that he loved.
What could he possibly do?
It not only made it harder to think, giving him such vertigo but left him afraid.

VII.

Bedelia ran, stumbling down the village main street, which was empty of people. She needed someone to help her. She needed a carriage or a horse. Somebody to get her as far away from here as possible. Bedelia cried for someone to aid her repeatedly, but nobody would come out and help.

Trying a shop door, she found it locked up tight. Was anyone in there? Were they just afraid to open their door to her?

The fog was all around her and she knew that she'd get lost in it. She hated not knowing how to find her way to London herself, let alone how to escape this damn curse.

What of her folks?

Her da was a fisherman. He would sail past the fog to get his catch before coming home each night. Though he and her ma never visited her, she was sure they still loved her. Bedelia ran as quickly as she could down toward her old home. At the door, she pounded furiously.

"Ma! Da! Help! My husband went mad! Da! Please! Open the door!"

The windows were dark. Nobody came to the door.

What the hell was happening?

Why wouldn't anyone help her? Where was everybody? She was sure the vampyres hadn't killed off everyone. They had to be around here somewhere.

"Bedelia?"

Bedelia turned to see Eireen at the gate.

"Where is everybody?"

"The priest took them down to the shore," Eireen said. "They're trying to have an exorcism to dispel the fog."

"Eireen. Please take me to them."

Eireen slowly nodded. "A'right, Bedelia. Follow... me."

Bedelia followed Eireen closely as they made their way to the bay shore. She watched the buildings around them, waiting for vampyres to appear out of the fog to get them. She asked herself if she believed that a priest could drive away this curse. Bedelia didn't really know. Eamon Macrae could be possessed by a demon, but he was very much real. She was sure Eamon would break the priest's neck before uttering much of his Latin.

The bay was a crescent of sandy shoreline with cliffs off to the north and south. The villagers were all there... all cluttering the center shore, watching a priest in his ceremonial vestment robes shaking holy water from a holy water sprinkler toward the village.

Bedelia hadn't been to one of Father Brian's masses since marrying Eamon Macrae, but she recognized him right away. She couldn't believe that he was finally standing up for the people of the village.

"Saint Michael the Archangel, defend us in battle. Be our protection against the wickedness and snares of the devil; May God rebuke him, we humbly pray; And do thou, O Prince of the Heavenly Host, by the power of God, thrust into hell Satan and all evil spirits who wander through the world for the ruin of souls. Amen."

As Father Brian continued on, Bedelia caught a glimpse of someone in the southern rocks—the formations that would rise up into the southern cliffs. A man.

Who was that, and what was he doing?

Curious, she looked back to see that Eireen was joining the villagers in singing a hymn and decided to go see what the man was doing so far away from the group. She left the crowd and made her way, climbing between rocks as she went until she saw a man in his fifties or so, raising his hands out to the sea.

Not wanting to be seen, Bedelia ducked down behind the rocks and watched the man hold out a dagger and a smoking bowl that filled the sea air with strange, wonderful scents.

"I call the Sprites of the Wind and Air. I summon and stir you to my whim. Listen to me. Swell and blow. Take this Devil's Breath!"

Bedelia's eyes widened in shock. She started seeing humanoid forms—half invisible or partially transparent—floating in the air around them, flowing with the wind. They were whipping up and going in and out of her sight, sometimes formed and sometimes formless. They all screamed in unison and the man pointed the dagger up.

As if the strange entities were waiting for this very action, they flew up, following the point of the dagger, and Bedelia could feel the winds, coming in from off the sea, getting stronger. Bedelia laid herself flat, holding onto the rocks and the skies cracked with thunder.

"Ventus ictu ictu!"

Bedelia was never so scared in her life, but when she looked up, she could see the fog stirring around.

She was in awe. This man was driving the fog away.

The man flew back, falling to the ground and rolled back against a rock. The bowl landed nearby, and the smoke went out. His dagger landed near Bedelia, sticking in the ground near her head.

Worried that the man wasn't alright, Bedelia crawled to him, and she checked his head. He was out. Part of his head was bleeding, but she could feel his chest as he breathed.

She decided to stay with him, watching the cursed fog blow away out to sea.

Hopefully, it would never return.

Something was happening here, she thought. *Changes in the air.*

The vampyres were feeding, barely anything left inside of Maggie, when the siofra slipped into her. The bonding was immediate. Having been attuned to Cherry Fox, the siofra was imbued with part of her, including her blood. When it blended itself to what had become of Seagrass Maggie, Maggie could feel some of Cherry Fox's power light up inside of her. From a weakened, sickly feeling, she suddenly felt a rush of good health and strength. It was an orgasm of vitality.

Cherry Fox was sharing her fata, and it was like a mortal's life force, only boosted by the Primordial. It elevated her body's resolve. It was a culmination of vigor and a relief from all the pain.

Seagrass Maggie shook the vampyres off of her with a violent throe, their teeth tearing off chunks of meat from her. Maggie could feel the life of the Bod Mór and called it.

With this strength, Maggie thought, she can get out of this. And once she did, Doran Dunn wasn't going to fool her anymore.

She flew through the water, her spiny-finned tail propelling her swiftly through the icy-black waters, tackling one of the sisters back until she collided with the walls of the cave. The force was so strong that the vampyre's head hit the wall, exploding in an underwater cloud of brain and blood.

The other sisters shrieked. Maggie watched as one moved to let Muirgen free from her cage, but Maggie didn't stop. She charged the other vampyric sister and got her into a sleeper hold. She pulled until the flesh of the vampyre's neck tore wide. She bit into it as the vampyre's blood flooded out, and Maggie gave it a little extra effort to pull the creature's head clean off.

It was as if she were not only one with the sea and its currents, but the sea was using her access to her new divine nature and *moved through her.* The sprites danced and played around them—celestial, partially humanoid forms moving through her, giving her their magic.

How did you suddenly become strong? You were next to death! Muirgen cried out in her mind. You have killed my sisters!

The Bod Mór penetrated the water and flew to Maggie's hand. She pointed it at Muirgen.

This is where we end this.

Muirgen hissed and started rushing her, arms reaching with clawed hands. Murder in her raging eyes.

She could kill me, Maggie thought. She was still a queen and amongst all of them, Muirgen was fueled by her pain.

What was she going to do with her? Swinging a club through the water wasn't going to work so well. So, what next?

Through the water... Maggie had a sudden idea.

Maggie looked at the surface and bolted upwards, the vampyre close behind her.

Cuán quietly sobbed in a dark recess he found in the main cavern. He didn't know why the monster—the one that killed the vampyre that threatened him—hadn't yet come for him. He didn't care. Cuán didn't understand why none of the other brine vampyres came up for him either. He didn't care.

All he could think about was Maggie. What happened to her? Where was she? Was she coming back?

His mind reeled back to the day he found her on the shores of Kilkee, pale and wrapped in long strands of algae. How she first smiled at him in the caves, or played with his giant Irish wolfhound, Ponc, when his faithful dog was still alive. He remembered the first time they kissed when she graduated from school. Wasn't that his twenty-first birthday? Maggie had been so happy, and she looked so lovely in the sun. How could he ever forget the taste of her lips or the warmth of her body pressed against his? Or like the day before, when they were stuck in the magic box on a train, and she selflessly gave him such intimate pleasure to pass the time? Maggie was not only the love of his life—she cared for him, and she was his... savior.

She should have come up by now.

The pool of seawater inside the cave gushed upwards, and he saw the sea-green creature's body break the surface, flying up into the air between the rusted chains that suspended the cages in the water beneath.

Cuán realized that her body had changed: it was darker with spiraling rings of bluish bioluminescence all over her. She had spiked purplish fins over her scalp, down her back and—

...tail?

The tail was straight, helping her propel into the air.

Muirgen's ashen form shot up from behind her out of the water, reaching for her.

Seagrass Maggie's monstrous form twisted in the air, suddenly swinging a black cudgel-staff around. The staff's goldish bulbed cap smacked Muirgen in the head with a large *thock* sound. A cloud of black ichor spraying out from the vampyre's head.

Both creatures fell back into the water with another splash, which sprayed him as he tried crawling backward, away from it.

He waited, hoping to see Maggie come up again. The moment was longer than he liked. They were battling. Maggie was alive. But Muirgen looked like she was just as strong.

Come on, Maggie... Don't let her win.

Once they splashed back down into the engulfing depths of the cave water, Maggie could see the crushing blow she made in Muirgen's head. The vampyre shook, but Muirgen reached out for her, grabbing her arm and scratched her. Maggie cried out, feeling its nails carve out flesh, and rushed her own body into Muirgen's. They collided in the water, spinning, and Maggie fought to get her arms around Muirgen's neck. The vampyre's black hair got in her face, and she felt the vampyre claws rake down her ribs and under arms.

You're going to go to hell with me, Maggie!

Maggie cried and twisted with all her might.

There was a cracking sound and Maggie couldn't feel Muirgen fighting anymore. Angry because of the wounds and all the pain this vampyre put her through, Maggie couldn't stop herself from twisting Muirgen's head clean off until the body sank to the bottom of the cave, leaving her head in Maggie's arms.

Not today, I'm not, Maggie shouted into the psychic atmosphere.

Maggie grabbed Muirgen's black hair and held it up so that she could see Muirgen's lifeless eyes. There was nothing left inside her. Relieved, she remembered that Cuán was in the caves above her, probably terrified. She looked one more time at the head, deciding that she was claiming the head as her trophy. Muirgen was conquered.

She wanted to see Cuán more than anything, so holding tight to the hair on the vampyre's severed head with one hand and the Bod Mór in the other, Maggie started for the surface waters.

Cuán crawled to the water's edge and saw the redhead surface, her hair pasted to her scalp, her lips peeled back, showing lots of daggerish teeth.

She turned around, looking for him, so he wiped his eyes and crawled over to her.

"Oh, were you cryin'?" she said.

"I'm an Irishman, Maggie. We never cry. Shut up," he said, wiping his eyes.

Maggie held Muirgen's head above water, obviously removed from the rest of her body. She was holding it by the hair.

Muirgen's face was frozen in horror and blood dripped from her torn neck. Part of her skull had caved in. Cuán was sure he could see brain matter and his stomach twisted up and he looked away.

Maggie tossed it onto the cave's dry bank and swam to it. Cuán helped her crawl out of the water and onto the rocky embankment. She was still holding onto the cudgel-staff tightly. Her lips still dripped blood.

Did she—?

Though Maggie's body was monstrous at first, Cuán could see these bodily changes beginning to withdraw slowly. While he would never say it aloud to her, it was a relief to see that the Maggie he knew seemed to always return to him.

He kissed her deep, pushing his tongue into her warm mouth, savoring her, and she responded happily. Cuán tasted the blood in her mouth, but he didn't care. Holding her small wet body against his, he was only too happy to have her back.

Maggie broke the kiss finally, suddenly looking worried. "I'm not horrid to you?"

Cuán remembered being terrified of what she could do. The alleyway with the thugs that attacked them, and the way Maggie told him that she was going to bite Deirdre's head off with such assurance.

"Never," Cuán said.

Maggie grinned at him, and he looked at her sharp mouth, seeing how deadly her teeth were. He didn't fear them anymore.

"What about Deirdre? Ambrus?"

"I think I saw the arrachtaigh," Cuán said. "It's back there. It tore up one of the vampyres when it came after me. I don't know why it didn't follow."

Maggie nodded and put her hand on his cheek. "Let's go take a look."

They went deeper into the cave. Eventually, they came across the body of the creature. On top of it was another body. They recognized the red hair immediately. Deirdre. Her face was next to the skeletal remains of Myrna's old skull, exuding from the creature's body, Myrna drooling blood and mucus into her dull eye, both of which were staring off into nothing.

"Oh my God!" Maggie cried, climbing to touch Deirdre. She hugged her body, sobbing. "No, no. My *sister*."

Cuán felt a heavy lump sitting on his chest. He felt so badly for Maggie.

"This is an awful thing," Maggie told him.

Cuán nodded and shook his head. *Aye, it was.* He was glad that Maggie could come around.

"We lost Róis. Myrna killed her, so *I* killed Myrna," Maggie said. "But this creature was part of her! Look at it. It has parts of her body and parts of someone else... I should have made sure she was dead, but I didn't. I didn't know she could do this."

Cuán nodded again. "Possibly the commissioner, if Eireen Hearn was correct. It looks like Deirdre found out who it was. And I don't think Myrna really had this power. It was Doran Dunn."

Maggie wiped the blood and mucus from Deirdre's eye and gathered Deirdre's body up in her arms. Cuán moved to help her. They sat her body near the water in the cave. Laying her down, Maggie noticed the gold locket dangling on a chain between Deirdre's breasts. She took it off her and slid it over her own neck.

Maggie's lips trembled, and she let out more sobs. "Oh gods, I loved them all, Cuán."

Cuán put an arm around her. "I'm sorry, Maggie. I really am."

After a moment of silence, Maggie started to smile.

"Maggie?"

Maggie looked at him. "Having the siofra inside me binds me to Deirdre in a strange way. I can feel Deirdre inside of me. She was happy with herself. She beat the arrachtaigh. She killed it for all of us."

Cuán didn't know what to say, but it didn't matter because Maggie frowned again. "Doran Dunn. The bastard."

Epilogue

I.

"While you were in the caverns, Father Brian gathered some of his flock, and they had a full-on rite of exorcism at the cliffs," Ambrus said. "They worked on driving the devil out of the village. While he was doing that, I spent my time below—on the shoreline in the bay. I did my best to stay away from the docks and out of sight of any doggers going by. Once I was sure I was alone, I put out my ritual things and I called the sprites of the wind. I ruffled them up and made them blow. So, when Deirdre killed the arrachtaigh, it could no longer pull the Devil's Breath in. The wind carried it away, and Séala Bán is free of its curse.

"I'm not sure what happened after that. The wind blew me off my feet. Luckily when I awoke, there was a young blond woman there to help me back to town. Greatest thing ever. Seeing someone smile at you in gratitude when you can see in their eyes that they've been sad for a very long time."

Maggie sighed and threw an arm around Cuán's neck, draping his shoulder. They were now sitting in the carriage with Deirdre's money, a bag with a severed head in it, escorting Ambrus back to the train station in Galway. "The sun looks so glorious when it's out in full. Hopefully, it stays that way for a while."

Cuán's leg was wrapped up. Unable to quickly heal like Maggie, he was still feeling the vampyre's painful bite and was rubbing it.

"What about Doran Dunn?" Ambrus said. "Surely you can't forget that he's still a problem?"

Maggie couldn't forget when she and Cuán were still in the caves. She was still shaped in her monstrous form with the tail and teeth, while she and Cuán were looking for an easier way out than the Feat Pit in the ceiling. Maggie was working on transforming back into her human form, but she found it a slow process.

Eireen's daughter appeared in a white gown, leaning on a walking staff in front of them. Maggie could sense that inside Nola was something else. Something divine and powerful. Her Primordial essence was a burning aura around her.

"Now that you have acquired the siofra, you must return it to Doran Dunn," Nola said.

"Are you the Cailleach?" Maggie wondered, not feeling the witch anymore. *Something else* was inside her now.

Nola shook her head, smiling. "No. I am Brigid. The Cailleach sleeps."

Maggie looked at Nola's shadow, seeing that it was of an old woman.

Once she'd seen it, Maggie's mind switched back to what Brigid was actually saying.

"And give him such a powerful gift? I think not!" Maggie replied. She was still holding the Bod Mór, and she held it out between them. "That fecker is goin' to pay for all the misery he's brought to me and mine."

Nola hissed at her. "Do not make the same mistakes Sionnach Silín made. If she hadn't gotten involved in the first place, you would have not been taken by the fomori."

Nola disappeared as if she had never been.

Now in the carriage, thinking back at that moment, Maggie looked at Ambrus Kárpáti. "Maybe we do as Brigid asked."

"That sounds like a good way to die to me," Cuán said.

Maggie nodded. "It does. But I really don't want to make the same mistakes Cherry Fox made."

"But she was able to get out of it and return to her Cycle," Ambrus pointed out.

Maggie smiled. "That's right! Somewhere here in Ireland, there's a baby being born with her soul."

Cuán smiled at her. "And that baby is Sionnach Silín."

"Deirdre," Maggie said.

"Okay. If we do this, we do it the safest way possible," Cuán said. "We don't go to Dublin."

Ambrus nodded. "I think I know what you're thinking. May I help with this?" he grinned menacingly.

They all laughed together.

"Right. So, we'll need a place to stay in Galway for a bit," Cuán said.

Maggie looked at Cuán as he looked at Ambrus. Cuán, disheveled from the hell they'd been through, was as handsome as ever. She kissed his cheek.

Her mind turned to who she was. A *Maris Demidian*. Whatever that meant. She and Cuán would have to look into it and see what they could find. If she learned anything over the last few months, she was never going to be a normal girl. She might as well embrace who she really was. With the vampyre problem over, the only thing to fear now was the Fomorians themselves. She wondered what they'd do next.

Doran was in his study, making his plans for his visit to see the London branch of *MacKay & Dunn*, when Felim came in and dropped a wooden box on his desk. It was painted blue and had yellow, heavy serifed typeface: THE GREAT KÁRPÁTI!

"What's this?"

"I don't know," Felim said. "It came from the parcel service."

"Well, open it."

Felim nodded and started tapping the doles out on the sides. Once he was done, the sides fell down, revealing a pale, severed head of a woman with long black hair. Her face was frozen in horror. Her scalp was partially caved in.

"What the bloody hell?"

Doran saw something in her mouth, so he used his fingers to spread her purple lips. What he saw was a mass set of long, sharp teeth.

"Dear God," Felim said. "What is that thing?"

"A brine vampire. Fomorian," Doran said. "It looks like the queen."

"Is it sweating?"

"Sweating?"

Where before the head seemed pale and dry, it did now seem as though drops of water were running down its face. Getting frightened now—was it going to come to life?—Doran stepped back.

But it was too late. The water was only the beginning as a semi-transparent and gelatinous caul seemed to exude quickly from the flesh. It sprung up and landed on Doran's face.

He felt the siofra climbing into his skin. He was absorbing it.

Doran screamed and Felim ran from the study in terror.

Suddenly the study doors slammed shut, and a giant, hunched young lady crouched there before him, head wreathed in flowers, filling his study with her very size. Her burning eyes frightened him, making him draw back into his study as far as he could go, against his bookshelf, as far away from the giant maiden as much as possible. He knew who this was—Brigid the Maiden.

Brigid grinned. *"Now, let's try this again, Doran Dunn. And make no mistakes this time. I have a different babe I would like to acquire, and this one is far more important."*

II.

Elieris steamed. Once the vampyres were destroyed and Brigid retrieved the Cailleach's siofra, the Maiden Goddess etched sigils on a stone at the base of the island along the coasts of Kilkee. The sigils were hidden from the mortals, deep under the waters. When he sent fomori to get past the sigils to end Maggie's life, the barrier proved too strong for even his power.

He sent eels to rub against the sigils every day, attempting to rub the surface of the stones clean. If he could erase them, the power would fade. However, this was slow going. No matter how many eels he sent, the etchings were still to be seen.

He would have to lure her out, he decided. While Elieris was known for his patience, he didn't want Maggie to have time to come up with more ways to protect herself before he got to her.

It would take some planning. Maggie was clever, and she knew that he sought her. She wouldn't make it easy for him.

Elieris grinned, too.

It did make things entertaining, didn't it?

He reached out with his mind, seeking a way to lure the little Demidian out. Elieris wouldn't stop until he found something. Nobody made a fool of Elieris. Nobody survived his judgment.

Not even this little bitch.

He grasped the relic on his chest. The Derdriu Shard. Given to him by the fomor, Fangtooth. It was made from a piece of her spirit essence. Her *shine*, as they called it. With it, he had no doubt that it wouldn't be long before she succumbed to his might.

III.

Once Maggie and Cuán delivered the news that Deirdre had died, there were questions, but they stuck behind the idea that they didn't know themselves how it happened, only that her body was never found. Eventually, Column and Mona accepted it, which, of course, broke their spirits. Cuán pulled Maggie aside and they decided together that leaving was a bad idea with everyone hurting so much right now. At first, Maggie protested against his idea, knowing how badly he wanted to go to the university. Knowing it was his dream.

"Maggie. I want yeh with me. I'm not leaving without you," he said. "I can wait. Right now, yer parents need you."

This also broke her heart, but she took it selfishly. She needed it.

Though Maggie stayed with Oona, who loved her as a mother, Maggie spent as much time as she could to help the Ó Fionnáin's move on with their lives without Deirdre. Oona didn't question Maggie's desire to be with the Ó Fionnáin's from time to time, believing that it was just who Maggie was: someone who cared about those around her. While the Ó Fionnáin's never completely healed from Deirdre's loss, Maggie made life so much better for them. And they enjoyed having her around.

"I'm proud of you, Maggie," Oona said. "And if I *had* a daughter, I would have liked her to be very much like you."

Maggie could sense the sigils on the stone under the coastline, carved by the Cailleach. It didn't take her long to realize that they were meant to keep her safe from the fomori, but she knew she couldn't stay there forever. Cuán had dreams to follow and she had dreams to follow him until they found the life they were looking for.

Sure, she had questions. Were there other Demidians like her out there? What about the other fae? Had they all left the world behind? A part of her wanted to find someone else that could teach her more about the world to which she belonged. She would need it to keep Cuán and herself safe.

For now, that's what mattered to her.

© Copyright 2020 Charles Allen

Glossary & Pronunciation

Aos sí—[*Ehs shee*] The aos sí are the descendance of the Tuatha Dé Danann. They were all born earlkings, but many become twergs over a great amount of time. Most of the aos sí are women who live modestly in the Otherworld.

Arrachtaigh—[*AR-rock-tog*] A general term for an Irish monster.

Athraithe—[*Ah-REE*] An 'Altered One'. A human chosen to be subjugated by the fae and modified physically for certain tasks.

Balor's Eye—[*Bay-LOR*] Balor is one of the most powerful fomor ever born. Lugh struck him down with a sling-stone and Cherry Fox finished him off when he crawled off to heal. Balor's Eye is the blight that brings death to nations and to gods themselves.

Cailleach—[*CAL-lee-ehk*] The Queen of Winter, one of the oldest goddesses of Ireland. Her name is often used to refer to witches. She saved Maggie from the fomori when she was still a child.

Cinniúint—[*kin-noo-ent*] The fate of mortals woven by their Vital Essence.

Croí—[*cree*] The magical lifeblood of the Primordial, the Creator Force of the universe. The fae naturally gather croí to their *fata* essence, giving them the ability to cast Eeries (magic).

Demidian—[*deh-mi-dee-ehn*] A mortal with divine blood. Either a demi-god (born half-blood) or gifted with divine blood. Demidians do not have *fata* essence, so they cannot use the Eeries, but they can learn Accordances that mimic some of these powers.

Déantán—A fetish idol of a god.

Derdriu Shard—[*der-droo*] Maggie Connell was originally born Deirdre Ó Fionnáin, so when the fomor Soulforger, Fangtooth, fashioned the Shard from a piece of Maggie's soul (her píos anam), it was called the Derdriu Shard. The shard itself is slight, but it allows anyone to connect with Maggie wherever she is.

Devil's Breath—Also called Ostium. When the Suspirium (spirit world) and the Material realms collide (often because of portals or pocket realms). So called because the majority of portals in the modern world are created by demons—agents of the Commination.

Eagla/Eeries—[*eeg-lah*] The Eeries are natural powers that the fae may use by weaving their croí. The fae only have access to Eeries within their nature. Eeries comes from the Gaelic root Eagla, meaning fear. Mortals feared the power of the fae, and still do to this day.

Elieris, the Fomorian King—[*El-ay-res*] The God-King of the fomori, who has become the dwellings for his people since they were banished from Ireland by the Tuatha Dé Danann. He seeks vengeance against the Tuatha Dé and the Gaels (Irish) for taking fomori land.

Fae—A term for any Primordial Being (including fomori, fir bulg, the aos sí, etc.). Those with the *fata* essence.

Féth fiada—A fairy mist created by croí. Sometimes the Devil's Breath is misconstrued as féth fíada.

Fomor (sing.), **fomori** (pl.), **Fomorian** (nation)—The demons of the sea. Once a tribe of fae who ruled Ireland many centuries before the Gaels arrived.

Glamour—Croí can be made to manifest through the physical fundament, creating a magical substance called glamour. Glamour can shape appearances and form magical materials (called glamour tokens). Magically enhanced matter, it can break the laws of physics and form powerful illusions that actually manipulate all five senses. Glamour tokens can remain with an astral projection in the Hollow.

Great Contracts, the—After the Milesian Battle, the Tuatha Dé gained respect for the Gaels who fought for their place in Ireland. Mother Danu forbid the Tuatha Dé from destroying the Gaels and instructed them to the Final Recant (withdrawing into the Otherworld from the physical). In order to make it so, thy constructed a magical peace treaty with conditions that vibrate in the souls of both fae and the Irish.

Hollow, the—The psychic atmosphere hidden all around us, created by the sentience of all living things. Sorcerers tend to call it the agasha, or Akashic Records. The Hollow can be travelled via astral projection (a projection of their Psyche Essence), where people become doorways to their inner mindscapes.

Homunculus Alteration—The potion created by the sorcerer and alchemist, Doran Dunn, to create a human form that can supersede human fragility and give him control over their minds.

Imbolc—[*Im-boh-lk*] A Gaelic festival that marks the beginning of spring, traditionally February 1st. Also called St Brigid's Day.

Maighdean Uaimh—[*Mi-dun oo-ev*] Brine vampyres, created by the fomori to serve them.

Nathaira—[*nah-thair-uh*] The Great Oilliphéist (Sea Serpent), daughter of Caoránach—the Mother of Demons.

Piocadh—[*pee-oh-kah*] Someone who has been 'picked' or 'chosen' specifically.

Píos Anam—[*peas AH-nom*] A piece or shard of one's soul.

Siofra—[*SHIF-rah*] An unborn of the fae that can take the shape of others. They are often used as changelings and are protected by the Great Contracts.

Sióg—[*SHIG*] The Irish catchall term for the fae.

Siúracha Seacht dTobar—[*Shoor-ock-ah Shock-t TAH-boer*] The Sisters of the Seven Springs.

Thar An Naoú Tonn—Irish Gaelic for Beyond the Ninth Wave. The old sailor's adage that the ninth wave was always killer because it existed between both the physical world and Otherworld. This border area between both worlds is where the merrow tend.

Tír na nÓg—[*Tear nah NOG*] The Land of Youth and the central realm of the Otherworld.

Tuatha Dé Danann—[*Too-ah dey DAN-nahn*] The first few generations of Mother Danu and Father Allód. The Tuatha Dé are known as the ancient gods of Ireland and also the fairies of the mounds. They are the tribes of people who fashioned the Great Contracts with the Milesians (Gaels) and the rightful heirs of Ireland.

Token, Glamour—A glamour manifestation mimicking a physical object. It can be a sword, clothes, a coin or anything else imagined. Glamour tokens are impossible to discern by most from a real physical object that it's based off. See Glamour.

Postface

St. Peter's Church on Aungier Street, Dublin, where Cuán and Deirdre visit to plot Maggie's escape from Granya's, no longer exists. Though it was a real place. It was a former Church of Ireland, built in A.D. 1280. It became the largest Church of Ireland parish in Dublin. The churchyard was used until 1883, the remains be reinterred to Mount Jerome cemetery in the 1980's.

The first photograph published in a newspaper—actually a photomechanical reproduction of a photograph—appeared in the Daily Graphic on March 4, 1880. So, I took some liberties with the timeline for photographic images in print. Additionally, the earliest known fashion photographs date back to the 1850s, in the court of Napoleon III, but the use of photography as an advertising tool did not become popular until the early 20th century.

In the Victorian period, pornography on the market boomed, and was produced in abundance. Before 1864, pornography was described as "obscenity". It was characterized by paradox of rigid morality and anti-sensualism but also by an obsession with sex. Victorian anti-sexual attitudes were contradictory of genuine Victorian life, with sex underlying much of the cultural practice.

I wanted to thank all those who helped me deliver this book. Alpha and beta readers include Larcy Allen, Chase Reineke, and Paul Allen.

Others who were a great help to me over the course of writing this book are Rebecca Brewer (development editing), Greg Darwin (proofreading the Irish translation), and Susan Russell (copy editing and proofreading).

Let's also not forget the wonderful cover artist, Matt Barnes, who also did all the inside full-page, chapter-facing art as well. Gorgeous work, man.

If you love tabletop roleplaying games, you can find VICTORIAN GOTHIC at DriveThruRPG (www.drivethrurpg.com). Seagrass Maggie takes place in that world. In fact, characters appearing in this book also appear in that game setting, like Ambrus Kárpáti. You can find these products at this link:

www.drivethrurpg.com/browse/pub/17342/Arcanus-Press

A gothic horror game in the gaslight era. Play a Hunter, Investigator, Psychic, Spiritualist or Sorcerer. You have come across your First Encounter with the supernatural, and you have found a new path in life. Unfortunately, this path has many dark shadows, mysteries and hidden dangers that may lead you to an unwanted end. An ominous Miasma has risen up, the undead have awakened, and werewolves prowl and hunt the full moon nights. Will you break free of your curse, or be devoured by it?

Maggie's story will be continued in
THE ORDER OF THE RED GOD.

Excerpt from THE ORDER OF THE RED GOD
The Seagrass Maggie Trilogy, Book II.

I. Dark Visitations

July—1855

-1-

The air was brisk, filled with moisture from the western sea, and the cliffs stood proud against the crashing waves below. There were several herring gulls looking for shelter against the rocks, seals making their way among them along the coastline, and the sprites in the air stirred, sensing the pungent likes of the Deep Dens.

They were coming.

Malformed, ghastly arms reached out from beneath the waters and grasped the rocks with their clawed hands. The horribly twisted and ominous-sized creatures lifted their hulking bodies from their natural element and breathed in the air as if grasping for something that they never knew they needed.

Inside their heads, the Fomorian King—Elieris—spoke to them.

Find her. Bring her back, or kill her if you have to.

They started the climb up the cliffs, their tongues flicking over their sharp teeth. Oh gods, this was their divine purpose, and it thrilled them more than the savagery of copulation. Serving Elieris served themselves in almost every way.

No one fools me, Elieris said to them. *She is mine.*

-2-

Thunder was sudden around her, and she could feel the electricity in the sea air. Thrilled, Maggie looked behind her, having left Oona in bed for the night, hoping no one had seen her leave home. Luckily, Cuán, the absolute love of her life, was off in Dublin, where he was setting up a home for them. He knew her very well, and if he knew she was out here, he would probably fret and criticize her for being so careless.

She wore a simple white gown and nothing else, though she hung the straps of an old, beaten leather bag (that belonged to Oona's husband—now gone, gods rest his soul) over her shoulder. At the cave, she pulled her gown over her head and stuffed it in the bag, leaving it in a dry spot as close to the exit as she could. Bare-skinned, she delighted in the wind and went running for the swelling waves. Her naked feet *splipped* and *splashed* through the cold water, hitting her calves and then her thighs. Soon the swells were around and between her legs, pushing her back and then pulling her toward its dark, leviathan form.

Diving forward, she allowed her body to change. Her skin darkened to a deep sea-green, and the symbolic scars she received from the Fomorians when she was but a babe deepened. Her hands and feet both grew webbing between the digits and long, black claws. Her mouth grew jagged, incredibly sharp teeth. The Fomorian scratches etched upon her body started to glow a cyan, revealing their occult significance. Along the top of her skull through her curly red hair, and down her back she grew purplish spiked fins that continued down her long tail that swung between her legs, helping propel her quickly through the oceanic waters.

She was a human-serpent hybrid—*Seagrass Maggie*.

The sea life around her spread out, sensing her predatory instincts, though she was not inclined at the moment to hunt them. She dove deep, following the island's bottom as it deepened into the Atlantic Ocean. She felt the pressures increase around her, and she could feel her body easily adjusting to them at the same time.

Maggie had come to realize that she was a powerful creature, and though she knew there were worse things alive around her, she learned that she was not easy to kill. Living all those long years with the fomori in the Deep Dens had changed her natural mortal body, touching her with the fae essence, transforming her into something different. Having escaped the Fomorians with the help of the Cailleach, she found herself hunted by a sorcerer working for the Fomorian King, Elieris, who wanted her back for breaking the Great Contract. The sorcerer was Doran Dunn—a maniac that also happened to enlighten her, that she was now a Maris, a Demidian of the oceans. Someone with divine blood.

Over the next couple of years, once Dunn was dealt with, Maggie and her lover, Cuán, explored more of her powers and sought others of her kind. However, these were no longer like the ancient times—the fae all but retreated to the Otherworld, leaving only a few behind after the Great Contracts made with the Milesians.

Swimming still deeper, moving swiftly between a few basking sharks and the hairy-looking orange blob of a lion's mane jellyfish, she thought about Killian. He was the only fae she had met who actually spent a lot of time socializing with mortals in their world. While he refused to say too much about himself, he was the only one she really learned to trust. Other fae creatures lived in the shadows, refusing to speak. They were spread out, usually living hermit lives, mostly running away as she approached them. Even though she could sense their natures, it was still difficult to find them, and even more difficult to communicate.

Over the last few months, however, she swam farther from the island. Farther and deeper. Beyond the Celtic shelf, she encountered other beings. Humanoid and yet alien. Some were as frightful looking as the fomori; only, unlike those terrible creatures, they were often beautiful in some alien way that not even Maggie understood. They also had these gorgeous red bio-luminant veils about their heads—gelatinous and transparent, they opened like balloons about their heads before folding and collapsing when they moved about. Their *cohuleen druith*. In folklore, it was described as a red cap and Maggie could see why some may think that.

The creatures kept themselves mostly hidden, staying in the murky veil in the distant waters, but they looked at each other for as long as each dared and then they would be gone before Maggie could find the courage to approach them.

She suspected they were the merrow.

As Maggie approached the last location she'd seen them—only a few nights before—she stopped and hid amongst the rocks on the seafloor. They stood up around her like standing stones. There were so many that it was easy to hide within them, making her feel certain that she couldn't be seen.

She waited, hoping to see one again. Maggie wondered what Cuán would say about all this. She truly wanted to show him these marvels, and she often wished she could bring him down here with her. Except, after the dangers Doran Dunn put them through, he was reluctant to let her do anything treacherous.

A coldness ran through her. Maggie's body always adapted to both the pressures and temperatures of the ocean, so when she got a chill, it wasn't the waters. It was something in them. Her senses told her she might be in danger.

Maggie looked around, frightened that she had let her guard down, not realizing her life could be in immediate danger until it was too late.

She froze when she saw it: the smooth head, the shiny silver eyes, and the masculine torso. It was alien to her. Almost metallic, like a school of shimmering bluefin tuna. Only it was a beautiful man with fins and a wide mouth, ribs fanning the waters as he breathed. There was a tendril of red behind his head; his *cohuleen druith*. He watched her for a moment and then dashed away. Behind him, several merrow that she didn't even know were there, followed him just as quickly. There were females with long flowing hair, naked breasts, and long, elegant and colorful-fined tails. (*Mermaids*, Maggie thought). But they were gone almost as quickly as she noticed them.

Maggie swam out of her hiding spot, wanting to communicate that she wasn't a danger to them, but she waited there and didn't see them again. She swam around the rocks with her powerful tail swishing back and forth through the waters, feeling the ocean rush through her hair and her fins, and looked for them.

They disappeared, leaving no trace of their existence.

Disappointed, Maggie decided she would try again another day. Beneath the waves, Maggie often lost track of time. For all she knew, Cuán could be over to have breakfast and wonder where she was.

Maggie started back, swimming as quickly as she could. The muscles in her body jetted her to the coastline in very little time, her supernatural vigor outlasting any ache that she would normally imagine. On the shores, she let her body shift back to its human form: the short, freckled redhead with ghostly pale skin. She could not see the sun on the horizon, but she was sure it was soon upon her.

She climbed up the rocks to her cave and went to her bag.

Only the bag was not there.

In the deeper, dark part of the cave she heard a sloughing breath. Its unnatural sound scared her. Maggie didn't know what to do, so she stepped back toward the mouth of the cave. She was naked and alone with no weapons to protect her.

"Seagrasss Maggie!" came a deep, sloughing voice.

"Who the feck is there?" she said. Maggie told her body to change, and in a moment, she had her claws, her fins, her tail...

"Oooooh, Maggie. You don't remember us?" The mouth that formed the words sounded like it popped and sloughed again.

About the Author

Charles Allen has worked as a game designer, filmmaker and photographer but telling stories comes most natural to him. He is the author of the tabletop roleplaying game VICTORIAN GOTHIC. He resides in northern Idaho with his wife, Jen, and youngest son, Bentley, a mixed terrier (Murphy), and two tabby cats (Oscar and Willow).

The Seagrass Maggie Trilogy

Seagrass Maggie (2023)

The Order of the Red God (2024)

A Graveyard of Ships (2025)

Milton Keynes UK
Ingram Content Group UK Ltd.
UKHW020852131123
432470UK00021B/1158